3 9082 06602185 1

10638378

DARK DESTINY III:
CHILDREN OF DRACULA

Edited by Edward E. Kramer

Dark Destiny III: Children of Dracula is
a product of White Wolf Publishing.

White Wolf Publishing
780 Park North Boulevard, Suite 100
Clarkston, GA 30021
World Wide Web Page: www. white-wolf.com

Printed in Canada

This tome is dedicated to Bram Stoker (1847-1912); father of darkness, purveyor of light...

CONTENTS

Foreword

Slavic folklore tells us that a vampire is a malign spirit that refuses to join the ranks of the dead, but instead takes possession of a body in order to continue enjoying the pleasures of the living. Rising from its grave each night, it feeds off the blood of innocent (and not-so-innocent) victims, which in turn become vampires after death. Traditionally, they are the ghosts of criminals, heretics, and suicides—and can be put to rest only by having a wooden stake driven through their hearts.

In 1887, Abraham Stoker compiled one of the most potent stories ever to haunt the imagination. A tale of Gothic romance, it provided a veritable sexual lexicon of Victorian taboos (seduction, rape, group sex, necrophilia, pedophilia, incest, adultery, oral sex, menstruation, venereal disease, and voyeurism). Considered his most autobiographical work, Stoker projected himself into all of its major characters, dumping the signposts of his life into a supernatural cauldron called *Dracula*.

Unlike H.P. Lovecraft, who chronicled the Cthulhu mythos to support his vision of the world's origins, Stoker's relationship with the *World of Darkness* was less clear. His source for the Dracula legend was Prince Vlad, who fought bitterly against the Turks and, because of his sadistic cruelty toward subjects and Turkish prisoners alike, was dubbed Vlad the Impaler.

His father was known as Vlad Dracul (Vlad the Devil)—hence the son's name, Dracula, son of the Devil.

In the novel, a Dutch metaphysician and scientist named Van Helsing is summoned to deal with the menace, and ultimately kills the vampire. To this day, however, there are those who do not accept Dracula's demise. In many regions of Europe, wreaths of garlic still hang over doors as protection against evil spirits of the night; undead that draw both blood and life from those asleep within. This collection you now hold follows Dracula's descendants throughout history. Step inside and meet the *Children of Dracula.*

— Edward E. Kramer
June, 1996

Introduction

by Brian Yuzna

A hundred years ago, Bram Stoker chronicled the evil force that is Count Dracula, bringing him out of the dark, superstitious Eastern European Old World past and into the modern industrial western world, to infect us with his parasitic seed and haunt our waking dreams. Since then vampire legend has thrived, spawning countless shapeshifting progeny which have successfully survived and prospered as our secular postmodern rock-and-roll apocalyptic cyber-culture barrels headlong into the millennium. The tales collected in this anthology are a testament to the enduring power of the Dark One to adapt himself to our changing culture, insidiously and effectively feeding on the lifeblood of our imaginations, all in the name of entertainment. And yet, as an enduring icon of fear, dread and blasphemous desire, Dracula, Vampyre, Nosferatu, Vlad the Impaler, the Undead, represents much more than a thrilling diversion. There is something mythical about the person of Dracula, in the sense that his story has taken root in our collective unconscious, becoming a part of the building blocks of our psyche. In this way he is more real than our everyday natural world, because it is from these building blocks that we create our objective reality. So, Dracula actually is an evil force and the authors of these stories all serve as his Renfields, just as Bram Stoker did before them, preparing his way into our lives, laying sod from his homeland in our cities. Like traitors to our mortal kind these stories nurture the darkness, announcing his arrival, making the introductions, inviting him into our lives—all from the creative madhouses of the fiction writers' minds.

Just what is evil about Dracula? It all starts, I think, with the contemplation of rotting flesh after life has fled. The vampire is a rejection of temporality. It has always fascinated me, the cannibalistic and shapeshifting origins of vampirism in medieval superstition, the undead prowling unhallowed ground in search of brief carrion respite from their eternal hunger. Certainly in these early incarnations the vampire expresses all that is decayed and despicable, a creature of the night weakened by the light of day, capable of transformation into batlike and lupine creatures. Stinking of putrefaction, unable to digest normal human sustenance, sexually perverse, inhuman, a soulless, godless predator, feeding on all that is pure and corrupting all that is good, he incestuously breaks the familial contract, a patriarch seducing the virgin daughters, all the while supporting the Holy Roman Church's dogma of the transubstantiation of blood. A blasphemous, damning communion. In fact, it is the Church's symbols, the cross and holy water, that are generally the most powerful defenses against the vampire.

The strength of this folklore is evidenced by its enduring influence in a western culture dominated by science and Judeo-Christian monotheism, and increasingly, secular existentialism. The vampiric legends spring from our deep psychological archetypes into that part of us that believes in transmutations, afterlife and miracles, the word made flesh, evil and redemption. Dracula made this horror more appropriate to the twentieth century. Not the vague gruesome horror of his dark origins—Bram Stoker appropriated for him a history. He was Vlad the Impaler, an historical ruler of specific Transylvanian ancestry. As the wealthy Count Dracula in London he smoothly preys upon the English virgins next door. It is the forbidden, but seductive, sheen of sexual license that Bram Stoker gave full expression to in his vampire, that is Dracula's special appeal. This makes Dracula a cultural danger, but a bit less than evil. Ultimately, it is his soullessness that irredeemably damns Dracula and his kin as purely evil. For all of Bram Stoker's success in transforming the vampire from the brutish monster of legend into a suave, well-mannered, attractive aristocrat, beneath the smooth surface, we know, is an evil, inhuman, decayed demon. Incapable of being killed, he must be destroyed, staked to the ground, beheaded, stuffed with garlic, burned. An evil that has always been our shadow, tempting us with a sensual and materialistic immortality, for which we only have to give up our humanity and our chance of spiritual redemption. But, as the world changes, becomes more secular, postindustrial, so has the Dracula of a hundred years ago. The stories in this book continue the reincarnation and reinvention of our favorite demon.

When I first read *Dracula* in high school it immediately gave me the creeps. *Frankenstein*, on the other hand, took me until I was grown up to be effective, and *Dr. Jekyll and Mr. Hyde* was interesting—but *Dracula*—wow, it was scary. The first part of it, Jonathan Harker in the castle, provides the elixir of dread and dark sexuality that is altogether satisfying to the fan of horror and the supernatural. Bram Stoker brought it to London, to our modern world of psychology and transfusions, of democracy and asylums, of love and commandments, of moral relationships, science and progress—and we invited him in, over the threshold, to quicken the dark stirrings banished to the deepest recesses of our souls. Imagination has done the rest.

Throughout countless novels and short stories, theater plays, television and cinema, Dracula and his spawn have been resurrected, reinvented and mutated in innumerable incarnations of every conceivable sort. From its first publication, Dracula struck a nerve with the public, and was embraced in print and on stage with a passion equaled only by the denunciations of critics and self-appointed guardians of the public morality. Inevitably, the public prevailed, and Dracula has been our dark companion ever since. After Bram Stoker there was Anne Rice. Her writings carried the children of Dracula into our nuclear postpsychedelic world with a widespread popularity that dwarfed the devoted readership of such inspired interpreters of the bloodsucking legend as (some of my particular favorites) S.P. Somtow, Les Daniels and George R.R. Martin. In Anne Rice's vampire chronicles we could really sympathize with the monsters. How they forsook old world theism, their immortality freeing them to enjoy exhilarating powers and unbridled sensuality, free of bothersome ethics and morality, but, doomed to suffer exhaustive and mind-blowing confrontations with existential dread. The beauty of the undead, the horror of eternity. Freed of the dogmas of the Church, a secular audience can admire and sympathize with the existential angst of these vampires, these dark heroes. It is this dramatic evolution that provides a context for the stories in this volume.

Dracula is the most chronicled character in the history of cinema. From the nightmarish bloodsucking demon of F.W. Murnau's *Nosferatu* to Bela Lugosi's romantic aristocrat, Christopher Lee's incestuously blood-drenched Hammer Films incarnation and even David Bowie's androgynously elegant Undead, we have seen ghoulish vampires, erudite vampires, high fashion vampires and funny vampires, vampires with heart and vampires who eat hearts, vampires in New York and vampires in outer space. We've had suave vampires, men, women, gay, black and lesbian vampires; lovers and monsters, children and comedians. The variations are so wide-ranging that it almost becomes impossible to logically say what Dracula and his kind actually are. Which is just as well because it really isn't logical, anyway—evil isn't logical. It has more to do with instinct and inspiration, art and religion, image and dream. If anything it reinforces the notion that Dracula is a bloody powerful and pervasive icon of our increasingly confused and violent times.

It all has something to do with blood. (That is, until psychic vampires rear their paranormal heads.) Sucking the blood of another. The living, pulsing, life-giving blood of a warm, breathing human being. Killing to live, often sexually, sensually and romantically. How we love that image of the victim swooning into the bloodsucker's arms, nape of the neck arched vulnerably upward, tenderly proffering the pulsing vein.... Like an addict enamored of her corruption, death-love, a hunger for debasement and oblivion. If orgasm is the "little death," how much more seductive is the long slow death of coupling with our dispassionate vampire lover. Eternal night drawing us in, to drift in the shadows forever. A blood-red river of no return. The stuff nightmares are made of.

And nightmares are what this book is all about. Chronicling the vampire plague and reveling in it is what the authors of the tales that follow delight in. Afflicting our imaginations with their dark visions. American, British, Thai, the authors are about as diverse as the worlds that they describe. You may be surprised at the extent to which Dracula and his children infect the history of humankind. From prehistory to the close of our century these tales expose the workings of the vampire in Sodom and Gomorrah, Oxford, England, Hollywood and the Civil War South. You will discover Bram Stoker's relationship with the Count himself and be repulsed by the vampire soldiers of the war between the red and white Russians. And you will meet Lizzie Borden, Thomas Edison, Rasputin and Lawrence of Arabia. Dracula touched all of their lives. His children contributed to the demise of the dirigible as a means of transportation and they are teenagers in our suburbs today. You will encounter vampire villains, and, popularly these days, vampires as heroes. In fact, would you believe, a mensch Jewish vampire who will only suck the blood of Gentiles? But, let us not forget Santa Claus(!) and the breathlessly phantasmagoric Gregor and Ivan soaring deliriously o'er the sundrenched and goresoaked California desert. A veritable cornucopia of bloody fun, a tantalizing sampler of gruesome excess, a wellspring of dark dreams and fearful treasures. A family album of Clan Dracula. Please, read on....

Peking Man

Robert J. Sawyer

The lid was attached to the wooden crate with eighteen nails. The return address, in blue ink on the blond wood, said, "Sender: Dept. of Anatomy, P.U.M.C., Peking, China." The destination address, in larger letters, was:

Dr. Roy Chapman Andrews
The American Museum of Natural History
Central Park West at 79th Street
New York, N.Y. U.S.A.

The case was marked "Fragile!" and "REGISTERED" and "*Par Avion*." A brand had burned the words "Via Hongkong and by U.S. Air Service" into the wood.

Andrews had waited anxiously for this arrival. Between 1922 and 1930, he himself had led the now-famous Gobi Desert expeditions, searching for the Asian cradle of humanity. Although he'd brought back untold scientific riches—including the first-ever dinosaur eggs—Andrews had failed to discover a single ancient human remain.

But now a German scientist, Franz Weidenreich, had shipped to him a treasure trove from the Orient: the complete fossil remains of *Sinanthropus pekinensis*. In this very crate were the bones of Peking Man.

Andrews was actually salivating as he used a crowbar to pry off the lid. He'd waited so long for these, terrified that they wouldn't survive the journey, desperate to see what humanity's forefathers had looked like, anxious—

The lid came off. The contents were carefully packed in smaller cardboard boxes. He picked one up and moved over to his cluttered desk. He swept the books and papers to the floor, laid down the box, and opened it. Inside was a ball of rice paper, wrapped around a large object. Andrews carefully

unwrapped the sheets, and—

White.

White?

No—no, it couldn't be.

But it was. It was a skull, certainly—but *not* a fossil skull. The material was bright white.

And it didn't weigh nearly enough.

A plaster cast. Not the original at all.

Andrews opened every box inside the wooden crate, his heart sinking as each new one yielded its contents. In total, there were fourteen skulls and eleven jawbones. The skulls were subhuman, with low foreheads, prominent brow ridges, flat faces, and the most unlikely looking perfect square teeth. Amazingly, each of the skull casts also showed clear artificial damage to the foramen magnum.

Oh, some work could indeed be done on these casts, no doubt. But where were the original fossils? With the Japanese having invaded China, surely they were too precious to be left in the Far East. What was Weidenreich up to?

✢

Fire.

It was like a piece of the sun, brought down to earth. It kept the tribe warm at night, kept the saber-toothed cats away—and it did something wonderful to meat, making it softer and easier to chew, while at the same time restoring the warmth the flesh had had when still part of the prey.

Fire was the most precious thing the tribe owned. They'd had it for eleven summers now, ever since Bok the Brave had brought out a burning stick from the burning forest. The glowing coals were always fanned, always kept alive.

And then, one night, the Stranger came—tall, thin, pale, with red-rimmed eyes that somehow seemed to glow from beneath his brow ridge.

The Stranger did the unthinkable, the unforgivable.

He doused the flames, throwing a gourd full of water onto the fire. The logs hissed, and steam rose up into the blackness. The children of the tribe began to cry; the adults quaked with fury. The Stranger turned and walked into the darkness. Two of the strongest hunters ran after him, but his long legs had apparently carried him quickly away.

The sounds of the forest grew closer—the chirps of insects, the rustling of small animals in the vegetation, and—

A flapping sound.

The Stranger was gone.

And the silhouette of a bat fluttered briefly in front of the waning moon.

✠

Franz Weidenreich had been born in Germany in 1873. A completely bald, thickset man, he had made a name for himself as an expert in hematology and osteology. He was currently Visiting Professor at the University of Chicago, but that was coming to an end, and now he was faced with the uncomfortable prospect of having to return to Nazi Germany—something, as a Jew, he desperately wanted to avoid.

And then word came of the sudden death of the Canadian paleontologist Davidson Black. Black had been at the Peking Union Medical College, studying the fragmentary remains of early man being recovered from the limestone quarry at Chou Kou Tien. Weidenreich, who once made a study of Neanderthal bones found in Germany, had read Black's papers in *Nature* and *Science* describing *Sinanthropus*.

But now, at fifty, Black was as dead as his fossil charges—an unexpected heart attack. And, to Weidenreich's delight, the China Medical Board of the Rockefeller Foundation wanted him to fill Black's post. China was a strange, foreboding place—and tensions between the Chinese and the Japanese were high—but it beat all hell out of returning to Hitler's Germany....

✠

At night, most of the tribe huddled under the rocky overhang or crawled into the damp, smelly recesses of the limestone cave. Without the fire to keep animals away, someone had to stand watch each night, armed with a large branch and a pile of rocks for throwing. Last night, it had been Kart's turn. Everyone had slept well, for Kart was the strongest member of the tribe. They knew they were safe from whatever lurked in the darkness.

When daybreak came, the members of the tribe were astounded. Kart had fallen asleep. They found him lying in the dirt, next to the cold, black pit where their fire had once been. And on Kart's neck there were two small red-rimmed holes, staring up at them like the eyes of the Stranger....

✠

During his work on hematology, Weidenreich had met a remarkable man named Brancusi—gaunt, pale, with disconcertingly sharp canine teeth. Brancusi suffered from a peculiar anemia, which Weidenreich had been unable to cure, and an almost pathological photophobia. Still, the gentleman was cultured and widely read, and Weidenreich had ever since maintained a correspondence with him.

When Weidenreich arrived in Peking, work was still continuing at the quarry. So far, only teeth and fragments of skull had been found. Davidson Black had done a good job of cataloging and describing some of the material, but as Weidenreich went through the specimens he was surprised to discover a small collection of sharp, pointed fossil teeth.

Black had evidently assumed they weren't part of the *Sinanthropus* material, as he hadn't included them in his descriptions. And, at first glance, Black's assessment seemed correct—they were far longer than normal human canines, and much more sharply pointed. But, to Weidenreich's eye, the root pattern was possibly hominid. He dropped a letter to his friend Brancusi, half-joking that he'd found Brancusi's great-to-the-*n*th grandfather in China.

To Weidenreich's infinite surprise, within weeks Brancusi had arrived in Peking.

✢

Each night, another member of the tribe stood watch—and each morning, that member was found unconscious, with a pair of tiny wounds to his neck.

The tribe members were terrified. Soon multiple guards were posted each night, and, for a time, the happenings ceased.

But then something even more unusual happened....

They were hunting deer. It would not be the same, not without fire to cook the meat, but, still, the tribe needed to eat. Four men, Kart included, led the assault. They moved stealthfully amongst the tall grasses, tracking a large buck with a giant rack of antlers. The hunters communicated by sign language, carefully coordinating their movements, closing in on the animal from both sides.

Kart raised his right arm, preparing to signal the final attack, when—

—a streak of light brown, slicing through the grass—

—fangs flashing, the roar of the giant cat, the stag bolting away, and then—

—Kart's own scream as the saber-tooth grabbed hold of his thigh and shook him viciously.

The other three hunters ran as fast as they could, desperate to get away. They didn't stop to look back, even when the cat let out the strangest yelp....

That night, the tribe huddled together and sang songs urging Kart's soul a safe trip to heaven.

✠

One of the Chinese laborers found the first skull. Weidenreich was summoned at once. Brancusi still suffered from his photophobia, and apparently had never adjusted to the shift in time zones—he slept during the day. Weidenreich thought about waking him to see this great discovery, but decided against it.

The skull was still partially encased in the limestone muck at the bottom of the cave. It had a thick cranial wall and a beetle brow—definitely a more primitive creature than Neanderthal, probably akin to Solo Man or Java Man....

It took careful work to remove the skull from the ground, but, when it did come free, two astonishing things became apparent.

The loose teeth Davidson Black had set aside had indeed come from the hominids here: this skull still had all its upper teeth intact, and the canines were long and pointed.

Second, and even more astonishing, was the foramen magnum—the large opening in the base of the skull through which the spinal cord passes. It was clear from its chipped, frayed margin that this individual's foramen magnum had been artificially widened—

—meaning he'd been decapitated, and then had something shoved up into his brain through the bottom of his skull.

✠

Five hunters stood guard that night. The moon had set, and the great sky river arched high over head. The Stranger returned—but this time, he was not alone. The tribesmen couldn't believe their eyes. In the darkness, it looked like—

It was. Kart.

But—but Kart was dead. They'd seen the saber-tooth take him.

The Stranger came closer. One of the men lifted a rock, as if to throw it at him, but soon he let the rock drop from his hand. It fell to the ground with a dull thud.

The Stranger continued to approach, and so did Kart.

And then Kart opened his mouth, and in the faint light they saw his teeth—long and pointed, like the Stranger's.

The men were unable to run, unable to move. They seemed transfixed, either by the Stranger's gaze, or by Kart's, both of whom continued to approach.

And soon, in the dark, chill night, the Stranger's fangs fell upon one of the guard's necks, and Kart's fell upon another....

✠

Eventually, thirteen more skulls were found, all of which had the strange elongated canine teeth, and all of which had their foramen magnums artificially widened. Also found were some mandibles and skull fragments from other individuals—but there was almost no post-cranial material. Someone in dim prehistory had discarded here the decapitated heads of a group of protohumans.

Brancusi sat in Weidenreich's lab late at night, looking at the skulls. He ran his tongue over his own sharp teeth, contemplating. These subhumans doubtless had no concept of mathematics beyond perhaps adding and subtracting on their fingers. How would they possibly know of the problem that plagued the Family, the problem that every one of the Kindred knew to avoid?

If all those who feel the bite of the vampire themselves become vampires when they die, and all of those new vampires also turn those they feed from into vampires, soon, unless care is exercised, the whole population will be undead. A simple geometric progression.

Brancusi had long wondered how far back the Family went. It wasn't like tracing a normal family tree—oh, yes, the lines were bloodlines, but not as passed on from father to son. He knew his own lineage—a servant at Castle Dracula before the Count had taken to living all alone, a servant whose loyalty to his master extended even to letting him drink from his neck. Brancusi himself had succumbed to pneumonia, not an uncommon ailment in the dank Carpathians. He had no family, and no one mourned his passing.

But soon he rose again—and now he did have Family.

An Englishman and an American had killed the Count, removing his head with a kukri knife and driving a bowie knife through his heart. When news of this reached Brancusi from the gypsies, he traveled back to Transylvania. Dracula's attackers had simply abandoned the coffin, with its native soil and the dust that the Count's body had crumbled into. Brancusi dug a grave on the desolate, wind-swept grounds of the Castle, and placed the Count's coffin within.

✠

Eventually, over a long period, the entire tribe had felt the Stranger's bite directly or indirectly.

A few of the tribefolk lost their lives to ravenous bloodthirst, drained dry. Others succumbed to disease or giant cats or falls from cliffs. One even died of old age. But all of them rose again.

And so it came to pass, just as it had for the Stranger all those years before, that the tribe had to look elsewhere to slake its thirst.

But they had not counted on the Others.

✠

Weidenreich and Brancusi sat in Weidenreich's lab late at night. Things had been getting very tense—the Japanese occupation was becoming intolerable. "I'm going to return to the States," said Weidenreich. "Andrews at the American Museum is offering me space to continue work on the fossils."

"No," said Brancusi. "No, you can't take the fossils."

Weidenreich's bushy eyebrows climbed up toward his bald pate. "But we can't let them fall into Japanese hands."

"That is true," said Brancusi.

"They belong somewhere safe. Somewhere where they can be studied."

"No," said Brancusi. His red-rimmed gaze fell on Weidenreich in a way it never had before. "No—no one may see these fossils."

"But Andrews is expecting them. He's dying to see them. I've been deliberately vague in my letters to him—I want to be there to see his face when he sees the dentition."

"No one can know about the teeth," said Brancusi.

"But he's expecting the fossils. And I have to publish descriptions of them."

"The teeth must be filed flat."

Weidenreich's eyes went wide. "I can't do that."

"You can, and you will."

"But—"

"You can and you will."

"I—I can, but—"

"No buts."

"No, no, there *is* a but. Andrews will never be fooled by filed teeth. Ever since Piltdown Man, filing is the first thing people look for when they see an odd specimen. And, besides, the structure of teeth varies as you go into them. Andrews will realize at once that the teeth have been reduced from their original size." Weidenreich looked at Brancusi. "I'm sorry, but there's no way to hide the truth."

✠

The Others lived in the next valley. They proved tough and resourceful—and they could make fire whenever they needed it. When the tribefolk arrived it became apparent that there was never a time of darkness for the Others. Large fires were constantly burning.

The tribe had to feed, but the Others defended themselves, trying to kill them with rock knives.

But that didn't work. The tribefolk were undeterred.

They tried to kill them with spears.

But that did not work, either. The tribefolk came back.

They tried strangling the attackers with pieces of animal hide.

But that failed, too. The tribefolk returned again.

And finally the Others decided to try everything they could think of simultaneously.

They drove wooden spears into the hearts of the tribefolk.

The used stone knives to carve off the heads of the tribefolk.

And then they jammed spears up into the severed heads, forcing the shafts up through the holes at the bases of the skulls.

The hunters marched far away from their camp, each carrying a spear thrust vertically toward the summer sun, each one crowned by a severed, pointed-toothed head. When, at last, they found a suitable hole in the ground, they dumped the heads in, far, far away from their bodies.

The Others waited for the tribefolk to return.

But they never did.

✠

"Do not send the originals," said Brancusi.

"But—"

"The originals are mine, do you understand? I will ensure their safe passage out of China."

It looked for a moment like Weidenreich's will was going to reassert itself, but then his expression grew blank again. "All right."

"I've seen you make casts of bones before."

"With plaster of Paris, yes."

"Make casts of these skulls—and then file the teeth on the casts."

"But—"

"You said Andrews and others would be able to tell if the original fossils were altered. But there's no way they could tell that the casts had been modified, correct?"

"Not if it's done skillfully, I suppose, but—"

"Do it."

"What about the foramen magnums?"

"What would you conclude if you saw fossils with such widened openings?"

"I don't know—possibly that ritual cannibalism had been practiced."

"Ritual?"

"Well, if the only purpose was to get at the brain, so you could eat it, it's easier just to smash the cranium, and—"

"Good. Good. Leave the damage to the skull bases intact. Let your Andrews have that puzzle to keep him occupied."

✠

The casts were crated up and sent to the States first. Then Weidenreich himself headed for New York, leaving, he said, instructions for the actual fossils to be shipped aboard the S.S. *President Harrison*. But the fossils never arrived in America, and Weidenreich, the one man who might have had clues to their whereabouts, died shortly thereafter.

Despite the raging war, Brancusi returned to Europe, returned to Transylvania, returned to Castle Dracula.

It took him a while in the darkness of night to find the right spot—the scar left by his earlier digging was just one of many on the desolate landscape. But at last he located it. He prepared a series of smaller holes in the ground, and into each of them he laid one of the grinning skulls. He then covered the holes over with dark soil.

Brancusi hoped never to fall himself, but, if he did, he hoped one of his own converts would do the same thing for him, bringing his remains home to the Family plot.

Brimstone and Salt

by S.P. Somtow

And what, you ask me, did they do in Gomorrah?

It's a reasonable question. We all know what they did in Sodom. They sat around buttfucking each other until God, in his wrath, rained down fire and brimstone, and blew the place to kingdom come. Everyone knows that, right? It's all there in the Bible. An angel told Lot that if he could find ten righteous and upright men in all of Sodom and Gomorrah, the twin cities would be spared; Lot couldn't, and that was that. Boom. Apocalypse. Mushroom cloud hanging over half of Mesopotamia.

Of course, Lot's own righteousness was pretty questionable; the Bible tells us that he screwed his own daughters, so he was probably not the very best judge of character. One wonders what gave him the right to pick ten honest upstanding citizens out of that double den of iniquity.

As usual, alas, the Good Book has it all backward; and we must, in fact, look elsewhere for the facts. Ask me anything. I know. I was there.

Don't laugh, Mr. Big-shot Shrink. You run a tight support group. Melvin the Multiple's pretty damn entertaining, and Mildred's regressions to her four-year-old closet of satanic abuse are truly *Hard Copy* material. Nothing to complain about there. Maybe Jack-in-the-Box, who doesn't do a fucking thing except rock back and forth, isn't that much of an asset to the group, but on the rare occasions when he does talk, he goes wild. One of these days I'm going to get *Entertainment Tonight* in here for you, but for now, we just have each other, don't we? As if that weren't enough.

I've been watching you guys go at each other for three weeks now. You know I haven't said anything. I've sat, and I've watched, and maybe you people think that my hundred bucks an hour are wasted because I haven't had the chance to spill my guts all over the plush white carpet of your elegant art deco office. Tonight, my friends, you're going to get your money's worth. This is one child abuse survivor support group that's never going to be the same.

Melvin, you had such a hideous time when you were four years old that your mind fractured into a dozen personalities. I've had a thousand. And not because of one cruel stepfather—because the entire world hurt me. To survive, I've become a thousand people over the years. Oh, Melvin, you have me beat on one thing—all your people are inside your brain now, fighting among one another. My personalities came one at a time. Each of them grew up, grew old, and died, yet I went on.

As for Jack, rocking back and forth—I like you. You had a narrow escape from a serial killer when you were seven years old, so you don't talk much. Look into my eyes. I'm a lot worse than the one you escaped from. I've dined on the kind of man who made your life a living hell. I'm a serial killer's serial killer.

Mildred: maybe you were a victim of that satanic abuse bullshit, and maybe not. False memory syndrome is a big thing right now, and your last analyst is being sued by half her ex-patients. I don't really believe it personally. You think you hung out with Satan? Satan was a personal friend of mine, back in the days when he was somebody.

So here I am. Just a visitor, in a sense, although I too am a survivor of what happened to all of you; I just happen to have survived a few thousand years longer than any of you have. Don't laugh, Mr. Shrink; I am not delusional. I am not suffering from any psychosis, though, after all these centuries, I probably ought to be. I'm not some rich bitch paying through the nose in order to play elaborate mindgames or live out arcane fantasies, two evenings a week.

I am a vampire.

I am Shoshana, the youngest daughter of Lot.

I am probably the oldest incest survivor in the world.

You want the support group confession to end all support group confessions? You want a night to remember, full of spectacle, bloodshed, debauchery, greed, insanity, shame, lust, angst, orgies, bellydancers? Hold on to your horses, my friends. Tonight, after five millennia or so, I finally feel like talking. And you, my friends, are a captive audience. Not because I compel you to stay, but because we of the ancient Kindred possess a seductive glamour that makes it nearly impossible for you to resist us. You fear us, but you desire us too.

Look at me, Mr. Big-shot Shrink: am I not beautiful? Is it the moonlit pallor of my complexion, the lurid carmine of my lips, the dusky splendor of my shoulder-length hair? Or is it perhaps the sensuous contralto of my voice, or my indefinably foreign accent, or the bizarre way that I lisp sometimes, as if the air had been trapped in my lungs for decades at a time, because I don't seem to need to breathe? Surely it's not the way I dress—about four centuries out of style—passing for gothic chic in today's strange, alienated youth culture? I am, you know, forever young. And I do mean forever.

Maybe you want to know, if I'm really this immortal creature of the night, why I need to be here with you at all. You're beyond all this, you tell me. You're not even human. Psychiatry is about helping human beings come to terms with their humanity, is it not? If you're really a vampire, presumably you don't have to worry about such mundane things as night terrors, bad dreams, neuroses, obsessive-compulsive behaviors.

But you have to understand that before I changed into what I am today, I once was human, and the bad thing my father did to me started long before I even knew vampires existed....

✠

It was at Ur that my father first came to me in the middle of the night. We had come for the funeral of Enkidu, the king's lover. Our people had long since been displaced from the land we called Eden, the fertile valley of the Tigris and Euphrates, by a technologically superior people, smelters of bronze, builders of cities; the desert had become our home. We lived in a manner not much different from the Bedouin tribes of today; but in theory the King of Sumer had suzerainty, and now and then it was necessary to send an official mission to the court. A formality, really. Abraham, the patriarch, didn't need to go himself, so he sent Lot.

My sister and I came with him, sharing a camel. We were not important. They didn't even lodge us in the palace, but allowed us to set up our tents in a walled garden that had once been part of the royal harem.

As the lowliest of the subject peoples, my father was not even granted an audience with Gilgamesh. But on the morning of the funeral, they gave us a perfunctory tour of the city. We were a convoy of litters, each one carrying a visiting party from some distant outpost of civilization, and they were doing their best to impress us with the splendor and spectacle of their superior culture. But everyone was in mourning, so there wasn't much to see. The marketplace was closed, and all the houses shuttered; from inside came the constant sound of weeping. The king had decreed that anyone caught not acting suitably doleful would be impaled.

The only action within the city walls was at the temple of Ishtar, which couldn't very well be closed down. Our palanquin moved slowly past it, and our guide, a minor court functionary named Turak, lectured us about sacred prostitutes. I had no idea what he was talking about. But my father covered our eyes with his fat palms.

"Abomination, abomination!" he murmured. "Don't look!"

"But father," I said, trying to pry his fingers off my face, "you're looking. In fact, you've got that look in your eye. The one that usually gets you in trouble."

My sister Rachel was a lot less defiant than I. She turned her back on the temple and squeezed her eyes tight shut. But I got in a good look. It was a spectacle! There was a ziggurat in the midst of a plaza, and it was all limestone, shimmering in the sun. On the front steps of the temple sat women of all shapes and sizes. Most were young—some as young as me, even—but a few were haggard and hideous, and there were one or two leviathans among them. They weren't wearing very much. Except for their makeup, that is: they were kohled and rouged and powdered until they looked more like statuettes than human beings.

One of the women winked at me and beckoned with a languid hand. She was, I thought, very beautiful. The thick layer of makeup made her seem quite unreal. My sister saw me gawking and poked me in the ribs. "Don't let abba catch you staring," she whispered.

"But he's staring himself," I said.

"He's a grownup," she said. "Not like you."

Turak was explaining to us bumpkins, in a self-important drone: "When a girl reaches the age of her initiation, she must come to the temple of Ishtar and wait to be deflowered by the first man who desires her.... "

"What's 'deflowered', abba?" I asked my father.

He slapped my face.

My sister began giggling. "You'll soon find out," she said.

My father grew very red. "Faster," he said to the litterbearers. "Faster. We don't need any of this heathen nonsense." And he flailed at the nearest one with a little lead-tipped flagellum. The slaves marched a little faster. They narrowly avoided a six-palanquin pileup with a little fancy footwork. The streets in Sumer were narrow, the buildings leaning inward, mostly in that white adobe style you still find in places like Tunisia.

Enkidu's funeral was an obstreperous affair, with bevies of women beating their breasts, and slaves, animals, ex-wives and catamites of the deceased being drugged and buried alive along with him. We, the visiting diplomats, watched the whole thing from a specially erected pavilion. We caught a glimpse of Gilgamesh, the god-king, but he was wearing a golden mask of grief, so we couldn't be sure if it was really him or whether it was some priest, subbing for him so he could sulk in his private apartments.

As is customary at funerals, the last clod of earth shoveled over the dead (and the half-dead) was the signal for a different mood, a kind of desperate merrymaking. There was a banquet to be held in the throneroom, and yes, there were plenty of dancing girls and all sorts of food and drink. Gilgamesh didn't bother to show up.

My father drank deeply of the wine, which was cooled with snow that had been brought down by runners from mountains, they said, a thousand leagues away. He was in a foul mood. Ambassador though he was, he wasn't being well treated. And the incident at the temple of the goddess seemed to have put him into a severe depression. My sister was deep in conversation with some Akkadian prince, which didn't please my father either. I loved my father, and I hated to see him this way. So I took it upon myself to sit by him, to fetch him a fresh beaker of wine now and then, and to cool his brow with a piece of damask dipped in spring water.

Turak, our erstwhile guide, had taken a shine to my father, for some unearthly reason. Perhaps it was because he was being snubbed by everyone else at the party. In between gnawing off great mouthfuls of leg-of-lamb, he insisted on informing us who all the guests were. Not that I really had any idea what was going on.

A long time after sunset, when half the guests were already sprawled out snoring on pillows stuffed with rose leaves, there was a brief commotion. Conch-trumpets blared. My father rubbed his eyes and bestirred himself a little. Several acrobats and fire-swallowers entered the throneroom, followed by slave girls strewing flower petals.

I overheard some of the guests talking: "The impertinence! Getting here this late, how can they get away with it, not even showing up at the funeral itself," and other gossip that I didn't understand. It was at that point that the mystery guests entered the throneroom.

One was a young man dressed as a woman, his hair delicately hennaed, his eyebrows brushed with kohl. "Abomination!" my father whispered, and tried to cover my eyes again; but I was able to peep through his half-separated fingers, and I thought the man-woman was really very good-looking. "Such a creature has no right to exist on this earth! It is an abomination; it should be stoned to death."

"Nonsense," said Turak. "You Hebrews are so provincial. That is the King of Sodom, you ignoramus. Their priest-kings take the form of the Sacred Hermaphrodite out of respect for their god, who possesses both sets of genitalia; he is said to have impregnated himself, grown himself inside his own womb, and at length given birth to himself."

"What arrant superstition," said my father.

"You think your little tribal thunder-god, whose name you don't even dare utter, is any more believable?" Turak said, laughing. My father simply fumed.

At that point, I took a good look at the other guest. She had long black hair that went all the way down to her knees, and it was artfully draped around her body. To my amazement, I realized that it was the only thing she was wearing, apart from her earrings. Her skin was as pale as the snow on the mountaintops on a moonlight night; her hair was blue-black, like a raven's feathers. Her eyes had an unearthly glow about them, and when she smiled something glistened in her mouth, shiny and pointy-sharp.

I found myself staring at her. Amazingly enough, she appeared to be staring at me too. I saw her whispering to some confidante, perhaps trying to find out who I was.

I did not have to ask; Turak was already explaining. "The Queen of Gomorrah," he said. "The less said about Gomorrah, the better."

I went on staring at her, and I thought I could hear her voice inside my head, murmuring of cool springs and fragrant gardens, telling me of a land of eternal starlight, of perpetual night.

Later in the evening, I found her seated next to me. I didn't see her move across the room. She touched my shoulder. Her hand was icy. She said, "You are beautiful, daughter of Lot. You are wasted on these ill-mannered nomads. One night you should come to my city. Then you'll know what love really means." And she smiled, and I turned to see my father scowling.

That was the night my father stumbled onto my pallet, his breath sour with alcohol and vomit. That was the day he caressed me with gnarled hands, tossed aside the coarse woolen covering, and lay next to me, touching me in places where no man had ever touched me. I lay awake, but dared not open my eyes. My father started to speak in a harsh, strained whisper: "Oh, Shoshana, I'm a wicked man, I'm a man who's drawn to abomination and darkness, but you shouldn't have stared so hard at the sacred whores of the goddess you bitch cunt whore look what you're making me do you bitch oh, oh, Shoshana, I can't help myself, you're such a fucking bitch you cunt you whore.... "

Oh, god, it got worse. He ripped open my sleeping robe. I felt something hard drive into my body. I felt torn up somehow. I knew I was bleeding. I couldn't help crying out. My father whispered, "Go to sleep, go to sleep, nothing's happening," and at that moment he began to shudder and—most heinous of all—began to utter the sacred Name of our tribal thunder-god—"YHWH!" he cried out. "There, I've done it, just as I do it every night with the other bitch, and you haven't struck me down, you haven't turned me to stone, you haven't seared my abominating body with a lightning bolt, YHWH YHWH YHWH," and each time he screamed out that word he thrust deeper into me and once I opened my eyes and I saw that his eyes were the eyes of a madman and I thought to myself, This is the worst moment of my life and I wish I could go away far far away....

It was in that moment that I saw, in my mind's eye, the face of the Queen of Gomorrah, saw her thin-lipped smile, saw her eyes grow wide and bloodshot, and heard her voice inside my head again, speaking of endless night. And I was comforted.

In the morning, there came gifts to my father's tent from the court of Gomorrah: a pound of salt for my father, and a terra-cotta doll for me. My father made me smash the doll in little pieces. "It's a graven image," he told me. He divided the salt into several pouches and put it away in a cedarwood chest. "Salt, after all," he said, "is the most valuable thing in the world. It's only because of salt that the people of Sodom and Gomorrah can be so arrogant, so blatant in their public disregard for propriety and godliness."

Nothing was said about the happenings of the previous night.

✢

So far, it was all very '90s. The drunken father sneaking into the bedroom, the silence the morning after, the blame being cast on the child, even my father's little attack of Tourette's Syndrome while he was violating my innocent person. Nothing, you say, has changed in five thousand years. But that is not quite true.

We had no support groups in the Bronze Age.

We had no runaway hotlines, no battered children's shelters, no psychiatrists, no *Hard Copy*. I had no way of knowing that my fate was not unique. My mother was dead, and there was no one else I might consider talking to; my sister was moody and self-involved, and seemed to have a boyfriend in every oasis, despite my father's efforts to keep her chained to the hearth.

My father's visits became more frequent.

I think I was about ten years old, although we measured time differently in those days, not being tied, as the city people were, to the cycles of moon, sun, and river. Our tribal god had rejected agriculture in favor of the hunter-gatherer lifestyle—that's why my great-uncle Cain had been exiled from the fold—but that's why our people had become so backward, wandering the desert instead of living in shiny cities, lacking a real notion of the passing of time. But I did grow taller, and my father grew crazier.

One night—

It was after one of my father's nocturnal visits. It was full moon night and I suppose I couldn't stand the pressure anymore, so I ran out into the night—a bitter cold night as many desert nights are—wearing only a shift of Egyptian linen. The stars put me in mind of the Queen of Gomorrah. It was bitterly cold, and I hid from the wind by snuggling against a line of tethered camels, comforted by their toasty, rancid body odor.

Presently, I saw that the patriarch's tent was aglow, and that shadowy people were moving around inside. I got curious. I crept along, lifted the tent-flap, and crawled among the sheepskins that were draped over everything. There were voices, and they were coming from deep within. Flickering light, too. Around me, Abraham's wives and concubines huddled together for warmth. I moved toward the inner tent, conscious that I was doing something very wrong, very unwomanly; the Hebrews were perhaps the most chauvinistic culture of that period, and we girls were certainly not allowed to trespass into the holy of holies.

The patriarch was sitting on a woven reed mat, and my father was with him. In the background, surrounded by veils, were the emblems of our tribal thunder-god, which few had ever gazed upon and lived, which had been ours ever since the big flood.

I watched them, knowing that I'd probably get a severe whipping if I was caught—Dr. Spock had not yet informed the world's parents about how traumatizing it might be to beat your children—and I saw the patriarch in a foul mood, rubbing his beard and now and then glancing askance at the holy of holies, as though afraid it might emit a thunderbolt at any moment.

"I've been hearing voices again," said Abraham. "Voices from, you know, behind there." He pointed to the sacred veils.

"What are we supposed to cut off this time?" said Lot. "Our dicks?"

I narrowly avoided giggling. My father was referring to Abraham's recent vision in which our god told him that all the men would have to slice off their foreskins as a sign of servitude to him. Well, it could have been worse; some gods require the sacrifice of one's firstborn, and others expect female clitoridectomy; I hoped that idea had not occurred to the patriarch.

"No, no," said Abraham. "It's Sodom and Gomorrah. We have to teach them a lesson."

"So what is the Lord God planning to do?" my father asked. "Have us take over the salt mines?"

"Our Tribal Deity," said Abraham, "is going to blow those twin cities off the face of the earth as a punishment for their iniquity." He said it as casually as you or I might talk about snuffing a candle. That's what made him the patriarch, you know; he could make the grandest of concepts seem almost trivial; crossing Sinai was like crossing the street.

"Quite right," said my father. "Nothing but abomination. Should have taken care of it during the flood."

I hadn't realized that our patriarch's voices were now claiming responsibility for the great flood that almost wiped out Mesopotamia a few generations before. I wondered whether they'd be taking credit for creating the universe next.

Don't gape, Mr. Big-shot Shrink. The world was a lot different then. Monotheism was still in the future. Every little society had its own god in those days, but no one had gotten around to claiming that other people's gods didn't even exist. That was a level of theological abstraction to which we hardworking nomads had yet to aspire.

"I want you to go to Sodom," Abraham told my father. "Scout the place out. I've told the Lord God that if you can ferret out ten worthy men in all of the twin cities, I'd like him to spare them the cataclysm."

"Good move," Lot said. "That way you don't lose face if—heaven forfend—no cataclysm actually takes place. Ten honest citizens won't be hard to find."

"True," said Abraham. "And while you're there, learn all you can about the salt business. You know, we're not going to be a bunch of desert-faring nobodies forever. One of these days, I see us taking over every city in the world—running the banks, the entertainment industry—taking charge, the way a Chosen People ought to take charge." I gasped. Another of his childishly simple, earth-shattering concepts. Talk about ambition! "Take your daughters," the patriarch continued. "Settle in. Keep an eye out for anything unusual. You'll be guests of the King of Sodom, so you'll have diplomatic immunity. Try to keep kosher if you can. And whatever you do, don't go over to Gomorrah."

"Why not, patriarch?" said my father.

Abraham leaned over and whispered something in Lot's ear. My father's eyes hardened; in the sooty light of the oil lamp he looked crazy, the way he looked sometimes when I sneaked a peek at him and saw him lumbering over me, sweating, in the night.

And once more, I thought of the Queen of Gomorrah, and wondered whether I would ever see her again.

Ur had been a dull city, all white and featureless. Sodom was beyond belief. Sodom had a night life—torchlight burning until the wee hours, taverns overflowing with wine. The salt mines had made the upper classes rich. People had slaves for everything. Even the public punishments were ostentatious—beheadings were accompanied with psaltery music and dancing girls, and whippings were performed by trained flagellants, wearing dark robes and golden goat masks. Nothing so simple or so interactive as a stoning.

Salt permeated the city. Their food was oversalted. The water held a hint of brine. Even the heaps of camel dung in the streets were encrusted with salt crystals. Salt caked the alley walls; you always saw a few dogs licking at the limestone.

Abraham had told us our host was to be the king, but as usual we were palmed off to one of his lower-echelon retainers; we were lodged in an apartment in the mansion of one of the royal salt accountants, who measured the salt into earthenware containers and employed a staff of six to tally the amounts on clay tablets. They went through a lot of tablets a day, and once I visited the archive, with its stacks of cuneiform-covered documents. Being a girl, I could not of course read—those were chauvinistic times—but it was fascinating to stare at the little wedges, and wonder what they meant.

Gomorrah was dark as Sodom was colorful. Separated from its sister city by a narrow stream so briny from the nearby salt mines that no fish could live in it, Gomorrah was permanently in the shadow of a thundering mountain—the only active volcano in the region. The city's walls were black basalt; Sodom's were limestone. When any of the inhabitants of Gomorrah emerged, it was only at night. Sometimes they showed up at one of the nightly orgies which, as visiting diplomats, it was my father's tiresome duty to attend; but they never ate, and they never drank wine.

I suppose it was only inevitable that I should become obsessed with the idea of Gomorrah.

In the first place, I had been very strictly brought up. I knew nothing of fleshly things—strange to you, maybe, considering my father's now almost nightly invasion of my most private world—but think about it. We didn't have Sex Ed in those days. I assumed, in my subservient way, that I'd been a very bad girl, and that I was simply getting what I deserved. It's not that surprising that I should become more and more drawn to that which was forbidden.

My sister Rachel, on the other hand, seemed to blossom in this place. The more my father came to me by night, the less depressed and moody she became; it was hard not to think there might be some causal connection between those two things. She took bellydancing lessons from one of the king's minor concubines (contrary to popular belief, buggery wasn't the only form of sex they practiced in that town) and soon became the life of the nightly orgies. My father never even bothered to scold her, though often, after she'd been particularly exhibitionistic, or ate too much barbecued pork, he would come home and beat me senseless with a cedarwood cane he kept especially for that purpose.

I remember the cane well, because it had a curious knob in the shape of a dog's head, and it had come all the way from Troy. I also remember it because of some of the painful uses to which my father put it in those wee hours of the morning, sometimes not even bothering to anoint it with camel fat beforehand.

I don't want to dwell on it, but I think it's fair to say that I wasn't having a very good time in Sodom. If you check your Torah, the book of Genesis claims that "it" only happened once, that I got my father drunk, and that he never noticed a thing; well, that's what you get when the history books are written by male chauvinist pigs.

I started to wander the night.

It was safe to leave the apartments as soon as my father left my side; within minutes I would hear him snoring. My sister had taken to staying out all night, painting her face, and indulging in all the other Sodomite activities; my father no longer really gave a shit. Wandering alone in the streets, a young girl who had yet to even have her first period, I was self-conscious at first. But I found that if I kept to the shadows, if I darted quickly from alleyway to doorway, from pillar to gatepost, few ever noticed me. Sodom was a tolerant city.

One night, I found the pit of discarded slaves....

It was by the eastern gate, the closest point in the city to Gomorrah. It was the stench that first attracted me. There was a temple dedicated to their hermaphrodite god by this gate, and a cloud of frankincense smoke, billowing out of the front portal, almost masked the odor of rotting corpses. The steps of the mini-ziggurat were lined with vultures. There was no one on the street, which was strange; in this town, no matter how late at night, you always ran into some drunken partygoer quirting his litterbearers, or a prostitute primping in a doorway.

Past the temple stood a low wall, and when I looked down I saw them: emaciated bodies heaped up, arms and legs and bony faces, staring eyes; in the bright moonlight the eyes glittered like polished onyxes.

Have you ever seen some of those Holocaust photographs? This was just the same. Except that no one thought it particularly immoral. I gazed, but I did not condemn. We all had slaves. I was impressed at the quantity of the dead, the conspicuous consumption of the society. I was too young to feel much pity. But presently I heard the clatter of a cart, and I ducked behind a statue of Ishtar that overlooked the pit. An old man was pushing the cart, which contained a fresh load of corpses. He dumped them unceremoniously over the side of the wall, and left.

I heard a noise. Someone—or some creature, perhaps a jackal—was prowling through the piles of corpses. I heard the patter of its feet. Yes. Definitely an animal. It sprang from heap to heap, sniffing, searching for something in particular. I'm not afraid of jackals; they are cowardly creatures for the most part. He stopped now and then and howled. He listened. I froze. He ran up a body that was tilted up, arm hugging the lip of the wall, and now he was on the other side of the statue, a little upwind of me; I hoped the wind would not change.

Then it was that the eastern gate creaked open, and there came through the portal a palanquin completely draped in black. The litterbearers were all Nubians, and their loincloths and headbands were also black. I shrank back in my hiding place. The eyes of the Nubians were glazed, as though they had been drugged or were in some magical trance. They carried the litter to within spitting distance of where I was. I crawled between the statue and the wall, between the breasts of Ishtar. I tried not to breathe. The jackal was suddenly right next to me.

It snarled. I was trapped between the goddess' breasts. I could smell its hunger. It was salivating, shuddering. I didn't want to scream, but when it leapt up onto me and began tearing at my garments, I let out a startled whimper. Because there was something about the jackal that was a little like my father—the look in his eye, a faint whiff of desire—we did not know then about pheromones, Mr. Shrink, but we could certainly feel their effects. That animal was embracing me in a parody of what my father had done that night, itself an obscene parody of love.

When the jackal bit me on the breast, I did scream, and then I felt powerful arms pulling me out, felt the sharp stone graze my elbow, found myself suddenly face to face with the Queen of Gomorrah.

The jackal was whimpering. I saw a deep red scar on its back, and the queen was handing her gold-handled whip to an attendant. "You should know better," she said to the jackal. "Roaming the slave-pits at night! Stupid, stupid, stupid."

In the moonlight, losing my terror, I saw that there was something human about the jackal. It was cowering from the queen. At length, it slunk away. She turned to me. "We meet again," she said, as though she had been expecting it all this time. "I see you have been bitten. Are you ready to come to Gomorrah?"

"My lady," I said, "the patriarch forbade us—"

She laughed. The sound was like the clatter of clay pots. I felt a certain comfort in that laugh. I dared to look her in the eye. I saw myself, twin images of a girl in those eyes, and I thought: How young I look, how vulnerable, how sad. And I knew she was thinking the same thing.

"You mustn't let men do all your thinking for you, Shoshana," she said. "Men see everything in black and white, and always in an adversarial relationship. Good and evil, man and woman, life and death. There are, you know, twilight areas where opposites intermingle; shadowlands you might call them. Sodom is such a land: in Sodom, the distinction between man and woman is blurred, and that's what your father calls abomination. But in our kingdom, it is the line between life and death that is crossed, you see."

"What do you mean?" I asked her. "How can something be both dead and alive at the same time?"

She touched my hand. Cold, cold, cold; I had touched a dead man before, and I knew that cold. "My daughter," she said softly, and I thought she was about to weep.

"I cannot weep," she told me.

"Do you read minds?"

"No," she said, "but after the passage of a few centuries, one learns to guess what humans think; their emotions skitter across their faces; you can smell their thoughts, sometimes before they even think them."

"Humans?" I said. "You speak as though you are not one. Are you a goddess?" I knew that the gods took human shape sometimes. Our own god used to take long walks in Eden with Adam and Eve, our forefathers.

"I am more real," she said, "than any goddess."

She lifted me to my feet—in my confusion I had fallen on my knees before her, as though she were that very goddess she claimed not to be—and caressed my cheek, my hair; her hand moved slowly down to the wound in my breast, an ugly welt that showed through the tear in my sleeping-robe.

"Oh," she said, and her icy fingers tensed a little, "I see that the vile creature has already… embraced you. That was not according to my plan… but never mind. It's time you visited Gomorrah."

She enveloped me in her arms. I flinched. Her skin was bitterly cold. I buried my face in her bosom, heedless of the burning iciness that seeped into my pores, that seemed to invade my very veins. Even this cold comfort was better than my father's hot embrace. She kissed my brow. It was as though she were branding me with the imprint of her frozen world. I knew then that I loved her. That was what I had felt when I first looked on her face, long ago, in the city of Gilgamesh.

"Did you like that kiss?" she asked me. "Is this what you have longed for, secretly, in the middle of the night—to be sucked into a world deeper than death, colder than the grave, darker than shadow?"

"I don't know," I said, "but I know it's got to be better than the world I know." And she drew me by the hand and led me to her palanquin; a slave made a back for me to step up; I reclined against cushions made of human skin, stuffed with the feathers of exotic birds; and I lay in the darkness and let the queen kiss me, again and again, not even crying out when her kisses drew blood.

Thus it was that I shared the palanquin of the Queen of Shadows, and came to the city of night, and learned the darkest secret in the world.

✠

Things became a little better after that. My father remarried—rather, he purchased a plaything from the slave-market, and scaled new heights of perversion and sadism with her. I never found out her name, never attended the ceremony, which was a Sodomite one in any case and therefore not actually binding on us. I suppose her name is of little interest; nobody thought it important enough to record in the Torah.

They left out my name, too, and I'm supposedly the ancestor of an entire race.

Gomorrah—

By day, a tomb. The basalt mansions, some carved out of the side of the volcano itself, were desolate. Volcanic ash lay over draperies, furniture, statues, dimmed the once-bright murals. The citizens of Gomorrah lay sleeping; some in a communal catacomb, a network of tunnels that burrowed into the mountain; others in splendor, in sarcophagi of granite or marble or pure gold. The houses were like tombs, their contents piled up; treasure-hordes were guarded by skeletons in armor; statues of gods and heroes lay in disarray; there was no food or drink, except for the occasional depiction on a mural. A smell of brimstone lingered in the air, perhaps because they had burrowed deep into the side of the volcano, exposing clefts that spewed out fumes of sulphur now and then.

By night, the court of the Queen of Gomorrah was lavish beyond all I had seen in Sodom. As the sun set behind the volcano, the courtiers would emerge from their hiding places. The megaron of the grand palace was cloaked with cobwebs and carpeted with dust; it was hard at first to get used to the darkness, but when I did, I saw that a different light suffused these creatures' existence. The phosphorescence of their skin, the dust-motes scintillant in the starlight, the silvery radiance of the moon over burnished mirrors of bronze—the flecks of gold dust on their black cloaks—the crystalline intensity of their eyes—all these things illuminated a world that never needed lamp or torchlight.

On the third night, the queen led me by the hand to a garden in the heart of her palace. It was overgrown with blackened, twisted vines; here and there, a red rose bloomed; and in the center of the garden stood a mirror-still pool, bordered by four dragons sculpted from lapis and malachite. Incense spewed from their jaws, a bitter odor, mostly myrrh, I thought.

"Your father," said the queen, "has a god who speaks from behind a curtain, through the lips of a befuddled old man. Would you like to meet our god?"

"I've never met a god," I said.

She chuckled. "Don't be afraid."

She led me to the edge of the pool and told me to look into the water. The water was quite still. And now, the queen took a pebble from a little basin beside the pool, murmured words in a mystic tongue, and cast the stone into the water. "Now," she said, "repeat after me—Dracula, Dracula, Dracula."

"What does that mean?"

"It is a magic formula whose resonance opens up a gateway from the present into other times, other places."

She cast the stone into the pool. I repeated the words; they rolled richly off the tongue; they were words of power; I shivered, trying to blame it all on the cold, for Gomorrah was a cold city, even in summer.

The water shimmered in the moonlight....

Then, kneeling over the edge of the pool, I started to see things. I saw a man on horseback, darkhaired, with a drooping mustache and a helmet of some unfamiliar metal. He looked out at me. I heard him whisper in my head: *Greetings, daughter from the distant past.*

"Who are you?" I cried out. "What kind of god are you, that condescends to speak even to an unlettered girl?"

I am your people's future.

"My people?" I said. "You hold the destiny of the Hebrews in your hands? But I thought that our tribal thunder-god—"

He laughed. *There are a people even more chosen than your own,* said the god. *Believe me. You are the ones who will influence all the events of the future. Nations shall rise and fall; empires, religions, and races shall came to power and be overthrown. But behind all these great events will be yourselves—the eternal ones—the ones who have embraced the world of darkness.*

I turned to the queen in disbelief. "I don't understand," I said. "What is he telling me—that I will live forever?"

"If you take good care of yourself," said the queen. "We are not gods precisely; we can't change the laws of nature; there are ways to kill us. But there is no reason you shouldn't survive for a thousand years."

"The way people used to," I said, "before the great flood."

She laughed again. "How superstitious you are," she said at last.

"Images in pools—isn't that some kind of heathen superstition?" I said. "Our patriarch says we shouldn't trust gods we can see and touch, but only the invisible one behind the curtain in the tabernacle."

The queen said, "Let me tell you something of our god, then. He is not so much a god as a visitor from the future. The word of power came to me in a vision long ago, when I was still mortal. In his time, he is some kind of great king, a *voivode*. He is feared. He impales his enemies by thousands and dines while watching their death-throes. A great mage captured his spirit in this pool, so that we can speak to him through the chasm of time; to him, in the time beyond, it seems as though he is dreaming. Because to him we are figures of history and legend, he knows more about us than we do ourselves; to us, he can serve as a kind of oracle. If you want, ask him a question about your future... it will come to pass, I promise you."

There was really only one thing I wanted to know. But I was afraid to say it out loud. I have not divulged my shameful secret to anyone until tonight. Oh, I wanted the god to tell me whether my torment would ever end, but to do so I would have had to confess that this torment existed. So instead I asked about something I cared far less about. "Are there," I asked the god, "ten upright men in all of Sodom and Gomorrah? My father is on a mission—"

Dracula glared at me across the gulf of time. *Our father*, he said, *is wasting his time*.

I said, "You mean that he might as well pack up and go home, that he won't find what the patriarch has sent him to look for?"

No, daughter of Eve, he said, *I merely mean that his search has become irrelevant. There are some things even the gods have no control over.*

The queen took me by the hand once more. "Talk to me while I bathe," she said, "and I will tell you more."

We went into an inner chamber hewn out of the basalt, and there she commanded an attendant to draw her bath, which was a curious thing; for there were twelve young women chained to columns, and the attendant bled each one into an earthenware pitcher, and emptied its contents into the tub. The victims were drugged, perhaps; they stared dully ahead, not seeming to care that their lives were being siphoned away from them. She stripped, stepped into the frothing blood, and began languidly to scrape herself with a lump of pumice.

I sat beside the bath, handing her cloths and unguents as she requested them, waiting. One always had to wait with vampires; they have so much time on their hands; they do not move that fast, unless it is to attack, immobilize, and drain their prey's blood. I tried making light conversation. "Among our people," I said, "when a woman has her monthly bloodletting, she takes a ritual bath, a *mikvah*, to cleanse away every trace of blood… but you are doing the opposite…. " She only smiled.

"Don't chatter," she said. "Enjoy the profound silence of night."

I listened. The room was quiet, save for the groans of dying slaves. The walls were thick. At first I heard nothing more. Then I realized I was hearing more than I had ever heard before. Somehow the acuity of my hearing had increased. I could make out individual crickets. A nightingale halfway down the mountain. I thought I could hear the grass grow… and yes… if I really listened… there, there, my father's drunken snores, and the quick, sharp breathing of his Sodomite woman.

Finally, she said, "The god is right. You see, Shoshana, our mages have been studying the mountain for some years now, and we are certain that it is on the verge of erupting—in a matter of days."

So it had nothing to do with divine retribution at all.

"But what will you do about it?" I said. "Will your people pack up all your belongings and found another city somewhere?" If, indeed, the inhabitants of Gomorrah knew that they were going to be buried under tons of lava, why didn't they seem remotely worried?

"Oh, some of us undoubtedly will leave," said the queen, "but for most it will be at best a minor inconvenience. The mountainside is honeycombed with tombs. We will sleep a little longer than usual, perhaps, but what is a century or two, or even a millennium, to those who must contemplate eternity?"

"What about the Sodomites?" I said.

"Why worry about them?" said the queen. "When your farm's burning down, are you going to waste your time rescuing the cattle? There'll be other prey."

I still couldn't believe this, couldn't grasp the long view that the vampires took of history. The queen smiled sadly. She touched my cheek, my forehead. She was no longer cold; the blood had warmed her body almost to burning, and I winced; but then, when a rivulet of blood dribbled down toward my lips and I tasted the smooth salt fluid, I felt something I'd never felt before. Orgasm only hints at its intensity. I shuddered. The warmth shot down my throat and seemed to rush directly into my arteries. I could hear my heart pumping, could hear the river of blood as it gushed through the capillaries of my brain.

"YHWH!" I cried out. I was shocked at my own perversity. To let the sacred name pass my lips... yet there was no thunderbolt. "What's happening to me? Have I become a vampire?"

"You are not completely changed, my daughter. But a time will come when the daylight will cause you grief...."

"The blood! The blood!"

She gripped my wrists now and drew me into the tub of blood with her. She caught me in the slippery embrace of gore. Blood seeped into every orifice of me. I was on fire. The room careened about; everywhere I saw the lifeless eyes of the chained slaves. I could not tell terror from ecstasy. With a slender finger she traced on my young breasts the outline of an apple. With her other hand she plunged down to my most secret places, touched what only my father had touched before; but he had not sought to kindle any flames in me. The queen's deft fingertips skirted my nether lips, snaked upward to caress a certain mound that made me tingle and finally quake and scream, and I profaned the holy name several more times, heedless that if one of my people heard me I might well be stoned to death; I no longer feared death; I knew that the woman who held me in her arms was death, that death was a new way to say love.

Before dawn, I went once more to the oracle of Dracula. I threw in a stone and repeated the magic formula, and once more I gazed into the visage of the impaler from a future time.

Daughter, he said, *I dream of you again*.

"Show me this future they're talking about," I said. "I suppose it's too late for me now, there's no going back, I don't know if I've chosen wisely, but—"

The water rippled softly. The moon was obscured by the mountain. Incense rose from the brazier. Through the wisps of smoke, in the undulating water, dimly lit by candlelight and starlight, I saw vague images. I saw the volcano burst, the city buried, the people screaming in the streets. I saw new cities, always new cities, bigger, shinier, dirtier, more and more crowded. I saw wars that spanned whole continents. Death was everywhere. Dracula's own victims cried out from their spikes. I saw my own people driven from their homeland time and time again—from Egypt, from Judaea, from Poland, from a thousand places with unpronounceable names; I saw them die by millions; I saw a weapon that killed more people in a single hour than the entire population of our known civilized world; and I knew at last the truth of the legend of Adam, my ancestor and the patriarch's; that man is a fallen creature, that our god is infinitely wrathful, destructive, and uncaring.

The only light in the world's future came from a place of ultimate darkness....

I saw the Queen of Gomorrah emerge from a thousand-year slumber, shatter her igneous prison, break out of the walls of obsidian. I saw her in the night, her skin luminescent in the starlight. I saw vampires everywhere—though I could not know what the scenes represented then, I now know what I saw—Auschwitz—Hiroshima—London in the Black Plague—Naples during the cholera season—vampires. Standing watch at the foot of a cross where a man was tied up and nailed alive; ruling in the courts of Egypt and England, Constantinople and Kazakhstan. I saw vampires dancing in the neon night of a thousand cities. I saw vampires in theaters and opera houses, vampires in darkened movie houses, vampires feasting on the numberless hordes of humans who populated an exploding world. I even saw myself. Yes. Sitting in an art deco office of the future, pouring my guts out to a roomful of strangers. No, I didn't understand any of these visions. It was a kaleidoscope of alien landscapes.

Daughter of Lot, the dark god whispered in my mind, *do you like what you see?*

I couldn't answer. I was bursting with new emotions. All my life I had hungered for something without even knowing that I hungered. The taste of blood lingered on my lips. I felt fulfilled. I wasn't just some insignificant female anymore. I had a destiny.

✠

Two messengers were at my father's house a few days later. The Septuagint calls them angels, but angelos just means messenger in Greek; those Greeks do have a knack for fancifying the mundane.

They came from the patriarch, who was encamped in an oasis nearby. It was a day of tumult and festivity, the annual ceremony of their god-king's sacred marriage to himself, which was also the city's fertility ritual, signaling the commencement of spring. Drums, conch-trumpets, harps and dulcimers could be heard coming from every direction. People jammed the narrow streets; palanquins rammed into one another; merchants jostled one another as they peddled shish kebabs and wine.

A parade was streaming past our apartment; we sat on a balcony, watching it go by. Abraham's messengers were young men, twins, and very attractive; my sister Rachel had been making eyes at one of them all through breakfast, and now my father's wife was winking suggestively at the other as she broke bread and poured out salt.

In honor of the hermaphrodite god-king, it was the custom for the men and women of Sodom to cross-dress. It was not unlike the Mardi Gras in New Orleans; drag queens everywhere, and music pouring from every tavern; the only difference was the constant death-gurgle of the sacrificial victims from altars all around town, for the sacred hermaphrodite god was propitiated by the flaying alive of dozens of young boys and girls, mostly culled from the children of the slaves who worked the salt mines. The flayed skins were hoisted up on poles and carried aloft by dancers;

the smell of death mingled in the hazy air with the tang of salt and the odor of sweaty bodies.

Abraham's messengers weren't particularly disturbed at the bloodshed *per se*; you have to understand that this was before our tribal god banned human sacrifice.

The patriarch's wife, you may recall, bore a child at a very advanced age; it was naturally incumbent upon Abraham to sacrifice his first legitimate son, but one of those revelations from heaven conveniently intervened—that's how it is when you have a direct hotline to the Lord God—and soon everyone was denying that the Hebrews ever practiced human sacrifice at all.

It was the scale of human sacrifice that appalled the two messengers—I mean, this was their first time in the big city—and the stench was making it hard for them to keep their breakfast down. They complained loudly about the abomination of it all, and my father chimed in now and then in hearty agreement.

At that point, a group of revelers stopped beneath our balcony and started hooting and whistling at the two messengers. The celebrants were drag queens to the nth degree. One wore a flounced skirt in the Minoan fashion, with fake breasts made from two large conch shells; another was dressed like an Egyptian, with a wig, blackened eyes, a chain of scarabs around his neck that rested athwart another pair of artificial boobs, these ones made from gourds; a third was actually in the costume of a Hebrew matron, which is to say that she was very plainly and concealingly attired.

It was the pseudo-yenta who cried out, "Who are those handsome young studs up there in the apartments of the Hebrew ambassador?"

"Send the fresh meat down," said the one in Egyptian garb.

"Yes," said the Minoan, "we want them for the sacred fertility orgy."

"Is it true you Hebrews are all circumcised?" said the yenta. "Show us yours and we'll show you ours, honey!"

Lot cried out, "Abomination! You would practice your craven lusts even upon the angels of the lord?"

They hooted and jeered, and the messengers looked suitably embarrassed, and Lot got up and did what every good Hebrew does when confronted with abomination; he rent his robes and howled. I was glad he did not put on this exhibition too often; with the amount of abomination in this town, he would have had to spend all our barter goods on clothes.

At length, the procession moved on. At noon would come the solemn nuptials of the god-king. I wanted to go to the palace to watch, of course, but my place was at my father's table, waiting on the guests hand and foot; even now, I was oiling their feet as my father discussed the salt business and how our people might want to get a piece of the action.

"What about the patriarch's ten upright men?" said the first angel. "How's that going?"

"Oh, it'll be fine," said Lot. "I got a list from the king's treasurer of the most honest men in the city—they pay their taxes, are faithful to their wives, and don't indulge in any more abomination than absolutely necessary—so we can easily pick ten at random."

"Good," said the second messenger. It was the politically correct thing to do, to satisfy Abraham's mysterious voices while simultaneously managing to do business.

"Daughter," Lot said—I honestly think he could not remember my name at times—"Hurry up and finish drying the guests' feet; you're so slow—are you sick?"

"No, father," I said. "It's just the sun. For some reason, it's really hurting my eyes. I think I'm burning up."

"Not even that hot," my father said. "You'd think she'd never been reared in the desert at all, she's become so spoiled by their soft city ways," he went on, but it was true that I was finding the sun almost unbearable, and I was glad that I was able to crouch under the shadow of the breakfast table. "I'll write a note to the patriarch," he said, "and tell him the ten good men are no problem; he can call off the apocalypse. The Sodomites will no doubt be very relieved," he added, winking.

I don't know why I even opened my mouth. Girls are supposed to be seen and not heard. But I had acquired a new self-esteem during my visits to the Queen of Gomorrah. I piped up. "Father, the volcano is going to blow any minute. I don't think you'd better find any upright citizens in this town. You wouldn't want the Lord God to make a mistake, now, would you?"

"What?" my father screamed.

"I know," I insisted. "I've been to Gomorrah. I've spoken with the Dracula oracle, the voice from the future. You've never spoken with any god; you just listen to whatever Abraham says; every little whim he has is the word of YHWH."

My father gasped to hear the sacred name pass my lips, and the two messengers looked very sheepish. My father's wife, knowing nothing of Hebrew customs, just looked bewildered.

It was my sister who shrieked, "You stupid little girl. Don't you know you can be stoned for saying—"

"And who's going to stone me?" I shouted. I got up, hurled the basin of expensive oil at the wall, quickly backed into the shadow of the doorway, away from the sunlight. "It's not like there's a couple of hundred tribesmen here to pick up rocks. I mean, look around you. These people are civilized. They don't go around stoning people just for saying YHWH."

My father slapped me resoundingly. I tasted blood. And that taste rekindled my memories of the night I spent in the Queen of Gomorrah's bloodbath; instead of cowering and backing down, I got right in my father's face. His breath, stinking of wine and garlic, brought back a flood of memories of traumatic nights, and I shrank back, but only for a moment. I looked him right in the eye and said, "YHWH, YHWH, YHWH, father, I don't see any thunderbolts descending from the sky; if that was true, you'd be burned to a crisp by now."

That was how my father found out that I'd been conscious all those times, that I knew what he was, knew him to the core. He exploded. He started to slap my face over and over, and finally he shoved me through the doorway into the apartment. "Go to your room," he said, "and you will receive neither food nor water until you are ready to apologize."

"Go fuck yourself," I said to my father.

He just gaped. I started to laugh. For the first time I felt that I had power, real power; that I was a real woman and not some defenseless child. I could just imagine what the two messengers were going to tell Abraham when they got home.

✠

By sunset, my father was more drunk than he had ever been in his life. I could hear him shouting and throwing things, and cursing at the messengers. With my attenuated hearing I knew everything that was going on; heard the wine splosh out of the jug, heard my father's heavy breathing, my sister giggling, my father's wife pacing back and forth in confusion.

I lay on my pallet, brooding. At length, my father stormed into the bedchamber. He saw me in the half-dark, thought I was asleep.

"Bitch!" he shouted. "Whore! I'll teach you your place. You think that you're a woman now? You think you can defy me, little girl? You think that because I've neglected you of late, I can't come right back and give it to you all over again?"

He hulked over me. Seized me by the shoulders. Out of force of habit, I squeezed my eyes shut, waiting for the invasion of his touch. Sweat ran over my shoulders, slicked my narrow breasts. He shook me. His fingernails drove under my skin and I could feel blood welling up, and the smell of my own blood maddened me.

I bit him.

He raised his hand to slap me down.

At that moment, the volcano began to rumble.

There came an eerie red glow through the window-slats. I caught a whiff of burning sulphur. I opened my eyes. I didn't care anymore. My father looked defeated, spent, consumed with inner torments I had never seen before. He let go of me and crumpled down to the floor.

Then he left the room. I heard him shouting. "Rouse the messengers! Tell them to get word to Abraham that ten good men could not be found in Sodom! Get our camels—we're getting out of the city!"

He did not even bother to summon me. But I crept out of bed, and I too began gathering up a few pots and some fresh bread out of the oven, and a basin full of salt. My sister and I worked feverishly together with a new kind of solidarity. I knew she had heard everything in my room; she had a newfound sympathy for me. "You too, Rachel," I said softly.

"Yes, Shoshana; me too."

And we embraced; it was the first tender moment we sisters had shared in many years.

In the streets, the drunken revelry was still going on. Only a few were surreptitiously marching in the direction of the westerly gate. The volcano, I suppose, had rumbled before, without much effect. But now, as I looked eastward toward Gomorrah, I could see that the mountaintop was coated in brilliant vermilion, and that smoke was funneling up toward the moon.

My sister and I and my father's wife sat in a cart; my father drove the camel; the messengers, riding a chariot, were disappearing into the distance. We reached the gate; the gate-slaves opened it; we entered the plain; we moved on without speaking.

We were only about a mile away when the explosions began.

"Don't look back!" said my father to us all. "The abominations are being wiped out! Great is the Lord God, the Lord of Hosts! Holy is he, the Lord of Sabaoth! Don't look back or you too will be consumed!"

We were traversing a ridge now. Below us were the salt mines. Slaves were still working them by torchlight, and overseers still stood with whips. The ground was quaking. We hastened. Our camels grunted.

"I have to go back," said my father's wife. "You think I want to live in a stinking sheepherder's tent for the rest of my life?"

"You'll die!" my father said.

She leaped from the oxcart and began running down the slope, toward the salt mines. Behind her, Sodom was in flames. The sky was black with ash. The lava was hurtling down the mountain now. The twin cities glowed. Even from this far I could hear the screams.

If we didn't hurry, we too would be buried alive. My father urged us on, but I stood and watched her. I knew that I was not wholly human, and that even if I was buried in the ashes I would find a way to come back.

I saw the earth open up. I saw the mines collapse. Slaves blowing into the air, arms, legs, decapitated heads flying. I saw Lot's wife, standing there with her arms outstretched, gazing at Sodom, saw the hail of salt and brimstone descend upon her, whiten around her, turn her into a statue in mid-scream. I felt my sister grab me by the arm and drag me back to the cart. Heard the wheels clattering, felt the cart bumping over the stones;

at length, when the plain evened out a little, the rhythm of the cart put me into a deep sleep, and I dreamed of the Queen of Gomorrah, and of nights of blood and shadow.

✣

We lived in a cave. My sister and I were pregnant; I died in childbirth and they walled me up in that selfsame cave and returned to the tents of the patriarch; by then the story of Sodom and Gomorrah had grown to—dare I say it?—biblical proportions.

Why, then, am I here? Listen. I've ridden into battle alongside Vlad the Impaler, stalked the catacombs of Rome for lost Christians, gorged myself on the battlefields of Waterloo and Gettysburg. But always I was haunted by my father's face: not only the face of rage as he violated me on countless nights, but also the expression of helplessness and defeat on the night I finally overcame him. I was alone for a thousand years, and then I encountered the Queen of Gomorrah at a party in Antioch; she smiled, we talked of old times; but you know, we had drifted far apart in that thousand years. Since then I have known crowned heads and white trash, presidents and slaves, and I feasted on their blood. But buried deep within me… somewhere… there's an angry little girl.

For a hundred bucks an hour, I want someone to hold her, soothe her, wipe away her tears. For a hundred bucks an hour, I would like to learn to weep again. I've lived with this so long I don't know what I'd do if I could be cured, but I think the time has come for me to try.

Can you help me, Mr. Big-shot Shrink? Can you hold Shoshana's hand? Can you read her a bedtime story?

Can you love her?

The Death-Sweet Scent of Lilies

David Niall Wilson

The sound of dripping blood was hypnotic, drawing him away from the reality of the moment and into the recesses of his mind—of his memory. The stakes surrounded him like a small forest, their grisly cargoes twisting and turning slowly downward as the sharpened tips worked their way through flesh and around bone with the help of gravity. The dying sun drew grisly shadows that trailed away from the corpses and drained into the growing night.

Only a couple of those impaled had the strength left to fight. Only one of them still lived. He was vaguely aware of the woman's eyes, glaring down at him, struggling through the pain to concentrate on him, as if desiring to take his image to the hereafter, where they might meet again.

He paid her no attention. Let her die with her fantasy, he would die with his own nightmares, and they had come for him again, though he was awake and aware, dragging him inward.

✢

The cell in the sultan's palace had been cold and damp, but the chill that had set into the marrow of his bones went far deeper than physical discomfort. He had been punished before, many times, and yet this time, somehow, he knew it would be different. This time he felt his life teetering in the balance. While the thrill of it was delicious, still he feared.

It had been a small thing. One of the princes of the palace had wanted a particular girl—Myrna; Vlad had wanted her as well. Myrna had chosen Vlad. Officially he was a guest at the palace, though all knew the truth of it—that he was hostage against the good faith of his father, he and his younger brother Radu. If it had ended at the girl, all would have been well, but of course, it had not.

Ahmen, the prince, had not been satisfied with defeat. He'd come upon Vlad in the gardens, weapon drawn, and he'd insisted that they fight. He would, he'd said, avenge his honor on this "son of a dog"—thus making it personal. Vlad was no stranger to fighting—he'd done more than his share of it since arriving at the palace—and he'd set about teaching the young prince a lesson; that lesson was that a dog is no mean adversary.

The cuts, and the young man's pride, would heal, though there would be a scar on his cheek until the day he died to remind him of Vlad Dracula. The sultan's anger was less easy—less malleable. There was no fighting allowed, especially no fighting wherein "guests" injured princes. No matter the cause of the dispute, Vlad was at fault, Vlad would be punished.

They had brought him to the cell in the early afternoon, leaving him with nothing but a skin of warm, brackish wine and his thoughts. He had never been in this particular section of the dungeons, and his sense of direction, usually without peer, was failing him. He knew only that his prison bordered a garden, or what had once been a garden, before decay had set in, and that the barred window in the far wall looked out over that barren, lifeless place.

There was something about the way the light slipped through and over the court, but never seemed to touch it, the way the shadows held their ground and relinquished nothing to the dying rays of sunlight, that sped his heartbeat. The hairs at the back of his neck were standing, prickling, and he nearly jumped from his boots when a key slipped into the lock and the door grated noisily behind him.

Turning swiftly, he found that the sultan himself had entered the cell, alone, and that the door was closing again behind him.

"Your eminence," he said, barely hiding the sneer in his voice. "This *is* a surprise."

"Oh, this moment has been long in coming, young Vlad, but it was as inevitable as death." The sultan's voice had a merry lilt to it, as always, but his eyes were cold, like those of a serpent.

"I trust you have had some time to think over your transgressions.... do you know why you are here?

"To soothe the wounded pride of a very stupid and physically inept prince, I believe," Vlad snapped.

"Oh, that... " the sultan made a dismissive gesture with one hand. "You may have actually done Ahmed a favor. He is much too quick to provoke a fight, and now he has learned that when you do so, you risk losing. He is lucky it was only his pride."

"Then," Vlad's tone changed, his brain racing, "why *am* I here?"

"You remind me too much of your father, young Vlad. He had been nothing but the greatest of thorns in my side, and I see him in your eyes, only it is much more dangerous because, where your father is wild, impetuous, and strong, you are all of that and much more intelligent."

Vlad said nothing, his senses on full alert for a sudden movement, or a trap.

"This leaves me with a problem, you see," the sultan went on. "You will be free one day, assuming your father manages to keep himself in check long enough to ensure it, and on that day we will no doubt become enemies. Do not try and deny it, it is in your blood.

"I have something to show you that I hope will help to even the odds. There are secrets even your father cannot have told you, things very few know of, things that make a difference. Do you believe in God, Vlad Dracula?"

The question took him completely by surprise. He had been raised in the church. All that his father stood for, all that they fought for, was so heavily enmeshed in the church that it was part of their lives, their souls. Did he believe in God?

"I do not know," he answered slowly. "I have been taught to *fear* God, and that is a hard lesson to unlearn. In that respect, I believe in God."

"I will show you a new fear," the sultan said softly. His voice was still light, but his eyes were dancing now, and deep within their depths, Vlad saw the fear the man spoke of surfacing.

His own heart speeded accordingly. This man had locked him here, was threatening to teach him fear, and yet he feared himself. Whatever was to come, it was either safe for neither of them, or simply horrifying enough that, even without personal risk, it made the sultan nervous. Vlad grinned.

"You will show me something that will bind me to you?" Vlad asked slowly, not wanting to let his true feelings show, his contempt. He could imagine nothing, death included, that could bring such a thing about.

"I will show you something that will bind you to nothing," the sultan replied quietly. "I will show you something to shake your belief in yourself, your God, and your world. I will show you something to pale the threat of death.

"You are wise and strong beyond your years, Vlad Dracula, but you have not lived those years. Your experience limits you."

The sun had fallen steadily as they talked, and the shadows that had ruled in the corners and nether-regions of the ancient courtyard beyond the window stretched forth to swallow it whole. Vlad could think of nothing to say, and he was afraid, in any case, that a catch in his throat might give away the dread that was stealing over his soul with the vanishing of the light. He stood in silence, and the older man came to stand at his side, watching.

Suddenly, there were sounds in the courtyard, the scuffing of feet, the rattling of chain and the scrape of metal against metal. There were soft curses and a whimpering, keening cry—muffled, but forlorn and so bereft of hope that it stood the hairs on Vlad's arms and at the nape of his neck on end. He reached up to grip the bars on the ancient window, fought to split the shroud of darkness to see what, and who, was there.

They came into sight moments later, illumined by a soft glow of moonlight that had begun to trickle down through the withered trees. He could make out three figures. Two were larger, men, and the third was dragged between them. He could just make out a woman's robes... no, only a girl. She struggled wildly in the grip of her two captors, but to no avail. She was bound, hand and foot, in chains.

As they drew closer, Vlad could make out the soft lines of her face. It was Myrna, she over whom he and Ahmed had fought, and her eyes were wide with unbridled terror. He could see their whites as they tried to roll in upon themselves. What would instill such fear?

"Is this some sort of joke?" he said, spinning to the sultan in anger. "The girl means nothing to me; do you think her death will change me?"

"I have not grown to this age by being a fool, young Vlad.... you would do well to keep that in mind. Watch. Learn. Fear. The girl is nothing."

This wasn't exactly true. Vlad could still remember the softness of her skin as they'd pressed together the night before, the touch and taste of her lips, the soft, flower-scent of her hair. She was not important, not exactly, but the point that was being made of her, at his expense, that was an insult that would be repaid. He kept his silence, and he watched.

The two men released her from her shackles, one at a time, but they held her tightly by each arm, as if awaiting some sign. Vlad looked out and caught Myrna's eyes, just for a moment, and they held his—begging him, beseeching him. The futility of her trust in him angered him further, and he felt the muscles in his arms tense, felt his hands gripping the bars so tightly that either the metal, or skin and bone, would surely give.

What could they be planning? Rape? Torture? Were there wolves to be set free, or was it all a show to see if they could get him to react? What kind of lesson could this man, this "Turk," be planning? The man might be a dog, but he was no fool, as he himself had pointed out.

There was a high, keening cry from above, and the men, their own eyes awash in sudden dread, released their hold, throwing Myrna to the ground. They melted into the shadows quickly, and before she could rise to follow, they were gone. She was alone, except for her silent audience of two. Vlad's breath quickened.

Myrna did not move immediately. She seemed pinned to the ground, trembling and weak. Looking about frantically, she searched the encroaching shadows, never locking her gaze on any one point. She sensed something—they all sensed something—but there was no direction to it, only the acrid, bitter stench of danger. It burned at Vlad's eyes, dripped from him in the sweat that stained his tunic and froze, clammy against his thighs.

There was a skittering sound, like claws against stone, and the fluttering of a thousand moths, trapped against the glass of a lantern. Vlad could not tear his eyes from Myrna. She shivered now, melting to the ground without form or substance, unable to rise. Her gaze was devoid of thought or intelligence. He saw the animal in her, stark and unchained, and it was not a predator he saw, but helpless prey.

Then his heart stopped. The window was blocked, no, not blocked. There was a face in the window, a creature, grasping the bars from the other side, eyes feral and yellowed, fangs bared in an evil grimace that mocked a smile. The creature let loose the high, keening screech once more, this time directly in his face, and he felt the heat of its breath, smelled the stench of decayed flesh and generations of death washing over and around him, trapping him.

The thing had its claws wrapped around his fingers where he grasped the bars, and he could not tear his hands away. He could not release his eyes, either, as he felt himself dragged easily into the thing's gaze. Behind him he was vaguely aware of the sound of scraping stone, aware that the sultan, for all his bravado, was making his exit. There was no time to spare for the man now. All was focused on those eyes, on the points where cold, icy flesh gripped his own, and the madness of the power he felt emanating from the thing.

As the door behind him slammed back into place, he wrenched himself free with a mighty tug, falling heavily back and slamming into the stone of the opposite wall. His head connected hard with unyielding stone, but somehow he managed to stagger to his feet. He tottered back to the window, careful to keep his hands from the bars, and he gazed into the courtyard.

His heart was hammering so fiercely that he felt it would burst from his chest, but he had to see—had to know. Whatever that thing was, whatever it was going to do, he had to know. He had looked into its eyes, and he had not seen his death; he had seen hunger, damnation far beyond the physical release of death—madness. He had to know.

The thing had left the window as he fell away, swinging to face Myrna, who was pressed so tightly against the ground that she seemed no more than a small lump in the courtyard. Her eyes were as round as saucers, wider and more filled with dread than any Vlad had seen, and they were locked onto those of the creature. It advanced with mincing, prancing steps across the court to where she lay prone, and yet she did nothing to move from its path, did nothing to try and escape.

"Run!" he cried, putting every ounce of strength he possessed into the scream. For one long second, she seemed to acknowledge him, to hear. She turned slightly, letting her gaze return to his eyes, and in that moment he knew fear. It was not the exhilarating fear of battle, or the fear that riding a horse through the woods at full gallop might bring. Those fears he knew and reveled in—this was unclean. It was a fear so deeply rooted, so all-encompassing, that he had to force himself to continue to breathe. The weight of it pushed down upon his breast, punishing, grinding into his soul.

The creature paid him no attention, and Myrna's gaze returned almost immediately to her attacker. Miraculously, she managed to rise to her knees as it approached, then to stagger to her feet as it reached out with clawed, shriveled hands to take hers in its grasp.

Vlad wanted to scream again, to scream a negation, either of the scene before him, or of the knowledge he would now take to his grave, the fear that had been thrust upon him. He knew this creature, though until that moment he'd thought it legend alone. He knew the *vrykolakes*, the *vampyr*. He knew, and wished to the depths of his soul that he did not.

The thing was drawing Myrna closer, bringing her against itself in a parody of an embrace, or some demented dance. Myrna did not resist. If anything, she seemed drawn to it, entranced. She moved as a lover, now, not a victim, and the fear had melted from her features, leaving them slack and lethargic, though her eyes were as wide as ever.

His heart cried out to her, to what she had been. He was helpless in his cell, would probably be so in the courtyard, and she was beyond his words. It was like watching the bizarre courtship ritual of some gigantic insect, one that fed, like the spider, on its mate.

He saw the thing dip its head in a lightning strike, saw Myrna's head yanked roughly back by the hair and heard her tiny cry. It had her by the throat, fangs ripping through soft flesh, both arms holding her in a tight embrace as she squirmed weakly. The thing drank her down in moments, great heaving, gulping draughts of her, pumping her dry with the enormous strength of its arms.

Vlad retched violently, falling to his knees, then clawed his way back up the wall, tearing skin from his fingers and breaking nails with the effort. He rose without bothering to wipe the bile from his face or clothes, forced himself to watch. He was beyond fear now, beyond anger, even. He was recording each moment, each emotion, for revenge. He was etching the scene into the fabric of his psyche. He was setting the course of his destiny.

The thing had stopped its convulsive feeding. It still held Myrna's cold form close to it, but almost tenderly. Slowly, she was lowered to the ground, and it turned again, facing the window, seeking Vlad's gaze.

Again, his heart skipped a beat. It was no hideous ghoul he faced—nor was it quite human. The thing still wore its tattered clothing, draped over thin shoulders like the wrappings of a scarecrow, and yet there was no comparison. Where the hair had been patchy white shocks, barely clutching the sides of a ruined skull, blond hair had sprouted, long and lush. Where yellowed, glowing eyes had stared out moments before, deep gray orbs, flecked with ice, called out to him.

The mincing, dancing steps had become even and sure, and the thing was advancing on the window again, reaching out a long, slender arm, gesturing for Vlad to come near. He took a half-step forward, nearly reaching for the bars again, nearly reaching through them, then stopped. Sweat ran from him in small rivers, coating his skin, soaking his clothing, but he did not move closer. He fought.

Beyond the thing, a broken lily against the dark, shadowed ground, he could see Myrna's prone form. She did not move, and her skin, if anything, was paler than the white, filmy gown that she wore. He latched onto the sight of her, the memory of the way she'd been the last time they'd been together, and he lurched away from the window.

You will come to me, Vlad Dracula, the voice trailed after him, soft, sibilant, provocative. *In some time, in some way, we will be bound, you and I. By the blood.*

Then there was silence. Nothing. He did not feel the chilling dread that had accompanied the thing, nor had it made any discernible sound in leaving. He remained where he was, leaning heavily against the wall beside the window, heaving in immense lungfuls of air and expelling them as quickly as he could, trying to wash the taint of the thing's touch, the memory of its eyes, from his soul.

A long time later, he managed to turn his face toward the window again. Myrna was gone. There was no trace in the court of her body, or of her assailant. Nothing. It was as empty as the shadows that filled it were black.

Vlad laid back on the rough, wooden cot and placed his arm across his eyes. A weariness was creeping over him that overcame even the discomfort of the cell, the chill of the air and the weight of memory on his heart. Closing his eyes, he passed from consciousness, falling into a nightmare world of claws and yellowed skin, fangs and crumpled flowers that became women, then blossomed and flew into the night on wings of wicked laughter.

When he'd awakened, he found the sultan there, watching him from the other side of the room and waiting. He sat upright in a swift motion, rising to his feet and coming within a foot of the older man before he stopped. He knew the ice of anger was in his eyes, that his own death might be imminent; it didn't matter. He was through with this game, this horror.

"Now you have seen," the sultan said simply. "They are here, Vlad, many of them, and they feed in the night, despite what we might wish. With some we have a pact—we don't hunt them, they don't hunt us. We provide sustenance when it is scarce, or when we have a suitable sacrifice."

"The girl had done nothing," Vlad grated. "You should have shooed your dog of a prince out there—at least he earned the fate."

The sultan's eyes went hard for just an instant, but his control was phenomenal. "I am not here to banter back and forth with you, young Vlad. I need you as the leader of your people, and I need your support—and theirs—to continue my own rule. What I have done is simply to ensure that this is possible.

"There are those among us who would do away with the *vrykolakes*, given their way. Your church would certainly do so, but it is not so simple. Some among them have done me great service, service that has gone beyond the confines of death itself. A man such as yourself can see the beauty of such service.... the honor of it.

"These would come for you, if I bid it, young Vlad. This is my lesson to you. Remember this night, remember the eyes that held you and the beauty of the death dance. They will come for you if you fail me. You will be one of them, not dead, not alive, no salvation for your soul possible. You will do as I bid, or you will never die.... that is a promise to chill even *your* hot, Wallachian heart."

A breath passed in which, if the sultan had uttered another sound, consequences be damned, he would have died. Vlad knew the message was clear in his eyes, and he saw the momentary quiver in his captor's smile. Very slight, very quick, but no less real for all that.

"I will do as you say, sire," he answered calmly, "because I believe it best for my people. I will live as my father lives, doing as you bid, as long as what you bid serves the common good. You have spoken of honor—it is obviously not a concept you cherish, or you would know that, horrible as your threats have been, dizzying as the reality of these creatures is to my heart and mind, I will not be your slave. Do not think to make of me your dog, sultan."

"I would never consider such a thing," the sultan smiled. "Go to your quarters, Prince Vlad. Clean yourself and get some wine. Find another girl. Just see that you do not forget.... wherever you go they can find you. There is no escape."

Vlad knew that there was no way that he could share this experience with anyone. He could tell his brother, little Radu, but Radu was weak. He had always been the weak one, and if he believed the tale at all, it would only add to that weakness. He might tell his father, were they to meet again in this life, but to what purpose?

So he had an enemy. A new, very powerful enemy. An enemy that dropped from the shadows and drank the very life from your blood. An enemy that he did not know. Of these facts, only the last was intolerable. Only the last could he do anything about.

Without a word, he slipped past the sultan and out of the cell, being careful not to go near any portal or window that looked as if it might skirt the border of that courtyard. It was daylight outside, and yet he did not feel as though he could face those bent and twisted trees. Nor did he feel the urge to approach the spot where Myrna had lain, or to search for her remains. What he wanted he could not have—freedom from the memory of what had happened in the night. Freedom from those eyes, those dripping fangs and that hypnotic voice.

✠

One of the corpses slid further down its stake with a sickening lurch, the sound bringing him back to the present. The horror of the memory lingered—transcended coherent thought. He knew the *vyrkolakes* now, knew them as no man living could know them, as no man living *should* know them. He felt their pain, knew where and when they would strike before they knew themselves. He had lived and breathed their lore, and he knew the ways of their deaths.

He had not kept his word to the sultan, as he'd known, in the end, he could not. He'd learned more of the church and its God as he matured, learned more of love, war, and hate than he'd believed possible. He'd learned death best of all.

Turks. Any of them could be the one, any of them could be the demon set to stalk him, to drag him into the realms of nightmare and blood. Any of them. He had no idea how many he'd killed, how many of his own people, seen through fevered eyes in moments of rage, that he'd added to that total. The stake was the only sure way, the only absolute in any of it. He could take no chances, could afford no weakness. If he were caught alone, or unaware, he would be theirs, and evil as he himself had become in their eyes, his people and those of the church needed him… his strength, his wisdom in battle—his ruthlessness.

He heard a creak, felt droplets of blood dripping down his neck toward his collar, and he turned. It was the woman. She refused to die—refused to meet her maker. As he watched, his eyes widened and his heart tripped like the drums at a festival, faster and faster, running out to become a trembling in his arms and fingers.

The woman was not sliding down the stake with the force of gravity. She was not *sliding* anywhere. She was reaching out, one hand after the other, and she was dragging herself down the pole. He watched in dark fascination as she struggled, heard the sickening wrench of the stake as she forced herself downward, clawing ever nearer, the madness in her eyes turning to a glow of purest hatred, and something—something deeper and older, more chilling.

"Do you… not know me, Vlad Dracula?" she hissed through blackened, twisted lips. Her words slid like sand over yellowed teeth—elongated teeth. Her hands became claws and her progress more pronounced, until at last her feet came to rest on the ground before him. Placing them firmly, she gave a great wrench, and the stake came free. Almost contemptuously, she dragged it the final two feet through her torso and at last tossed it aside.

"No," he said softly. "No. The stake should end your life—your death-life."

"It would be so," she hissed, taking a step nearer, "were I only what you believe me to be, Vlad Tepes, son of the Dragon. You truly do not recognize me, do you?"

His head was shaking back and forth, perhaps in answer, perhaps in negation only. His own hands were white with tension as they pressed into the arms of his chair—his crude wooden throne—readying his body to leap free, to run like the wind.

With a cackle void of mirth, the woman snatched at one of the bodies that hung near where she stood, ripping it downward. As the blood burst free of the corpse in her hands, she gulped it down greedily, huge, heaving swallows that inhaled more than was possible, more than he could believe. And she changed.

At first it was subtle, the lessening of the twist in her back, the glossy, gossamer soft hair sprouting—materializing?—where only gray patches had clung, a firming of the muscles. Vlad tried to send the message to his limbs that would carry him away, tried to galvanize his frame, to move as he had moved so many times, to fight yet again.

She turned. It was her. No mistaking it. Age and years had spun their web over the features of young Prince Vlad, but Myrna was ageless, beautiful. What had been bright and fresh, naive and endearing, was now tragically beautiful. A woman's eyes—or a demon's—stared from beneath arched brows. Her lips twisted in a smile so powerful, so erotic and enticing, that he felt himself growing hard, even as his blood ran to ice.

"Oh," she sighed, almost coquettishly, "you remember me now?"

He felt himself falling backward again, into time, into memories that battered at his sanity. He did not run. There was no power left to his limbs, no will to resist pounding through his veins. He stood, and he waited. That much dignity he maintained, though the urge to fling himself forward into her arms was ripping at his control.

"You?" He'd meant it as a statement, meant to fill his words with hatred, with bile. They came out soft, gentle, familiar as an old nightmare. It seemed so right, somehow, after years of fear, with lost lives and broken dreams scattered behind him like the dead shells on an endless beach. She had wanted only him. She had *chosen* him, over Ahmed, over life.

"There was nothing I could do," he said finally. "I was a prisoner, held against my will. I could not come to you, and you would not listen when I called to you."

"Oh, but I heard you," she laughed darkly. "I heard you, heard your terror, even through my own. Would you have truly come to me, Vlad? Would you have forsaken the light and life for me? I think not, but I'd like to dream it so."

As she spoke, she moved closer. He trembled, but he did not turn away, nor did he approach her. She was lovelier than he remembered. Her figure was the same, and yet somehow the curves had sharpened, become more voluptuous in their very angularity. Her skin, always fair, was pale like the moonlight.

He remembered his last image of her, a crumpled flower, wilted and torn. Torn for his benefit, to teach him a lesson, only, not for anything she herself had done. As her breath wafted over him, drowning him in the scent of death and decay, he imagined that he smelled the aroma of lilies—decadent, damp and rotten, lilies long on the grave, and yet sweet.

As she took him into her embrace, drawing him close and piercing him, even then, he pulled back—but not far. "How?" he asked. "The stake, it should have killed you… it should have brought you peace. How?"

"It is not the stake, Vlad," she whispered, letting her fangs brush once more against the skin of his throat, "it is the sunlight. You staked me, but at sunset—when my powers wax strong. You have killed many, but few *Vrykolakes*… very few, and all by daylight. You didn't even know them when they passed.

"Besides," she continued, running long, slender fingers through his hair, "I could never have left without you. From the moment I heard the sultan's promise, I knew it would be my charge to come to you, to bring you home. You have been mine all along, Vlad Dracula, mine and the night's."

He closed his eyes then as she grew silent and moved back to his throat, holding him with tenderness and strength beyond his wildest imaginings. He felt himself flowing out and through her, felt his senses dying and awakening at once… felt at last the chill, final touch of death—and beyond.

As the moon rose to her throne, the blood of Vlad the Impaler joined that of his final victims, soaking into the earth and disappearing. A lone figure walked away over the nearby hills. She was slight, slender and willowy, and her hair blew about her like the petals of a dark, blossoming flower. In her arms, like a child, she cradled a still form, carrying it away into legend.

Stoker's Mistress

Caitlin R. Kiernan

"My revenge is just begun! I spread it over centuries, and time is on my side."
—Bram Stoker, *Dracula*

Prelude
Whitby, Yorkshire, March 1841

The snow falling, drifting down like every crystal minute of his long life and death, filling up the churchyard above the sleeping village, and he leaves his footprints in the drifts. The woman walks a few steps behind, following in his wake, barefoot and naked except for the long necklace of emeralds and rubies and black onyx beads on her throat, his gift, and she reads the names and dates aloud. Like potent charms or nursery rhymes chiseled in stone, careless and considered words in the brogue that still shows through, litany of the bones beneath their silent heels. And "Here," she says. "Here's a sweet fresh one, 'William Scoresby born 1760 many years successfully engaged in arctic whale fishery died 1829.'" And she brushes snow from the top edge of the headstone. "Poor Billy. He's hardly been down long enough to get used to the company of the worms."

He pauses near the abbey ruins, stares down at the dark shrouded houses on both sides of the valley, the silver trail of the river Esk laced in-between, across the harbor and the headland stretching out to the storm-worried sea. Sleeping houses under snowy roofs, practical English dreams in an Age of Reason, and he thinks again how odd to be so far from home in a century so strange as this.

Behind him, the girl coos, "Ooooh, Sir, this one here. 'Edward Spencelagh, master mariner, murdered by pirates off the coast of the Andes,' it says and there's a skull and crossbones carved in it, like it was a bottle of arsenic." Pause and for a moment, nothing but the wind between the graves and stone walls, the surf pounding restless down below, and then she asks, "Where's the Andes?"

"Mountains," he says, "Far, far away. Mountains in the New World, Molly." And "Oh," she says, and "You don't suppose they brung him all the way back to England, then? And him already dead and all?"

"No, Molly. It is an empty grave," and she laughs at that, an empty grave, laughter that hides itself in the wind so only he can hear. Laughter that is innocence and the clank of swords in war, the chink of broken crystal falling on stone. He stands at the grassy edge of the bluff and the icy wind tangles itself in his long hair, ruffles and tugs at his fine English suit of clothes. Slides off the sharp angles of his face, but it does still have the power to sting his eyes and he looks back for the girl, calls her, "Molly," and she dances away from the leaning rows of stones, stones all more or less the same unremarkable shape and height, as if every man and woman laid in this plot of land were exactly the same as every other. And seeing how they're dead, he thinks, they might as well be, at that. Earth and mold and bones, skeletal cities of ribs and vertebrae for insects and vermin. And he feels old, never mind who or what he is, he feels old as the world as she dances her circles around him.

"You will remember everything I've told you, Molly," and she nods and smiles as she passes by. "Every word of my instructions," he says, "These things I've given are not free. They are your price. And if you fail me, Molly Breen, I can take them all, every one, away. And more."

And softer, "They'll not see this coming. And when they do, they'll think it a betrayal, the Tzimisce, all the Camarilla, until they understand.

And by then I'll be beyond their reach. I have been a man, and men die. I was made more than a man and I can still die. But when I am a myth, Molly, when I am made words on paper, nothing but fashionable phantasm and enduring symbol, I might live forever.

She dances away from him again, spins and leaps, scatters snow and lands without a sound to any ear but his, and now she sings a song he's never heard in a language he barely understands, sings gaily of dying as if it were birth, and, he thinks, for her, it may as well be."

Act I
Clontarf, Dublin 1854

This boy child born in a year of plague, Black '47 says his mother, and he dreams of the ocean he's never seen from his sickbed. Makes the dream from the words of his brother and sister and the cherished stories that his mother tells of the world beyond his walls. A dream where he walks and even flies like a bird high above the city. The streets and church spires down below, the Liffey flowing glittering dark between the quays on its way down to the sea, weary and broken from its painful long journey from the Wicklow Mountains. The moon gazing down with an old woman's grin and he rushes out across Dublin Bay. The ships with their tall masts and furled sails, and he wheels like a gull.

"Abraham," his name, he remembers and looks over his shoulder, his fluttering gown and something like ragged black wings close behind him, carried on the salt night wind, black wings without feathers that seem to stretch across the whole sky and she says his name again, "Abraham," and this time he opens his eyes wide and full awake in an instant, no fog between his worlds. Only the *sí* at the window, wild black hair around her white face, the face he never remembers until she's at his window and then he always feels silly and ashamed to have forgotten her. She raps once on the pane and he gives back her warming smile from his pillow before she fades and mist the endless color of autumn skies sifts beneath the sash, draws her in and melts away until it's only the fairy lady. Her cloak, flowing yards of velvet the same blue as the vanished mist and her feet bare on the floor when she moves silent as a kitten to stand by his bed; she bends and he sees her nakedness inside the cape, the curve of her white, white body and she kisses him lightly on the cheek.

Her breath smells sweet and dry, smells of dead flowers, dead flowers and dust.

"Hello, Bram," says the lady and brushes her fingers through his hair, and *hello, ma'am*, he says back to her. If she has a name, she's never given it. "I brought you a song tonight," she says, and he remembers that this is what she always says and remembers her voice, clear and sad and that it never wakes his sleeping family, never brings anyone to his room looking for the singer. And before she begins to sing, she leans close again, buries him in her hair and dusty pressed-rose breath and he thinks he remembers the sudden pricking pain at his throat, but it doesn't matter because the song is carrying him away. Farther than his dream of flight, not just away where but away when, years back, falling through her, time yarn bundled inside her, years before he was born and he walks the cobbled street of a village with strong legs.

And because she tells him, he knows that this is not a street in Clontarf or anywhere else in Dublin, late afternoon going to dusk in a village somewhere far to the north and west. Like the villages in his mother's stories of her childhood in Sligo, but finer, clean streets and healthy faces, shop windows filled with fine and pretty things, butcher's windows crowded with fat geese and hams and only the best cuts of meat, smiling fishmongers and a fat woman with a cart of bright flowers. Clatter of horse's shoes, dray and carriage wheels and from where he stands, the crest of a tall hill, he can see the whole town laid out before him, stretching this way on to the sea, that way on to green pastures with fluffy white sheep and fat brown cows.

"There, Bram. Look!" and he follows her pointing finger, across and over the rooftop shingles and grand towers. "Do you see? Out there, under the moon?"

And he does see it, vast shadow or simply a place where light can never go, something like a man and as tall as the sky, shrouded in a robe of starless midnight. Arms stretched wide to embrace the world, curling hands whose fingers trail away to ragged nothing and drip that darkness. The village like a thousand doll houses in its path, and he shades his eyes with his hand that he might see more clearly, though he wishes he could look away. Could turn and run, but she holds him there.

"It's a gift," she says. "To see such a thing when others can hardly see past their noses."

But he does try not to look at its face, that much at least, the blind, devouring holes where eyes should be. Pulls free of the lady and runs, tugs at the sleeve of a man standing nearby, tall man with spectacles staring down at his gold watch on its fancy gold fob.

"The giant," Bram cries, points to the east, darkening sky and the thing moving through the clouds. "Can't you *see* it's coming?" and the man frowns down at him, watch snapped shut and secreted away into a vest pocket, *Nonsense, it is very far off*, he says, *Berlin, Paris, nothing to worry yourself over, child.* And it makes no difference who he warns, the fat woman tying her bouquets of posies and forget-me-nots, the porkbutcher, the fishmonger, or that he has begun to cry. *It is far away*, they all say and smile or frown or send him on his way, *It won't be coming here.*

And then he stands beside a fountain and the sky is going out overhead, hushed flutter as all the birds in Ireland light around him, magpies and sparrows and great black ravens. Court of feathers and voiceless beaks, nervous, watchful eyes, and no sound now but the gurgling fountain and his own useless sobs, and he sees that the streets are strewn with the bodies of the dead and dying, black and cholera swollen faces. The coffin makers from door to door and he watches the traveler buried alive, miles from town and the sickness crawling on him, in him, the men who dig a deep pit and push him in with their long poles, cover him up quick, the dirt and lime dribbling down into his mouth until he is as silent as the birds. And the men dig trenches across the eastern roads as Bram walks between the birds who step aside to let him pass, him and the lady with him, and they walk nigh—swallowed streets, between burning barrels of tar and sulfur. Air thick with the smell of rot and filth, vile smoke and the jingle of the bells on the cholera carts.

When he looks up, straight up where the sky should be, he sees only the face of the giant looking down, and its nothing hands dragged hungry across the world.

And a long time later, after they have all died and the giant has moved on to visit other towns, the lady shows him other things before he opens his eyes and there is no one in his room but him. Grayness before dawn at the windows, and he knows he hasn't been alone, no memory of her but the dusty perfume of dried flowers, and he is so weak that he closes his eyes again and waits for morning.

Act II
Chelsea, London, 4 January 1881

The Irishman grown tall and strong and red-bearded, and past his years of ledgers and office monotony in Dublin Castle, past so many things, now; already three years since his marriage and the commencement of his managerial duties at the Lyceum. *Hamlet*, that first night, something comforting to remember now when he needs the comfort; three years, almost, to the day, the night, and the warm light of the braziers outside the theater on the crowds, the city's elite and their lines of carriages and fine horses, the rest filling in the pit and gallery, finally the curtain rising on Barnardo and Francisco. Who's there? —Nay, answer me....

The book in his lap, a time and finger-worn volume of Le Fanu, another, odder comfort, and the sizzle and crackle from the hearth. But he does not open the book, stares instead out the study window at the snow falling heavy on the street. White veil from a black sky, white blanket gathering below, and the wind whistling hard off the river.

He might have kept his temper, he thinks, might not have read anything but innocence into the gift of a crown of flowers. Opening night for The Cup and his Florence one of the supers, one of a hundred vestal virgins and the gift sent backstage to Ellen, two crowns and the note in Wilde's hand, explanation that one was for the actress herself and the other to be given anonymously to Florence: *...but you won't think she will suspect? How could she?* and *She thinks I never loved her, thinks I forget. My God how could I?* And Ellen might not have shown him the note, as well.

Even then he could have let it go. But later, after the performance and everything afterward, her so quiet, so distant on the cold ride back to 27 Cheyne Walk and when he tried to kiss her in their bed she turned away, not a word. And he spied the crown across the dark room, laid on her dressing table and maybe Ellen hadn't kept the identity of the giver a secret after all, had shown the note to Florence, as well.

"I don't understand," he said and she didn't answer, laid still with her back to him.

"I haven't the faintest idea what you're talking about, Bram," and he sat up, still staring at the flowers, the real flowers and the flowers reflected in her mirror. And before he thought better of it, "Do you still love him, Florence? Do you still love him? Is that why you refuse me, because you have regrets?"

And that time she said nothing, didn't answer, lay still and he pushed back the bedclothes, crossed the room and held the crown in his hands. There were other things, the small and golden cross she still kept, for instance, a Christmas gift from the poet.

"I have no regrets, Bram," she said after a time, him standing there, barefoot in the shadows, "Come back to bed."

But he set the flowers back and went downstairs, alone and only a few hours until morning, poured a glass of brandy and sat watching the snow with the unopened Le Fanu across his lap. Confusion and fear, fear that he doesn't have her heart after all. That he hasn't won her fully, that a part of her will never be his, another Dubliner's. Her heart held always prisoner by a scandalous poet, and he closes his eyes, tries to think of other things: work to be done and bills to be paid at the Lyceum, small imperfections in the first-night performance. And in a little while, he dozes.

He has not heard her enter the room, this tall, thin woman, porcelain face and hands, hair so thick and black it could never be anything but a dream, and her lips stark and the color of a wound. Feels cold air, though the fire stills sparks and the windows are shut tight against the night. And she comes to him, long legs and like an afterthought he realizes the woman is naked. Every inch of her that same skin white enough that his eyes can trace the veins underneath, faint tracery of Wedgewood blue, and she leans over his chair and whispers, "It is a sad pity and a waste, Abraham, that a handsome man such as yourself should want for a woman's passion." Her breath and voice drifting down over him, fog of flowers pressed between yellowed scrapbook pages, keepsake violets and roses.

"I do not know you," he says and the woman sighs, brittle sweet laugh and "If I sing to you, would you remember me, Bram? If I were to sing you a bit of the 'Raglan Road' or 'Carrickfergus,' would you be remembering me then?"

And her eyes, animal eyes and the eyes of a madwoman, of an angel, Heaven and Hell twined in those eyes.

"I do not know you."

"No," she says, "Neither of those. But you'll remember this one. This was one of your favorites," and she begins to sing, *Last night she came to me, my young love came in*, or he is only thinking that she sings because her lips do not seem to move, *So softly she entered, that her feet made no din*, ventriloquist's shoddy magic, her hand marble smooth against his cheek, and she came to me, and this she did say, and when her lips come closer, before the pain, he remembers, opens his mouth to cry out, *It will not be long....*

And he comes awake slow, sweating and the fire blazing high, the volume of Le Fanu tumbled off his tap to the carpet and lying open. His lips still parted, gasping, moving as if there are urgent words he can't remember, and sudden tears down his face as he rises from his chair. Stares down at the snowbound street, the storm grown more furious, and he sees footprints in the fresh mantle, the prints of small, bare feet that lead from the lamppost in front of the house and vanish in the street. In another minute, the storm has buried them entirely.

Act III
Nuremberg, July 1885

Scene 1: Alt-Nunberg, The Five-Cornered Tower (restored)

They have come to Germany and this city, business and holiday in one, precious time away from the Theatre and London, the bright Bavarian air and a chance to take in local color for the Lyceum's forthcoming production of Goethe's *Faust*; Henry Irving and Ellen, Bram and a scene painter, a few others.

"It's all perfectly monstrous, really," the actress says and Bram turns to look at her, comes slowly, reluctantly, back to the world from his contemplations, and Henry says, "Well, yes, Ellen, I suppose that was rather the point."

Bram smiles at such a purposefully bad pun and, "I don't mean to sound morbid, but there is a certain elegance to it, so much art turned to the business of torture. Art and science," and he turns back to his examination of the device, *Verfluchte Jungfrau,* the Iron Maiden of the Tower. Alone at the center of the chamber, dusty and rust-scabbed, crudest parody of a woman's form, subtle lines and curves cast in cold iron. He steps closer, inspecting her hollow, spiked interior laid open for all to see, to witness: each skewer placed just so, to pierce eyes and heart, belly and genitals, when she is closed again. And he remembers the jaws of an odd plant, an exhibition of carnivorous flora and the Venus flytrap brought from America. Something of those green jaws in this thing, something of this thing in the needle jaws of that plant.

"Ghastly," Ellen Terry says. "This whole drafty place is ghastly."

"This is atmosphere, Ellen. Priceless stuff," Irving says, examines the disorderly collection of headsman's swords gathered against one wall. "If we could only capture half the mood and implied violence of this place with our props and paint and tricks of light. Tell her, Bram."

But he doesn't answer, lets his eyes trace the Maiden's outstretched arms, the long and bristling knives set along their length and he looks down, then, to her feet, one a mechanism when touched by the executioner's boot caused the arms to spring closed, and there's another way to die at this woman's touch. Another way she drew blood.

"Prisoners who were to be put inside," he says aloud, thinks aloud without having meant to speak, "Those prisoners first were made to kiss her, their lips to hers," and "Bram, please," Ellen groans, "I think I've had enough of this dreadful place to last three lifetimes.'"

"Yes," he says, wondering if the old gears and springs have rusted fast, if the Maiden has been disarmed by time and neglect, inexorable corrosion of metal by the damp tower air. Or if she might still kill, if anyone were very foolish or unlucky.

"Bram," and he feels the gloved weight of Henry's hand on his shoulder. "There's still much of the Castle left to see, and I think almost all of it will sit much better with poor Ellen." And he follows them down the winding staircase, dim light and their footfalls, and Henry talking, stories about the castle's past, real and fancied: bottomless wells dug into the native rock by slaves condemned never again to see the light of day, and fearless outlaws, secret passageways and the intrigues of burggraves and knights and saints.

And the Order of the Dragon, let's not forget them, he says as they step out of the tower, into warm courtyard sunlight and air that smells of the city and summer gardens, but Bram only half listens, *Yes, another of those murky medieval Catholic armies*, still seeing the daggers on the Maiden's long arms, the spikes in her empty soul, *It's supposed to have held all its most secret meetings and ceremonies somewhere in the Castle.*

"Like the Knights Templar?" Ellen asks and that brings him back again, her voice and the smell of summer. He runs one hand across his face, through his beard, tries to push away the images of execution, flesh lips to iron lips, the creaking sound of hinges closing to bring absolute piercing blackness.

"Something like that, I suppose," Henry Irving says.

"Were they out for the holy grail as well?" she asks and Henry laughs, and Bram wants to glance back at the tower, to trace his way up the crumbling wall; "No," he says, instead. "Another defense against heretics and Turks."

"Bloody heathen Turks," Ellen says grimly, voice low and chin held close to her chest, and they all three laugh.

Scene 2: Beyond the Westthor Graben

In the carriage that bumps along beside the dark waters of the Pegnitz, a ride alone to try and clear his head. Because he woke in the night from a dream of death in a cold woman's bladed arms, because he's tired of talking *Faust*, tired of sausages and German hospitality and the steep and red-tiled roofs. Homesick and wants to shake off the uninvited obsession with the dank little museum in the Tower, display of vicious treasures salvaged from the Rathaus prison and the Vehmgerricht, and so he has left them all behind for an afternoon, has told Jacobb, his coachman who speaks English like broken crockery, to drive him into the forest, away from the city. Away from the Castle. "Ja, mein Herr," and soon they were rattling away from Nuremberg and the leaf shadows of the trees and the songs of birds are making him sleepy.

He considers closing his eyes for a time, not sleeping, *resting my eyelids*, his father would have said, *just resting my eyelids*, but the thought that he might be visited by the dream again and so he stays awake, watches the river, ducks bobbing there like white and gray feathered boats, until the road turns north and the trees close around them. Yews and oaks, cypresses that have grown here since before the first tower was raised at the Burg, bowed trunks and arthritis branches that would count their lives in centuries as years. And up ahead he notices a much narrower road turning off, feels the welcome goad of curiosity, something he hasn't seen before, something no one has seen in some time, perhaps, and he calls for Jacobb to stop.

Dust cloud and woodcreak, the horses seeming reluctant to stop here and Jacobb seeming offended at his request, but the carriage pulls to a halt, and the coachman leans down, speaks through his thick mustache, "Ja, Herr Stoker?" and Bram points. "Where does that road lead?"

"Ah," and a long pause while he gazes nervously at the neglected path, grass thick between its ruts and "Nowhere, that road leads," he answers, finally.

"Come, man, it leads *somewhere*, surely—"

"Nah, nowhere," Jacobb says again, insistent, and the horses straining in their reins. "No good place to be stopping for," he says. From where Bram sits, the road seems to drop away through a long, winding hollow. "I want to go down that road, Jacobb, and should very much appreciate knowing why this place is upsetting you."

And far away, filtered through the forest and across miles, an animal's cry or yelp, a dog, or wolf, perhaps, but nothing quite like either. Jacobb, face pale and sweating, struggles to calm the frightened horses, leaps down from the box when Bram climbs out of the carriage to get a better view down the road.

"No good place stopping for," he says again.

"Was that a wolf? Aren't we awfully near the city for there to be wolves in these woods?"

Jacobb is petting the horses, calming them with his big hands and whispers in their ears and he doesn't turn around to answer, "*Ja*, wolves," he says, and nothing else. Back to his ministrations with the horses, takes the bridles and leads them twenty or thirty feet further along the road. Bram follows, notices something at the crossroads, a stone cross fallen over and broken. Weathered granite and he steps off the road, brushes aside the creepers and tall grass and there is an inscription on its base: *Die Toten reisen schnell.*

"Jacobb, what is this place? What's in the valley?"

"Worse place than this," he says, still standing with his horses but looking back at Bram now. And Bram bends closer to read again the words cut into the stone, and he sees something else that makes him stop.

"Christ, Jacobb. What is this?"

An iron rod, rust-purple, rising from the shattered monument, iron finger aimed up at Heaven, or down.

"Who killed themselves," Jacobb says, wary, brittle voice, and speaking almost too quietly to be heard. "She who killed themselves and buried her here."

"You're not even making sense now, Jacobb," but he recalls something, then, old superstition and another shunned crossroads outside Andover in Hampshire, years ago. Burying suicides at crossroads, and he touches the protruding end of the iron spike. It is driven firmly into the earth and will not budge.

"We go back now," Jacobb says, firm and as if to prove his point, that cry again, and maybe closer this time, maybe a trick of the woods. Not a dog and not at all how Bram would have thought a wolf would sound. *Distance playing tricks*, and he steps back from the grave, says to the coachman, "Yes. But first you tell me where that road leads. *Then* we'll go back to the city."

The horses paw the ground and shake their heads and "It is unholy," the coachman says, and if his voice was brittle before, it is broken now. "That place down there."

"The *valley* is unholy?"

"A village, a village that was there, long, long… "

"The village, then, the village was unholy? Why?"

"Herr Stoker, *please*, I answer your question now."

Bram glances back at the impaled grave, the cross tumbled over, busted apart, and for the third time the cry drifts through the woods, lost and searching sound, lonely sound, almost human, and he feels the prick of gooseflesh beneath his clothes. Hesitates a moment longer. "That's not a wolf, is it Jacobb?"

"Unholy," Jacobb says, crosses himself and scrambles back up to his box. "I go back with you or not, now, Herr Stoker."

"Yes, Jacobb, I'm coming," and another plaintive cry as he climbs into the carriage, this one from the opposite side of the road he thinks, so two now, two at least, and he notices how deep the shadows have become, how close to dusk. And it will be night before they're even out of the forest, much less back within the city's walls. The horses rear and Jacobb has to whip them, biting leather swish of his crop in the still air and then they are moving past the crossroads, and Bram steals a last glance down that other way, *unholy*, and sees or imagines a stirring in the gloom. A hundred yards past the crossroads and the wheels of the carriage jounce and rattle as if they might slip from the axles and Jacobb is still whipping the horses; Bram begins to call out for him to slow the carriage, to ease up on the poor animals and he sees the inscription again, *The Dead Travel Fast*, epitaph or warning or augury, and he doesn't say a word.

And night comes, faster even than he'd feared. Black enough for night; maybe a last few rays of straggling daylight left above these trees but black enough below.

"Hurry," he calls out to the coachman, but knows that Jacobb hasn't heard him over the furious clop of hooves, the carriage racket. But he does become aware of another sound, a panting and the slap of softer feet on the road and he looks, fearful, and can make of the dimmest form running along beside the carriage. Never a wolf half that large. Eyes that burn the same hot orange as stoked coals or steel under the blacksmith's hammer, eyes that turn and look back at him, eyes that smile when they know he sees. He clutches his walking cane as if it might protect against eyes like that, makes the sign of the cross although it is not of his faith.

"There is something on the road," he calls out and is surprised when Jacobb answers, "Ja, Ja, something… "

And the road is rising ahead, darker place where the trees seem to twine together, braid of ancient boles, and the carriage begins to slow; Jacobb whips the frantic horses and he's cursing in German, calling the names and mercy of Saints and Bram hears the horses begin to scream, a sound almost as unnerving as the strange cries floating across the valley. And the thing with burning eyes slams into the coach, patch of utter darkness and those two fires where its head must be and it rams the carriage like an angry bull. The coach rocks up onto its two left wheels, almost capsizes, spilling Bram and the coachman into the road, bounces back down and springs groan and wood splinters loud.

And now there are other eyes in the night.

A smell like shit and death long under summer sun and its forepaws on the passenger steps, tilting the carriage its way, and Bram *can* see that smile now: black lips curling back and the teeth, grandmother, what big teeth you have, what *white teeth.* Raises his walking stick, fine oak but it may as well be a match stick and then he hears the woman's voice, Latin spoken sloppy fast in commanding tones and the Irish brogue coming through and Jacobb smacks the thing across the snout with his riding crop. It turns its head, its grinning jaws, away from Bram, but not toward the coachman, as if it hadn't noticed the blow, and the woman is shouting. Not one word can he make out and her voice so loud it hurts his ears.

The beast moves slowly away from the carriage, reluctant lion or tiger forced back by the trainer's lash, and a sound from far down in its throat, a hateful, cheated, hurting sound like a promise. Stands a moment longer on the road, facing the direction of the woman's voice, and other voices rise from the forest around them, other threats, and it backs away, one last glance toward Bram, those eyes, twin doors to Hell left open for his edification, and then it is gone. And the other eyes peering through the trees are gone, and the horses are racing forward.

As they pass, Bram catches the briefest glimpse of the woman, her skin like alabaster reflecting light that isn't there, hair black as the thing she has driven away, and he knows that face.

Act IV
Scene 1: The Beefsteak Room, The Lyceum, 30 April 1890

The curtain drawn on this night's performance of *The Dead Heart*, actors, take your bows, and afterward, backstage to the Beefsteak Room. Twelve years now since Bram, at Henry Irving's request, cleared away the old lumber and backdrops stored here, returned the rooms to something of their former glory. Renaissance, the turn of the last century when they'd been the meeting place of the esteemed Sublime Society of Beefsteaks founded by Sheridan, a retreat for men like the Duke of Norfolk and Lord Erskine, and they haven't done so bad themselves, these latter-day Beefsteaks, Bram and Henry and Mr. Harry J. Loveday. Have entertained their own host of luminaries, royalty, the toast of society, the art world, the theatre. The Prince of Wales, Lord Randolph Churchill and Alfred Gilbert, the exquisite Sarah Bernhardt.

Tonight Bram watches their guest across the table, unusual guest even for these chambers, the Hungarian scholar and Professor of Oriental Languages from the University of Pesth, adventurer, advisor to diplomats, spy, and for that he's been awarded Commander of the Royal Victorian Order. The man who followed the footsteps of Marco Polo across Central Asia, who, disguised as an Arab, risked his life in the Middle East. Arminius Vambery is more than no ordinary man. And the woman with him, as unnerving as he is a fascination, hair like a night without stars, face painted as if she is a White Chapel whore or has no color of her own. She smokes a cigar and drapes one arm about Vambery's shoulder.

"That portrait?" Henry says. "Oh, yes. That was done by Sargent, our own Ms. Terry as Lady Macbeth. Are you familiar with Mr. Sargent's work?"

"Certainly," says Vambery, tugging at one side of his gray mustache, admiring the painting with wide eyes the color of almonds, bright eyes that make Bram think of an owl or some other hunting bird, alert from all they've seen, from all that's left to see. Possibly the sharpest face Bram has ever seen, hawksharp nose plunging down toward the sharp chin beneath. Full lips and arched, almost womanly brows. His long hair tied back and hints of gray at the temples but no other clue to the man's age, though surely he can't be young.

And he's talking again about the East, his perils, and Bram asks him a question, the first he has allowed himself in spite of his curiosity, "Have you ever been afraid, sir?" Henry and some of the others at the table glare as if the asking is itself an insult, but Vambery smiles his disarming smile and his woman laughs her icicle laugh.

"Afraid? Afraid of death, you mean?" the faintest Magyar's accent and he tugs at his mustache again. "No, but I am afraid of torture. I always protected myself against that."

Bram squints at him through the haze of cigar and pipe smoke, and says, "However did you manage that?"

"I had always a tablet of poison, cyanide, fastened here," and he points to the lapel of his coat and Bram sips his champagne.

"Then you must be terribly afraid of torture, indeed."

"My studies and experiences have made me respectful of the pain that can be visited upon the human body, yes. Tell me, Mr. Stoker, are you familiar perhaps with the history or folklore of my part of the world?"

And Bram shakes his head, never mind that it isn't exactly the truth, for fear that Vambery won't continue. "Then you haven't heard the tales of Prince Vlad III, Dracula, Vlad Tepes, the 15th-century Wallachian? Vlad the Impaler, who ruled his people and any he conquered through the constant threat, nay, *certainty* that the most trivial disobedience would bring down upon them the greatest tortures he could devise." And it doesn't matter that Vambery talks like a player delivering lines in a particularly poor melodrama; he commands, and he speaks to a hard and hungry place inside Bram, the place that once drew him to a German museum of death and torture.

"Yes. He broke the bodies of innocent men beneath the wheels of oxcarts. He skinned men and women alive or roasted them alive over beds of red-hot coals. He hated foreigners, he hated the *boyars*, he hated his own people. Vlad massacred without distinction for his own pleasure and security. But he was most renowned for the torture that earned him his nickname," and Vambery pauses here, calculated pause for the effect, time for his audience to catch up and consider what he has said thus far.

"Tepee," he says, *tsepesch*, "Impaler."

And Arminius Vambery talks for hours more, on toward dawn, grisly tales of the warrior king, ruler of a wild land trapped between the crescent and the cross and crushed beneath the merciless hand of its own sovereignty. And somewhere toward the end, he begins to speak of this man dead more than four centuries as though he were a bloody Arthur or Charlemagne, a barbarian Roland, that the superstitious people of the Carpathians believe and fear he will come again. Or that he never died. Or that death has not kept him in his grave, that even Hell might have turned him away.

"Transylvanian peasants will tell you, Mr. Stoker, to this day, that Vlad Dracula's bloodthirst did not fall as his mortal body fell before a Turkish blade.... " and the woman whispers something in his ear, smoky whisper and he nods.

"Yes, you are right, my dear. I have kept these gentlemen far too long with my old stories," and "Forgive me," he says to them all, reaches across the table clutter of plates and glasses and ashtrays to shake Bram's hand. "We must be going, before we exhaust this hospitality. We will talk again sometime, perhaps?"

"Yes," Bram answers, "I would like that very much," and they all stand with Vambery and the black-haired woman who has never been introduced. And as she moves past Bram toward the door, he catches the scent, like a memory of dust and pressed flowers.

Scene 2: Chelsea, London, 1 May 1890

His dreams are crowded with the Hungarian's words, words fulfilled, made actualities, and he walks a battlefield under a violent sunset sky with the black-haired girl, who he remembers now. She holds his hand, her own cold and hard as if it is made of marble, and they step between the slain. Ground so drenched with blood that the earth is muddy red and clotting slime fills their footprints. At first he thinks they must be in a forest, the long shadows thrown around them the trunks of strange trees, and she says no, look around you, and he sees the stakes, then, the impaled hoisted ten and fifteen feet into the stinking air. The dead and those who are still dying as their own weight pulls them down the greased and sharpened poles stuck through their asses. The mouths of some already gape wide where the tip-ends have made their inevitable exits, and in the distance, the sound of many horses. A thousand, ten thousand stakes stretching away in every direction, and whenever one has fallen there are huge black wolves and rooks to worry and gnaw the corpses. Blood drips from the sky like rain.

And she stops, throws off her cape and stands naked, the falling blood stippling her shoulders, her arms, and she kneels before him. No, he whispers, sees the tower, ebony spire almost to the western horizon of this flat plain and knows that something is watching him from there. Utter patience in that gaze, and urgency, too, and she looks up at him as she unbuttons his trousers, takes his stiffening sex in her chilling hands. And when she opens her mouth the wolves and carrion birds stop their feast to see, gleaming eyes all around as her crimson lips pull back, and the animal teeth in her jaws close themselves around him.

Act V
Cruden Bay, Scotland, August 1911

Old man, and he cannot sleep again. Sleeps less and less, and even on holiday, which he can hardly afford these days, there's no escape from these black moods, the regret and failure fluttering around his head like sparrows. But his health not yet so far gone that he cannot walk and so he leaves his and Florence's lodgings at the Kilmarnock Arms and follows the narrow streets of the village toward the comforting surf sigh and crash, the song of the Water of Cruden. There is not much wind, and the night is bright, clear sky and the moon only a day or two until full, but his eyes have almost failed him, like everything else. He knows this walk by memory, through the dunes past fishermen's cottages and the slate-roofed sheds for drying herring, the line of dinghies turned up for the night, nets stretched high on poles, to the sandy flats and down to the sea.

The salt air is a hundred times better than any physician's draught or pill, and he breathes it in deep, catches the smell of wood smoke before he notices the bonfire glow south, off toward the granite promontory of Whinnyfold. Not far, so he walks that way, follows the tide line, firm sand and shellcrunch beneath his boots. Before long he can see the young woman sitting a short distance from the fire, her face orange in the light of the flames. And he calls out, "Good evening, Miss," not wishing to alarm her by appearing suddenly out of the dark. Her black hair in an elaborate bun and she is dressed simply enough, except for a velvet cape that flows away from her across the sand. Obviously another guest at the inn; she waves and smiles, he thinks, and when he comes closer, he can see she is reading a book.

"Good evening," he says again when he is standing close enough to feel the warmth of the fire, the crackling driftwood sending its ember offerings up to the pinprick white inferno of the stars overhead.

"Good evening, Mr. Stoker," she says pleasantly, an Irish brogue but not so heavy as his own, and he makes out the title printed across the cover of her novel, his latest, *The Lair of the White Worm.* Assumes that she has learned his name from someone, another guest or a servant, back at the Kilmarnock.

"Are you enjoying it?" he asks and she looks uncertain for a moment and then smiles again. "Oh, the book, you mean? Yes, it isn't bad, not so far. Though, I confess, I liked your *Dracula* better."

"Yes," he says, and stares out across the sea, thinks he can make out the treacherous and stony scatter of the Skares offshore, shipbelly rippers, black dots on the shimmering sea. "So did I."

"There is a long tradition of great worms in Scotland, you know? Though mostly in the lochs and rivers."

"Is that so?" he says, knowing full well it is, and turns back to the woman. And in that moment knows her, that pale face, unreal beauty, the spectral girl who has come to him since his childhood sickbed in Dublin. And it shows on her face that she understands his realization. The sudden certainty makes him dizzy, sets his heart to racing, and he sits down on the sand across from her.

"Then I'm not mad and you are not a phantom," not a question because he knows it's so, and "I never said either of those things," she replies.

"But they're true. I know that now. Holy Christ… "

She says nothing more for a moment and then, "And does the knowing make a difference, Abraham?"

"All my life," he says, and a log pops loud in the fire, releases a bright shower of sparks up through the smoke.

"It's something," she says. "To be chosen."

"Why?" he asks, why, and it doesn't surprise him when she shrugs, shakes her head, slow and almost sadly; he is past surprise.

"Because there was a sickness a long time ago and I was young and didn't ever want to die. Because a strange man showed a girl a beautiful necklace and offered her a way out. A man who needed a story told."

"Because there are strings on us all, Abraham."

He sighs loud, sighs years, and, "I can't give you any better answer than that," she says. "There are rules."

"Strings," he says, and she says, "Yes, strings."

She closes her book, *his* book, and before she leaves, kisses him on the cheek, musty nostalgia of her breath.

"You have been a good man," she says and is gone.

And he sits very still, watches the fire until it has burned away to gray ash and the sun is rising over the sea.

Finale
The Roxy, Manhattan, 12 February 1931

Thursday night, end credits and then the film is finally over, laughably dreadful thing that it has been, and Molly Breen sits next to her sire as the audience begins to rise and file slowly out of the theatre. Still not light but the unsteady glow from the screen and they are surrounded by the giggling pack of anarchs that are his entourage while he is in America, foppish casanovas, preening teases and their ghouls, undead reflection of a decadent and doomed culture; they have no idea who or what he truly is, only that they are being paid well in blood and money for their time and that's enough. More than enough.

"The German film was better," she says, and he raises an eyebrow, fine arch, laughs quietly. "Of course it was, but it hardly matters, Molly. Even that… " and he motions at the screen, "… that tawdry, flickering shadow show frightens them. But only until they are back out on the street with their electric lights and automobiles, and then they can tell themselves it was all make-believe. If they even *have* nightmares they'll laugh them away in the morning."

"They do not even look at us," she says, watching the people moving past up the long aisle.

"Of course not. We look nothing at all like that poor Hungarian fool in his opera cape. We no longer meet their expectations."

She watches them go, until the house lights come up and the huge theatre is almost empty, and then she says, "I'm sailing for Dublin tomorrow night. I want to go home for a while," and he nods, "It will probably be good for you." And after he has gone, the anarchs ahead of him and trailing out behind, making faces at one another, parodies of Lugosi and the other actors, she sits alone and stares at the drawn curtains until an usher asks her to leave.

Most of the Gaelic poets, down to quite recent times, have had a Leanhaun sidhe, for she gives inspiration to her slaves and is indeed the Gaelic muse—this malignant fairy. W.B. Yeats

The End

The Devil's March

By Philip Nutman & Anya Martin

Midnight September 1, 1864. Lieutenant James Tyler's Journal.

The battle for Jonesboro has tired us all. Those who have not battled today have been busy dismantling the railroad, but few men can be heard snoring tonight. Sleep is something unknown to them anymore. So none of us is awakened when thunder crashes in the distance but no rain falls. The sounds resonate familiar, shells exploding one after another, then a silence and more. What is more fearsome is that night hangs, a tapestry of darkness, and we do not know what is happening in Atlanta. Has General Hood swooped down upon General Slocum and his men? Or is something more evil afoot?

I watch old Tecumseh pacing, a bottle of whiskey clutched in one hand, a cigar in the other, and I can tell he is anxious to know. When he drinks, he drinks heartily and his tolerance is great, but he does not usually drink so much in the heat of battle. If we had not the letters in our possession, the dark, troublesome correspondences between the Confederate and a potential foreign ally, we might assume it was just the ways of war. With the horror we have seen from war alone in the past four years, that would be enough.

Journal of Wallace Baker, City Councilman, Atlanta.

We were all awoke by the thunder, so close, indeed, not just a mile away if that far. Not that any of us in our family could sleep, the heat hanging so heavy and stifling within the walls of our homes here on the edge of the end of the World. Just a few hours ago, the sun glowed blood red on the horizon as if foretelling something horrible. Now it is just after midnight according to Ma's old grandfather clock that still ticks on in defiance of all this war. But as I rose from my writing desk to the window, my eyes beheld a sight which I must put to paper, if only to chronicle this terrible night for generations to come.

Flames vaulted high above downtown Atlanta. The railroad yards exploded, giant fiery clouds shooting hundreds of feet into the night sky, debris hurled toward the depot and other downtown buildings. The air reeked with the rotten egg smell of sulfur and smoke wafting even to my window. It was like I imagine a volcano would look in the throes of an eruption, like Pompeii of the Romans. But our beautiful city was being wrecked not by nature's fury but by man's own. If General Sherman can indeed be called a man.

Has the Devil finally rode into Atlanta, sobbed my dear wife, Sarah, clutching at my bedclothes, tears streaming down her face. Helen, my daughter, also ventured into the study now in her nightgown, the noise raising her even from her sickbed. I stroked their tender cheeks, and with deep regret, I told them the bitter truth— Yankee shells could never do that much damage all at once; it is our boys in gray who are blowing up all our munitions so that the Yankees cannot take them and use them for their own benefit. The rumors were true. Tonight Hood's final troops were marching out of Atlanta, leaving us defenseless again the Devil's hordes.

My wife clung to me like I offered her only protection, and yet I knew I was none. A gang of Negroes we had never seen before passed our house below. Though they did not pause, it unsettled her further, for we know all the Negroes kept by our neighbors, and there was no white man with them. They walked slowly with a look in their eyes like whatever life that was in them was bleeding away. Just barely over the fire, explosion and panic, I could hear them humming an old funeral dirge that my mammy hummed when my sister was stillborn.

Some of Hood's troops still roamed the street below us, too, mostly drunk and careening from one side to the other. They were heading south, so they were leaving, stragglers of the main army. A red-bearded soldier careened close to our gate, laughing loudly, offending Sarah so much she shouted "Shame!" at him from our window. He laughed back at her, calling her a name which made her almost faint.

Just seeing them go, even this vulgar soldier, after seeing so many march out earlier just after sundown, filled me with even more bitter sadness. Then Helen reminded me gently that we still have a new ally who promises hope for the new rise of the Confederacy. She and I are two of the few privy to that knowledge, because this hope comes courtesy of her fiancee, the courageous Mr. Castle. I can only hope that she weathers her illness until her wedding day, which will now likely be long postponed.

I first questioned why any European country would come to our aid. If it were the English, that would make some sense. It saddened us all when the British had declined the chance to redeem themselves against the Union that had so sorely disappointed them in the last century. But when the shipments started to arrive from our patron, that gracious foreign lord, I began to feel my faith returning. His newest cargo would be burning now, too, because it had yet to be unloaded. The coffins were to be for our war dead, a symbolic gift but nonetheless well appreciated when we were burying officers with no coffin at all. But still, according to Mr. Castle, there is so much wealth in the hands of this nobleman, whose name we are forbidden to mention in writing in case our journals fall into the wrong hands.

Still, what a waste. General Hood should have known better. All it would have taken was emptying a few boxcars. Though rumors said Generals Johnston and General Hardee are still untrusting of our new benefactor. They felt to accept help from him is against God for some reason, but how can anyone who would aide the Confederacy be against the Lord? It is Lincoln and the Yankee who are evil, otherwise how could they so waste our homes and our people without any conscience. I have heard tell that General Sherman is often heard to declare that "War is hell." So appropriate since he is the Devil Incarnate.

Oh, my darling Helen, I hope you live to see the Yankee learn what true Hell is.

August 18, 1864. Lieutenant James Tyler's Journal.

Atlanta was quiet today if only for an hour or two. General Sherman had ordered the shelling ceased, though we all knew the siege would begin again tomorrow, the same strategy, random shells exploding without any apparent pattern so as to confuse the populace even further. I was playing poker with several soldiers with whom I had become acquainted, sitting under a big oak tree and gambling for Confederate coins, medals, and jewelry that we had all taken from the bodies of the dead. We did not feel good about such scavenging, but it was difficult to turn your head and walk away from any little bit of wealth one could take home to make life easier for your family after the war. After the war. It had such a nice melody to it, that phrase did. I only had my dear mother at home in Philadelphia. My darling Catherine passed away in childbirth, barely one year since we married, so I had neither wife nor child like many men do. I had the freedom to die without injuring the feelings of many.

Rodney Habersham threw down a full house, John Maddox a two-pair, Davey Puckett just one pair, and I won again, a straight flush, when Corporal Tom Taylor tapped me on the shoulder. "Uncle Billy wants a word with you," he said. That was our way of talking, not that the General minded such familiarity. Besides, I considered him my second father, given the attention and advice he had bequeathed to me during our long march from Tennessee. He had fought alongside my own father in the Mexican War, and therefore he felt he owed it to his friend to keep an eye on me. Though others may criticize his seeming lust for destruction, this is not so. No man was more honorable in this entire War than General William Tecumseh Sherman. And to this day, I will be honored that he put such trust in me. Nevertheless on that hot as Hell, balmy August afternoon, I never expected the conversation we were about to have nor the strange and terrifying course of events that would follow after we finally marched into Atlanta.

When we arrived at the command tent, Uncle Billy was not alone. With him was Captain Orlando Poe, his chief engineer, and General Henry Slocum, who greeted me warmly but seemed distracted in their manner. Sherman himself looked distressed, rubbing his red beard and fretting his lips as he studied a book at the old wooden desk. Hearing us enter, he bade me welcome and dismissed the Corporal.

"How'd your game go, Jimmy," the General said, motioning me to sit. His tone was not that of his usual animated self but more somber than I had ever seen it out of the heat of battle. Even then, he was known to joke and make light of a perilous situation. "I apologize for dragging you away from it."

"As usual, sir, I won most of the time," I said, taking a seat on the crate that served as the only other chair.

"Glad to hear you're not losing your touch," he said, pouring me a shot of whiskey. "Drink it down, boy. In a minute you're going to need it."

When I had downed the shot, he poured me another and ordered that I down it as well. He poured a third but motioned for me to save it.

"That's for after I tell you what I am entrusting in you," he added, with a dry chuckle, standing and beginning to pace. "These two men in this room are the only ones who know just how important it is for us to take Atlanta and take it as soon as possible, but I am not sure just three knowing is enough. I could use the bravado and perspective of someone younger, someone who could lead a discreet and elite corps of men who will be sworn to secrecy on what may be the most important task of this entire war. For it may mean the difference from the South transforming not just into another country but an enemy more severe and evil than brother fighting brother."

"I don't understand," I said, confused at this sudden grave and troubling declaration.

"Ever since I was a boy, I have read widely on a great number of unusual subjects, but some years ago, my friend, the great P.T. Barnum, introduced me to someone," he began, leaning his tall, lank frame, to look me straight in the eye. "You are familiar with P.T. Barnum, Jimmy, are you not?"

"The proprietor of Barnum's Museum in New York," I said, nodding. "He is the one who discovered and made famous General Tom Thumb and all those bearded ladies, giants, skeleton men, amazing animals, the Man-Monkey and the like?"

"Yes, he is a man fascinated with those humans and beasts that do not follow God's normal prescription," Sherman added, handing me two books, one called *Legends and Folklore of Central and Eastern Europe*, and another by a James Malcolm Rymer: *Varney the Vampyre or The Feast of Blood*.

I still could not follow his meaning and what in God's name these strange books had to do with Atlanta.

"What is a vampire, sir?"

"A man or woman who in exchange for the opportunity to live forever sacrifices his humanity and his chance to enter heaven by drinking the blood of his fellow man."

"But that's ludicrous, some silly superstition, sir."

For the first time ever, I questioned the sanity of the man who had led us so valiantly, with such genius as to the ways of war. And yet the other two men remained serious in their gaze.

"I would have thought so myself had not Mr. Barnum introduced me to one such gentleman, a man who claimed to be born in 1714 but yet looked no more than age 27," Sherman continued. "Even though this gentleman charmed us with colorful tales of visiting the court of Marie Antoinette, dining with George Washington and fighting at the Alamo, I laughed him off. And later I told old P.T. that he had been most surely deceived. Then Mr. Barnum told me a story that made me laugh even more heartily. This man was undoubtedly one of the most ambitious hoaxes who ever tried to make a buck with the aid of the master showman. For Barnum told me how this man had traveled widely across Europe in his youth and related to him how he had chanced upon the castle of an old Romanian aristocrat named Count Dracula."

"Romania? Is that next to Russia?" I tried to remember my European geography to no avail, conjuring only images of England and France.

"Just keep on listening, son, and when I am done you can tell me what you believe then. This Dracula never ate in his presence and always disappeared during the daylight hours. One night he came to the man's chamber and bit him on the neck and drained his body of all his blood.

He then had the man drink from a cut on his own waist and replace his life blood with that of Dracula. From then on, he neither could walk in the sunlight nor drink wine or whiskey. He subsisted only on the blood of victims whom he killed like a predator. The day after my dinner with Mr. Barnum and this gentleman, the 'vampire' disappeared, and Mr. Barnum never heard from him again.

"P.T., however, handed me these two books on loan, which I read with great skepticism and duly returned. Until a month ago when one of our spies in Atlanta at great danger to himself smuggled me a set of letters. I sent to P.T. to dispatch me the books again which he most graciously did, fine supporter of the Union that he has always proven to be. But the final line of the story is this. The name of the gentleman to whom I was introduced by Mr. Barnum was Mr. Benjamin Castle."

With that he handed me a small bundle of letters, motioned for me to read them, and pushed the already poured shot of whiskey closer to me.

"These letters were smuggled to us by one of the Union's finest spies back while we were still battling for Chattanooga. The spy was found later in the woods near our camp with his throat ripped open as if by the jaws of a wild animal and all of the blood drained out of his body."

I finished the shot in one quick gulp and began to read.

May 19, 1863. Letter from Mr. Benjamin Castle, Esq., Savannah, Georgia, to Count Dracula, Transylvania.

My Lord, I believe I have found the perfect place for you to establish your new residence. In all my travels, I have never found a province so barbaric and yet so chivalrous, a land whose settlement has been so recent, and yet thanks to the humid climate, the buildings are barely erected before they begin to reek with the mildew of old age. The denizens are exuberant in their pursuit of profit like pioneers in a new wilderness and yet dignified in their code of behavior. I know you have declared to me that the New World was far too new for your old ways, but I beg you reconsider. In the South of the United States, your wealth and flamboyance of dress will allow you to blend effortlessly into the languid lifestyle.

And their practice of holding slaves will make it possible for you to have your entire sustenance ready and waiting on your estate with no suspicion. You can bleed them slowly, feeding on a single one for years, my Lord. And if you seek the purity of a kill, there are numerous white trash that live in pitiful homesteads all over the countryside. They are often prey to disease and stray crime among feuding neighbors, so there will be no suspicion. Your privacy will be assured.

At this very time, the Southern states have recently separated from the United States and declared themselves a new country, the Confederate States of America. The Union, as the Northern states call themselves, and the Confederacy have launched a war between each other, but I feel confident that the Confederacy will triumph. Their military leaders, such as General Robert E. Lee, General Stonewall Jackson, and General Jeb Stuart, are among the finest this country has to offer, and they have already driven the Northern armies out of Virginia and onto their own land in Pennsylvania.

I ask you to think again about the prospects of crossing the ocean, and I look forward to your letter of response.

July 1, 1863. Letter from Count Dracula to Mr. Benjamin Castle, Esq., Atlanta, Georgia.

Thank you for your letter. I am intrigued by your proposal and wish to consider it further, but I have heard the Union army is much larger in size than the Confederate, and many feel that eventually the tides of war must turn to their favor. If, indeed, this proves to be, what will the Southern states become? News has reached me that if the Union triumphs, their President Lincoln will abolish slavery. As I said, the situation intrigues me, but I must reserve my final decision until the war proceeds and we see where the tides turn.

August 24, 1863. Letter from Mr. Castle to Count Dracula.

You may have heard that the South lost a major battle at Gettysburg, Pennsylvania. I am afraid that this news will dispose you to believe that the South's fortune has turned. This, my Lord, is not the case. Even now, the Southern generals are regrouping and planning their new strategy to turn the war's course back to their favor. However, if you still find the notion of settling here attractive to you, I suggest that you could take some action to aid the cause of the Confederacy in terms of money, supplies, and invulnerable armies. I know that even though for many years you have retreated from the affairs of mankind, in the past you have told me that you led armies and derived much pleasure from the punishment of your enemies. Let me continue.

I am still residing in Atlanta in the state of Georgia where many are not happy with the actions of Confederate president Jefferson Davis. Indeed, Atlanta hoped to be capital of the Confederacy had it not been for President Davis' affection for Virginia. Many in Atlanta would welcome the support of a foreign noble with wealth who would be nefarious and powerful enough to break through the Union blockade with military supplies and necessary civilian provisions. Do not tell me if your ship was stopped by Yankee sailors that any of them would walk away alive.

Meanwhile I can begin to create an army for you to lead against the Union, an army that would strike at night like a phantom stealing into their camps and slaughtering men in their sleep. This will cause panic and fear amongst the Yankees, allowing the human armies of daylight to strike their deadly blows in an environment of chaos.

I do not know that you would desire to be the President or that it would be practical given your circumstances and desire for a long term residency in one place without too much suspicion, but I venture to say that you would gain much power of influence and respect should we pursue this tactic. Let me know if I can approach the Confederate leaders in Atlanta with your kind offer.

December 1, 1863. Letter from Count Dracula to Mr. Castle.

Your suggestions fascinate me. Perhaps I have stayed isolated from the affairs of men for too long. Let the Confederate leaders know my offers, and I shall immediately arrange a first shipment of the finest firearms that can be purchased by an acquaintance of mine in Vienna. I will send rifles, ammunition, several cannons, and explosive shells. Also, I will instruct my agent to purchase sugar, flour, and wine, as well as some nice European hats for any ladies whose influence could be beneficial to our personal cause. Also, let them know that a second shipment shall arrive soon after the first, but this one is to be held until my arrival. Tell them I am sending fifty coffins for their honored war dead, but I must be present for the burial. And most importantly, no one should open these coffins until I have arrived. I trust you will convey my wishes in a way that will not make these people find my request unusual. As soon as I hear from you that these shipments have arrived in Atlanta, I will begin to make arrangements for my own journey.

August 18, 1864. Lieutenant James Tyler's Journal.

"Is this all?" I asked. "The letters abruptly stop last winter."

"Those are all we have intercepted, but we have reason to believe that there are more, including more recent correspondence," said Slocum, lighting a cigar.

"How then can we be sure that this is not some sly Confederate hoax meant to throw confusion upon us and make us look like fools?"

"I wish it were so," said Poe. "But I was the man who found the body of the spy. And he was not the only man we found. Several scouts were also found murdered in the same disgusting manner."

"You know, son, I am the last man who would seek to be called a fool, but this time, I wish I would find myself utterly ridiculed rather than face whatever beast ripped up these good men's bodies," Sherman said, sitting down again. He had continued to pace while I read. "I wish I hadn't seen the one who clawed himself out of his grave under the sight of several witnesses and later attacked me in my tent while sleeping. I thrust my sword into his heart and yet he did not die. He, one of my own men whom I knew well, raised the Rebel Yell of the Confederacy more harrowing than any yell I have yet heard on the battlefield. I finally remembered something of what I had read in Mr. Barnum's books and grabbed a wooden cane with a silver crook and plunged it into the heart of this vile creature that was no longer my soldier."

I tried to picture the attack in my mind, and I became suddenly sick to my groin that I had ever questioned the general whom I respected more than any other man. I felt sicker still thinking that the Southerners could hate us so much they would make a pact with the Devil himself to win the war. And yet I knew it was not all Southerners. It was a greedy few who would welcome in such creatures to fight their war for them.

"Why not tell everyone? It will only drive the troops to fighting harder to prevent such a terrible creature from establishing a foothold in this country."

"I wish it were so, son," General Sherman laughed now again. "But I think that most people would likely laugh like I am, like I did at old P.T. Barnum. Blood-drinking men who walk only after the sun sets with the power to transform themselves into bats and wolves? Pretty good joke, huh, Orlando? Henry?"

The two men laughed along with Uncle Billy, but they did not seem at all comfortable with the notion of laughing.

"You see the problem is not just this Mr. Castle and Count Dracula," General Slocum said. "It appears that Mr. Castle has been quite busy drinking the blood of both Atlantans and our Union soldiers for some time, according to our spy and a little of my own experience, as well as spreading his own peculiar malady to the newly dead. If we do not take the matter into our own hands soon, we may be facing an army of these creatures. While they can only fight during the night hours, they are invulnerable to bullets and can only be killed with a wooden stake through the heart and by sunlight. I fear many of our men would fall under such an attack. With their ability to regenerate their armies with fresh dead newly arisen, it would be like fighting an enemy whom the moment one was destroyed, two would rise in his place."

"Why me, sir, then?" I asked.

"Because I have every faith in your bravery and honor," said the General. "And I know if I ask you to swear never to tell a soul of this mission that you will keep your word. Right now, the menace may be stopped. This Mr. Castle is a sly devil, but I believe he can be curtailed if we are equally cunning. If this Count Dracula is allowed to arrive, our foe will be far more formidable, and it may not be so simple.

"I need you to pick twenty men whom you trust as greatly as I trust you. Men who are willing to swear on the Holy Bible that they will never divulge their mission even unto their deathbeds be that tomorrow or many years from now. Take these books and study them well for they will instruct you in all the ways to kill a vampire. Orlando here may be of some use to you in this matter since he is such a brilliant engineer. I fear, though, much of our strategy will have to wait until we get to Atlanta and see how severe the problem is. As for me, tonight, I have to get wild James Kilpatrick and his cavalry off of their high horses and down to Jonesboro to rip out some rails."

I began the task of gathering myself twenty honorable and not born too skeptical men. The thought that these "vampires" would appear to be men just as us and yet not die from a bullet deeply troubled me.

August 18, 1865. Letter from Helen Baker to Natalie Wendall, a friend in Charleston.

I do not know what to do. My sleep last night was interrupted by another troubling dream, a dream so unsettling that I feel I must put it to paper even though today I feel even weaker than yesterday and holding the pen is difficult. I have not had the dream in two weeks so I was hopeful it would not return. I can only think it has something to do with the Yankees being so close now, their shells falling upon us every day.

I was sleeping in my bed as the dream began, and then I heard a sound at my window, a tapping, first very soft. Gradually it mounted until the window itself blew open as if a sudden gust of wind had broken the bolt. The next thing I remember, a cloud of mist swirled through the window and around my bed. The cloud came together as if to form a column. No, it was the figure of a man in dark clothes. Red glowing eyes glared at me from the head. There was something familiar about his face, but I could not see the shape of his nose, only teeth, as he bent down toward me. I wanted to scream but could not. He kissed me with lips as cold as icicles. And then his mouth lowered to my neck. The next thing I knew, the sun was streaming in my window and it was morning.

Papa says Benjamin will come tonight to see me. He has been off with General Hood defending the city, but when the message got to him that Dr. Foster says I am getting worse, he insisted upon seeing me. Seeing him should make me happy. Surely I will feel better when he is here. Surely things will be better when the war is over, and we can finally be married, or so my dear Papa says. I hope he is right.

Much love, I miss you terribly.

September 2, 1864. Councilman Warren Baker's Journal.

After last night's horror, today has been tragedy. The only good news is Helen seemed better. She has not had that dream again since Benjamin came to see her a week and a half ago, and she seems to be gaining strength again. I so thought I would lose her, one of my life's two only remaining joys, she and her beloved mother.

Mayor Calhoun summoned all the members of the City Council and various other eminent citizens to a special meeting this morning even before dawn to discuss whether we should surrender. Many of us were loathe to doing so, though we had no method by which to defend ourselves with the army gone. And then much to the surprise of everyone, Mr. Castle arrived. We all thought he had gone south with General Hood. After all, why should he linger when he would be far safer with the troops.

Indeed, the man has such a mastery of words. There is no doubt he was raised in a family of wealth and breeding. "I know that I am not an Atlantan by birth, but then neither are any of you for this beautiful Gate City is so young," he said. "Please hear me then as one of Atlanta's proudest citizens. We can foolishly sacrifice our lives by fighting the enemy without an army. But if we surrender, it does not mean they have won the war, only that our women and children will be allowed to live. My lord is even now making his arrangements to travel by ship across the Atlantic with his own army to help him elude the blockade. If you will be but patient, my good gentlemen, surrender is but temporary. I assure you, the tide will turn, and Atlanta will rise again, the new capital of the Confederacy."

Mayor Calhoun called for a vote, and most of us voted for surrender, difficult as it was to accept. Yet Mr. Castle's words filled us with hope. When we turned to thank him for his counsel, he was gone, again mysteriously disappearing as is his way. For all his breeding, he is a most unusual man, but perhaps he is afraid the Yankees will take him captive when they march into the city. Mayor Calhoun, myself and several other members of the Council will ride to meet them.

September 3, 1864. Lieutenant James Tyler's Journal.

Atlanta is ours! The terrible noises of the night before last were General Hood's army blowing up the munitions stored in the railroad yard, and the Rebel army has marched south out of Atlanta. General Slocum is already in the city and Sherman will march in on the 8th of September after assuring that General Hardee is in flight and inspecting a hospital housing wounded Rebel officers in Jonesboro. He has ordered me and my men ride north immediately to begin our grave task. Our first assignment is to find Mr. Castle. I have but a description of a well-dressed gentleman with piercing blue eyes, blond hair and a goatee. Otherwise, I know only that he is engaged to the daughter of a City Councilman, Miss Helen Baker.

September 6, 1864. Lieutenant James Tyler's Journal.

Mr. Castle is nowhere to be found, but I have already seen sights that make my blood chill. The threat indeed is still here. Last night four of our men visited a local Madam and her ladies, and only one returned telling a terrible story of murder. All were drinking heavily, and as each man finished his whiskey, the ladies would pour another. There would seem to be nothing unusual about this since the ladies were laughing and flirting with the men as these ladies normally do. And then suddenly one of them kissed one soldier, then lowered her head and bit his neck so hard that she drew blood.

The other three rose to defend their fellow, but the women with them pushed them down with unusual strength for a woman and bit them as well. Only this one soldier escaped, wailing about how he plunged his sword into this woman's chest and yet she kept coming after him. He only escaped when he knocked her into a burning candelabra. Apparently she was not immune to fire. When my men and I visited the brothel, we found it still burning and made no attempt to douse the fire, only to prevent its spread. I can only assume the ladies who made their business there have escaped.

Yesterday, I visited Miss Baker under the auspices that we were making a general inspection of all homes to search for Rebel spies. Mr. Baker and his wife were polite but guarded in their answers, I could tell, especially when I brought up Mr. Castle. They could say no wrong about the man, only that he would make the perfect husband for their daughter. According to them, he was the son of a plantation owner from Alabama who had recently settled in Atlanta to pursue a trade as a banker. He was a man of honor and manners like no other, and there was no more that they would tell a Yankee. I told them he had a reputation for supporting blockade running of supplies and possibly mercenaries. They scoffed at this suggestion, but I could tell they were hiding something. I wondered though if they knew the full story, since they seemed such an average Christian family. I asked to search the house, and they begged me not to disturb their daughter as she was ill and had been so for many weeks. I apologized but said I must inspect every room, and so reluctantly they let me enter.

Lying in the lace canopy bed was what I could term only as an angel, for since Catherine, never had I seen a woman so fair. Even as pale as she was, a sweetness radiated from her smile, for though I was a Yankee, she treated me with the utmost politeness and grace. I asked her father the nature of her illness, and he told me even the doctor was unsure. She appeared to have some form of anemia that had struck suddenly in late July. Since then she had been plagued with nightmares, and her illness had only been made worse by lack of sleep during proper night hours. He insisted it was our fault for battering the city with shells every day, but she said, no, this was not so. She dreamed of a stranger with red eyes who came to her in the form of mist, and what could this have to do with men fighting men? Her father preferred to blame everything on General Sherman.

I wanted to question her further for I had a terrible feeling that her illness and dreams had a significance far more sinister. And besides I immediately enjoyed her company more than any woman I had met since Catherine's death. But her mother and father were becoming steadily more uncomfortable at my presence. I asked for just one minute alone with her, and they protested, but she insisted it would be all right. They reluctantly left the room, and when the door was shut, I asked her when she had last seen Benjamin Castle. I expected her to refuse to answer the question to protect her fiancee. But the very mention of his name filled her with a sudden air of discomfort as if his name frightened rather than raised longing for an absent love.

"I have not seen him since August 20," she said simply. "Honestly, Lt. Tyler, I do not feel I will ever see him again alive."

"Miss Baker, I can see that you miss him, but do you believe he is dead?" I asked her.

"Dead?" She laughed lightly. "No, I will be dead soon, Lt. Tyler. The next time I have one of my dreams, I am sure I will not wake up."

"But how can one die from a dream?" I started to ask her, but her father opened the door and demanded that I had spent enough time disturbing her and she needed her rest.

As I left, her mother pleaded I allow the doctor to continue to see her, and I agreed, even offering to post several of my men to protect the house against looters. Her father did not like the idea of having Yankees around, but her mother begged him to agree. I left John Myers and Tom Halligan, instructing them to keep a special watch on Miss Baker's window.

"If you see anything unusual, or that window should open for even a minute, I order you to enter the house and make sure she is all right," I ordered. "Don't allow her parents to give her fresh air at night and check the bolts carefully. If they ask why, just say I have ordered it."

I would return myself once it was dark, I decided, for this was where Benjamin Castle would come. I hated him, even though I had still to meet him, for seeking to corrupt something so pure, kind and innocent.

September 9, 1865. Lieutenant James Tyler's Journal.

I am relieved General Sherman is finally here. Tonight, he called a secret meeting at the John Neal House, his Atlanta headquarters at Washington and Mitchell Streets, a regal building fronted by Corinthian columns. Ostensibly, it is about the evacuation of the city he ordered on September 4. The date for all citizens to register their names at City Hall looms three days away. They will be permitted to take along clothes, a small ration of food, whatever furniture might fit upon a wagon, and any servant who by his or her own free will wishes to accompany them. By September 20, they must be gone.

"We must remove every man, woman, and child from the city during daylight," General Sherman said. "We will search their wagons to make sure no one smuggles any of these dead creatures out of town. And then we will know that any Southerner who is left is one of them. After which, the only course of action left is to burn the city to the ground to make sure that none of them survive."

He paused and I could tell he was not pleased with his conclusion. He had told me of the pleasurable time he had spent in Atlanta, even more a frontier town in those days and barely born, twenty years before as a young officer. Contrary to what any Southern historian may later claim, he did not relish the thought of leveling the city.

"We will let stand only the Masons' Hall, City Hall, and certain churches which may be spared for these are places of God, and if the legends are true, the demons cannot enter there. A minister will bless any hall or house that is spared that is not a place of worship."

After the others had left, I apprised General Sherman of my surveillance on the Baker house. I feared for Miss Baker's life should she be moved from the safety of our watch. The General agreed, noting she was the single most likely bait to attract Mr. Castle. I rode immediately to inform her family that due to her severe illness, they would be allowed to stay. While Mr. Baker is still no more than cordial to me, his wife seemed most grateful.

September 23, 1864. Lieutenant James Tyler's Journal.

All the civilians are registered and gone now. Indeed, the order for evacuation has brought to light some twenty of the undead, including the three escaped prostitutes. While searching the rear of a ladies' dress shop for loot, several soldiers discovered coffins and opened them to find the three women whom they recognized. At first they thought them dead, but when touched, one of them sat up suddenly and grabbed for the soldier's throat. He screamed and ran out into the sunlight to his fellows. I was called for, and my men soon put the women to rest with wooden stakes through their hearts. We then dragged their bodies behind the building where the sun consumed their remains in a matter of minutes, reducing them to ashes.

Several more coffins were found in the basements of residences, and General Sherman gave the order that all buildings be searched from basement to attic. I feel certain that we have found any and all of these vampires in Atlanta and am relieved that they do not seem to have numbered as many as we feared.

But where is Mr. Castle? And will Count Dracula arrive any day to make our work redundant? At least, Helen seems more cheerful today. She is regaining her strength daily, and I am hopeful she may after all survive Mr. Castle's malady.

October 14, 1864. Letter from Helen Baker to Natalie Wendall.

Even in the middle of this mess, I am happy to tell you all my news is good. I feel much improved the last few weeks, so much so I wonder if I may indeed survive this illness after all. And not a single nightmare. Mother and Papa are doing well, though Papa is very distressed about the way the war has progressed, and I think it will be difficult for him to live in a state dominated by Yankees. He still hopes for a miracle.

It distresses my beloved parents if I say this within their earshot, but I am so enjoying the company of Lt. Tyler. Even if he is a Yankee, he is truly a good man. Every evening, he makes a point of arriving just after sunset. He will then read to me a little, often from Charles Dickens. We are in the middle of *A Tale of Two Cities*, which is a very exciting tale of the French Revolution. I sometimes imagine myself as Lucie Manette, a girl caught in the middle of a revolution and a war between two dashing suitors. Then we will play a little game of cards perhaps, and sometimes my parents will graciously join in. I think they do secretly like him and are grateful to him for taking such care of me. Then we talk and he tells me of his life in New York and Philadelphia. It would be so exciting to go see a big city like that. Benjamin used to regale me with his tales of London, Paris, Vienna, St. Petersburg, his journeys through the wild hills of Hungary and Romania, but I think to travel to Philadelphia would be exciting enough to a sheltered Southern girl like me.

We never talk about the war at all as if it is some distant dream when we are together. It made me cry though when he told me about his young wife, Catherine, and that she died in childbirth. I feel so sorry for him being almost all alone in the world.

What I did not tell him is that I am afraid to be married because as you know, I do not love Benjamin anymore. He is handsome for sure and charming, and he has put a spell upon Papa. I was so in love. Remember how I went on and on about him? But now, especially the last time I saw him, he scares me in his zeal for the war, and especially when he speaks of his foreign benefactor whom he says is on his way to help us. I suppose I am not showing my proper allegiance to the Confederacy, but the way he talks. I cannot help but think it has something to do with my dreams, though that does not make any sense either, does it?

My apologies for rambling on so, but I must get this off my chest and you are the only person I feel I can trust. My love to your parents. Have you heard from Charley? You said he was fighting in Virginia now. I pray he is safe.

October 26, 1864. Lieutenant James Tyler's Journal.

We are most sadly and grievously mistaken. A month passed without a sign of the fiends, just the normal business of an occupation. But our search of homes has not eradicated the vampire from Atlanta; they have just lain dormant, lulling us into a false sense of comfort. We had even wondered if Mr. Castle had fled the city and had no intention of returning. After all, what was there for him here but one beautiful young lady? As I found myself in love with her, I hoped time and distance had eradicated his dark affection for her. Nevertheless, I kept my vigil every night with four men guarding her window, her door, every way anyone could enter the house.

But last night, we found out the vampires were not gone at all. Four of these fiends made their way to General Sherman's own bedroom window, killing seven sentries, and attempting a daring assassination. It was fortunate the dropping of a strand of pinestraw would wake the general. His eyes shot open to see not one but four of the very columns of fog described by Helen. He yelled for aid and grabbed his sword as the mist faded into four figures. Three were Confederate soldiers, still in uniform, the reek of death so strong it almost choked him. The fourth was a well-dressed man with blond hair and a goatee whom he recognized immediately.

The soldiers fell upon him, but he swung his sword in a circle, and they backed away for a moment, hissing.

"You cannot win, William Tecumseh Sherman," Castle said, laughing. The scurry of hurried footsteps could be heard outside the door. A foot soldier was dispatched to fetch me. "I have the power to keep that door shut and locked for at least the few minutes it will take to kill you."

"My men will break it down," Sherman said defiantly. "And even if you take me down, other brave men will assume my place."

"Bring you down?" Castle chuckled again. "When the naive Mr. Barnum first introduced us, I knew immediately that your honor and your ego would be your downfall. You should be humble before an enemy who is obviously more cunning and ruthless than even you. They dub you the Devil for all your burning, looting, and routing good folks from their homes. I can give you the power to be the Devil, to truly strike terror into the hearts and souls of every Union soldier when you assume the command of General Hood's army under the banner of my master. Hood was too weak-minded. He cared for people, and he was dreadful at strategy. But *you!* Just imagine how the South could rise again with you as their military leader!"

"*Never!*" Sherman declared. The battering at the door grew louder and more urgent. "How can you think I could just transfer loyalty like that, especially if the cost is to become one like you, feeding off the blood of the living and not allowing a man even the courtesy of an honest death in battle."

The Confederate soldiers moved in closer, and the general swung his sword again. This time, they did not draw back, the sword drawing blood from all three waists, but not causing any of them to pause.

"Or I could leave you at the helm of the Union forces," Castle suggested, rubbing his chin. "My lord just wants a change of scenery, and I think he would appreciate the irony. Think how powerful you would become with eternal life. You could run for President and rule a century."

"And what do you get out of it?" Sherman asked, his eyes on the vampire soldiers, his free hand fumbling in his pocket.

"Power," Castle responded. "One does not have to rule to pull the strings."

I was on the other side of the door by now, yelling at the guards for not pushing harder. But as I touched the door, I was stabbed by a pain that jetted into my fingers and through my body, forcing me to recoil. The pain dissipated as suddenly as it charged through me, and I turned and lowered my voice.

"Is there a room with a window next to the General's?"

Sergeant Thompkins nodded and produced a key immediately.

In the General's bedchamber, one of the soldiers reached forward to grab him by the shoulders. Sherman pulled a clump of garlic from his pocket and smeared it into the fiend's face. The creature recoiled, hurling its hands into its eyes and screaming.

The other two paused, the odor obviously distressing them. The General reached beneath his bedshirt and pulled out a crucifix from around his neck. They hesitated again, covering their eyes. But Castle was not so easily turned back. He reached forward and grabbed the cross from the General's hand with a mighty rip, smoke rising from his fingers as the cross burned them. His face froze in the pain of touching it even for a few seconds. Then he flung it across the room and out the window. At this point, I was on the ledge outside with two of my men following from the window next door. I leapt into the room, just as Castle was about to sink his teeth in the General's neck. The General was strong, but I could see that Castle had not the strength of one man but strength more than any man.

"Take your hands off him, you scoundrel!" I shouted. My men, Davey Puckett and Rodney Habersham thrust themselves through the window behind me. We were all armed with crossbows with wooden arrows, and I cursed that we had been so confident all the fiends were dead and had armed the General with such paltry weaponry as garlic and a tiny cross. Castle's head shot up from the General's throat, and a vampire who had been clutching his eyes when we came in, yanked his hands from them and moved in my direction. I shot straight for the heart. He fell to the ground, screaming loudly.

Another of the creatures approached, and Davey fired, hitting him also in the chest, forcing him to collapse onto the floor and the other vampire to hesitate. It shot a glance at Castle.

"All I have to do is move him slightly, and he'll take any arrow you aim at me," Castle said.

"Shoot me if you must," Sherman ordered, his voice almost a whisper. It was strange to see the General so disabled.

"We have got to separate him from Mr. Castle," I said. "Davey, now that you've reloaded, keep an eye on the other one. Rodney, follow me."

Sherman had taken Atlanta through a succession of flanking maneuvers, now our only hope for the General's life would be the same strategy. Davey approached the other creature, easing it to the left, as

Rodney and I moved to the right side of the bed, cornering Castle, still clutching the general on the other side of the bed. Then suddenly, the other vampire leapt forward at Davey, but his crossbow jammed and the creature grabbed it and hurled it across the room, plunging teeth into neck. Rodney separated from me, but the best aim he could get was the creature's back. The beast did not even wince, but kept on drinking at Davey's neck. My friend's eyes called to me in pain, but he did not seem able to scream. Rodney reloaded, pulling the vampire away from Davey. It looked up at him now, eyes glowing red in anger, flesh and blood from Davey's neck still clenched in its wolflike teeth.

"Die, vile spawn of Lucifer," Rodney yelled and let loose another bolt just as the creature lunged. This time, the shaft sunk straight into its heart, and the thing collapsed. Three down, only one to go. I spun back toward Castle. I had looked away for an instant, but he was gone, the General now lying across the bed massaging his neck wound. A column of mist rose from where Castle stood, and with a quick whoosh, fled out the window.

At the same moment, the door crashed open, and eight soldiers ran in, rifles poised, followed by Generals Slocum and Thomas.

"Oh my Lord," General Slocum gasped, bending down beside the General and helping him to sit up.

"I'm all right," Sherman said. "Just stop that assassin at all costs."

"Come with me," ordered General Thomas, taking five of the men with him. We could hear him yelling orders out in the hallway.

"He's dead," Rodney said, checking Davey's pulse.

"All right," Sherman repeated. "They won't strike again tonight, though I'm not going to stay in bed and wait and see. We have a problem, gentlemen, but that doesn't mean we ain't going to win this war. What do you recommend, Jimmy?"

"First, we've got to burn these bodies just to make sure they're really dead," I said. "Then, sir, you get a guard twenty-four hours a day even when you are sleeping. At least four of my men in your room. Finally, we have got to find where they sleep during the day and destroy every one of them."

"Damn right," Sherman chuckled. "Clear that boy out of here and make sure he gets a proper burial. I know it won't give his wife much comfort but maybe it will give her some when I issue him a posthumous medal and promotion for valor beyond the call of duty. Then I want a drink and a cigar, and then I am going to tell you what he said to me."

When he finished the story, all I could think of was Helen, and I damned myself for not thinking of her sooner. I ran back up the street, but it was too late.

When I returned to Helen's window, I found the soldiers I had left to watch her dead, all with the marks of the vampire on their necks. Entering the house, I found her father and mother dead in the parlor. I ran up the stairs to her room only to find her sheets tousled and her bed empty. Outside, dawn was breaking, and I prayed that this meant he had not had time to finish his vile task. I had a day in which to find her before she would be lost to Heaven forever.

October 27, 1864. Lieutenant James Tyler's Journal.

The streets were crowded with packs of stray dogs and cats as we made our way to Oakland Cemetery yesterday morning, an army of men with shovels. Every grave was to be dug up, every crypt entered, and any corpse found looking remotely like it could be alive, a stake to be plunged through its heart. It was not pleasant work.

Although the cemetery itself covered only six acres, the Confederates had been forced, through the volume of their dead, to expand beyond the boundaries. At the bottom of the small hill which crowned this hallowed soil lay a vineyard, and beyond that a rich tobacco field. Our foes had begun stripping the vineyard of its foliage, cutting back the frames to inter their fallen comrades in cramped rows, each body designated by a simple marker. This section formed a rough contrast against the backdrop of ornate stone mausoleums, crypts and granite slabs which formed the cemetery proper. Only fourteen years old, but the ravages of war, the shelling from the siege, had taken its toll. The place looked a shambles.

The men under my command, numbering forty, including Rodney Habersham, had been privately briefed by the General. They were among the most trusted and honorable who had served throughout this long and painful campaign. Excepting those who already knew the terrible and fearsome truth, the General explained our gruesome task thus: that a strange disease had contaminated many of the Rebels, inducing a state which suggested death prior to truly taking their lives. That, in haste, the Confederate forces were burying those unfortunate souls, and it was our duty to release them from their agony. No one questioned his order concerning the staking through the heart, such was their trust in his command.

Each grave was assigned a team of two men, digging in unison until the coffins were exposed. Two thirds of the company worked on fresh graves, the others on the older monuments.

By noon we had excavated perhaps a third of them and the stench of death floated above us, permeated our clothes, our very skin. This smell was, however, one we had grown accustomed to, particularly since we had entered this wild city. All of the older graves and mausoleums proved fruitless, their contents nothing more than bones and dust. The most recent graves, however, proved to be far more of a challenge. The sights and smells of those who had fallen tested the mettle of the most courageous soldier.

We toiled long and hard under such circumstances, a blessed breeze providing a brief respite from the stench and the fearsome heat of a hellish Indian summer afternoon. It was then, as we approached our hundredth grave, that those men who had fought so valiantly discovered a new face of the horrors of war.

Two young infantrymen struggled, a few graves away from my position under a majestic magnolia tree, with a particularly tenacious coffin lid. The pine casket suddenly shattered, exposing its inhabitant to the midday light. Both men recoiled as an incandescent flash of flame burst forth from the opening. As they stumbled on the bank of dry red earth, all eyes turned to the source of that terrible sound.

A flaming figure sat bolt upright in the coffin, clawing at its burning face, the mouth open wider than lips are meant to part, the scream issuing forth a shrill tea kettle wail of uncomprehending agony. Every man in the cemetery froze.

And in the blink of an eye, the screaming corpse exploded into fiery debris, the flaming remnants showering the two young soldiers. One cried out as shreds of burning cloth rained upon his exposed skin, as the other back-peddled wildly on the mound of dirt. His footing on the loose earth lost traction and he slid into the hole and landed face first into the glowing embers. His shrieks of pain and revulsion proved no match for the sound which had issued from the mouth of the vampire, yet were nevertheless chilling.

Before any of us could move to aid our comrade, a voice from the hill barked out a command: "Don't just stand there! Get the poor fellow out of that hellhole!"

I looked up and saw General Sherman standing beside an imposing crypt, surveying the grim tableaux beneath him. Without further thought, Rodney and I raced to the young man's side, slipping into the grave ourselves in haste to aid him. We floundered together in the scorched remains of the pine box and the ashes of the dead, my hands upon his chest as I tried to pull him from the hole. With Habersham's aid, I managed to drag the infantryman onto the grass. He had fainted from the shock and pain, his face blackened with ashes, the skin blistered from the burning embers. The General now was standing beside us.

"Get a doctor here, right now!" he commanded to Ira Templeton, who dashed back to the gates for his horse. Then he turned to the rest of us. "You men keep digging."

A murmur traveled through the group, and the General's eyes narrowed, his steel gaze silencing the discontent. He slapped me on the shoulder, gesturing for me to walk with him, out of earshot of the men. As we sat upon a horizontal slab of marble, he informed me more soldiers would arrive soon.

"This is taking too long," he stated. "And time is against us."

His words filled me with dread. All morning my thoughts had been consumed by poor, dear Helen, wondering what terrors that fiend Castle had condemned her to.

"It's past noon. We have only five hours of sunlight remaining."

His words hung over me like a funeral shroud.

Where was Helen?

We toiled hard throughout the hot afternoon, our tunics stained with sweat and soil. And yet we found nothing. Some of the men started to violate the bodies of the inhabitants of Oakland, removing gold teeth, wedding bands, and the silver plates adorning coffin lids. While we had stripped war dead in the field of their possessions, this offended me greatly, but my protestations to the General were met with a reasoned, but cold logic.

"These men have fought valiantly against great odds, and our casualties have been far greater than the Confederates'. And now I order them to do this. I think they deserve some reward for their ungodly labors. The lure of easy wealth will keep morale high and questions to a minimum. Many a fine young Union lad has died far from home and deserves to rest in hallowed ground. Once we are through here, I plan on having these bodies removed and our own interred. War is barbarous, Jimmy, never forget that."

With that he walked down the hill to give words of encouragement to our boys. At that moment, my feelings toward him were divided between dismay at his amoral pragmatism and respect for his strategist's mind. Still, unsettled by his reply, I wandered away from my position to take a brief rest. Standing atop the low hill, I saw the farm houses north of the cemetery, one a quarter mile distant, the other farther away, situated next to the blasted remains of the railroad Hood's men had destroyed in anticipation of our advance.

Every building still standing in Atlanta had been searched thoroughly since late September, but what if Castle had been one step ahead of us and had frequently moved his place of rest? Now, with the city inhabited only by troops, what better place to hide than in the most obvious—a house near the cemetery. This thought had less to do with logic than some deep sense Castle had been taunting us all along.

I questioned Corporal Taylor, who had been in charge of searching this area previously. The houses had been searched several weeks ago, he confirmed. I ordered him and two of his men to follow me.

The first house was as empty as a Confederate rations box, and seeing the sun lower toward the western rim, I was filled with despair. What if I was wrong? Despite Taylor's protestations that this was a wild goose chase, we set off at a trot toward the farthest house.

The wooden exterior had sustained considerable damage due to its proximity to the railyards and one wall was torn open, exposing the structure's innards to the feeble twilight. A quick search of the basement proved fruitless. As we raced upstairs, I saw that in the few minutes we'd been below ground, the shadows had lengthened and the sun was now below the horizon. We were almost out of time, but I ordered the men upward. There in the attic we found our quarry.

Helen's pale, frail body lay beside an ornate oak coffin, and as we entered the room I saw a hand emerging from beneath the lid.

"Get her out!" I shouted as I ran toward the box, stake held high, Corporal Taylor a footstep behind me.

Castle swept the lid from his resting place as I lunged for his chest, but his other hand batted away the wood as if it were a cobweb. The blow knocked me to my knees as the vampire rose from the box and grabbed Taylor by the throat, lifting him clear of the ground.

"James?" I heard Helen weakly exclaim.

Turning, I saw she was barely conscious, swaying like a rag doll between the soldiers' arms.

"Out! Now!" I cried as I scrabbled toward the stake.

"Fool," Castle sneered, crushing Taylor's wind pipe, silencing his gasps. He hurled his body through the small, covered casement window. And before the soldiers could make for the stairs with Helen, he was on them, faster than the eye could register. He broke the nearest man's neck and tore the other's face to shreds like a lion with his sharp fingernails, slashing the man's scream into silence with the other hand. Before I could move, the fiend embraced Helen, her back to his broad chest.

"You are powerless, Yankee," he said, his mouth stretching into a feral grin.

"James," Helen murmured as if she were half asleep, her eyelids fluttering.

"How touching," he hissed, one hand caressing her alabaster throat. He nicked the skin over her jugular with a nail, drawing blood. "The South falls for the North."

He spun her suddenly to face him, tilting that beautiful neck toward his vile mouth, and laughed.

I snatched the stake beside me and, with a cry befitting a primitive warrior, charged toward him. Again, the devil was too fast for me; he threw poor Helen aside toward the window like a petulant child discards a toy, batted away the wood, and broke my left arm with a chopping blow, then swept away my feet. I landed heavily on my useless appendage, my head striking the floor. My thoughts swam in lazy circles, numbing the pain.

"James!"

Helen, I saw through blurred vision, tried to stand but staggered. Her head had hit the plaster, and she swayed like a punch-drunk prizefighter. Winded, dazed, and in pain, I could not move.

"Before I kill you, Yankee, I shall make you watch her suffer," he leered down at me before taking three strides to Helen. "She who could have been consort to the right hand of Dracula."

I could do nothing other than lie and watch as he slid behind her, one hand around her neck, the other threatening to claw furrows in that delicate face I had grown to love. A concert of startled cries and shouts entered through the broken window along with a chill breeze.

"*Up there! Inside!*" The voice belonged to Rodney.

Castle spun his head at the sound as heavy, frantic footfalls assaulted the stairs.

"More cattle to the slaughter," he chuckled, then tilted his head as if detecting a distant sound beyond the thunder of boots ascending.

Then I, too, heard what his acute ears had detected: echoes of faraway screams erupting from somewhere in the cemetery. Castle spoke his final words to me as I slipped into unconsciousness.

✠

All is fair, they say, in love and war. Not so, I say, for Fate denied me the pleasure of watching Benjamin Castle die. Uncle Billy reminds me I am blessed that Rodney Habersham's quick actions saved Helen and I from certain, terrible deaths.

Helen's frail form now lies in the bed opposite mine, here in the secure confines of the Masons' Hall, a doctor constantly monitoring her pulse as he provides her with a further transfusion. My head hurts like all Hell, but I am too agitated to rest, and writing provides catharsis.

This morning, after the surgeon had reset my arm, Uncle Billy and Rodney brought me French brandy and cigars, and informed me of the outcome. Those we had sought were not in the cemetery proper but concealed in graves situated in the densest part of the vineyard, and thirteen brave men died in the attempt at laying to rest seven Confederate undead.

As for that hellspawn Castle, startled on seeing Rodney enter the attic with twelve men all armed with crossbows and stakes, he made to break dear Helen in two. But he underestimated Rodney's speed and skill as a marksman. Before he could do so, Habersham, as fine a marksman as you will find in this army, fired a crossbow bolt which caught the fiend in the neck, just above the collarbone. Enraged and surprised, he discarded Helen and spread his arms, and (this I truly am glad I did not see) transformed himself into a huge black bat. Yet as the creature prepared to take flight through the shattered casement, Rodney's men unleashed a rain of arrows which found their target and the vampire plunged into the line of troops commanded by the General below the window.

"Rest assured, Jimmy, that devil's back where he belonged," Uncle Billy informed me gravely as he lit my cigar. "And he burned like the fires of Hell itself, and I trust he's still burning now."

The winged, wounded beast landed in front of a dozen armed men who unleashed a tide of bullets and arrows into its foul body. Although obviously in great pain from its wounds, yet not quite incapacitated, the General didn't hesitate to stride forward and plunge his trusty cane deep into its heart.

"And then, my boy, it burned. Burned so bright, it could have been a Christmas bonfire," Uncle Billy added, the lines of his face heavy with relief.

Between the concussion and the brandy, I suddenly feel dizzy. I must rest now.

Please, dear God, let Helen live!

November 15, 1865. Lieutenant James Tyler's Journal.

Last night I dined next door to the fires of Hell, but compared to the experiences of the last few months, it was a friendly Hell. I sat with officers at the grand table in Uncle Billy's headquarters house. We smoked cigars, drank whiskey, though our meal was simple hardtack, sweet potatoes, bacon. Seated at the head of the table in a huge mahogany chair, Uncle Billy was in good spirits, joking about the pleasures of Southern belles and eating hardtack, though not in the same breath. Between hearty swallows and generous puffs on his cigar, he went on about Lincoln and General Grant, dictating telegrams and talking right over everyone else's conversations. I was happy to see him so animated, as if the horror we had experienced had never happened.

Outside a band from the Massachusetts regiment burst into song, and many of us rose from the table to the window. Behind them, explosions echoed and flames shot a hundred feet into the air as Atlanta died before us. The Ohio regiment had first blown up the stone roundhouse, the foundry, the oil refinery, and an old warehouse, but the fire generated by the massive explosion soon spread out across the Depot Square engulfing the Atlanta Hotel, dry-goods stores and theaters, Washington Hall, the fire station, the jail, the slave markets. The night air hung thick with smoke and the scents of sulfur and burning pine. Huge warehouses are exposed to their bones and dressed in red. Flames spread from one building to the next with no mercy.

The band switched then to the "Miserere" from *Il Trovatore*, a sad melody which Major Henry Hitchcock would later remark to me would always remind him of that somber night. For him, the tragedy began and ended then, and I envied him his lack of knowledge.

By midnight, the fires slowed, and we could make out the shadows of the Masonic Hall, the courthouse and a number of private homes that have been spared. On the streets, drunken soldiers dashed madly, some on horseback, dancing, singing, smashing glass windows, and generally cavorting. The final scent I remember that night as I walked those streets unable to sleep was the pungent reek of dead animal, horses, mules, dogs, cats, rats, whatever was unfortunate enough to be caught in the flames. I was glad that Helen was on her way to Philadelphia to stay with my mother and not here to see this final chapter to our campaign. After the war, perhaps she will marry me. At least now I was like other men with a woman to live for, who would write me letters, knit me socks, care whether I lived or died.

In the morning, with the dying embers of Atlanta behind us, we continued south on route to the ocean, Mr. Castle's final words echoing in my mind: "There are more of us. They are everywhere and you cannot escape them." Mr. Castle is crafty, and we know not whether he is telling the truth or merely taunting us so that we will never again sleep through a night without fear. General Sherman is prepared to burn everything in his path if only to make sure.

November 17, 1864. Letter from Count Dracula to Mr. Castle (intercepted by Union spies).

Thank you for your letter of mid-September apprising me of the current situation in Atlanta. I hope it will not be a great disappointment to you and your people, but I have decided, given the circumstances being now so bleak for your armies, to remain in Transylvania. I am sure General Hood's efforts in North Georgia are ambitious, but I feel it is too much of a risk to support a cause now so weakened. I have sent a friend such as you to England to investigate the possibility of finding me a home there. While not so wild and untamed as your New World with its slaves for the taking, I am intrigued by the arrogance of the Englishman in feeling that his tiny island is destined to rule the world. This barbarity is one with which I easily identify.

I am sorry if this disappoints you severely. If somehow your people's destiny has a change in fortune, if you would be so thoughtful as to write me again.

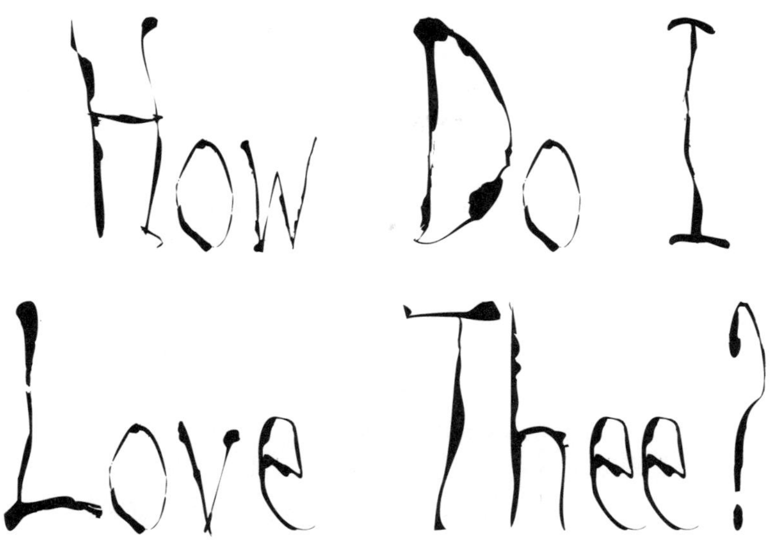

How Do I Love Thee?

by Rick R. Reed

My Dearest Maria,

There is blood on my hands. Thin, yet viscous rivulets of the stuff run down my cheeks, clot in my hair. My dress, black, reeks, yet even though the color shouts out, accusing, it is hidden. The smell, however is heady: the blood of the unwashed. Delicious, just as you promised. After the act was done, I bent to taste it, to discover the sublime warmth of it in my mouth, to see if I could feel what you feel when you take it. I licked the blood from my father's face, ran my fingers around in it, my stepmother's wounds opened for me, the warmth gushing over my fingers. Its coppery heat filled me, consuming. I know now what you feel, how the life flows from one vessel into another, its magenta vitality transferred. I have never felt more alive than when I was stealing life. Oh my love, your way is the true way, the path I long to follow.

I did this for you, my cherished one. Took the hatchet and stole their lives, freeing me to revel in the pleasures of Hedonism with you. I know that my offer, my sacrifice will open your eyes and let you see that my love flows for you, flows like the blood of my family, its hue deep crimson, its taste the taste of wine, of lovemaking, of your sweet lips.

When you receive this missive, I know you will return. Here in this dingy little backwater town, where the streets are crowded with the ignorant. Walking corpses who know so little. Filled with French and Portuguese immigrants who mock me, who could never understand the love we share. And then there are the ones who are supposedly like me: money grubbing, so-called members of "society." Their lives are filled with trivialities. All of them the walking dead.

All but two now, my love. Father rests in the parlor downstairs, his hideous, bloated body bearing mute witness to a life that knew no joy, knew only miserly ways and cruelty. And only feet away from my bedroom lies the body of the fat one, my stepmother. Felled by the bed, she lays, a corpulent mistake, something that should never have lived. And truly, has she ever lived? Has she ever known the kind of love we two shared and can share, through eternity? I think not.

I wish you could see them, my cherished one. I wish you could squat in your fine satin and lace and sup on their flesh, on their hot blood as it pumped from their bodies. Not since lying in your arms have I known such passion as when I took that hatchet in hand and split open their sad bodies, releasing the life essence within. My heart filled with joy as the hot blood splattered my face, my hands. And yes, oh yes, to taste them!

But by the time you return to me (as I know you will, for your passion runs as deep as blood lust, as true as our two hearts pumping through our veins the life of others less deserving of love and passion than we), the bodies of my father and stepmother will have turned cold. Will indeed have been hauled away by the so-called authorities to play their petty detective games, to find a soul to accuse. And fear not, my beloved: no one in this backwater will have the nerve to accuse me. Even if they did, they will never be able to prove that I am the one who did this hideous deed. Hideous in their eyes, love. In our eyes, we see only beauty… the magnificent scarlet beauty of the life force.

Bridget is outside, washing windows. Her stinking Irish work ethic never granting her a moment's respite from the heat, heat that has, these past few days, pressed in so close as to feel palpable, making any movement real effort. The fact that I did this for you, oh beautiful one, when my strength is sapped by the heat proves only how deep runs my love for you. I felt only joy as my sweat and their blood commingled. And Bridget will be the one the authorities will believe. Bridget will be the one who will be able to bear witness that it could never have been me, the dutiful younger daughter, who could steal life in a way the uninitiated could never comprehend.

Sister (you remember the mousy little shadow who watched us from the upstairs windows as we kissed, as you bit gently at my wrist, tasting me, drawing forth my essence so that we two could truly be one) is away for the first time in her life, at the seaside, with our cousins. Pity. She could have been the one to take the blame. Too weak to protest, she would have been the perfect culprit, putty in the hands of those obsessed with things like solving crimes.

But I am clever, as you know, and I venture to say that together we will watch as the mystery of my parents' deaths confounds generations. Delicious, isn't it?

And everything I have will be ours. Father's money, Maplecroft, and the land which he earned through deviousness, through meanness and trickery. No matter. We'll sell it all, traveling the world and tasting life wherever we go.

I will become one of you, just as you promised. You do remember, don't you, how you told me you could make of me one of you? Please say you haven't forgotten. Your silence tells me only one thing: you await proof of my love, proof of my worthiness to be with you, your clan, to be one of the chosen ones. The Hedonists.

And the proof lies in the blood pudding. Even without this letter, you will know of my act, know from the newspapers, from gossiping wagging tongues.

Wherever you are.

And when you know, you will understand at last how very much I love you and want to spend all my endless nights with you, arising at dusk to watch the blood-red moon rise above the horizon, to scurry at dawn back to the warmth of our lair, licking from our lips the sweet nectar, the blood of those less worthy than we.

You told me once as we sat by the Taunton River, its dark waters sending up the smell of life, of your father, the father of you all: Vlad Dracul, and how his dominance might prevent our being together through eternity. You told me that there were traditions in your world and that these traditions must be obeyed. One of the traditions was that it was wrong for you to make me one of you, so that our hearts might be intertwined forever. My sweet Maria, I have already taken the life of my own father and I could do the same for yours, should he stand in the way of our consuming passion for one another.

A less believing soul might suppose you gave me this speech as some sort of farewell, but I know you were only seeking to have me prove my worth to you.

I have done so. Taken the body and the blood. Won't you now come back to me? I long to feel your cold embrace and the ice chill of your kiss upon my throat. I long to lay in a mahogany coffin with you, the lid shut, closing out the world so that all that exists is each other.

Tell me what else it is you need from me, my Vampire Lover and I will do it. I will kneel at your altar for eternity, burn candles to your image, pray to you as the uninitiated pray to their Christ. I will pray to Vlad Dracul, if that is what you require. I will do whatever it takes to be yours.

The August heat rises up. I am weary. Soon, they will come and discover what I have done. Discover, but never comprehend. Only you can do that. Only you can appreciate my worth. They will call my sister, my Uncle John and the town of Fall River will be astounded by my handiwork.

I have already planted the seeds for my acquittal, should I be charged with what those who could never understand would call murder. Only last night, I went to my friend, Miss Russell and told her, cryptically, but enough to plant the seed of doubt: *I am afraid somebody will do something; I don't know what but someone will do something.*

So you see, my beautiful fanged goddess, I will be free to be with you.

Come to me, please, see me through this time of travail. I have no one, save for you.

Their blood is on my hands.

In closing, I repeat the words of Elizabeth Barrett Browning, who could never have known how closely her famous, lauded words could fit our situation:

I love thee with a love I seemed to lose
With my lost saints—I love thee with the breath,
Smiles, tears, of all my life!—and, if God choose,
I shall but love thee better after death.

Be with me, my beautiful one. I await your return and shall wait, my dear, until death washes over me.

Yours For All Time,

Lizzie Borden

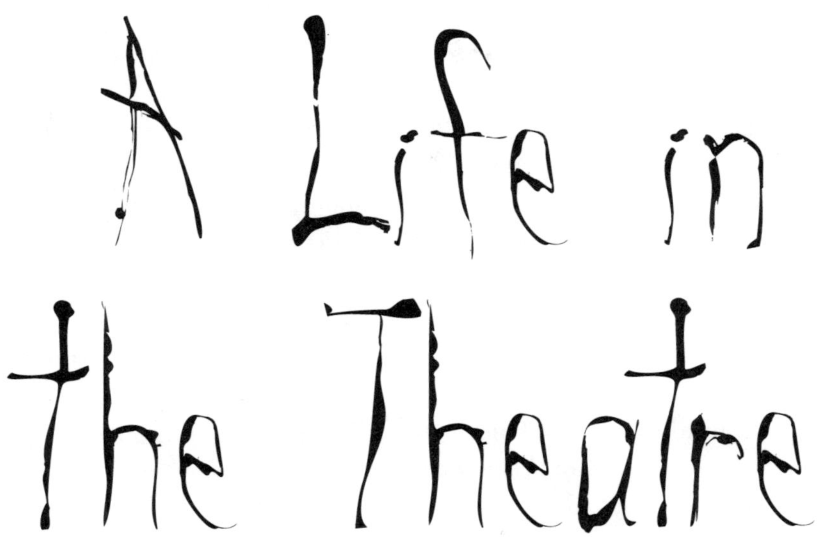

A Life in the Theatre

by Esther M. Friesner

The young man stood in the London rain across the street from the Lyceum Theatre and consulted a pocket watch of antique design. Lamplight illuminated the high planes of his cheekbones, the almost womanish curve of his lips, and played over the dark richness of his hair. Water streamed down the back of his neck, but he made no move to seek cover from the elements. He shifted the wine bottle in the crook of his arm, feeling its plain brown wrapping paper pilling away under the fidgeting of his fingers. He consulted the watch a second time, like a condemned man, knowing and dreading the appointed hour of his execution, yet unable to fix his thoughts on anything but the seconds jerking him toward oblivion by tick and tock, the inexorable erosion of time.

He sighed. He had dallied a good ten minutes past the appointed hour for his interview. "You're a fine one, Johnnie," he murmured. "A fine, bold liar to yourself. Why should a watch that's worked with perfect precision for years suddenly turn unreliable? Yet here you stand, utterly convinced that it's running fast. Oh, it simply wouldn't *do* to arrive at your interview early, would it? Makes a bad impression, that. Makes you look too eager, too—" He paused. "Whom do I think I'm fooling? I'm anything but eager. I know these symptoms well enough to give them their proper name." He lifted his face to the light and laughed without joy at his own weakness. "You'd think I'd be past stagefright by now."

A wayward gust of wind blew a scrap of paper against his ankles. He stooped to pick it up and examined it closely, a man desperate for delay. It was a handbill advertising a future performance by the great actor-manager, Sir Henry Irving, in a production of Shakespeare's *The Merchant of Venice*.

"The pound of flesh," the young man muttered. "There's a fine omen." He pulled the collar of his coat closer about his face, got a firmer grip on the bottle, took a deep, sustaining breath, and marched across the street and into the theatre.

He did not enter by the doors that admitted the glittering city crowds on performance nights. Instead he made his way inside through a lesser portal, one that left him standing in the building's dimly lit backstage warren. He shook himself like a dog. Rainwater flew everywhere, puddled from his clothing to the floor. He closed his eyes and filled his nostrils with the many scents of the theatre.

That single inhaled breath worked a cruel magic. It conjured up a host of illusions shining and keen as knives. They came rushing back over him, a gaggle of memories to flood not only his mind but all his senses. Amid the scents of sawdust and scenery paint, of snuffed footlights and costumes thick with sweat and camphor, a phantom stage arose in his mind's eye. It blazed and shimmered with handsome men, dainty women, their every movement a dancer's graceful pose, their every uttered word a note of music. And from the murmurous dark surrounding that gorgeous isle of bright perfection there rose up wave after wave after wave of a sound sweeter than all the rest: applause.

Alone in the half-darkened theatre, the young man made a sweeping bow to ghosts. "Gentles, we have parted company too long, but that is an oversight of Fate which I intend to remedy. I pray you, attend me." His eyes glowed as if reflecting stagelights some obliging hand had kindled.

"There you are." The voice that yanked him from his reverie was curt and harsh, seasoned with an accent that never sprang from the streets of London. It belonged to a red-haired, red-bearded man well set into his middle years. "You're late." He didn't look like the sort of person who appreciated or forgave being kept waiting.

The young man pulled himself up to his full height. From top to toe, his bearing was the picture of elegance, even if his garb had seen far better days. "I beg your pardon," he said, with a nonchalance that was all a skilled actor's well-played pretense. "The weather is terrible and I was unable to engage a cab. I misjudged how long it would take me to walk to the Lyceum from my—"

"American?" The older man cut him off abruptly, cocking his head like a robin eyeing a worm. "Your letter of introduction said nothing of that, though your accent certainly does. From the United States, are you?"

"I was born there," the younger man allowed, and his mouth twisted as if at the taste of something unspeakably bitter on the tongue. "But that is all well in the past, as is the appointed hour for my interview." He laughed lightly, though the effect was more of brittleness than easy good humor.

The older man grunted and then turning said, "It is a matter of no importance, Mr.... Brown, wasn't it?"

The younger man flashed a brief smile, striving to ingratiate himself. "John Brown, sir, at your service." The false name came as easily to his lips as the false smile. "I cannot express how gratified I am that you have consented to see me tonight, and at this hour. I've taken the liberty of bringing along this small token of my gratitude." He extended the wine bottle.

His attempts at charm were seed cast upon flinty ground. The older man shrugged heavy shoulders, ignored the offered gift. "You came highly recommended to Sir Henry's attention, although you requested an interview with me. I confess, I don't see why."

"My business is with you, sir, and not with your employer. If my initial letter of introduction was sent to him, it was solely that he might use his influence on you to ensure this meeting."

"Ah." He nodded. "Very well, then, Mr. Brown: The sooner we retire to my office, the sooner we may conclude this… business of yours." His tone made it clear that he regarded the younger man's affairs as more of an annoyance than a mystery. "Be so good as to follow me." He led the way across the darkened stage to the other side of the wings. The great curtain was up; there was nothing to block the view of loges and balconies and boxes.

The putative Mr. Brown trod the stage with a step so light that it called up no echo from the boards at all. And yet every pace he took reverberated inside his skull with the sound of a stone being rolled across the entrance to a tomb. He knew that if he allowed his glance to steal aside, out into the deserted theatre, the old magic would come upon him, a Medusa of memories to root him to the spot, all stone. He tried to keep his eyes fixed on the nape of his guide's neck, struggled to achieve that measure of discipline that seemingly had eluded him all the days of his life, and now…

Why should now be any different? He looked out from midstage. There were no houselights on, nothing to illuminate the theatre save the meager spill of brightness from lamps kept burning in the wings. To an ordinary man, the vast emptiness of the house should be no more than a great darkness filled with lesser shadows.

It was not so for him. He stood in the center of the stage and his eyes gave their own weird light to all within the compass of his vision. All that he saw was transformed by the mere act of his choosing to notice it. The Lyceum vanished, and the expanse of the Atlantic Ocean with it, both swept away in the great stream of years. He stood upon a different stage, in a different time, and felt the weight of greasepaint on his cheeks once more. There was a lowered curtain before him, but it was woven of the lost sights and ruined glories of his youth. He could see through it with no trouble at all, as if it were no more than smoke.

Beyond the shadow curtain, the seats and the aisles teemed with a bustle of people dressed in their very best. Crinolines rustled, ladies fanned their glowing cheeks, gentlemen conversed knowingly with their neighbors about the merits of this racehorse or that politician. A scent of wildflowers and good Virginia tobacco rode the murmurous wave of voices that washed up out of the audience to inundate the stage.

Then there was silence. The veil of shadow lifted itself from between the audience and the young man beneath the proscenium arch. He wore the well-remembered velvet doublet of Romeo, as he had worn it in a dozen cities of the ever-gracious South. He knew that this audience too would adore him, unlike those ham-brained Northern boors who only clamored for Edwin's appearances. He stood poised like the finest hunting hound, waiting for his cue. He took a step the footlights, one hand raised in a gesture of greeting, lips parted to deliver his first line.

"What's wrong?" the older man snapped from the wings. He stood there in an attitude of growing irritation, a living testimonial to the old wives' tale concerning the short temper of redheads. "Come along, if you please. We don't have all night."

"Ah." The younger man couldn't repress the half-smile that stole across his features. "Don't we." He intended the words for no ears but his own. He had found few people who shared his taste for irony. In a more audible voice he said, "I beg your pardon, sir. I was simply enjoying a bit of nostalgia. You see, I am an actor."

"An actor?" The younger man could see his guide's brows rise abruptly. The sight made him chuckle, which in turn only served to deepen the red-haired gentleman's frown.

"My apologies." The younger man made a bow as courtly as it was overdone. "It is a family weakness. My father and my brother also suffered from the affliction."

"No, no, you mistake me." The red-haired man grumped out the words into his beard as though he begrudged having to say them. "It is I who ought to apologize to you; I meant no disapproval of the profession."

"Certainly not. You could hardly have served so ably as Sir Henry's secretary all these years if you did not love the theatre." He strolled carelessly foward, adding, "Though to tell you the truth, for a moment you did sound like one of those village parsons who'd sooner plough up his churchyards and plant turnips than give an actor's corpse resting space."

"An actor… " The older man rolled the word around in his mouth as if tasting it and finding the savor strange. He regarded his caller narrowly for a time, then shook his head. "An actor's corpse indeed. No, no, that would be impossible."

"What would?"

"You bear a remarkable resemblance to—" Again he shook his head, more emphatically, and said once more, "Impossible."

The object of his scrutiny shrugged. "As you please."

"You have me at a disadvantage, sir," the older gentleman said as he resumed his role as backstage guide. His eyes flashed suspicion of all manner of crimes, and the hard line of his lips glimpsed beneath his well-trimmed mustache showed his instant readiness to condemn and eject this peculiar caller at the first hint of scandal.

Mr. Brown observed all this with an actor's trained eye for reading character from a person's unguarded face. "Sir," he said smoothly, "I see that you fear some illegality in my background. Certainly there is a great deal of prejudice in society against those who have run afoul of the law."

"Have you?" Sir Henry's secretary demanded brusquely.

"Whose law?" his caller countered lightly, shrugging his shoulders. "You have my word as a gentleman—if you will allow an actor that title by courtesy—that for as many souls that would brand me a criminal, there are at least as many stand waiting to hail me as a hero. When the great Junius Brutus brought down the Tarquin kings of Rome, was he an assassin or a man of valor? You look like a god-fearing man who knows his Bible. When the Israelite Ehud slew Eglon, the Moabite tyrant, was that murder or liberation?"

"Is that your crime, sir?" The older man's thickset body stiffened. "Murder?"

"The only crime I stand ready to admit is this," the other replied, and he dipped one hand inside his coat to draw forth a folded bundle of papers which he tossed onto the desktop. He took the same opportunity to thunk the wine bottle down beside them. The red-haired man leaned forward, for all the world like a cat sniffing charily at some alien thing fallen in its path. "What is it?"

"A play." Mr. Brown suppressed the urge to laugh at the older man's wariness. "Rather a scene from a play. I can produce the rest of the text for you, if this much of it proves of interest to you."

"An original piece?"

"Written by my own hand." The younger man laid a hand to his bosom and inclined his head modestly. "The crime of which I spoke, the only one I acknowledge. This is my business with you: To pique your interest in the piece sufficiently to have you recommend it to Sir Henry for production."

"Ah." The suspicious scowl softened a little, becoming an expression of plain puzzlement. "You have a roundabout manner of doing things, Mr. Brown; either that or a love of melodrama for its own sake."

"I come by it honestly," the younger man murmured. In a more audible voice he added: "At least as honestly as I came by that fine old port there. Would you do me the honor of sampling it?"

"Port, eh?" Now the older man's face relaxed almost entirely. He went so far as to give his guest the hint of a smile. His hand took up the bottle tenderly as a nurse might hold a newborn babe. "Now my interest *is* piqued, though perhaps not quite in the way you intended. How did you come to know my favorite wine?"

Mr. Brown persisted in his self-effacing attitude. "As you yourself said, sir, I know more about you than you do about me. However, I hope to remedy that situation over a glass of this excellent vintage."

"Well, well, if that's what it will take for you to place your cards on the table, I suppose we must." The older man did not sound at all reluctant to make that concession. He fetched a polished oak box from the lowest shelf of the room's bookcase and opened it to reveal four small cut-crystal glasses and a matching decanter. He extracted two of the glasses and held them up to the light. "Irish," he explained. "None finer, if you will permit me a little chauvinism."

"Pride in one's nation is not chauvinism," Mr. Brown stated.

Sir Henry's secretary produced a corkscrew from his desk drawer and applied it to the bottle dexterously. "Some men say that excessive national pride is a failing, not a virtue." The cork came out cleanly under his expert hand.

"Some men are fools, rogues, and hounds!" The words burst from the younger man's lips with so much vehemence that even he was startled by it. In a more subdued voice he added, "Who can dare to measure another's love for his native soil? Who has the right to judge the acts of a true patriot, or to condemn them as crimes, save another who has acted out of the same passions and suffered the same unjust condemnation?"

The older man passed his caller a filled glass. "You are a man of considerable passions, Mr. Brown," he remarked.

The other shrugged. "I am an actor." He watched intently as Sir Henry's secretary took the first tentative sip of the port, then a more substantial one. As for himself, he only allowed the wine to moisten his upper lip.

"Mr. Brown, I commend your taste in wines," the gentleman said, automatically helping himself to a second glass. "However, I cannot say the same for your taste in business methods. You've been pleased to call me honest; I would prefer to describe myself as *direct*. Allow me to be both: While I do relish your gift, I don't care for the tack you've taken concerning the future of this play of yours. It's far too byzantine, and not a little suspect. A letter of introduction on your behalf arrives here addressed to Sir Henry's attention. That same letter requests him to arrange for you to speak with me. And now that you have achieved the interview you desired, you say it was sought only so that I might bring your play *back* to Sir Henry's attention? I fail to see the need for such intrigue." He finished his second glass and with the air of a man in a dream poured himself a third.

"Have you ever observed a hunted fox, sir? How it doubles and redoubles back over its own tracks, confusing the scent of the pursuing hound?" A dark look fell over the younger man's face. "There are some hounds who would gladly hunt me down and tear out my throat if they but knew of my presence here tonight or of my ultimate aim for that." He gestured dramatically at the bundle of papers.

"Foxes and hounds? Gibberish." The word came out somewhat slurred. The older man blinked, momentarily bewildered at the sound of his own voice, and gave his glass a quizzical look. Nevertheless he drained it, as though refusal were now beyond his power. As if to compensate for this weakness, he made his tone all the sterner as he decreed, "I am a busy man; I believe you owe me a full explanation, and in short order."

"That is the least of my debts," said Mr. Brown. The last wisp of his former devil-may-care attitude had blown away, plunged to oblivion. His demeanor now brought the despair of a thousand lost souls into the little office. The man behind the desk jerked back involuntarily, as if avoiding a potentially fatal contagion of the spirit. His healthy color paled until his face mirrored his caller's for ashen hue.

"Mr.—Mr. Brown?" he ventured. "Are you well?"

"Ask for me tomorrow and you shall find me a grave man." His laughter sounded like a rustling of old husks. "Edwin often said I'd make a better Mercutio than a Romeo, but the public thought otherwise."

"Sir—?" The red-haired man's expression of puzzlement was now tinged with alarm. He rose partway from his chair and looked ready to bolt for the door, but once on his feet he stood swaying like a sailor on watch in a heavy gale.

"Oh please, my good man, sit again," his caller pleaded, his voice soft and persuasive. "I assure you of my sanity. Didn't I tell you that I am an actor? Surely you've worked with Sir Henry long enough to know more than a few of our profession given to… eccentricities of expression. Sit, sit. You shall have all the explanations you desire. All that I ask of you is that you allow me to make them in their proper place, my own time."

The older man resumed his chair, visibly grateful to do so. The other sagged with relief. "Thank you. We actors are all a little mad. We see things differently than you ordinary mortals. And yes, sometimes our visions take us roundabout to our goals, but what of that, if we accomplish them?"

"And your goal was—was to have me read this play of yours and suggest that Sir Henry—?"

"You have almost hit on it. Almost." The younger man's hand darted across the desk and snatched back the scrawled pages. "There is no need for you to read it. I would have you *see* it."

"See—?"

"See it, hear it. It will only take a few minutes of your precious lifetime. The words themselves as they now stand on the page—" He sighed gustily. "I fear they are inadequate. You are the one with the talent for words. I know what I want to say, what *must* be said, the warning that must be given before—" He took a deep breath. "And of course the only way, the best way for it to *be* said must be through the theatre, but—" The air fled his lungs in a shudder of regret. "Now you know why I did not present this offering to Sir Henry directly. Because it is a flawed thing. Because I lack the art to mold words to my purpose, though once they are set down I have more than enough talent to present them so that people will remember, will know. And they *must* know."

He rose from his place, his eyes burning like coals in the belly of a furnace. He struck a pose both dramatic and fearsome, lapped round as it was with words that flowed from a seeming madman's lips. "I have observed his plans already set in motion. He has seen fit to take me into his confidence, to permit me certain indulgences, certain intimacies… " The younger man's hands began to shake. His defiant stance curled in upon itself until he cringed against the side of his chair, Prince Hamlet beset by an unfeigned lunacy.

"*His* plans?" the older man echoed. He spoke as if his lips had turned to wood. "Who is—?"

"You will see," the other told him. "You will see because you *must* see." He regained full mastery of his limbs by degrees. "I thought him a hero. When he came to me at first, in the house where we all were wont to meet, he heard out my plans to capture the traitor Lincoln and praised them. But when those plans came to nothing, when I stood facing the cold truth of what I must do to save my beloved country, it was he who set my feet on the final path."

"Lincoln… Lincoln… " Sir Henry's secretary sat repeating the name as though it were a sovereign charm against a host of bogies and banshees. His forehead was shining with fat drops of sweat. He blotted them away with his pocket handkerchief; the square of blue linen trembled in his hand. The muscles of his face were slowly relaxing, letting his mouth sag open helplessly. His glance darted toward the empty wine glass before him, the full one at his caller's place, and a terrible look of realization flashed in his eyes.

The supposed Mr. Brown either ignored the older man's distress or else did not even notice it. "Do you know the enormity of what I undertook? To kill a man… I could not number for you the times that I dyed my hands red with slaughter, but that was only on the stage. And such a man! No matter what I thought of him, his office made him the equal of kings. I did not want to kill him. I did not dread the deed itself so much as I feared what would come thereafter: The flight, the peril to my own life, the utter vilification of my name whether or not I was apprehended. My name, sir! A name accustomed to the praise of audiences, of my fellow players, of—dare I say it?—the critics." He managed a sickly smile.

"I… do… know… you." Every syllable was an effort, fighting its way free against the pull of the drugged wine. Sir Henry's secretary was a strong man, but he had not always been so strong. His life had begun with years of immobility, bedridden, helpless, a childhood to be fled, not cherished. To be imprisoned in his own body once again brought back those awful years. He thought his heart would burst from the wild fury of its captive beating. Still he struggled to say, "Booth."

The younger man winced at the sound of his own name. "You make it sound like a curse. And yet you were among the throng that applauded my elder brother's performance when he shared this very stage with Sir Henry, not so long ago. I might have been there with him. I might have shared his fame instead of being the sole possessor of my infamy. I might have spurned the dark cup held out to me, turned my back, walked away—" He closed his eyes. "I could not. No more than you could resist a second cup and a third of that most special vintage, my 'gift' to you, once you had tasted the first sip. Some things *must* be."

He opened his eyes and reached out for the still brimming glass at his place. He held it up to the lamplight, studying the shimmering ruby heart of the drink as he spoke on. "I filled your mouth with wine to hold you; *he* filled my ears with words to capture me. He told me who he was, his true age, his true nature. I disbelieved him—What sane man would accept such a tale at face value?—until he gave me several... proofs of his veracity." His free hand strayed to touch his own cheek, then drifted lower to caress the smooth side of his throat. His eyes gazed on nothing that the little office held.

"He said he knew me for a hero. He was well versed in the ways of heroes. In his native Wallachia they named him so, they still spoke of him with reverence for his bravery in defending the land against the Turks. But others named him monster. The things that he did, the nameless acts, the bloody deeds for which he has been remembered—"

Without warning, a dry sob convulsed him. He dropped the glass. Irish crystal shattered on the floor, and the dark stain of wine spread at his feet. The phantoms that had drawn his vision all fled. He stared straight at his captive audience and cried out, "Ah heaven! And do I dare call myself an actor next to one such as he? When the grossest lies were on his lips, he made me believe them for the purest truths. What is that, if not the mark of a master thespian? He said that if I did this thing, took this life at his bidding, then I too would be remembered as a hero. My fame would be immortal. And then—then when he saw how I still hesitated, he offered more. Hero to hero, he would remake me in his own image, give me the same gift of eternal life he enjoyed—*enjoys*! "

"Dead." The older man's body began to sink down under its own weight, his muscles losing the power to sustain it. "I... read what happened... afterward... farmhouse... soldiers... fire... "

"They had me trapped." Booth lowered his voice, a witch-counseled Scottish king whose hour waits to strike, but will not wait too long. "My leg was broken. The doctor I deceived into setting it for me had done his job, but still, how could I run? I lay there in the straw like an animal. They fired the building. I knew that if I broke from cover they would shoot me down, less than a dog."

His fine white fingers closed on the top of the chair, the knuckles showing whiter yet. "And he was there. Sudden as the sound of a spark popping from dry brushwood aflame, like that, he was kneeling beside me. He told me that I had nothing to fear, that a true hero never knows fear, only rage against an unjust world. He said that together we would yet make the world pay for how it had treated us. He said that I had proved my worth, that he had come to fulfill his promise. And he did. By the time I fled the burning building and the bullets took me, I was his."

"His… " the older man repeated, and his eyes asked the question his lips no longer had the strength to form.

"His name?" Booth's mouth curved up ever so slightly at one corner. "Dracula. After all, my poor attempt at the playwright's craft is aimed at making his name as much a byword for evil as—as—" His voice dropped. "—as my own, thanks to him. Come." He held out his hand.

Despite the terrible weakness that pervaded his limbs, Sir Henry's secretary found himself rising from his chair, coming around the corner of his desk, clasping Booth's hand in his. It was hard and cold as iron. "Come," the actor repeated.

"Where—?"

"The theatre."

Booth walked, drawing his captive after. They moved through the air like water, slowly, with a stately grace that gave up no sound of footfalls. The older man's throat constricted with a scream he was unable to utter.

As he led the way through the wings, back onto the stage, Booth spoke on. "What are we to them?" he intoned. "Cattle. Puppets. Mayflies. And sometimes… amusements. They move in shadow, his children. They take what they will from us—not blood alone, nor life, but our very souls if that is what they crave to feed upon. And we? We do nothing. We do nothing because we suspect nothing, we proud and self-important men of breeding. Of intellect. If we do hear of such creatures, we relegate them to the world of bugbears and peasant superstitions. That is precisely how they would have it. He has taught his children to cherish our ignorance of them—of *him*—as the single factor most favorable to their continued survival. So it has been for uncounted ages, and now—" He glanced back and his sharp teeth flashed. "—now it ends."

The stage was no longer deserted. A chair had been shifted onto the proscenium and ranged around it stood two men and two women, all of the same outstanding pallor as Booth. Each held a sheaf of papers, and each fixed his gaze on him with something resembling love.

"My players," Booth remarked casually, steering his man into the chair. "Unemployed actors have often been my sustenance, now they are my help. They will perform what you must transform: my play. There is no better way to reach the masses than the theatre."

The older man was breathing heavily now, his eyes half shut. The four players took their places before him. They moved like people in a dream. The first to speak clasped one of the women by the hand and began to tell her how overjoyed he was to be safely back in England after a harrowing journey through the Carpathian Mountains to a remote castle in the wilds of Transylvania.

Booth stooped down behind the chair. "You will not forget this story," he whispered while the actors droned on. "It will give you no rest until you write it down. You will recount it far better than I ever could, and you will use your place in Sir Henry's service to make certain it is produced, performed. It is my warning to the world, but it is *his* story, his true nature set out plainly for any eye to see. Once men realize that such monsters as Dracula do walk in their midst, they will stand ready to protect themselves, to fend off the vampire and his brood. From self-defense it will be only a small step to outright war."

He stood tall, his eyes aglow with zealot's fire. In two strides he was between the players and their audience of one, hands thrust heavenwards, head flung back as he cried out, "War? Yes, it shall be war. A war we sorry pawns shall yet win. Do you hear me, Dracula? *We shall win!*" He whipped his burning gaze onto Sir Henry's secretary. Behind him, the entranced actors continued to play out their allotted roles, as insensible to Booth's grandiose interruption as he was to the fact that his own posturings were all that filled his captive's eye.

"Do you doubt me, Impaler?" He shook a fist at shadows. "Do you think I lack the mettle to see this scheme through because you have made me one of your inhuman swarm? Do you dream that I dread the true death?

Never! Never, while my sacrifice might buy the freedom of a nation, of a world!"

A few lines of the players' dialog managed to creep through in the subsequent dramatic pause he allowed. Then he shifted keys, dropping to one knee, the image of nobility in the face of doom. In a low voice whose pathos fairly shouted to the cheapest seats in the house he murmured, "And when I too fall in that great crusade of my own creation, I shall go gladly into the final dark. I shall go knowing that I have at least repaid humanity for my sins against her, that I have cleansed my true native soil—the earth itself—of traitors, and that at last I go to my rest a hero." He rose and in ringing accents declaimed, "*Sic semper tyrannis*!" before stalking into the wings and then out of the theatre.

It was still raining when he left the Lyceum. He crossed the street to stand once more under the lamplight and sighed with pleasure as the chill drops raved his upturned face. As much as he loved giving a good performance, it was always something of a relief to put it behind him.

A sudden, rhythmic sound behind him made him jump and turn sharply. A well-dressed man stepped out of the darkness, his hands coming together in slow, deliberate applause. "Bravo, Johnnie," he said. "I trust your show was a success?"

"You weren't there to see it, Lord? But you said—"

The other gave him a thin smile. "I am always there to watch over my favorites. You overplayed it somewhat for our Mr. Stoker, I think. Some of your tirades against me and our people, Johnnie… " He clicked his tongue.

"Another critic," Booth muttered. In a more audible voice he said, "I thought it would play better that way, impress him. He adores Sir Henry's style, after all, and if you ever saw how *that* man out-Herods Herod—"

"I care nothing for Herod or Sir Henry. I only occupy myself with results."

"Results? Oh, you'll have results, Lord," Booth said, all self-assurance. "Soon my players will finish acting out their scene. They will gather up and destroy the script I left behind, along with any other evidence of my visit. They will leave the theatre, go back to their dismal flats and come to their senses some time tomorrow, remembering nothing of tonight. As for Mr. Stoker, he too will recover full possession of himself even sooner than they, and with this difference: He will remember. Tonight will haunt him with visions of a man come back from the grave with a story to tell. He will set that story to paper and contrive to have it put upon the stage, and once that is accomplished—" The assassin laughed. "—we are safe."

"Safe," Dracula repeated with a somewhat skeptical lift of his brows. "So you promised when you first laid this scheme before me. Do not fear: I will not hold you to it."

The lines on the actor's face deepened. "You sound as if you've doubted my plan from the start. Then why did you allow me to go ahead with it?"

"I indulged your fancy only because I saw it could do us no harm, but as for it doing us any good—" His lips parted in a look of mild amusement just enough to show the keen fangs beneath.

Booth bridled, holding in the same anger that had twisted his vitals every time he felt Edwin's shadow fall upon him. Very slowly he said, "When people believed that witches soured milk, microbes lived in safety. Then Pasteur taught them otherwise, and now they ruthlessly seek out and destroy even such a tiny prey. But people will not bother hunting down phantoms, or myths, or the fantastic creation of Mr. Stoker's imagination. They'd fear being laughed at for a gaggle of credulous fools. Rather than risk that, they'll find a dozen new diseases to explain away our handiwork among them, just see if they don't! To go about our business ignored because no one believes we are there? To escape persecution forever? To finally be *safe*? Yes, I'd say that will do us some good."

"Safe… merely because of a story?"

"Oh, not just a story, Lord!" Booth seized his master's arm. "A play. That was why I chose him for the job, Sir Henry's faithful secretary, a man whose life is as given up to the drama as my own. He will write a play because he lives for the theatre. With his hand set to the task, you will be brought before the public in just such a way that even the most credulous among them will nevermore be able to think of you—of any of us—as more than the empty stuff of dreams!" He offered his master a smile the way a dog might offer its belly in submission. "I of all people ought to know, no one ever believes anything they see in the theatre."

"Then I suppose we must be grateful that our Mr. Stoker will not write a book instead." And Dracula's laughter made the streetlights shiver as he and Booth walked away into the night.

The Wizard and the Dragon

Richard Lee Byers

The big double doors of the laboratory building had warped in their frame. Edison had to force one open. In recent years his hearing had deteriorated to the point where he couldn't actually hear the neglected hinges squealing, or the bottom of the door scraping across the floorboards, but the noises were easy to imagine.

Stepping a bit warily into the foyer, his breath steaming in the cold December air, he raised his kerosene lantern. Shapes swam out of the darkness: the dusty, glass-fronted cabinets which had once held telegraph keys, Morse sounders, and galvanometers; empty bookshelves; a jumble of old, prototype inventions and patent models, rusted and useless now, which the Boys—his assistants—had been accustomed to dismantle for spare parts; a Long-Legged Mary Jane dynamo in equally poor repair; wires and lightbulbs, shrouded in cobwebs, dangling from the gas fixtures. The building smelled of grime, decay, and an infestation of mice.

It gave him a pang to see the laboratory falling into ruin. He supposed his lawyer had been right, he should have made provisions to keep the place up. Or better still, never relocated to West Orange in the first place. Lately it had often seemed that when he'd deserted Menlo Park, he'd abandoned his luck along with it.

For a moment it appeared he was alone. Then, suddenly, three white faces appeared in the gloom at the rear of the building, where the carpenters' shop had been. Startled, Edison caught his breath.

As the trio advanced, the inventor's eyes were drawn to the man in the middle. Rawboned and lantern-jawed, with webs of wrinkles surrounding his steel-gray eyes, the stranger wore a plumed, wide-brimmed hat, a long curly wig, and layers of ruffles at his throat and wrists. The outfit made him look as if he'd just stepped out of Restoration England. His companions, on the other hand, had opted for conventional attire in the form of long overcoats and bowlers. They stalked along half a pace behind him, their expressions impassive and their eyes continually moving, as if they were his bodyguards.

After a moment Edison noticed that none of the strangers had steaming breath. He wondered why not.

The man in the plumed hat smiled. "Thomas Alva Edison," he boomed. "The Wizard of Menlo Park. What a pleasure to meet you at last. My name is Palmer Guice."

Edison blinked. He'd been rattled by the trio's sudden appearance and perplexed by Guice's antique clothing, but he was astonished now. He could hear the other man's rich bass voice more clearly than he'd heard anyone in years, as if something had cured his deafness, or an invisible telephone wire were carrying the sound directly into his skull. He wondered what sort of acoustical trick or hidden apparatus was responsible.

Guice extended an ivory hand and Edison shook it. The stranger's grip was firm and his flesh cold, possibly chilled by the frigid weather. "I must confess," said Guice, "I was worried you might decline an anonymous invitation to a clandestine meeting. After all, there was at least a remote possibility that I'd turn out to be a kidnapper intent on holding you for ransom."

"I was willing to risk it," Edison replied, setting the lantern on a workbench, "given the things I've glimpsed over the past few weeks. Sewer rats waltzing and doing tricks like circus animals. A dog—or was it a wolf?—pawing sentences in the dirt. A woman lifting a freight wagon over her head. My curiosity wouldn't let me stay away. I only hope you can explain it all, as your letter promised."

"Spoken like a true scientist," said Guice. "Rest assured, I intend to account for every last wonder, and with your permission, I'll commence with a demonstration." He turned to the bodyguard on his left, a blond young man with a prim little slit of a mouth. "Mr. Symons, your firearm, if you please."

Symons removed a double-barreled derringer from his pocket and passed it to his employer.

"Now hold up your hand," said Guice. Symons obeyed, whereupon the man in the plumed hat calmly fired a shot through the center of his minion's palm. Symons's stoic expression didn't change. Edison gasped.

"Please, don't be alarmed," said Guice, his mellow tones so jovial, so soothing, that to Edison's surprise, he actually did recover from the shock. "I assure you, we're not deranged, and my associate will be fine." He took hold of the inventor's forearm and drew him closer to Symons. The acrid smoke of the gun stung Edison's eyes.

"Inspect the wound," said Guice, laying the derringer aside. "I want you to be satisfied it's a genuine injury, not a conjuring trick." He extended his index finger and worked it through the bullet hole, still without eliciting any sign of distress from the younger man. The digit emerged red with blood.

The sight made Edison queasy. "I'm satisfied," he said.

"Excellent," said Guice. He withdrew his finger. "Heal yourself, Mr. Symons."

The bodyguard's pale hand glowed ruddy pink, as if a disproportionate quantity of his blood had flowed into his arm. Yet paradoxically, his wound stopped bleeding and began to pucker, drawing in on itself until it closed altogether. For a moment a grayish scar remained and then it dwindled away to nothing, leaving Symons' palm unblemished beneath its streaks of gore. Edison goggled in amazement.

"You see?" asked Guice. He drew a handkerchief from his ruffled cuff and wiped his finger. Symons retrieved his gun and stowed it back in his pocket. "The prodigies you've witnessed, that we arranged for you to see—there was no machinery or trickery involved, no magic lantern or any other sort of contrivance. The explanation lies elsewhere."

Edison struggled to get past his stupefaction. To start thinking again. He swallowed and said, "What is the explanation?"

"Do you believe in the supernatural, Mr. Edison?"

The inventor cocked his head. "I believe there are powers at work in the universe that mankind doesn't know anything about yet. I studied one of them, the etheric force, myself, though my experiments didn't get very far. Are you saying that Mr. Symons healed himself with psychic energy?"

"In a sense," said Guice, "but that's the least of what I have to tell you. Centuries ago, my companions and I were as you are now. Then we had the good fortune to attract the notice of a hidden elite, who saw fit to initiate us into their company. Our benefactors were—are—an exalted form of humanity blessed with eternal life and miraculous powers. A race that calls itself the Kindred, though mortal legends refer to us as vampires." He smiled, displaying upper canines which had lengthened into wicked fangs. After a moment they shortened again, evidently retracting into their sockets. "Do you believe me?"

His heart thumping and his mouth dry, Edison struggled to retain his composure. He had a feeling it might be dangerous to show fear. "Yes. You've given me proof. The question is, why? Most people *don't* believe in you anymore, and that's obviously because you want it that way."

"Quite so," Guice replied, "and thus you reason that I wouldn't reveal the truth to you unless I meant to ensure you didn't survive our *tête-à-tête*. That I lured you here to indulge a taste for the vitae—the blood—of geniuses." He smiled. "But you're mistaken. Mortal mythology has slandered my kind. We're people, not devils. As a rule, we obtain our nourishment without inflicting lasting harm on anyone, and I certainly have no intention of killing you tonight."

Once again, Guice's voice was so full of warmth and reassurance that Edison found himself relaxing. "Then what is this about?" he asked.

"I'm surprised you haven't guessed," Guice replied, "though I realize

I'm giving you a lot to take in. The opportunity my sire offered me I now extend to you. Join us."

Edison gaped at him. "You want me?"

"Of course. You're the greatest mind of your era. The Napoleon of Invention. And you'd like to be immortal, wouldn't you? Why should a scientist surrender himself to the grave, still ignorant of most of the secrets of the universe, when he could continue discovering and inventing until the day there's nothing left to learn?"

Edison shook his head. "You were right. This is too much to absorb all at once. Naturally I've wished I could live forever. I guess everyone has. But I have a life—"

"Forgive my bluntness, my friend, but you're already in your fifties. You have the melancholy final *act* of a life to play out—failing health, bereavement, and all the rest of it—and then, almost within the blink of an eye, the curtain will fall."

"Even so," Edison said, "I have a family, friends, a business. I'd have to walk away from all of it, wouldn't I?"

"I'm afraid so," said Guice. "There's no other way to preserve the Masquerade, the appearance that the Kindred are only a myth. And only you can decide whether what you now possess is more precious than immortality." His gray eyes gazed into Edison's. For an instant the inventor felt light-headed. "Tell me, do you have a *happy* marriage?"

Edison grimaced. "Once upon a time I did. But for the past few years, since General Electric bought out my power company, I've been in the iron ore business. I used to beg Mina to come stay with me at the mill in Ogden. She wouldn't, though. I guess she hated the dirt and the rough living more than she loved me."

Guice nodded sympathetically. "Dare I hope you have a closer bond with your children?"

Edison thought of rebellious Marion, whining Tom Jr., and the shiftless Will. "I wouldn't exactly say that," he answered bitterly.

"And I understand you've often been disappointed in your friends as well. Supposedly there was a man called Gilliand… "

"Ezra Gilliand. Everything he had he owed to me, and he tried to swindle me out of the phonograph." And Gilliand had only been one of many who'd betrayed him. Lippincott, Tomlinson, Insull, Johnson, Dickson—the names echoed in his head as if to mock the very concept of loyalty.

Guice sighed. "That would seem to leave business as a source of satisfaction. Specifically, your mine."

"Shut down," Edison said. "Even with my innovations, I couldn't compete with the big conglomerates. I don't know how I'm going to pay off the debts I ran up trying."

"It's not my place to judge," said Guice, "but I must say, I truly don't see that you have all that much worth clinging to. Among the Kindred, you could find companions worthy of you, the keenest minds and noblest souls who ever walked the earth, purged of pettiness and spite by the lofty perspective immortality affords. And you'd never have to fret about money again. We've been amassing wealth for millennia. We have more than we could ever need."

Feeling dazed, overwhelmed, Edison bowed his head and tried to think. Give up his humanity to become some sort of legendary creature? How could anyone truly assess the implications of such an act? The whole idea seemed reckless to the point of insanity.

But perhaps it wasn't, really. Not if a man feared his current existence was becoming unbearable. And though he did his best to hide his growing despondency, to be the energetic, self-confident "Wizard" the public expected, Edison often felt as if the walls of his life were closing in on him. That the glory days and, even worse, the great ideas and inventions were all behind him.

If there was any possibility that joining the Kindred could bring them back, then maybe it was worth the risk. And Edison had never been afraid to take a chance. Suddenly feeling eager, vibrant, as if he were immortal already, he lifted his head, just in time to see Guice and the bodyguards lurch around.

Puzzled, Edison looked where they were looking. Smiling sardonically, hands beating together—applauding slowly, the deaf man realized—a man dressed in a black Inverness lounged against the wooden stairs leading to the second floor. A stovepipe hat sat on a riser, next to his elbow. Edison got the eerie feeling that the newcomer had been loitering in the room unnoticed for some time, eavesdropping on the conversation. He was a sallow man of medium height, with high cheekbones, a crooked blade of a nose, and large, deep-set eyes framed by arched eyebrows above and deep hollows below. A long, straight mustache covered his upper lip, while the bottom one was so red and thick it looked swollen. A round gold medallion graven with the image of a dragon hanging prostrate on a double cross gleamed beneath his batswing bow tie.

"Bravo, Justicar," he drawled. His voice lacked the magical resonance of Guice's. Edison had to strain to hear him. Nonetheless, his instincts warned that this man too was a vampire. "A splendid performance. You almost had *me* believing it."

Recovering from his surprise, Guice smiled. "I do believe I have the honor of addressing Prince Dracula."

Puzzled, Edison frowned. If he wasn't mistaken, *Dracula* was the title of a gruesome English novel, one that had just been reprinted in America.

The man in the caped coat straightened up. "How gratifying to be recognized."

"Gratifying, perhaps," said Guice, "but dangerous. You're an outlaw. Among other crimes, you breached the Masquerade."

Dracula smiled. "Stoker did a good job, didn't he? His success exceeds my wildest expectations. Nevertheless, your accusation is rubbish. Thanks to the book, the kine are more inclined to regard us as creatures of fantasy than ever before. They're particularly certain that Vlad Dracula himself is a figment of a writer's imagination, which, needless to say, was the point of the exercise. Still, you can try to arrest me if you deem it appropriate. Your office grants you the authority, if not necessarily the power."

Guice hesitated. "Mr. Symons and Mr. Fielding are Archons," he said at last. "The three of us are quite capable of overcoming you. But as it happens, we're engaged with other business. Go now and you may depart unmolested."

"How kind," Dracula replied. "But alas, I too admire Mr. Edison's achievements, and thus your business is my business also. In other words, you can't have him."

Edison was reluctant to intrude on the vampires' confrontation. But he also resented Dracula's presumption, and felt ashamed of his own timidity. He took a deep breath, then said, "It's my choice to make, *Prince*. And I've decided to accept Mr. Guice's invitation."

His cape swinging about his shoulders, affording Edison a glimpse of its scarlet lining, Dracula pivoted toward him. "You wouldn't have," the Kindred said, "not this rashly, not if Guice hadn't subtly bewitched you. There's a kind of magic in his voice."

Edison blinked in dismay. Could Dracula possibly be telling the truth? There was *something* strange about Guice's voice....

"That's a lie," said Guice.

"He's the liar," said Dracula, still gazing at Edison. "Or at least he's been selective about which facts to reveal and which to withhold. It's true that if you became Kindred, you'd possess superhuman powers and live a long time. But the good Justicar neglected to mention the Hunger, the terrible thirst for human blood that overwhelms even the gentlest of us at times. No matter how humane his intentions, every Kindred eventually becomes a murderer many times over." He grinned. "Not that this bothers me. But I suspect it would trouble you."

Edison looked at Guice. "Is he telling the truth?" he asked.

"No," said the gray-eyed vampire. His voice was more musical than ever. Edison made a reflexive effort to resist its spell, if, indeed, it was exerting one. "I concede we have powerful appetites, but there are ways to indulge them safely. One simply has to employ certain precautions."

"Will you also deny misrepresenting the true nature of your segment of Kindred society?" Dracula asked. "You made it sound sufficiently egalitarian to delight even Mr. Edison's American soul. But you and I know it's a rigid feudal hierarchy, with sires dictating to their childer, the ancient exploiting the young, and the strong oppressing the weak. Proud and independent as he is, he'd loathe every aspect of it."

His fangs indenting his lower lip, Fielding, Symons' fellow Archon, a hulking, pockmarked man missing the last joint of his right thumb, shot Guice a questioning glance. Edison surmised that the bodyguard was asking permission to attack Dracula. The Justicar gave his head a tiny shake.

"More distortions," said Guice. "Naturally, Mr. Edison, as your sponsor, I'd help you navigate your way in Kindred society. You'd want me to, wouldn't you? And yes, we do have a government, and functionaries to enforce its laws. But so has every community since the dawn of time."

"The regime to which he refers," said Dracula to Edison, "is called the Camarilla. It exists primarily to twist mortal institutions into the forms the mad old Clan Ventrue elders, its masters, think they ought to take. Which is to say, to make certain that the kine, the *cattle*, the human beings such as yourself, never cast off the yoke of their self-styled owners, no matter how much murder and misery that entails. I very much doubt you'd enjoy being obliged to labor in such a cause."

"If this—Camarilla—is so evil," said Edison, "then why did Mr. Guice approach me as he did? Why didn't he just attack, transform, and enslave me? He could do that, couldn't he?"

"I could indeed," said Guice, "but I'm not a barbarian."

Dracula laughed. "I wish we had the leisure to discuss a few choice incidents from the Justicar's career," he said to Edison, "so you could appreciate just how funny that statement was." He reached inside his coat. Symons and Fielding tensed until he brought out a box of matches and a silver cigarette case, which he opened and proffered to his companions. The bodyguards ignored the invitation. Guice and Edison declined it by shaking their heads. "No one? Pity, they're quite good. A fellow in Istanbul makes them for me. Turkish tobacco is about the only good thing that ever came out of the foul place. But as I was saying, mortal, our friend in fancy dress would be quite capable of assaulting you if he deemed it expedient. But he's Ventrue. A politician to his bones. He'd much rather beguile you than resort to vulgar force, particularly since he's afraid of you."

Now it was Guice's turn to laugh. "I beg you, Mr. Edison, don't take offense. I'm not laughing at you. But the idea of one unarmed mortal posing a threat to three of us is ludicrous in the extreme."

"But that's why you're here," said Dracula, striking a match with his thumbnail. The yellow flare kindled pinpoints of light in the depths of his dark green eyes. He lit a cigarette. "Even you hidebound Ventrue fossils have finally realized that science and invention aren't the docile, sluggish beasts they used to be. They've grown into rampaging behemoths. They've transformed the world in a single mortal life span and they're going to keep changing it, so frequently and radically that before long your senile cabal of puppet masters won't know how to twitch the strings. In time, I suspect, they'll even grant the kine powers which dwarf our own."

Dracula exhaled a plume of pungent smoke. "The sad thing," he continued, "is that you Blue Bloods are still so befuddled and out of touch that you think recruiting Mr. Edison would put you back in control. Even if you could commandeer his genius, he's only one of many. I assume you have at least heard of Bell? Muybridge? Swan? Tesla?"

"Most assuredly," said Guice, "and I know that Mr. Edison is the greatest of them all. The one most deserving of immortality. And I daresay he'd prefer to enjoy it as a member of my sect, a fellowship which, despite your slurs, strives to promote peace, enlightenment, and prosperity on those rare occasions when it opts to meddle in mortal affairs at all. He certainly doesn't belong among you madmen of the Sabbat. He's devoted his life to civilization and progress, not savagery and destruction. Which is to say, *you* can't have him."

"You mistake me," Dracula said. "I didn't come—"

Guice gave a nod. The bodyguards lunged at Dracula. Startled, Edison recoiled.

Dracula thrust his pale hand back into his Inverness and brought out a long pointed stick, possibly scrap wood he'd scavenged in the carpentry shop. In the same instant, his muscles swelled and his body grew taller, tearing his garments and splitting them at the seams. His skin turned a glistening, oily black; a ridge of spines shot out of his backbone; and the bottom half of his face extended into fanged saurian jaws. A fetid stench suffused the air.

Seemingly undaunted by this metamorphosis, Symons and Fielding kept coming, the former charging straight at the towering ogre and the latter darting sideways to flank him. Grasping his stick as if it were a sword, Dracula thrust at Symons's breast. The blond vampire dodged and kicked his adversary in the knee. Despite his deafness, Edison heard bone crack.

The burly Fielding faded from view like condensation melting off a windowpane. A moment later something flashed and banged repeatedly. Already staggering from Symons's assault, Dracula reeled. Edison realized that Fielding had become invisible, then emptied a revolver into the giant.

For a second it looked as if the Archons had already defeated Dracula. But the troll-like figure hopped and regained his balance. His damaged leg bulged and rippled, repairing itself. Pivoting suddenly, he lashed out with a hand the size of a shovel. The backhand slap caught Symons on the cheek, flinging the smaller Kindred across the room and almost certainly breaking his neck.

Agile as a leopard, Dracula pursued him. As, his head flopping on his shoulders, Symons attempted to scramble up from the floor, the huge creature gripped the stick in both hands, swung it over his head, and rammed it down, driving it into the center of the other vampire's chest. Bone crunched, blood splashed, and Symons sprawled back down. His blue eyes rolled wildly, as if he were still alive, but with a stake through his heart he evidently couldn't move.

An instant later Dracula stumbled forward as though something had smashed him in the back. He started to turn and staggered again. Then he leaped sideways, evidently avoiding a third attack. Perhaps he'd heard that one whizzing through the air.

Blood streaming from the bullet wounds in his side, tattered clothing flapping, Dracula began to circle, duck, and dodge. He stayed close to Symons as if afraid that, given an opening, Fielding would yank the stake out of his partner's breast. Much of the time the giant vampire looked as if he were shadowboxing. But periodically an invisible attack connected, rocking him and carving a fresh welt in his slimy hide. Or else he pounced, his immense, clawed hands rending and slashing, and splashes of gore, springing from nowhere like a magician's bouquet, arced through the air. Soon his arms were red to the elbows, and crimson spatters mottled the floor. One of his blows knocked Fielding's bowler off. The hat popped suddenly into view and tumbled across the room.

At first Edison could only stare, fascinated and appalled. But eventually it occurred to him that the Kindred were fighting to determine the course of his future.

The realization infuriated him. He wasn't a trophy for anyone to win. He was a man, a great man according to some, at any rate a man who'd always charted his own course, and he had no intention of giving that up. Somehow, puny mortal though he was, he had to decide the outcome of the conflict.

The trouble was, he didn't know whom he *wanted* to win. Whom should he choose to initiate him into the world of the vampires—Guice or Dracula? Was the Camarilla benign and the Sabbat malevolent, or was it the other way around?

For a moment he nearly despaired of discerning the answer. Because there didn't seem to be a shred of evidence either way. Then he realized that, his gray eyes narrowed and intent, Guice was watching the battle as idly as he was. Keeping himself out of harm's way while his agents risked destruction on his behalf. Displaying a selfishness consistent with the accusations Dracula had leveled against him.

Edison studied the battleground, noting the drops of blood falling out of empty air, and the footprints appearing in the crimson smears and puddles on the floor, until he was fairly certain he knew where Fielding was. Trying to keep the bodyguard—or rather, his apparent location—in sight, the inventor lunged for the lantern.

Guice cried, "Stop!"

Edison froze. With the Ventrue's voice echoing in his skull, drowning his own thoughts, he didn't seem to have a choice. Then a surge of visceral fear and rage broke the spell and propelled him onward. He snatched up the lamp, whirled, and realized he didn't know where Fielding was anymore.

Peering desperately about, terrified that Guice was rushing up behind him, Edison finally saw a telltale trickle of blood spatter to the floor. He swung the lantern over his head and threw it with all his might.

The missile smashed into an unseen barrier and exploded into flame. An instant later Fielding appeared inside the blaze. He had a long chain in his hands, but, reeling, he dropped it to slap madly at the fire.

Dracula pivoted, picked up a ten-horsepower Baxter engine, and used it to batter Fielding without risking catching fire himself. In three heartbeats he reduced the bodyguard to a broken mass on the floor, still writhing, but too mangled to have any hope of extinguishing the flames. A sickening smell of burned meat rose from the conflagration.

Remembering Guice, Edison spun back around. But the vampire hadn't closed in to attack him. He was simply scowling in vexation.

Dracula shrank back into his human form, then rearranged his tattered clothing as best he could. Sneering at Guice, he said, "I see the passage of time hasn't made you any braver."

The Justicar shrugged. "Haven't you heard, these days generals don't risk themselves on the front lines. They devise strategies and their troops carry them out. You see, we Ventrue are capable of adopting modern ways. What now, prince? Are you going to attack me? I assure you, I'm more formidable than my lackeys. A tough nut for even the celebrated *voevode* of Wallachia to crack, particularly when he's already wounded and weary."

Dracula smiled. "Oh, I think I could manage. But go now and you may depart unmolested." A livid bruise on his forehead faded, and a bullet hole in his ribs stopped bleeding. "Provided you give me your word that you and your associates will leave Mr. Edison alone."

"What about Mr. Symons?"

"You can return for him tomorrow night."

Guice grimaced. "Very well. Since the kine has already chosen to cast his lot with you, there seems little point in remaining. But I promise you, prince, we will meet again." He nodded to Edison, turned, and sauntered out the door.

Though by no means as frightened as he'd been during the battle, Edison still felt jittery and awkward. "I guess you have to bite me, don't you?" He fingered the kerchief knotted around his neck. "Should I take this off? Or roll up my sleeve?"

"No," Dracula said.

"Aren't we going to do it here?" the inventor asked.

"Neither here nor elsewhere," Dracula said, firelight flickering across the sharp planes of his face. "I have no intention of giving you the Embrace. I was trying to say as much when the Archons attacked me. I only came to keep you out of Guice's clutches."

Edison gaped at him. "But... why?"

"Because, as I said, I admire you." He put on his top hat, which looked absurd in combination with the ragged, bloody remains of his Inverness and suit. "Good night." He turned toward the exit.

"Wait!" Edison cried. Frowning, the Kindred pivoted back to face him. "Please! I only sided with you because I thought you meant to change me, too. Don't you understand, I *want* to be a vampire!"

"Even after everything you've seen and heard?" Dracula shook his head. "For a genius, you're a great fool. Trust me, immortality wouldn't suit you."

"How can you know that?"

"I'm not going to tell you," Dracula replied. "You know too much about my kind already. But I am willing to tell your fortune, and I see you have some good years left. You and your wife will mend your quarrel. You'll make staunch new friends and new discoveries. Unless you try to involve yourself with the Kindred, in which case I'll destroy you."

"But—"

Somehow, seemingly in the blink of an eye, Dracula vanished.

✠

Dracula maintained three havens in London. The most secure was a subterranean temple excavated during the Roman occupation. A refuge buried so deep that by the time he alit from the final flight of stairs, even his hypersensitive ears could no longer discern the myriad sounds of the great hive of humanity overhead, just the gurgle of a nearby underground stream.

A pair of coffins, two steamer trunks, and a clothespress occupied one corner of the electrically illuminated chamber, near a crude carving of Mithras slaying the bull. But most of the space was given over to a laboratory much like Edison's, crammed with workbenches, machinery, bookshelves, and racks of jars and bottles. The harsh odors of corrosive chemicals, hot metal, and burning insulation mingled with the scents of earth and stone.

Sitting hunched at his favorite table, hampered by shaking hands, Faraday was bolting some sort of electrical device together. His skin was white as paper, his eyes shone feverishly, and his fangs were fully extended. He clearly hadn't fed in days or perhaps even weeks. If Dracula had been similarly famished, he wouldn't even have been able to think of anything except satisfying his Hunger. But Faraday seemed as oblivious to his condition as he was to his sire's entrance.

"Hello," said Dracula. "I'm back."

Faraday jerked around on his stool. He tried to reply, noticed his fangs were out, preventing coherent speech, and retracted them with difficulty. "Hello," he croaked.

Dracula wondered if his childe even realized he'd been away in America for the past five months. Moving closer, he said, "Come up into the city with me, Michael. You need vitae."

"Please," said Faraday, "later. I'm on the verge of a breakthrough. I can feel it." Eagerly, stumbling over his words, he began to babble about his latest efforts to turn electricity into antigravity, the quest which had consumed him since his metamorphosis three decades before.

Dracula glumly recalled the days when he'd attended to such discourses with rapt fascination. Why not? Faraday had been the greatest mind of his era, the man who'd isolated benzene and invented the dynamo. That was why Dracula had chosen him to head a projected corps of undead scientists, whose discoveries ought to give him unshakable dominion over kine and Kindred alike. And why it had taken him so long to recognize that the poor wretch was spouting gibberish. His scientific acumen had perished at the moment of his transformation. Only the increasingly obsessive need to exercise it remained.

Dracula had often wondered why this should be so. The Embrace didn't extinguish other forms of creativity. The poets of Clan Toreador wrote masterpieces. Tremere sorcerers concocted spells and arcane rituals. Why, then, could no vampire improve on the current model of the atom, or invent a new type of engine? Perhaps it was the Creator's little joke. His way of ensuring that, though the Kindred would have their dark and bloody hour, the kine would rise and destroy them at the last.

It was unfortunate, Dracula reflected, that he couldn't simply have explained to Guice the futility of transforming Edison. It would have spared him considerable discomfort. But the Ventrue would never have believed him.

He looked down at Faraday and realized what had to be done. He raised his hand and the scientist fell silent. "I apologize," he said.

"For what?" Faraday asked.

"For thirty years of needless torment. God rest you." He seized the younger vampire's head and wrenched it off his shoulders.

Uroborus

Victor Rodriguez

The primal sunrise enflamed the eastern sky with a majestic panoply of deep orange rays, illuminating the front doors of about two dozen humble wood-and-stone buildings. The tiny village was encircled by the jagged, gray peaks of the nearby mountain range, resembling a cradle made of thorns. A massive castle dominated the smaller buildings from its position above, set against the face of the surrounding Alps.

The medieval fortress had been built in times of savage war by the hands of enslaved nobles. Almost five hundred years later, the castle stubbornly refused to show signs of entropy, except for the darkening of its stones.

The villagers sluggishly emerged from their houses, trudging across the wet earth to attend another day of farming duties. From the castle's roof, the tall, neatly dressed new master watched them carefully through the viewfinder of his tripod-mounted camera. Slowly, he panned across the entire village, his left hand steadily operating the crank that turned the spools of film inside. He took a full minute to savor the fluid motion of the shot, then took a step back to admire the full splendor of the scene with his own eyes.

It was so much more breathtaking in color! He gazed at the golden reflection of the sun against the chiseled angles of the mountain peaks and the structures of the valley below. It reminded him of a frozen fire.

His voyeuristic passion for moving pictures went far beyond an amateur's keen interest. He loved the weight of the camera in his hand and the smell of hot metal and film that accompanied the soft whir of its operation. Most of all, he loved to watch the motion of the flickering images as they played upon the silver screen. He felt that all of life's mysteries could be captured in this new art form. The world's most talented filmmakers could make the fleeting images of the real world seem even more tangible by displaying them on the screen. Unlike memories, these images were frozen in time, making it possible to experience their purity forever.

He would have brought professional 35mm gear with him, but the enormous equipment would have filled an entire train boxcar. The rail lines only reached as far as the town of Des—over 60 kilometers away. The remainder of the journey was only possible by horse-drawn carriage over rough road, which coiled around the local mountains until it finally terminated in the valley now laid out before him.

Stuffing his gloved hands into the warm pockets of his deep-pile camel-hair coat, he took a sharp breath of cold air. The small puffs of steam that emerged from his thin lips and nobly sloped nose ceased as he held his breath, carefully unlocking the camera from the stainless-steel tripod upon which it sat. He looked out across the battlements at the valley one last time to admire its coarse beauty, then went inside, closing the balcony doors behind him.

With long strides, he walked across the highest room of the castle tower and descended a narrow, stone staircase back to the central area. The interior was icy and dimly illuminated by a gaslight pipe system which had been installed over thirty years ago.

Cradling the camera as he would a baby, he hurried through the dark, ornate hallways to the main suite of rooms, where he felt welcome heat radiating from the huge stone fireplace that had been burning all evening.

The steepled, segmented windows made the patterns of the rising sun fall in elongated cross-hatched patterns along the polished antique furniture. Waiting to attend him were two servants: a tall, white-haired man and his plump daughter. The bright sun shone through a window behind them, making him squint, but the master identified their familiar silhouettes.

"Good morning." His voice was deep and soft. The formality of their bows made him a bit uncomfortable.

"Master Alicanto, will you require breakfast this morning?" the young woman asked. Per the instructions of the new American master, she omitted the word "sir" whenever she addressed him.

"Thank you, Zita, yes. Please bring it down to the darkroom," Alicanto replied. His Romanian was showing signs of improvement, she thought.

"Shall I take the film into town for you, sir, or will you be riding there yourself?" Zita's father asked. The old man was not as able, or willing, as his daughter to change how he addressed the master or any other formality of his speech.

"Thanks for the offer, Dimitri, but I think I'll take it into town myself."

"As you wish, sir."

"This is the first day that the sun's been out in over a week. I'd have to be an idiot not to take a ride before the next thunderstorm moves in," Alicanto explained.

"It won't be long before that happens, my lord, considering the time of year." Dimitri had a sharp wit, but knew better than to debate the willful young man on something he had already made up his mind to do. Alicanto had a classic Ivy League education, which Dimitri felt closed his eyes to practical and traditional thinking.

The old man had been a housekeeper all his life; he was devoted to God first and the castle second. He considered the master's health as part of the latter. Staying out past nightfall might have been perfectly fine in an American city, but out here it was a sure way to shorten one's life span.

Alicanto nodded to Dimitri before descending the basement stairs. He would often sequester himself down there for hours at a time, developing film in the dark, or tinkering with his technological inventions. If they didn't bring food to him, Dimitri thought, the man would simply go hungry.

He had been wary of the American when he had arrived just over a month ago. He possessed papers proving his inheritance of the castle, but did not act like a proper Romanian lord. There was no doubt that Alicanto had Romanian blood in his veins, but he kept his emotions under tight control. His modern beliefs were strange and unorthodox to them, as he placed his faith not in God, but in science and philosophy.

They might have perceived him as a social threat, but the public opinion of Alicanto was tempered by the fact that he showed respect for their ways, and rarely attempted to impose his own. Some of them had noticed that the more time Alicanto spent in the village, the more he adopted their ways. Perhaps he would belong, in time.

The darkroom was the first place Alicanto had furnished when he had arrived. Even before he had set foot in his bedroom, he had unpacked numerous crates of sensitive, bulky development equipment, leaded glass chemical jars and steel containers filled with processing fluid.

Alicanto unlocked the room and flicked on a local generator, which made a terrible metallic rattle and bathed the room in a dim, crimson light. His long fingers gently removed the film from the camera body. He gradually worked through the exacting process of properly packaging it for its long journey to Kodak in the U.S., where the tiny black-and-white images would be developed to form a motion picture. It was hard for him to leave the darkroom once he had set foot inside, and he spent the next few hours working on his own development equipment. One day soon, he would be able to develop his own film. Then he could avoid waiting the several weeks it took to ship his film to Kodak in New York, develop it and ship it back.

It was an hour before sundown when he came back up from the basement, package in hand ready to be mailed. He donned his black riding gear, strapped the package to his favorite horse and thundered down the damp mountain trail on his way to the village post office.

As Alicanto approached the building, he slowed his pace, surprised to see an elegant, dark-brown carriage parked in front. The tiny village didn't often have visitors due to its isolation from surrounding cities. It kindled his curiosity.

The post office doubled as a village inn and was proudly run by Mirella and her husband, Stephan. As Alicanto was lashing his horse's reins to the bench, a quick, black-bearded man with massive forearms cautiously opened the front door. He smiled broadly when he saw Alicanto's lean face.

"My lord, what a pleasant surprise!" The man extended his usual friendliness to Alicanto, who took off his thick, leather riding gloves to shake the innkeeper's hand.

"Good evening, Stephan. I just finished another roll of film, and I thought you could take it into town tomorrow. Unless… " he gestured at the carriage.

"Ah, yes, we have guests! Perhaps you would like to have dinner with them tonight," Stephan replied, taking the package Alicanto gave him. "Please, come in, my lord, and have tea with us. Mirella was just brewing some."

"Stephan?"

"Yes, my lord?"

"Please don't call me 'my lord'—it doesn't suit me very well."

"As you wish. Perhaps someday it will," Stephan said, being careful not to offend him.

"I doubt that. All men are created equal, Stephan. Social classes are quickly becoming a thing of the past." Alicanto believed in hope for an idyllic future where any man could climb society's pyramid if he so desired.

"As you wish, Mister Alicanto. I did not wish to make you uncomfortable." If Alicanto spoke the truth about vanishing social classes, Stephan thought, Romania would probably be one of the last places to change. Hundreds of years of European tradition could not simply vanish overnight.

They walked into the main room, which was rustic and warmly decorated. The front desk was beautifully polished deep-red mahogany, and the air carried a faint scent of burnt sage. Small Christian objects were placed strategically about the room to act as tiny guardians against a nearly forgotten ancient dread. Alicanto's riding boots sounded on the hardwood floor as Stephan led him across the room to his best table.

"Mister Alicanto," Stephan said in a low voice. "You must meet our new guest. She is most, ah, fascinating."

"She?" Alicanto was surprised that the owner of the carriage was a woman.

"Oh yes, *definitely* a woman." Stephan had never beheld a specimen of womanhood so captivating as his new guest. "Lady Katalin is her name—I believe the lady is Hungarian."

"Really. Is she married?" Alicanto's question got a knowing smile out of Stephan.

"No, I don't believe so," Stephan said. A door closed upstairs and a solid man with tiny eyes walked down the creaking staircase. Under his arm was a folded copy of *Az Est*, a Hungarian newspaper.

The man took a seat on the opposite side of the room and Stephan politely excused himself from Alicanto's table to attend to him. At that moment, Stephan's wife, Mirella, conservatively dressed up to the chin beneath a freshly washed apron, emerged from the kitchen bearing a freshly brewed pot of tea. Stephan, meanwhile, retreated behind the front desk where he rummaged through the latest mail.

"Mister Alicanto," Stephan called out, his voice muffled behind the desk, "A large package came for you today, from Bukarest."

Mirella served Alicanto first, pouring the sweet herbal mixture into a hot cup of tea in front of the appreciative man, who was still a bit chilled from his brisk ride. Stephan approached Alicanto with a wrapped shipping crate about the size of a suitcase and propped it up on the chair next to him. The small-eyed guest peered curiously over the top of his newspaper.

Alicanto examined the package carefully, puzzled as to who might have sent it. The rain-soaked postage badges indicated it had indeed passed through Bukarest, but closer inspection revealed an obscured stamp from its primary point of origin: Nuremberg, Germany. He furrowed his brow, still associating that country with the enemy he had fought against during the Great War. Hellish thoughts of the battle-torn trenches of western Europe exploded from his memory. The peace with Germany was still freshly inked as far as he was concerned. In fact, it only dated back a few short years. That was the past, he told himself. He pushed the dark thoughts from his mind as he tore off the mysterious crate's wrapping.

Stephan assisted him in prying open the crate's lid and Mirella hovered by the table, pouring fresh tea into Alicanto's brimming cup. After they worked the lid free, Stephan and Mirella looked on, wide-eyed, as Alicanto carefully examined the contents of the crate. Nestled securely in packing straw were a small teakwood box and an ornate sword.

The sword caught Alicanto's eye first, and he lifted it out of the crate into plain view. He judged it to be of Spanish origin, dating back to the Middle or Dark Ages. Its ornate scabbard was decorated with various

Christian symbols fashioned from forged steel. He gripped the pommel of the weapon and withdrew it in a single, careful motion. He was impressed by the blade's fine craftsmanship and sharpness; while closely examining its edge with his thumb, he drew a painless bead of blood. The viscous liquid ran down the length of the blade and collected at the engraved hand-guard before he produced a white silk handkerchief to carefully blot it. There was no doubt that he held in his hands the proud weapon of a prince.

He carefully put the sword to one side of the crate. Alicanto then gently took out its traveling companion, the box. Roughly the size of a thin loaf of bread, its beige, smooth-grained exterior had an iron-hinged lid with a simple clasp to keep it shut. The lid was emblazoned with his family's heraldic shield: a rampant dragon. Inside the box shone a brilliantly polished bronze medallion. It depicted the dramatic image of a coiled dragon crucified upon a double-cross in the form of an uroborus, consuming its own tail. Alicanto's eyes widened as he felt a strange pull toward the image. He tried to suppress the odd feeling, focusing his mind on the symbol in an attempt to identify it. He recalled an ancient religions class he had taken at Brown University, where he learned that the uroborus was a symbol that dated as far back as Ancient Egypt. Religious and mystical societies of the world had used it to symbolize cyclical repetition: the perpetual process of death and rebirth.

Stephan, Mirella and the small-eyed man exchanged glances as they watched Alicanto holding the ancient medallion, which gleamed even in the dimly lit corner of the inn.

"Incredible," was all Alicanto could say. He searched the package for an accompanying letter, but it was otherwise empty, leaving him mystified as to who might have sent it.

"They suit you, my lord," Mirella said, in a thick voice. Alicanto looked at her blankly, his mind still thinking about his recently acquired possessions.

"Thank you," he said in a low voice.

Mirella pulled Stephan away from the table and off to the kitchen, where he helped her put the finishing touches on dinner.

Alicanto held the medallion at eye level and devoured the intricacies of its design. Slowly, he raised it over his head and put it on. He was overcome by an odd sensation of *deja vu*, though no particular images came to him. For the first time since his arrival, he felt truly comfortable here. He smiled and tucked the medallion under his shirt.

In his peripheral vision, he noticed the small-eyed man put down his newspaper and stand up, looking to the top of the stairs. Alicanto looked up as well, and he beheld a slender woman dressed in a maroon-colored velvet-and-lace dress. She drifted down the staircase slowly, approaching the small-eyed man's table, who stiffly bowed to her and pulled out a chair to seat her. She did not even acknowledge her servant's presence.

Alicanto found it difficult not to stare. The usual shyness that he had around women had vanished. Feeling the weight of the medallion under his collarbone, he fastened the sword on his belt and approached her. She met his gaze with clear blue eyes that urged him forward. He did not notice another of her servants appear at the top of the stairs and start down.

The small-eyed man got up and defensively watched Alicanto approach the table. Lady Katalin gracefully rose and extended her supple hand. Gently, he took it and touched his lips to her knuckle, detecting the scent of a rare Parisian perfume.

"Enchanted," was all Alicanto could say. He had never before seen such rare beauty.

"Don't you look dashing," the lady replied. Her voice was low and resonant. In the blink of an eye, she glanced him over, taking in thousands of details about his appearance.

"Allow me to introduce the Lady Katalin," came a deep voice from behind Alicanto. A black-haired man with a thick mustache had descended the stairs and approached the table.

"These are my bodyguards," Katalin revealed. "Why don't you join us for dinner?" Her boldness surprised him. She must have been a photographer's model, he thought, or perhaps a European actress. She spoke perfect Romanian.

"You are the new owner of the castle, are you not?" She sounded hopeful.

"Indeed I am," he replied.

"Ah, Lord Alicanto. Splendid." Her lips curved. Feline instinct looked out from behind her eyes. She must have inquired with Stephan or Mirella about him, he thought.

"Please, call me Daniel." He stumbled at informality. She indulged him.

"Very well, then you must call me Katalin. I am passing through here on my way to Bulgaria." The look in Alicanto's eyes asked for further information. Young men are so curious these days, she thought.

"Family matters," she said, hoping the vague reference would satisfy him. It did.

"I've only recently arrived myself." He tried his best to conceal his American accent.

"From the United States?"

"Providence, Rhode Island," he specified, admiring her powers of perception.

She nodded. Even many years of urbane living could not thin this man's blood, she thought. Behind his civilized exterior was the soul of a warrior. There was no doubt that she had found a direct descendant of the Romanian throne.

"You *are* aware of the history behind your new house, aren't you?" she playfully inquired.

"I understand that Prince Vlad had it built himself," he said, somewhat cautiously. His fascination with the medieval Romanian prince was a scholarly one, though it was true that he was a distant relative. History had taught him that Prince Vlad had been Eastern Europe's most bloodthirsty tyrant. The morbid life of the legendary prince had been partially resurrected thirty years ago by the popularity of the macabre fictional novel *Dracula*, written by Irish novelist Bram Stoker.

Alicanto found it fascinating that native Romanians did not have the same negative picture of Prince Vlad as the rest of the world. In fact, older families even lionized the man, considering him a distinguished leader of heroic character. It seemed that she was not intimidated by the castle's imposing history. This greatly relieved him.

"Would you like to see the castle?" She would surely be impressed, he thought.

"I'm afraid I must leave soon," she said. Her statement pained him, as if she were his long-lost lover.

"Then tonight, perhaps."

"Daniel, I've heard wolves running in the woods near here, and it *is* after dark… would that not be unsafe for a lady?" She gave him a coy look.

"Bring your bodyguards. We'll make sure you arrive safely. It's just up the mountain." Alicanto tried to inspire her with his confidence. Katalin hesitated, weighing what he had just said.

"I would only agree if you could prepare a guest room. It would be far too late to return to the inn after you have taken me on a proper tour of your beautiful house." Katalin leaned back in her chair to let Alicanto get a good look at her. He could not possibly refuse her, she thought.

"I would be honored," came his reply. Her red lips curved into a smile.

After dinner, Katalin's bodyguards put on their riding gear and sabers, following Alicanto to the castle. He escorted the carriage past the forged-iron entry gate and into the roundhouse just as the sky gave birth to a terrific thundershower. Torrents of rain poured down relentlessly as Alicanto led his new guest through the castle's massive double doors. He shielded her from the downpour with his cloak as they stepped onto the marble floor of the foyer.

Dimitri and Zita attended to them immediately, taking their cloaks and the wet riding gear of the carriage driver. In accordance with custom, both pairs of servants gathered around the huge, crackling fireplace. Meanwhile, Alicanto began to guide Lady Katalin through his home's gothic, lancet-steepled passageways.

As the pair toured through a high-roofed study, Alicanto remembered that this is where he had left one of his Hawkeye snapshot cameras.

"May I take your picture?" he asked. She hesitated a moment before answering. She had a genuine distaste for modern technology, but decided to indulge him, amused by the irony of his wish to possess an image of her that would not age.

"Very well," she said. "But I must request that you stand a good distance away with your flash powder." She had read accounts of the occasional burn accident occurring during a photography session.

"Of course," he reassured her. With care, he set up the tripod and extended the folding bellows on the Hawkeye. She chose to stand in front of a Jacobean mahogany table. A faded medieval portrait loomed above her.

With his thumb on the tip of the extended, flexible trigger, Alicanto had her pose for a score of shots, each composition featuring a different, ravishing angle of her lithe figure. His desire for her grew with each photograph he took, gradually pushing everything else out of his mind except a singular, sexual need to possess her. He imagined her lying next to him, her soft skin illuminated by candlelight, making hushed sounds as she stroked the lean surface of his chest with her slim fingers. Her beauty was intoxicating.

"Katalin?" Alicanto peered at her over the top of the camera. "May I… adjust your hair?" Concealed yearning dripped from his words.

"Yes."

She heard his heart pounding as he moved behind her and felt her own temperature rise with anticipation. Hands slightly trembling, he caressed the curls of her hair and laid them with care over her shoulders. Her warm flesh screamed to him from beneath the flimsy lace adornment of her dress. When she turned to face him, he saw his own desire reflected in her eyes.

"The resemblance is really quite incredible," she whispered. He had no idea what she was talking about.

"Resemblance?"

"The portrait," she said, making a casual gesture toward the wall. He now stood between her and the aged painting, and she nodded, admiring his face next to the one in the portrait. There were a few cosmetic differences between the faces of the two men, but they shared the same dark, ardent eyes and the same pronounced nose. It was as if the prince had returned.

"Ah," he realized, turning to the painting. He didn't wish to look at anything other than her. She lifted her right hand, placed her fingertips just below his collarbone, then lightly traced a line down to his belly button. She was looking into the open book of his desires. He leaned toward her and she let him taste her lips.

It was searing and delicate. He closed his eyes and drank in the sensation. She slowly pulled away, a bit shy, perhaps. When he leaned toward her again, she titled her head to one side and kissed his throat.

He felt her soft lips, then her tongue and then a slight sting. Ecstasy electrified him, shooting down his arteries to fill every extremity. He put his arms around her to hold her close to him; the warmth of her body felt so good. Drowsiness soon overcame him and he felt a sensation like sinking into warm water.

The small woman supported the tall man's weight with ease. He trembled in her arms, lost in the euphoria of the moment. Something within him, however, made his eyes drift open. He gazed down to see her holding him in her soft, unyielding embrace. Something was not quite right. He smelled something coppery and heard tender, sucking sounds.

His pupils focused with the sudden realization of what she was.

She greedily quenched her hunger with his blood, swallowing it as quickly as the two tiny fountains in his neck flowed into her mouth. He had given her almost all that he had, but in that one brief moment of lucidity, his will fought for his body's survival. All of his muscles strained against her and he pried himself free. The shock of the action took her by surprise and he jerked away, his back slamming into a heavy bookcase filled with leather-bound volumes. Hot blood spurted from his neck, showering the portrait and Katalin's exquisite face. Her canine teeth were extended to twice their normal size.

Alicanto clasped his left hand to his wounded neck and stared incredulously at her.

"Katalin!" He did not want to accept what his eyes showed him. His wet fingers kept reminding him this was real.

"Daniel," she stared at him without blinking as she spoke in a low voice, her head angled downward. The power behind her eyes paralyzed his legs.

"You are of Vlad Tepes' blood," she continued, approaching slowly. The tone of her voice began to darken.

"For centuries, I've awaited vengeance for what he did to my clan. You carry his sword. You wear his medallion. The Tzimisce will not tolerate another Dracula!" Her voice seethed with a hatred she had been nursing for five hundred years.

"But, the legends… " he choked. "Wasn't he one of you?" He summoned enough strength to start backing away from her, toward the doorway. Echoing from the main hall, he heard chilling screams. Her soft voice drowned them out.

"You know so little, Daniel. Vlad Dracula acquired the name *Tepes* because of his favorite form of executing prisoners. He killed those who rose up against him by impaling them on blunt, wooden stakes. Not all of them were human. Some were *Shilmulo,* like me. Vampires, Daniel." She advanced slowly, letting him fully comprehend his impending death. His realization would make his remaining drops of blood tangy with fear, a particular taste that Katalin had learned to appreciate over the years.

His hand felt the space of the open doorway behind him and he bolted out of the room, making his way down a narrow corridor toward the main hall. She laughed as she came after him, her strong, quick legs overtaking him easily. When she was almost upon him, he spun around, drawing the ancient sword from its sheath. His instincts and accuracy did not fail him; he gashed Katalin across the neck with enough strength to behead a normal man. The force of the swing even drove the sword's tip into the stone of the corridor wall. Her head, however, remained secured to her body. His cut opened a wound the size of a mouth in her neck, out of which blood merely trickled.

She stopped and put a hand against the opposite wall, steadying herself. Alicanto pulled the sword free and continued to run in the direction of the screams. He stumbled into the main hall in time to see Katalin's bodyguards hacking at the dying bodies of Dimitri and Zita.

Alicanto knew he would soon be dead from blood loss, but he still possessed a clear mind. His lust had transformed into rage, fueling his weakening limbs with new power.

He summoned enough strength to attack. Katalin's bodyguards rushed him, brandishing their bright sabers. He surprised the small-eyed man with a low sword stroke that split open his belly. The huge bodyguard sank to his knees, his bowels uncoiling onto the floor. The man with the mustache turned his weapon's blade on its side and ran Alicanto through. The point of the saber slid between his ribs, narrowly missing his heart. As the bodyguard pulled his weapon free, Alicanto slashed upward, bisecting his opponent's face from chin to hairline. The man with the mustache dropped his weapon onto the stone floor, palms pressed against his blood-filled eyes, and began to scream.

Alicanto's face was washed in red, except for his white teeth and eyes. Rage kept his weak heart pumping. He dropped the sword and wove his way toward the warmth of the fireplace, listening to the rain blaring against the huge windows and the screams of the dying man. Unfortunately, the fire, along with his plan to burn Katalin, had been extinguished by her guards. The screams coming from the mouth of the split-faced man gradually became weaker and stopped.

Suddenly, out of the darkness of the corridor, Alicanto saw Katalin rush out toward him, charged with supernatural alacrity. Her face was contorted into a bestial parody of her former beauty as she lunged, ready to rip every last drop of blood from his body. In a final, desperate exertion of willpower, the dying Alicanto gripped the fireplace poker and held it out in front of him, bracing his back against the stone mantelpiece. She slammed into him, the force of the blow snapping several of his ribs. The last thing he felt as unconsciousness overcame him was Katalin's razor-sharp teeth sinking into the flesh of his neck.

Suddenly, Alicanto's body lurched with violent life. The iron-tipped mahogany poker had punched a hole straight through Katalin's heart, immobilizing her and spattering Alicanto's face with her vampiric blood. The tiny droplets burned his tongue and sizzled down his throat. His eyes sprang open.

No sensation he had ever felt in his thirty-two-year-old life rivaled his newfound hunger. Disregarding his open wounds and broken bones, he pulled Katalin's body to him and drank deeply of the precious vitae that gushed from her generous chest. As he gulped it down, he felt his wounds closing, his bones mending themselves and all five senses screaming with heightened perception.

When the last drop of Katalin's blood was drained, he effortlessly tossed the undead corpse aside and looked up at the ceiling. Kneeling, with arms outstretched, he let out a primal sound of emotion and horror, filled with the realization of the monster he had become. The scream echoed through the castle. Dracula was reborn.

✠

Time was static as Alicanto stared at the image of the sun flickering on the silver screen. He was alone in the castle now, and preferred to languish in the cold room he had converted into a small film theater, rather than enjoy the pleasant company of mortals. The carnage of that blood-drenched evening was long since over, but not forgotten. From time to time, he would receive visitors, but those occasions would become less frequent as the months passed. The villagers suspected and accepted the truth and his custody, just as they had accepted Prince Vlad's five hundred years ago.

The smoke from his cigarette drifted into the cone of light that shone out from the whirring projector. His sharpened, supernatural eyes now intensified even the dimmest illumination and exploded every detail of the brilliant, scarlet sunrise that his camera had captured on film. He wished he could ignore the fingerprints, wandering lines and specks of dirt that played across the screen, reminding him this was a film and not reality. With the blood of the vampire in his body, he now had many superhuman abilities at his command. The blessed light of the sun, however, was forever lost to him. Even the most slender shaft of light would blind his eyes and burn the flesh from his body.

A few months after his battle with Katalin, when his mind could tolerate the horror of his new existence, Alicanto had become determined to see the golden hues of the rising sun once again. He had enclosed himself in his basement darkroom, toiling in complete darkness with heightened perception and steadfast diligence. Many nights later, he emerged with a working model for color film that he had begun years ago. He sent his ideas to Pathé Laboratories in France and Kodak in the United States. Within the year, portable color film cameras were commercially available in many parts of the world. He ordered one of the first models for himself, and had asked one of the villagers to film the sunrise.

The strip of film completed its cycle through the mechanism of the projector and now rhythmically flicked around the rear reel. The screen suddenly glowed white, its unwelcome brightness making him wince.

Flicking off the projector's lamp, he eased back in his high-backed leather chair as light fled from the room. The ember of his cigarette slowly burned out, the red reflections in his irises fading along with it. Darkness gently enveloped him with its hushed promise of serenity and he closed his eyes, finding solace in the purity of shadows.

Bloodlover

Victor Koman

The wanderer, clad in the black robes of a *starets*, strode into St. Petersburg with a name that had preceded him. Grigory Yefimovich Novykh smelled of vodka and laudanum, which—given the atmosphere in 1905 Russia—did not invalidate his status as an unordained man of religion. In fact, Novykh had been to the capital of Holy Mother Russia two years before. He had returned to make his mark. A permanent mark.

When he entered the tea room, a hush fell over the members of St. Petersburg's high society. Not because the unkempt man seemed out of place amid the show of wealth, but because many already knew him. The whispers began at the doorway and followed him as he walked slowly, broodingly toward the rear of the establishment. The balalaika player's fingers froze in midnote, seizing up the bright music as if all gaiety had been sucked from the room.

"Rasputin," whispered one, then another, and another.

"The *starets* from Pokrovskoye… "

"Immense occult powers… "

"A flagellant, a Khlysty!"

"Pilgrim… "

"Debaucher of women… "

"I hear he gained his powers on Mt. Athos, in Greece… "

"So filthy. So haunted. So exciting!"

Several women swooned. Impressing these women, however, did little to serve Rasputin's plans. Only one woman mattered: Tsaritsa Alexandra.

Toward that lofty goal would the man seated at the farthest table at the rear of the tea room steer Novykh, the man called Rasputin.

The man rose upon sighting Rasputin. He stood a head shorter than the *starets*, and about a foot wider. A broad grin spread across his face. Arms outstretched, he greeted the newcomer in a stage whisper.

"Grigory! Best of health to you, my—"

The dark wanderer gazed at the little man with black eyes that were nearly all pupil. They looked straight through him as if Rasputin were solid matter and he—the banker Manus—were but a shade in the night. His smile evaporated and he bowed his head.

"*Batushka, batushka,*" he muttered, almost praying, but whether to the heavenly father or to Rasputin no onlooker could tell. "I have what you wrote me for. A meeting this day with Archimandrite Theophanes, whom you met in your visit here two years ago." The smile returned, but it now appeared ingratiating, that of a servant, not a comrade. "He travels now among the élite," he added encouragingly.

The dark eyes gazed at him unceasingly. Manus trembled, knowing Rasputin could demand anything of him and he would obey. Then, in a swirl of laudanum-scented, sweat-drenched robes, the dark figure turned about and departed, leaving behind him the whispers and nervous titters of an entranced aristocracy.

✣

The Empress of Holy Mother Russia, the Tsaritsa Alexandra Fyodorovna, gently cradled the frail child in her arms. Alexi Nikolayevich, her only son, carried in his veins the curse of her bloodline. She admitted privately no understanding of the disease hemophilia, but she knew that Alexi's condition was grave, and that the future heir to the Romanov dynasty could die from as little as a pinprick.

"Irina Pavlovna!" she called out. The wet nurse trotted into the baby's room, soft leather slippers shuffling across the tiles. Hand over her blouse, she came ready to produce a milk-swollen breast at the tsaritsa's command or at the vocal pleading of the tiny tsarevich. Over a year old, the infant looked more like a weak six-month-old, pale and drawn.

The tsaritsa gently handed the child over to Irina, who nursed him and cooed. Upon seeing this, the normally stern expression of the empress relaxed into a sort of calm warmth. She sat back, adjusted her thick white robe, and let her thoughts drift to the realm of the spiritual, in which she dwelt more and more these troubling days.

A scratch at the door to the chamber failed to rouse her from meditations on Theosophy and its relation to the eastern influences of Orthodoxy.

The wet nurse cleared her throat. "Tsaritsa Alexandra," she murmured, lest the suckling child in her arms grow disturbed. "A visitor."

The scratching grew louder. Irina rose slowly and quietly glided over to open the door. Beyond its portal stood a man in black, tall, gaunt, with a beard longer than most priests'. He smelled, but the musky, manly scent traveled straight from her nostrils to each of her womanly parts, setting them a-tingle. Then she gazed into his eyes and felt herself pulled into a blackness from which she did not want to escape.

He inclined his head ever so slightly in a gesture of humility completely inconsistent with his demeanor. "This humble monk," he intoned, "has been sent by the Synod to minister to the needs of Tsarevich Alexi Nikolayevich."

Irina backed away, holding the infant closer to her breast.

"Please," he said softly. "May I enter his room?"

Irina feared that if she let this dark stranger into the tsarevich's nursery, the child would be plunged into mortal danger. She sealed her lips and said nothing. From behind her, though, came a voice of confidence.

"Enter, *batushka*, please, if it be your will!"

"Thank you, my empress." He crossed the threshold and walked past the wet nurse toward the tsaritsa, where he knelt and lowered his head of long, oily black hair. "This humble servant of our one Master begs to assist your highness in ministering to the needs of the young heir. I have learned much in my travels pertaining to matters of blood." He turned his eyes upward and pinioned Alexandra with an obsidian gaze. "I can provide him with a long life. A very, very long life."

"And what is your name, *batushka*?"

"I am Grigory Yefimovich Novykh." He smiled a charming, self-deprecating smile. "Some, who differ with the Khlysty teachings regarding sin and redemption, have called me Rasputin."

The wet nurse gasped.

Alexandra, heart pounding in her breast with a mixture of elation, fear, and exhilaration, breathlessly said, "They call you a debauchee?"

"It is unearned, I assure you. A debauchee enjoys his sins. A Khlysty sins in piety, that he may gain redemption thereby. Know that I have paid myself by the lash for every act." He smiled that smile again. It chilled Irina's blood yet seemed to exert some powerful influence upon the tsaritsa.

"And you have the skills to aid my son, the future tsar?"

He stared deeply into her with eyes that had become pools of pure night. "I have the skills… and the power!"

"Then save him from this curse upon the house of Romanov!"

Without further word, Rasputin lifted Alexi from the stunned wet nurse's grip and cradled him in his black-sleeved arms. The child voiced no objection, but instead began to coo.

"Listen!" the tsaritsa cried. "My Alexi sings!"

"Praise to our Master," Rasputin intoned.

✠

Alone with the infant in an adjoining room, Rasputin whispered to Alexi in a deep, hypnotically soothing tone.

"Little Grand Duke, you have been put into my hands by a power far greater than you can imagine. I alone can offer you the gift of eternal life. I alone can cure you of this sickness in your blood. And when I have won, you will kneel in allegiance to the one Master of us all."

Then he whispered the name of his Master into the baby's ear. Alexi began to whimper, but Rasputin quieted him and rocked him gently, knowing that the battle was half won already.

✠

Tsar Nicholas II tugged at the waxy ends of his mustache and pondered Russia's fate. It had been a terrible year, beginning with Bloody Sunday in January. His July success at an alliance with Germany despite also being allied with its enemy France was somehow viewed as a sign of weakness, magnified by the humiliating defeat in the war with Japan and President Roosevelt's miserable Treaty of Portsmouth in which the Tsar—and hence Russia—lost Port Arthur on the Liaotung Peninsula, the South Manchurian railroad leading to it, and half of Sakhalin Island.

He would have them back, he swore, even if it took decades.

The Duma had been in existence for less than a year, and the October manifesto less than a month, yet already the constitutional regime he had promised these senseless dreamers began to irritate him. He would see an end to this Duma and its flirtation with representative politics. Witte was a fool to advocate such a thing. Making him prime minister was a mistake. Perhaps replacing him with Governor Stolypin…

A sound at the door caught his attention. It was Olga's distinctive scratch. His eldest daughter entered the chamber at his exhortation looking troubled. She was tall and regal in a simple white gown, her dark hair up in a decidedly American Gibson style.

"Papa?"

"What is it, Olga? I have many problems on my mind."

"Then I apologize for bringing you another." Her voice possessed a deep sadness through which her inner strength radiated.

The tsar sighed. The tsarevna spoke.

"Mother has allowed a *starets* from Siberia into the court. He claims to be a holy man, but I fear he does not serve the same Lord as we."

"Why is he here?"

His daughter let go a weary breath, then said, "He is to care for Alexi. He claims that he can relieve his suffering."

Nicholas, distracted by other thoughts, nonetheless regained his focus when the tsarevich's name escaped her lips. "My son? He can cure my son of his illness?"

Olga spread her hands in dismay. "Yes, no. All I know is that he has taken a room next to my brother's and has been at his side for a week now."

"And Alexi?"

"He no longer cries. His skin is more pink, he seems to be thriving. But there is something I do not like about the *starets*."

The tsar listened carefully. "What?"

"His look. His manner. Most of all his name: Rasputin."

Her father uttered the name slowly.

"I fear," she said, "that he shall bring about the fall of Romanov."

Nicholas smiled, then gently said, "The house of Romanov shall stand for an eternity."

✢

The house of Romanov stood, albeit shakily, for a decade, during which Alexi grew safely through boyhood under the watchful, dark eyes of Rasputin. The tsaritsa saw a weak but certainly not feeble grand duke in her son. In him, she also saw the next tsar.

If, that is, the current tsar could hold things together. Alexandra mused on this as she, her son, and Grigory sat in the warm orange glow of the grand ballroom's fireplace.

She loved… no, she *abided* her husband, obsessed for a year now with the Great War and having assumed control of the Russian army as supreme commander. Lord knows that he had abided her over the years, especially when the scurrilous rumors about Grigory erupted almost immediately upon his arrival at the palace in St. Petersburg.

And such rumors! The thought of a holy man leading a double life—humble and penitent in court, a licentious seducer outside—made her livid with rage. Just the other day she had been forced to take Grand Duke Dmitry Pavlovich to task for disputing Rasputin's role in suggesting replacements for the ministers and officials who dared to question his influence in domestic affairs!

She knew of all the shocking innuendoes about their relationship. Four years before, the circulation of spurious letters implying that they had shared intimacies forced the Duma to debate his supposed evil influence. And the reports of young women found dead and drained of blood! How could such things be laid at Grigory's feet? The implication!

She gazed at the two of them: Alexi, so robust and radiant in the fire's light; Grigory, so pale and holy in his dark robes. With Christmas less than two weeks away, how she would enjoy gifting him with the special Fabergé egg Carl had designed at her request.

Rasputin paused in watching the fire, turning to gaze at the tsaritsa with those black, infinitely deep eyes of his. "I must be leaving soon," he said, which made her stiffen in alarm.

"Leave?" she asked, hand above her heart.

"A midnight tea at the home of Prince Felix Yusupov. I shall return well before dawn."

She always wondered about his midnight teas. They were not uncommon among the Russian élite, and in fact the Romanovs were night people. But whenever Rasputin was out at night she worried. This time was no different.

"You will wear the beaver coat we gave you?" she asked. "It is deathly cold out there at this hour."

"Yes, my empress," he said in a most humble tone.

The motor coach turned onto the property of the Yusupov palace on Moika Quay. From inside came the sounds of revelry. The long driveway was icy, and Rasputin gripped the hand-strap over the door for most of the trip.

He had his suspicions about Yusupov, but, lately, the pressures of dismissing insurgent ministers and replacing them with more trusted acquaintances brought upon him the need to retreat into his holy world of sin and repentance. Sin first. It was a filthy endeavor, but his faith required it.

"What guests have you tonight, Felix?"

"A small circle of friends," said the prince—a relative of the tsar's by marriage. "Grand Duke Dmitry Pavlovich. Vladimir Mitrofanovich Purishkevich—"

"Since when have you friends in the Fourth Duma?"

Yusupov smiled. "These are trying times. One finds friends where one may." The coach slowed to a stop and footmen opened their doors. "Oh," the prince added almost parenthetically, "and a Dr. Lazovert, who once studied under Dr. Abraham von Helsing." He gazed at Rasputin as if expecting some sort of reaction. Seeing none, he entered his apartment in his father's mansion with the *starets* at his side.

Rasputin recognized the emperor's nephew, Dmitry Pavlovich, reflected in an astonishing number of mirrors immediately upon entering the anteroom. He greeted the grand duke with appropriate humility and walked into Felix's vast apartment, pausing only to face an ornate crystal-and-bronze Italian crucifix on the eastern wall, cross himself, and interweave his fingers in prayer.

Yusupov introduced him to Purishkevich, whom he knew only by reputation as a conservative in the new Duma. Lazovert—a small man with a trim goatee and intense gaze—was a total enigma. All through the night, as tea, wine, and vodka flowed, the doctor appeared obsessed with hovering around. First he offered Rasputin a glass of tea that smelled horribly of garlic. Repelled by the nauseous brew, he tried to depart from Lazovert and turn his attention to a lovely young woman dressed all in sapphire blue.

The ploy failed, as Lazovert stumbled toward him holding a small phial of liquid. He tripped and the contents of the phial splashed against Grigory's forehead.

"*Svolotch!*" he cried, wiping a sleeve over his face. The liquid felt like water kept at body temperature and smelled of hyssop. "Why does a doctor carry around holy water like a priest?"

"Grigory, Grigory," Yusupov interceded. "Please excuse Dr. Lazovert. Have some more wine!" A lovely young servant girl offered a tray holding a single glass. Rasputin downed it in one long draught. He tasted something more than wine. He tasted cyanide.

Rasputin knew the taste of cyanide. Through much of his life he took daily doses—small enough at first not to kill or even sicken, but gradually increasing in strength until what would kill a horse affected him not at all. He knew that someday such an immunity would come in handy.

"Traitors!" he cried out, casting down the crystal flute, shattering it against the floorboards. "Poisoners! Enemies of the Tsar!"

"No!" Yusupov screamed, drawing his Browning pistol. "You are the traitor! Seducer of the Tsaritsa! Corrupter of Alexi!" He aimed at Rasputin's heart. "Even poison will not slay the servant of the vile lord Vlad Dracul!"

"What?" Rasputin stared at the pistol in utter bafflement.

"Vampyr!" Yusupov screamed and pulled the trigger.

"Wait!" shouted Lazovert.

The muzzle of the revolver unleashed fire and lead. The bullet punched into Rasputin's chest, pain searing him only mildly through the alcoholic haze. He ran into the garden, fumbling for his own pistol within the folds of his robe. A pack of the prince's retrievers howled at the dark figure that disturbed their sleep.

He squeezed off a shot toward the apartment and only succeeded in felling a dog. He cursed the drink that clouded his vision, the poison that knotted his stomach, and the madness that gripped Yusupov.

The others burst through the doors into the snowy night. Purishkevich gripped a revolver and held aim on the bleeding man.

"You see?" Yusupov cried. "Even bullets do not kill the monster! We must drive a stake through his—"

Purishkevich fired four times at Rasputin. The last two hit vital tissue. The world swam before Rasputin's eyes but still he refused to die.

"Stop this!" Lazovert cried from behind them.

To the east was a dim glow. "See that?" Yusupov yelled. "The sun comes! Your master's enemy! Face the eye of God and die for all eternity!"

"He is not vampyr!" Lazovert screamed, throwing himself bodily across Rasputin. Looking up at the conspirators, he breathlessly raced through his words. "He rejected the garlic, yes, but the holy water had no effect, nor did he recoil from the mirrors. And he wears a crucifix, you fools! I was called here to see a vampire and I find instead a mere man. Yet you act without even waiting for my diagnosis!"

Purishkevich spoke, his tone moderated hardly at all by the doctor's revelation. "Well… he is still traitor to the emperor. I'm glad to have slain him!"

Rasputin took a rattling breath to whisper, "I'm not dead yet."

"Poison and three bullets!" Yusupov muttered. "I say we dump him in the Neva just to be sure."

As the prince and the grand duke held him down, Purishkevich bound the still-living Grigory Yefimovich Novykh with royal-purple drapery cords.

Rasputin's ebony eyes—glazing now as life escaped him in the frigid December dawn—still held power as he gazed at Yusupov to issue a final prophecy. "You have destroyed Russia in your mad attempt to save her. The house of Romanov will fall and take all of you with it because of the evil my holy powers can no longer contain!" He stared dully at the rising sun. "The east is red!" he gasped. "Red as blood!"

It took over an hour to smuggle the limp, twitching body of the mad monk to the Petrovsky Island bridge over the Neva River. Grand Duke Dmitry Pavlovich and a young officer, Sukhotin, dragged the body to the ice-crusted shoreline while Dr. Lazovert looked on, merely shaking his head. How von Helsing would have laughed, he thought, to see such incompetent vampire killers expend so much energy to wind up killing a mere human.

Icy mist escaped Novykh's lips as they swung his body back and forth to fling him into the dark waters. With the last spark of remaining life, the bound man gazed up at his killers to say, "I pray my Lord and Master Jesus Christ to deliver Mother Russia from the plague you have unleashed."

Fingers released their grip. Rasputin sailed a few feet through the air to break through the thin ice at river's edge and slip into the frigid, slow waters of the Neva.

"So," Grand Duke Dmitry muttered, "Rasputin is gone. And with him, Russia's nightmare."

✠

The leader of the Bolshevik squad guarding Ipatiev House, Yurovsky, nervously sipped at a glass of tea. Czech troops were rumored to be marching on Ekaterinberg to liberate the ex-tsar and his family. The July evening was calm and clear, as was his purpose. In the sixteen months since Nicholas' abdication, the royal family had proved nothing but an embarrassment. Their show of dignity and courage during the trial revealed nothing of their decadence to the world at large. Even during their house arrest at Tsarskoye Selo and in Tobolsk they evoked such courteous treatment as to allow them to go about unmolested.

That changed after last November, and the *Cheka* guard had voted to solve the problem of the Romanovs once and for all. Only then could Russia emerge into its brilliant red dawn.

He took his small detachment of men and descended into the basement. Ordering the door unlocked, he strode in only to recoil at the stench escaping from the cramped room. Tsar or peasant, he mused, the smell of stale urine is the same.

The small dungeon, unlit but for their electric torches, held Nicholas, Alexandra, their five children, three servants, and a doctor imprisoned with them. They all stared at the armed men entering their domain. They had been led downstairs only a few hours before, but their faces—haggard from months of abuse—looked like those of war prisoners returning from the front.

"Your relatives have tried and failed to rescue you!" Yurovsky announced, gazing at the fallen monarchists with flinty eyes. "In the name of the people and their soviets, you must all die!" With the stroke of a hand, he ordered his men to aim their rifles.

"Fools!" the doctor cried out. "You cannot kill these—"

"Shut up, old man!" The stern command issued—surprisingly—from the mouth of Tsarevich Alexi. Pale and drawn, he nonetheless evoked a chilling majesty. Standing, he continued to speak while staring at the assassination squad with cold delight.

"Our hosts, the Bolsheviks, will finally quiet your meddling tongue and free me to feed once more. Rasputin may have restrained me with his holy powers, though at least he let me partake of a peasant now and then. But you, lickspittle to von Helsing, kept me weak with your malicious science."

"Kill them," Yurovsky cried, suddenly fearful of the little hemophiliac's confident calm. "Kill them all!"

"Through the heart!" were Dr. Lazovert's last words as machine gun fired exploded in the tiny basement.

For more than a minute the *Cheka* troops sprayed the room with lead, laughing as they dispensed the people's justice. They were young, and they saw the coming of a new world. When the smoke settled, though, the remnants of a world older than they could imagine still stood.

Most of their victims lay crumpled on the stone floor, at least some of the bullets penetrating and rupturing their hearts. Then the sound of laughter replaced the fading reverberations of gunfire.

"Did you think that a branch of the royal bloodline of *Prince* Vlad Dracul could die so easily? That my need for blood—my *love* of it—could be stopped with as base a metal as lead?"

The swirling, choking smoke diminished enough that the shocked troops could see both Tsarevich Alexi and Tsarevna Anastasia still standing, their royal garments shredded by gunfire, their bodies riddled with bullet holes, yet not a drop of blood issuing from their wounds.

"The good doctor told you to aim for our hearts," the tsarevna said as she turned to kiss her hell-spawned brother. "Come, my love, flesh of my flesh. Shall we away?"

"Indeed." He turned to face the failed regicides who stared at him, uncomprehending. Smiling now so that his long canine teeth reflected the torch light, he said, "The color of your revolution is red. I find that blessedly ironic, for under my secret reign your future shall be redder than blood." With that his shape—and that of Anastasia—began to change, to darken, to shrink. With the last of his remaining human form, he whispered, "We fly to Omsk, my sister, my lover. The White Army is amassing troops under the command of Rear Admiral Kolchak. Surely *he* will welcome and protect the last of the Romanovs!"

The bloodlovers transmogrified into dark, leathery shapes—huge bats that beat fleshy wings to propel their demon forms into the Russian night. Toward the east. Toward a crimson dawn.

White Terror

Rick Hautala

Distant gunfire made soft popping sounds in the frozen winter night. After a lifetime of conditioning as a soldier, Markku Lahti crouched down in the deep snow. Beside him stood his master, Baron Johan Linderman, wrapped in a heavy fur coat that hung like a cloak from his wide shoulders. The Baron remained standing, his shoulders erect as he scanned the night-drenched forest. The distorting echoes from the forest made it difficult for Markku to get a direction on the gunfire, so he stood up again. He looked for telltale muzzle flashes but saw none.

When more shots rang out, he ducked low again and, turning to the Baron, smiled thinly.

"An ambush," he said.

"Do you know who's slaughtering whom tonight?" the Baron asked. His voice was tinged with a cool, aristocratic disdain that, even after so many years of serving the Baron, Markku found mildly irritating.

"Does it matter?" Markku asked wearily.

He watched the puff of steam that was his breath hover for a moment in front of his face before it dissolved into the darkness. He also noticed that, whenever his master spoke, no such evidence of warm breath appeared.

"True," the Baron said. "Their blood is just as red, whether they're Red soldiers or Whites who are dying out there." He nodded solemnly, then beckoned to Markku with one hand. "Come."

The deep snow tugged like a surging tide at their knees as the Baron led Markku across the small, moonlit clearing and then deeper into the night-drenched forest. The snow around them glowed eerily blue with dense, moon-cast shadows. The trees of the old forest rose like narrow, black spindles. They towered with a dizzying perspective against the frozen, star-sprinkled sky.

The sporadic sound of gunfire grew louder as the Baron and Markku made their way through the forest. Probing fingers of cold wind tugged at their coat collars, but the Baron seemed not to feel it.

How could he, Markku thought to himself, when he's already dead?

When they saw a small yellow flash from up on the low hill ahead, followed by a soft *crack* sound of a rifle, the Baron signaled for Markku to take cover.

"I can manage from here," the Baron said, smiling wickedly. His eyes glowed eerily in the darkness as he ran his tongue over the curved points of his extended canines.

Although Markku knew that, with his master's Tzimisce blood coursing through his own veins, he was much stronger than any mere human, he himself was still mortal, so he took cover in a snow-filled gully and watched as the Baron dissolved like mist into the night.

As Markku waited, the wind howled mournfully around him, swirling snow between the trees and carving out jagged, scalloped drifts and ridges. The sound filled him with a deep sense of sadness as he recalled that winter night so many years ago when he had first met the Baron. He cursed himself—as he had so many times over the intervening years—for allowing the Baron to turn him into the monster that he had become—a slave to the powerful vampire. But even now, Markku couldn't stop himself from licking his lips as he imagined the warm, sharp taste of blood that he would receive from his master if his master fed tonight.

And Markku had no doubt that his master would feed.

So far throughout the winter of 1918, the hunting had been very good. In January, civil war between the Communists and Imperialists—the Reds and the Whites—had broken out in Finland. Black-cloaked Death stalked the country. On occasion Markku found it almost amusing to think that the poor farmers and peasants who lived in this area on the Hanko Peninsular had no idea that his master, the Baron Johan Linderman, was simply one of many manifestations of Death. Before the winter was over, they would see and experience many other forms of death, including plague, starvation, and much worse.

The gunfire continued in intermittent bursts, cracking like whips in the night. The echoes rolled and faded away like distant thunder into the darkness.

Shivering inside his heavy coat, Markku was filled with a gnawing tension that might be hunger… or thirst… as he waited. The long minutes seemed to stretch into an eternity, but eventually he saw a dark, cloaked shape moving through the trees toward him. Hands trembling, he slipped his pistol from the holster at his side, in case it was an enemy soldier on patrol. Before long, though, he recognized his master's looming silhouette.

"It is the Reds who are dying tonight," the Baron said, delicately wiping his upper lip with the tips of his fingers.

Markku saw that his master's face was streaked with gore which looked like a thick wash of black ink as it dripped from the corners of his mouth and down his chin.

"But, as I said," the Baron added with a soft chuckle, "it doesn't really matter. Their blood is red… and warm."

Moving soundlessly, the Baron stepped closer to Markku. Placing both hands on his shoulders, he drew him closer.

"Come," the Baron whispered with a breath colder than the night wind and reeking of death and decay.

He raised his right arm and pulled back the sleeve of his coat to expose a thin, white wrist. Using the long, curved fingernail of his left forefinger, he made a delicate incision along the inside of his wrist. Dark liquid issued from the vein, bubbling up like hot tar. Markku felt the Baron's right hand take hold of the back of his head and begin pressuring him forward as he raised his arm to Markku's lips and said, "Drink... Drink, my friend... "

✠

Firelight flickered in the dining hall of Suommenlina, the stone fortress located on an island in Helsinki harbor. A half-dozen upper echelon members of the Baron's Tzimisce clan had gathered that evening, as they did every evening, to feast and to talk.

Chairs upholstered with crushed, purple velvet lined two of the walls. In the center of the room, manacled together, stood half a dozen young men, all of them soldiers wearing the ragged military clothing of the Red Army. Beside them, also chained together, stood three young peasant women—girls, really—who whimpered like frightened animals, which, Markku knew, was exactly what the Baron and his guests considered them. The girls clutched each other desperately and looked fearfully around the room as if they could read their imminent fate in the leering glances of the Baron's guests.

Standing at attention by the doorway, Markku heard a soft rapping from without. After excusing himself from the Baron, he walked down the long, stone corridor to answer it.

The instant he opened the heavy wooden door, a frigid blast of wind blew snow into his face. Through the sudden flurry, he saw a thin, white-skinned man, wearing a heavy fur coat and the kind of fur hat the Russian Imperialists once favored.

"Good evening," the man at the door said in flawless Russian as he bowed deeply. "I have urgent business with the Baron. May I enter?"

Waving the flurry of snow away, Markku looked past the man to see how he had arrived but saw no evidence of horse or carriage. The nearly full moon shone down on the castle's battlements, touching the granite edges with a vibrant, blue fire.

"Your master is expecting me," the man said as he regarded Markku with a long, steady stare.

Markku instantly recognized the hypnotic gaze of an aristocratic vampire. Bowing low and sweeping his hand in a graceful gesture, he said, "Please, your grace. Enter."

After hanging up the man's snow-dusted coat and hat, Markku led the new guest down the long, dimly lit hallway to the dining hall.

"How may I introduce you?" Markku asked as they paused outside the closed door. He could sense that this was a man who stood on ceremony.

"I am Count Yugo, from Romania," the man said sonorously. One corner of his mouth curled in a slight sneer as though he found conversing with a mortal repugnant.

Markku opened the door and led the Count over to his master just as one of the Baron's guests—a general named Urho Salminen, wearing the uniform of the White army—was making his selection. Taking one of the captive soldiers by the arm, General Salminen embraced the young man firmly and then quickly twisted the man's head back to expose his neck. Without any hesitation, the general opened his mouth wide and sank his fangs into the man's throat.

Only for a moment did the Red soldier resist. His legs thrashed, and his body twitched wildly as the lifeblood drained from him, but before long, he lost all strength and slumped into the general's arms. The general fed greedily.

The other guests continued talking amongst themselves, barely taking notice of the sudden attack that had occurred. The peasant girls were too stunned, too horrified to make a sound while the other Red soldiers, their eyes gleaming more with unspoken terror than hatred, stood stoically by, watching as their comrade died.

"Master," Markku intoned as he indicated their new guest with a flourish of his right hand. "May I present to you the Count Yugo, from Romania."

"Count Yugo!" the Baron called out jovially, his face instantly lighting up with pleasure as he rose from his seat to shake the Count's hand. "So, we meet at last. Come. Come. Sit. You must be exhausted after your journey."

Count Yugo maintained the thin sneer on his upper lip as he bowed stiffly to the Baron.

"Tell me. How is your uncle, Count Dracula?" the Baron asked eagerly.

"Well, I hope? It's been years—almost half a century since we've seen each other."

With a quick wave of his hand, the Baron indicated that he wanted the Colonel seated next to him to move to another chair to make space for his social better.

"My uncle is well and sends you his best regards," Count Yugo replied in a dull, nasal monotone.

Without another word, he took his seat beside the Baron. Sitting with one elbow resting on the plush chair arm, he stroked his narrow chin as he surveyed the captives chained in the center of the floor. Markku saw and recognized the lustful gleam that sparkled in the Count's eyes.

"I see that the spoils of war are treating you very well, Baron," the Count said, letting a thin smile curl his upper lip. His face looked pale and waxy in the flickering firelight.

Knowing that everyone in the room was either a vampire and trusted ally or else fated to die soon, the Baron smiled in open acknowledgment.

"Indeed," he said. "The war against the Communists has given our Tzimisce clan a rich opportunity. We would be foolish to let such… such riches go to waste. Wouldn't you agree?"

Count Yugo said nothing as he continued to gaze at the chained prisoners. Having finished drinking, General Salminen let the drained body of his victim, still manacled to the living, slip heavily to the floor. As he walked back to his seat, he took an embroidered silk handkerchief from his breast pocket and gingerly wiped the blood from his mouth and chin.

"We have much to discuss," the Count said, leaning closer to the Baron and whispering in his ear so only he and Markku could hear. "Perhaps, after you and your guests have quenched your thirst, we can retire to your private chambers to discuss… certain matters."

"Are you not thirsty after so long a journey?" the Baron asked, leering wickedly at the Count.

Yugo flickered a quick glance at the Baron, but, like a magnet, his gaze was immediately drawn back to the prisoners. His eyes fastened on one of the peasant girls—the most attractive of the three—who had a healthy scarlet hue to her cheeks. Her blue eyes stared back at him, shimmering like ice.

"Yes," Count Yugo said, speaking hesitantly. "Perhaps I shall indulge my hunger."

Moving with a smooth, liquid grace, he rose from his chair and walked over to the trembling girl. She whimpered and shied away from him when he reached out with both hands and caressed her face with the tips of his fingers, then ran his hands down the length of her neck. The other girls squealed and shrank away from him, tears streaming down their faces.

"Beautiful... so beautiful," Yugo whispered as he brushed the girl's long blond hair away from her slender neck and studied the pale, white skin. In the firelight, it looked as smooth and hard as polished marble.

Suddenly the Count grasped the back of the girl's head firmly, twining his fingers in her hair so she couldn't pull away. The girl looked too terrified to resist, but she screamed when the Count flicked his tongue out lasciviously and brought his face closer to hers. Her eyelids fluttered as she fainted dead away, but the Count caught and supported her in his arms as he nestled his face against her throat and punctured the skin with his elongated canines.

A loud, gulping sound filled the room as the Count drank greedily. Standing behind his master, Markku was nauseated by the sudden savagery. The other women were all screaming shrilly, but the Count seemed not to notice, so lost was he in blood ecstasy. The other women tried to pull away, but even combined, their strength was no match for him.

"Good, healthy peasant stock," the Count called out to the Baron over his shoulder, laughing as he released the girl and let her drop to the wooden floor. It was the first time Markku heard anything close to emotion in the Count's voice.

The girl wasn't dead. She appeared to still have plenty of blood left in her, but apparently the Count's immediate thirst had been slaked. His complexion looked less pale, his face less gaunt as walked back to his chair next to the Baron and sat down. A cruel smile touched his lips as he watched the other girls shrink away from him as though fearful that they, too, would provide a meal for him. One of them was kneeling down, tending to the unconscious girl.

The Baron watched his new guest with a steely remove for a few seconds and then, with a flourish of his hand, called out, "Come, friends. Let's all dine."

Moving as one body, the Baron and his vampire clan got up from their seats and rushed the manacled prisoners. For the next several minutes, the room was filled with the sounds of futile struggle and the greedy slurping noises the vampires made as they feasted.

Watching from the corner of the room, Markku was filled with disgust. He understood his master's desires and, having tasted vampire blood, could tolerate them, if not accept them, within moderation. But this wholesale slaughter of bound and helpless prisoners sickened him even though it was an event which had been a nightly occurrence for the last two months in Suommenlinna.

After watching his master and his guests drink, Markku retired, shaken, to the adjoining room. Alone in the darkness, he sat down on the cold, stone floor and blocked his ears with his hands, but even that wouldn't completely muffle the sounds of death issuing from the dining room.

✠

"My master will see you now," Markku said later that night as he opened the door leading into the Baron's private study and stepped to one side to allow Count Yugo to enter before him.

"Come in. Come in," the Baron called out as he waved a hand in greeting and rose from the plush leather chair behind the desk.

A fire was blazing in the stone-lined fireplace on one wall, its light casting a radiant orange glow over the rich, mahogany furnishings. Three of the walls, including the one penetrated by the door, were lined with ceiling-high bookcases. The fourth wall was taken up almost entirely by a multipaned window that looked out over the battlements to the wide Baltic Sea. A short distance across the water glimmered the city lights of Helsinki.

Yugo nodded politely as he entered the room, but he waited until the Baron had invited him before sitting down in the chair to one side of the desk.

Standing at the door unnoticed, Markku eased the door quietly shut and took up a position to one side of the door. He was often present when his master met with his guests, especially when there might be a threat of trouble. Markku was curious why Count Yugo had come here and what his urgent business with the Baron might be.

"I know that you didn't travel all this distance just to sample the thick, red blood of these northern people," the Baron began, laughing heartily as he glanced over at Markku.

The Count regarded him with a narrow, steady stare. Even in the firelight, his face had a smooth, white pallor, like marble. He glanced over at Markku, as if asking permission to speak in front of him. The Baron waved his hand causally and said, "You may speak freely."

"To get directly to the heart of the matter," Count Yugo said after clearing his throat, "I bring a word of caution from my uncle, Dracula, and the council of the Inconnu."

"Caution?" the Baron echoed, sounding slightly amused by the notion.

He sat back down behind his desk and, steepling his fingers together, narrowed his eyes, studying the Count carefully.

"Ever since this civil war began," the Count intoned, "you have been ostensibly fighting for the Whites."

The Baron nodded curtly.

"Of course," he said. The firelight made his eyes sparkle with energy. "We have fought long and hard against the Communists this winter. And—yes, to save you from a weary recitation of events in this country, I have instituted several camps, particularly in the southern sections of the country, to detain the Red enemy which, after much bloodshed on the battlefield, we have reduced in great numbers."

"Indeed," the Count said, his face implacable.

"Your uncle and the Council should be happy that we are striking a solid blow for the aristocracy," the Baron said. "After what happened so recently in Russia… "

He let his voice trail away, but the silence that followed was meaningful.

Scowling slightly, the Count nodded his understanding; but Markku could tell that he was not satisfied with the Baron's answer.

"There is a grave concern, Baron, that you are exploiting this situation and using it as an opportunity to expand the influence of your clan and, more importantly—and dangerously, in the opinion of some—your own personal power and influence within the Kindred."

"Is that your opinion?" the Baron asked, leaning forward, his eyes hooded.

The Count didn't reply, but Markku noticed that he was the first to break eye contact.

"I am merely a soldier, doing my job as I see it," the Baron said.

"You must understand, sir, that I do not judge you myself," the Count said, choosing his words carefully. "I come as an emissary for my uncle simply to ask you to attempt to curb your depredations."

"My depredations?"

The Baron's leather chair made a loud creaking sound as he stood up. His eyes flashed dangerously.

"This is *war*!" he said in a voice as hard as steel. "There are, as you say, many *depredations* on *both* sides."

Again, Count Yugo nodded his agreement, but before he or the Baron could continue speaking, Markku stepped forward.

"If it please, your grace," he said, bowing humbly. "Permit me to add my voice to that of the Count's."

He fixed his gaze on his master, almost withering under the merciless stare his master gave back.

"I have been advising you for some time now, master, that day by day, the situation here in the south is gaining international attention."

Before he could continue, Count Yugo turned and glared at Markku for the presumption of his interruption. His black eyes glowed with a dark fire that frightened Markku into silence.

"The Inconnu will not stand quietly by if what you are doing here draws attention to the existence of the Kindred," Yugo said, ignoring Markku as he turned back to the Baron.

"Are you threatening me?" the Baron asked pointedly.

Count Yugo sniffed with laughter and shook his head.

"As I said, I am merely a messenger, nothing more."

"Well, then, perhaps the *messenger* could use a little... friendly persuasion so he can see it from our perspective."

Before the Count could respond, the Baron reached below his desk and pressed a button that caused a hidden panel in one of the bookshelves to slide open. The Count turned to see a shallow niche revealed in which a young woman was chained, naked, to the stone wall. Her long blond hair flowed like silk across her breasts, and her pale blue eyes were wide with terror. Her mouth was open, but the only sound that came from it was a faint whimper.

"I have no intention of challenging the decisions of anyone in the Inconnu," the Baron said softly, smiling as he watched how eagerly the Count's gaze fixed on the captive woman. "But there are... *opportunities* here. Opportunities that someone in my—and your—position would be foolish to ignore."

For an instant, the Count's shoulders stiffened. Markku watched as he turned to face the Baron, eyeing him cautiously. He could see that the Count suspected this was a trap, but hope flared inside him that the Count's words would carry weight where his had not.

"I, too, have no intention of defying the decisions of the Council or the instructions of my uncle," Count Yugo said. "The concern among the Inconnu is that your actions are drawing undue attention to our kind, and that it is foolish and dangerous to be so... blatant in the face of world opinion."

As he said the last word, he turned his head again and looked at the woman, bound by iron chains to the wall. Her breasts heaved as she struggled futilely against her restraints.

"She is yours, if you want her," the Baron said, lowering his voice to a murmur that was as soft as an ocean breeze. "She and dozens... hundreds like her are all yours for the taking."

The Count lowered his gaze. Gripping the arms of the chair in which he sat, he shook his head in adamant denial. But even as he did this, the

Baron saw the tip of Count Yugo's tongue flick like a serpent's as it ran across his pointed fangs.

"Perhaps you will find it more rewarding to join with me," the Baron whispered, his voice low and seductive. "There are, as I said, opportunities here that your uncle and the Inconnu know nothing about."

Markku cringed to see that Count Yugo was still staring at the young woman, unable to tear his gaze away from her soft, blood-filled flesh.

In a sudden rush of motion, the Count leaped from his chair and ran to her. Balling her hair up in one hand, he yanked her head back savagely and sank his teeth into her exposed throat while his other hand caressed her breasts. For several minutes, other than the snapping sound of the logs burning in the fireplace, the only sound in the room was the greedy, slurping sounds the Count made as he drained his victim of blood.

Markku stood by the door, staring at his master. He was filled with a loathing and despair when he saw the supreme satisfaction in his master's expression. He realized now that his secret communications with the Inconnu had been futile. By the time Dracula realized that their messenger had been seduced into the ranks of the Baron, it would be too late.

The entire nation of Finland would be bled white before the Baron would stop, and his clan was the most powerful of the Kindred.

✠

The cloying stench of death hung like a dark shroud in the air as great tongues of flame from numerous bonfires reached into the night sky. Beyond the concentration camp, marked by a tall metal fence topped with rolls of barbed wire, stood the dark, brooding forest. Armed guards patrolled outside the fence with German shepherds on leashes and watched from the towers placed at intervals along the perimeter of the camp.

The Baron strode boldly through the prison camp with Count Yugo at his side and Markku following a few paces behind.

It had been five weeks since the Count's arrival in Finland, and in that time, the slaughter of prisoners and peasants alike had increased tenfold. This camp on the Hanko peninsular was one of many.

All around him, Markku could hear the low groans and whispered prayers of the dying. Everywhere he looked, he saw the blank, hollow eyes of the dead, staring at him accusingly. Corpses of men, women, and children were piled head-high, waiting to be thrown into the gaping pits that were being scooped out of the frozen ground by other prisoners. The work continued, day and night. Many of the living had the same empty stares as the dead, knowing on some deep level that soon enough they, too, would be covered over with a thin coating of frozen dirt. Some of the bodies in the heaps of corpses still twitched as if reluctant to let the last shreds of life slip away, even in such misery and pain.

"It's hard to determine what's killing them fastest—the fighting, the flu epidemic… or us," the Baron said, laughing heartily as he clapped Count Yugo on the shoulder.

The younger vampire smiled as he wiped a trace of blood from his mouth with the back of his gloved hand. He nodded, but not for a second did his eyes stop scanning the ranks of prisoners. It seemed to please the Baron that Yugo was already scouting for his next victim. In the time since he had joined his clan, the Baron had told Markku that he was apprehensive that Yugo's cooperation and loyalty were no more than a ploy by the Inconnu to entrap him and bring about his downfall.

But he seemed no longer to have any doubts about Yugo's easily swayed loyalty. As the Baron had promised, the feeding here was good. Yugo looked considerably healthier than he had on his first night in Finland.

"Your underlings may be satisfied with this… this fodder," Count Yugo said, his lip curling into a sneer, "but I find that far too many of these people are weak and malnourished. Their blood is thin and doesn't come close to satiating my… *deeper* hunger."

"What can you expect in a time of war?" the Baron asked, shrugging as though helpless. "There is so little food throughout the country."

"I expect that," Yugo replied disdainfully, "as long as there is blood to drink, I will be satisfied."

Markku, who had been listening to this exchange, suddenly interrupted.

"If I may be so bold," he said tentatively. "Perhaps what you need is to hunt."

Both the Baron and the Count stopped short and turned to face Markku. Their faces glowed orange in the firelight. For a moment, Markku feared that one or both of them were going to strike him for his impertinence; but after a lengthening moment, a sly smile spread across the Baron's face.

"Perhaps my thrall is correct," he said, licking his lips.

Placing his hands on his hips, he surveyed the camp. It was a horrible scene, like a glimpse into the pit of hell. Vampire soldiers bearing rifles prodded the emaciated prisoners who were digging the mass graves to work faster. All of the prisoners had strips of cloth tied across their faces in an attempt to block out the terrible stench, but many of them dropped to their knees and vomited. The vampires, on the other hand, seemed to luxuriate in the stench of death that surrounded them. In the last several weeks, hordes of vampires had joined the Baron's clan.

"Perhaps that is *exactly* what you need, Count. You lust for the thrill of the chase. This—" He sneered as he waved his arm to include the vast expanse of the prison camp and its miserable occupants. "This is all too easy."

"It's not that," Count Yugo said. "The blood here is too scant, too thin. I need... *richer* blood."

"I know a place not far from here where there are healthy, well-fed farmers," Markku offered. "I could take you there tonight if you'd like."

He looked back and forth between the Baron and Count, still afraid that one of them was going to strike him for imposing. His master took a threatening step forward, but before he could say or do anything, the Count held up his hand to stop him.

"Where is this farm?" he asked, his voice tight with emotion.

"The village is not far from here," Markku said quickly. "And I know of a farmhouse not far beyond that where the farmer and his wife have been hoarding food. They have a young daughter who's as healthy and robust as you could want."

Markku smiled inwardly when he saw the lambent glow that brightened the Count's eyes as the tip of his tongue played hungrily across his lips.

"No, this is foolish," the Baron said, glaring at Markku. "We have everything we need right here."

He grabbed the Count by the arm and tried to lead him away, but the Count shook him off and turned to face Markku.

"How far away is this farmhouse?" he asked, unable to mask the rising excitement in his voice.

"No more than twenty kilometers by car," Markku said.

"How do you even know of this place?" the Baron asked, eyeing Markku suspiciously.

"I found it last week, when I went into the surrounding villages to requisition food for the camp," Markku said before turning to face the Count directly. "I thought of you, Count, the instant I saw this young woman. She struck me as the kind of woman you seem to be… attracted to."

"We will go tonight! Right now!" the Count said, turning to the Baron.

Markku could see that his master was caught in a dilemma, wondering if he could depend on Count Yugo's loyalty if he denied him what any vampire considers not only his right, but essential to his continued existence.

"You yourself have told me that we should be more discrete," the Baron said to the Count. "These prison camps are one thing, and they are starting to gain international attention. If we begin to prey on the countryside, our existence will be even more likely to be uncovered."

"Peasants die all the time," the Count said casually, doing a poor job of masking the scorn in his voice. He turned to Markku and, grasping him by the shoulder, said, "Bring the car around. We shall leave immediately."

✠

Markku was filled with a tight, winding tension as he drove the sleek, black limousine along the rutted dirt road. The twin circles of light from his headlights bounced and waved about like searchlights sweeping the head-high snow banks and dark woods beyond. Above the black line of trees, the sky was luminous with stars. A thin, crescent moon rode low in the west, indicating that dawn was only a few hours away.

In the back seat, the Baron and Count Yugo sat quietly. They had spoken little throughout the long drive to the village. Their silence only made Markku all the more nervous. He had not expected his master to come along. The Baron's presence changed things, but only slightly, Markku decided.

He knew exactly where he was going because he was heading toward the village where, nearly forty years ago, he had been born and raised. Even after all these years of war and darkness, he recognized every hill and valley, every tree and stone. A deep sense of loss and regret filled him, and it spiked every time he glanced into the rearview mirror and saw the Count and his master, sitting silently in the back seat, their forms almost lost in the darkness except for the animal gleam in their eyes.

Markku had to drive slowly because the road was in such disrepair, but a half hour or so out of the village, he saw the farmhouse across the field and slowed the limousine to a stop. He turned off the headlights but left the motor running.

"There it is," he said, leaning forward and pointing out the passenger's window.

He heard the creaking of leather in the back seat as the Baron and Count Yugo looked to where he was pointing. Against the dusty backdrop of the night sky, the farm was a small, black block with only a single pinpoint of light in one window. A plume of smoke curled like a gray ribbon from the chimney and dissolved into the frosty night air.

"Wait here," the Baron said as he opened the door and stepped out onto the frozen dirt road. A numbing draft of cold air swirled like water into the limousine, making Markku shiver as the Count got out on the other side and shut the door quietly.

Markku watched as the two vampires moved, as silent as phantoms, across the snow-covered field, heading toward the small farmhouse. A rising expectation filled him as he watched, both dreading and hoping for what would happen next.

He soon lost sight of the Baron and the Count, so he could only imagine what happened when they arrived at the farmhouse. He kept glancing at the sky to the east, fearful of the coming dawn. After what was less than fifteen minutes, but which seemed like an hour or more, a sudden bright glow filled the windows of the farmhouse.

A jolt of panic shot through Markku. His first thought was that his master and the Count had set the house on fire after slaughtering the inhabitants, but as he stared at the glow across the field, Markku saw the front door of the house open. A dark shape came outside and stood, looking down at the road.

Markku gripped the steering wheel tightly and wanted to cry out as he watched the figure raise an arm and wave to him. Clasping the collar of his coat tightly around his neck, he opened the car door and stepped out into the night. A wild shiver raced through him as he started out across the field. The thin crust of snow broke with every step, crunching loudly beneath his feet.

"Hurry," a voice called out in Finnish. It rang in the night like a gunshot, echoing from the distant woods.

Markku increased his pace, but the snow was deep and kept tugging at him, slowing him down. His breath burned in his lungs. When he exhaled, clouds of steam left his nostrils and mouth, obscuring his view of the farmhouse until he was close to it.

"We have them," the man in the doorway said excitedly, "but they are not quite subdued."

"Lord save us," Markku said as he burst into the house, his eyes open wide as he tried to take in the scene in a glance.

The Baron and Count Yugo were lying on the ground with long wooden stakes protruding from their chests, pinning them to the dirt floor of the farmhouse. The Baron's arms and legs thrashed about wildly, scraping up the dirt and raising clouds of dust that glittered in the firelight while the Count lay stiff and still, like a corpse laid out in a coffin. Around them stood a ring of five men, all squat, muscular Finnish peasants armed with an assortment of long knives, pitchforks, and wooden clubs. Their low brows shadowed their eyes as they looked at Markku. Beyond the men, an elderly woman and a young, attractive girl huddled beside the fire.

Their faces were as pale as death. They each clutched a crucifix to their heaving breasts.

"You missed his heart," Markku said angrily as he leaned forward and stared at the entry points of the stakes.

He found it almost impossible to ignore the steady gaze of his master as the Baron reached up feebly with a clawed hand and tried to grab him. The Baron's face contorted with fury and pain.

"It was dark," said the farmer who had greeted Markku at the door. He shrugged apologetically. "We had to strike fast."

"I realize that," Markku said, "but unless the wooden stake pierces his heart, he won't be totally paralyzed. You obviously have only grazed this one's heart."

"Traitor," the Baron said, his voice strangled and raw. A thick, bloody foam ran from the corners of his mouth, staining his coat collar.

The insult sent a charge of anger flashing through Markku. He found it much easier than he would have expected to look his master straight in the eyes.

"No, Baron," Markku said, trembling wildly as he spoke. "It is *you* who is the traitor."

"Release me… this instant," the Baron growled, "or else… you will taste… eternal sting… of death."

The Baron's body trembled violently as he tried raise his arm, clawing at the air.

"You will… need to… drink," he rasped, but Markku smiled grimly and shook his head.

As much as his master's gaze entranced him, he filled his mind with thoughts of the horrors for which his master was responsible. As much as he was a slave to the terrible drink he obtained from his master's veins, he knew that—even if it cost him his life—he could not permit the slaughter of his countrymen to continue.

"I wasn't the only one who tried to warn you," Markku said, indicating the catatonic Count with a curt nod of his head. "I contacted the Inconnu and asked them, pleaded with them to find a way to make you to stop, but—obviously—they considered you already too powerful to act directly. So they sent him."

"And it… didn't work," the Baron gasped weakly.

"It didn't work because he was weak. He gave in to his own weakness," Markku said.

"No," the Baron said. "He gave in to… my… power because the… the power of life and death… is the only true power."

Uncontrollable tremors shook the Baron's body. His eyes glazed over with pain as a flow of thick, black blood from the wound in his chest ran to the floor and soaked into the earth.

"No," Markku said coolly, only vaguely aware of the others standing around, watching all of this. "You were seduced by that power, too. You couldn't see what was happening—the danger you were bringing down on yourself and all of the Kindred. You wouldn't listen to me! I tried to make you understand that what was best for my country was also best for you and the Kindred."

"You… still… need me," the Baron said, sounding weaker. "You will… need to… drink."

"No. I won't," Markku said levelly. "I have a new master now."

"But you… must… " the Baron wailed, his body thrashing violently from side to side. Several of the men stepped forward, weapons raised, ready to strike if they had to.

"We merely have to wait for dawn to finish what we've begun," Markku said to them. "As soon as the sun comes up and shines through the window, he and the other will be destroyed, and all that he has done will be at an end."

The house was filled with silence as Markku and the other men waited and watched. Every now and then the Baron would renew his efforts to break free, but it was futile. Beside him on the floor, Count Yugo lay still, his eyes wide open and staring at the ceiling. Markku knew he was still conscious and that, were he not paralyzed, he also would be fighting to escape.

After what seemed like a torturously long time, the sky to the east began to brighten. Long, slow minutes passed until—eventually—a line of bright light touched the eastern horizon. As the strong, steady light of dawn shone through the window, a thin line of sunlight fell across the two bodies that were staked to the dirt floor. A low, sizzling sound filled the farmhouse as trails of foul-smelling smoke began to drift up from the exposed bodies of the vampires. The Baron let out a horrible cry of pain while the Count lay silent, his eyes clouded with pain beyond endurance.

With a silent nod to the occupants of the house, Markku pulled up his coat collar and left by the front door. As he was walking down to where he had left the limousine, he tried to block out the shrill screams that carried across the wide, snow-swept field; but try as he might, he couldn't. They rang out in the frigid air, feeling like spikes being driven into his ears.

Shaking like a man gripped by fever, Markku got into the limousine and started it up. He backed the car around and, as he drove away, tried to console himself with the thought that it was now truly over. The orders of Count Dracula had been carried out. The deaths of the Baron and Count Yugo would hopefully be the last that his country would have to suffer.

But as much as he tried to convince himself of this, Markku knew in his heart that he was wrong.

The civil war was a product of forces much larger than him, forces which were outside of his or anyone else's control—even Count Dracula's. The slaughter on both sides would continue, as would the epidemic and famine. Hundreds if not thousands more people in his country would suffer before winter was over. The most Markku could content himself with was the thought that he had at least done what he could to stop it.

As the morning sun rose higher, touching the tops of the pine trees with a bright orange glow, Markku felt a powerful sadness grip his heart. He licked his lips, thirsting for the drink that his dying master had offered him, and which he had refused.

Gripping the steering wheel tightly, he pressed down hard on the accelerator, smiling with satisfaction as the limousine's powerful engine revved higher and higher.

The trees lining both sides of the country road sped past him in a blur as Markku forced the limousine to go faster and faster. The chassis bounced and rattled over the rutted dirt road, but he paid no attention to it.

Up ahead, he knew, was a sharp corner. He didn't slow down as he approached it. Instead, he stepped down on the accelerator, pushing it all the way to the floor. Markku let out a wild scream just before the limousine careened into the forest. It slammed to a stop when it hit the thick trunk of a pine tree.

The impact propelled Markku through the windshield, but as the engine exploded and flames lapped up from under the hood of the car, it was with sightless eyes that Markku Lahti, his body broken and sprawled across the black hood, looked up at the dawn that was stealing slowly across the clear, blue morning sky.

Avenging Angel

Doug Murray

"They say he's coming here next!"

The assertion spread, and, within an instant, whispered conversations wafted through the quiet darkness of the Bey's crowded seraglio.

"They say he's seven feet tall!

"With manhood to match!"

"And such hunger!"

Cackling hens! Tsigrine sighed. *Always gossiping about something!*

Sometimes even idle gossip hides a kernel of truth, Tsigrine. The words seemed to be whispered into her mind. *You should understand that better than most!*

The dark-haired girl stiffened. *Durga Syn?* Her mind broadcast the query even as her eyes searched the shadows. *Is that you?*

Who else would look for you in such a place, child? There was the suggestion of quiet laughter.

What are you doing here… Tsigrine peered around the corner of her cubicle, looking for the face of the old Kindred. *In the land of the Turk?*

I might ask the same question. A vision floated through Tsigrine's mind, a vision of pain and humiliation. *In the past, you suffered much at the hands of the Turk.*

Tsigrine's mind floated back, set suddenly adrift in time. She had been young then. So young…

It had just turned spring, the first warm and sunny day after a long, cold, mountain winter. She had lived in a small village then—one scarcely worthy of the name—just a meager collection of huts built together for mutual warmth. But to Tsigrine and her brothers, it was the whole world!

"…Race you to Lech's tree!" Bela laughed as he screeched out the challenge, already winging his way across the field with an impossible lead.

"That's not fair!"

I was fourteen then. The girl in the harem shook her head sadly. *Fourteen…*

Tsigrine stamped her small foot as she shouted after her brother. "You're cheating!"

"Don't be mad, little sister." Mircea's hand fell on her shoulder. "He knows he can't win any other way."

The girl whirled to face the older boy, face twisted. "Then he shouldn't make the challenge."

"You're right." Her big brother nodded, then shrugged. "But how are you going to convince *him* of that?" As she considered an answer, his face suddenly lit with a huge smile. "Come on, if you want competition, why don't you race *me* to the tree!"

Tsigrine glared at the tall form for a moment, but was unable to stay angry in the face of his good spirits. She sucked her cheek for a second, considering, then ventured a shy smile. "Will you give me a head start?"

He nodded.

"All right then." She stared at him a heartbeat longer, then pulled up her skirts and began to run. "Catch me if you can!"

Those were the happiest days of my life, Tsigrine realized.

They were about to end.

She raced toward the tree, but before she got even half the way, she noticed shadows at the edges of her vision. *I thought it was Mircea, caught up to me already*, Tsigrine remembered. *Would that it had been.*

The shadows turned into riders. Big men with long spears and dull, dented armor.

Turks.

"Father!" Tsigrine shrieked as one of the men rode across her path. He used his leg and the shoulder of his horse to knock her to the ground, leering as he ran hard eyes over her long legs and athletic torso. She tried to scramble to her feet, but before she could rise, the soldier rolled his leg off the side of his mount and dropped to the ground right next to her.

"So!" He reached down, his callused hand closing around the soft upper arm of the terrified girl. "There *is* booty—even in this godforsaken backwoods!"

"No!" But her pleas meant nothing against his strength. In an instant, she was pulled to her feet, arm locked in the man's iron grip. Tsigrine tried to fight, tried to kick the man, tried to pull free.

It was hopeless. Then…

"Let her go!" Tsigrine's shocked face turned to find Bela, eyes wide with anger, hurtling toward her captor, a wooden pitchfork held tightly in his hands.

"Oho!" The Turk's right hand dipped to his belt, came up with a long, curved sword. "The little bird has a defender!" He held the sword up. "And with such a weapon!" He never loosened his grip on Tsigrine as he stepped forward, sword scything across the throat of the youngster.

Bela stumbled forward, makeshift weapon slipping from arms that had suddenly lost all their power. His eyes went wide with surprise as he fell to his knees, hand fumbling toward the flow of blood spurting from his throat. Tsigrine could only watch as his life drained into the fertile ground.

The soldier grinned as Bela finally crumpled motionless to the earth, then pulled Tsigrine closer, swordhand reaching for her bodice.

There was a sudden roar from behind—and Mircea was there, smashing at the Turk's head with a rock-filled fist. The armored man, shocked at the suddenness and savagery of this new attack, was never able to bring his sword into play. Mircea didn't give him a chance, just smashed at the man's head and face, over and over, until finally, features pulped beyond recognition, the man dropped limply to the ground.

"Come on!" The boy hissed at his sister, eyes searching for other soldiers. "We've got to get out of here!"

"But Bela... and Father... "

"Forget them!" Mircea pulled again. "We must... " There was a buzzing sound, as if hornets had suddenly surrounded them.

Then Mircea was falling to the ground, three short bolts protruding from his back.

Tsigrine found herself frozen as if in ice. Unable to run, unable to even look up as more of the Turks surrounded her, pulling at her clothes, pushing her to the ground...

I have not forgotten what the Turks did to me! Tsigrine stood to her full height, eyes fiery now as they searched the seraglio for Durga Syn. *I will never forget what they did to me.*

Then why, the mental voice hesitated. *No. We have not the time for that now.* Another hesitation, then, as if a decision had been made: *I carry an urgent message—and request—from the Lord Dracula...*

Lord Dracula! Again her mind reached back across the years...

Bloodied and bound, Tsigrine had been forced to watch as the soldiers slaughtered the other members of her little village. They spared no one else, taking only Tsigrine with them when they marched back into the mountain wilderness that surrounded Transylvania...

They kept me always naked, led me like some animal with leash and collar. Her mind hardened. *Subject to the lusts of each of them...*

When they finally returned to Turkland, she found the Court of Murad II no more comfortable. *They made me a slave. Servant to their bodies and their appetites.* Tsigrine's mind darkened for an instant. *Turkish appetites...*

But her beauty was never marred, and, such being highly valued in the land of the Turk, she soon found herself a concubine in the harem of the Sultan.

Where she first met the younger son of the Dracul...

He was so young, so lonely...

So is the one called El Aurens!

What have I to do with him? Again Tsigrine searched for the old one. *She must be nearby*, she told herself quietly. *But where?*

Foolish girl! The chuckle came again. *I would never allow myself to fall into the hands of the Turk—and never into one of his harems!*

Don't judge me, old one! Tsigrine's eyes burned. *I have my reasons for being here. Besides*, she looked around, still searching for the old woman. *What is the alternative? Sure death in that white hell of a desert?!*

So that is the way of it...

Aye! Tsigrine's mouth set in a hard line. *This War has cut off all civilian water traffic to the continent—and you know the reasons for not going overland.*

And so you let the Turk have you again!

Again...

Tsigrine had soon learned to hide the hatred she felt toward her captors. The floggings had taught her that much—but she still searched for a way to escape, a way to regain her freedom.

A way to get revenge!

It consumed me, she remembered. *Sat like a hot coal in my belly.*

Then I met the Dracula...

The young prince was not like his brother. Tsigrine had already met Radu—and been forced to serve his lusts in the dark recesses of the Harem. *Dracula never seemed to notice the harem—or the ways of the flesh...*

The younger son of the Vlad spent his time learning what there was to learn—and finding ways to torment those who were his captors. Until Tsigrine caught his eye...

He knew I was one of his people—and that knowledge gave them something they could use against him...

The young Dracula had made sport of his teachers, and his captors, aware that the Sultan would not allow any harm to come to his person.

But Tsigrine wasn't protected by the Sultan—and there were many ways of punishing a man.

I would gladly have suffered any agony for his sake, she realized. *But he would not allow it—not when he saw what they were doing to me.*

That night would always be seared into Tsigrine's memory. She had been dragged from the Harem, taken by palace eunuchs to a dank room under the central fortress. There, what little clothing she wore was torn from her and she was bound with her wrists attached to a hook. Before she could breathe, she was hoisted into the air, where she swung in tight circles, pain already starting to fill her muscles and tendons.

That was not enough for the Turks. They tied her feet with thin cords, then pulled her feet out straight and tied weights to each of her toes.

Tsigrine began to sob as the pain racked her body, growing steadily worse as she hung there, her shoulders stretching toward dislocation.

Then his teachers brought the young Dracula in—and forced him to watch as they brought out a long lash and began to whip the helpless girl.

"This is *your* fault!" The chief instructor told him, letting Tsigrine's screams punctuate his words. "This is the punishment *you* would have earned if you weren't under the Sultan's protection."

Tsigrine's screams grew louder, more hopeless, as the lash continued to tear at her, again and again.

Young Dracula watched, eyes hard—but he didn't say a word.

"She will be punished—in worse ways than this," the teacher told the young man. "Every time you break one of our rules."

The lash kept falling.

"Do you understand, young Dracula?" The Turk nodded toward the writhing body of the girl. "*She* will suffer—and we will make *you* watch."

Dracula nodded—and the lashing stopped.

He never said a word to me…

But he remembered. Tsigrine caught a wry smile in the words. *And he did what he could to repay his debt to you.*

Tsigrine remembered that as well. It had been years later. The young Dracula had long since left the court, and Tsigrine had received no more punishments for him—although there were enough of her own to endure. She had made enemies at the court—Turkish enemies—and they enjoyed heaping pain and humiliation on their helpless enemy.

Then Lord Dracula had come.

And it was a good thing for you he did!

Tsigrine nodded her head. It had been a terrible night. The "head girl" of the Harem had been executed for treason—a common enough occurrence in a court which was noted for its intrigue—and the new favorite of the Sultan was consolidating her position.

And she hated you!

The new head girl, Tsigrine searched her mind for a moment, *What was her name?* She couldn't remember. *Ah, well, she died many years ago.* Tsigrine smiled a hard smile at *that* memory. *And whatever her name was, she did not die well.*

She decided to rid the harem of any "subversive" elements. The old voice showed a hint of amusement. *Like you.*

Tsigrine's lips pursed. *Like me.* And being Turkish, the new head girl wasn't content to merely kill her enemies.

You ended up in that room again.

The torture chamber. Tsigrine had screamed for what seemed like days as the eunuchs tormented her. First with floggings, then the lash, then hot coals.

I was sure I would die there, she remembered.

And you would have, Tsigrine heard the certainty in that voice. *If Lord Dracula hadn't wanted you saved.*

That salvation had come suddenly, without warning. One moment, the eunuchs were amusing themselves, placing heated coals on Tsigrine's naked breasts, the next they were lying on the rock floor of the room, their heads almost separated from their bodies.

A *man* stood in their place.

"Who… " Tsigrine's vision was blurred with the tears of pain, but the man looked familiar.

"I am Vlad Dracula." Strong hands tore away her bonds. "And I have long owed you a debt."

"Lord Dracula," Tsigrine tried to stand, found she lacked the strength. "You… you must leave." She gathered all her strength. "Great danger… "

"Not for me, child." He bent closer to her, touched his lips to her neck. "And soon, not for you either."

He gave you the kiss.

Tsigrine nodded. *Yes.*

Without *the Blood Bond.*

Another nod.

True freedom.

Tsigrine's eyes searched the room once more. "Until now."

Until now.

Tsigrine sighed. *What would he have me do?*

✠

His Arab fighters called him 'El Aurens'. He had come to Derah hoping to free it from the Turks.

And lost his own freedom instead.

The Turkish Bey had caught sight of him as he roamed the streets—and, although the man had not for a second recognized a British Officer in the tattered rags before him, he had seen something else.

A vessel for his lusts.

He thinks I'm a Circassian, Lawrence told himself, huddling in the tiny cell they had thrown him into. *A light-skinned Arab.* A giggle escaped his throat. *Can't let him know otherwise.* The giggle got louder. *Although what difference it would make, I don't know…*

The Bey had ordered Lawrence stripped, then, when the Englishman refused to do what the Turk ordered, *although I was tempted—very,* ***very*** *tempted*—had ordered him flogged and imprisoned.

The giggle came again. *It's like public school all over again!* Then he shifted slightly—and gasped as the wall rubbed against the welts on his back. *Only more so.* He looked around his cell, searching for a way out. *Sheriff Ali will be waiting for me.* He nodded his head once, let the certainty fill him. *All I have to do is get out of here.*

The giggle grew louder still. *Maybe if I just do as the Bey wants.* It almost escaped from his lips. *After all, when in Turk-land…*

The cell door opened and Lawrence found himself facing a shadowy figure.

"You are the one called El Aurens?"

Lawrence struggled to his feet, wincing at the pain in his back, sudden fear lancing through him. "No, Effendi, I am a mere… "

A hand grabbed the front of his torn robe, pulled him, with shocking strength, out of the cell. "We don't have time for that."

Lawrence found himself face-to-face with a woman, her face painted with the cosmetics of the harem. "Who… "

"Later," she turned away, and Lawrence saw her kick aside the body of one of his jailers.

That's the Turkish Sergeant! Strange feelings flooded through him. *He was the one who used the cane so expertly*. The giggle came back to the surface. *Too bad…*

The woman glided through the rest of the guard house, heading for the office at the far end. "Follow me."

"Where are we going?"

"You have a friend waiting outside."

Sheriff Ali! "A friend?"

The woman turned, eyes glinting. "Don't play stupid with me! I know who you are—and I've already paid a price to get you out of here."

Lawrence looked around the guardhouse, he saw three, *four*, bodies. "A price?" *I didn't know I had supporters in Derah.*

"Yes." The woman reached the office. "This one's life." She lifted a lifeless body from the desk there. Lawrence saw the dark features of the Bey.

Too bad, he thought. *It might have been interesting*. He forced the giggle down deep inside himself. *A bit painful, perhaps…*

The woman sighed, staring at the dead eyes. "He was no trouble at all." She cast a knowing look at the Englishman. "Only liked boys—especially those with light skin." She dropped the body. "The next one might like women." She shrugged. "I'll just have to retrain him."

"Just who are you, Madame?"

The woman looked at him, eyes suddenly bottomless pools of night. "I'm the one who saved your life." She blinked, and turned away. "Now you have to do your part."

"And what is that?"

She opened the door. "Get out of here." She motioned to the solitary figure standing outside. "And win this war."

"I'm afraid I can't do that." Lawrence stopped next to her, face apologetic. "I don't have the power...."

"Not the whole war." She shook her head. "Only this part of it—the war in Arabia." She smiled, and he saw drops of blood still clinging to her lips and teeth. "The war against the Turks."

He nodded, pushing a hand through his unkempt blond hair. "Kill the Turks." He glanced back into the room, settled his robe more comfortably on his welted and bleeding back. "Yes, I'll be happy to do that." He reached out, took her hand. "And where may I find you?"

"You won't." She smiled as he kissed her knuckles. "You'll never see me again."

"Pity." He gave a smile of his own then—a genuine smile. "After meeting you, all other women will seem so dull."

She shrugged. "Do you really care?"

His smile widened. "Not really." He stepped through the door, waving at the figure of Sheriff Ali.

✠

You have done it!

Tsigrine gave the ghost of a nod. *Yes.*

Lord Dracula will be pleased.

Good. Tsigrine sat on the edge of her bed, taking a deep breath, savoring the smell of the Seraglio.

Do you plan to stay here? There was shock in the voice.

Why not? Tsigrine lay down. *It's quiet here—and dark enough.*

But the Turks!

There are many ways to kill one's enemies. Tsigrine smiled. *Lord Dracula taught me that.*

But the battle…

I have survived battles before. Tsigrine smiled. *I will survive this one.*

And El Aurens?

Just another man. The smile vanished. *Not as much of a man as some.*

I don't understand you.

What is there to understand? Tsigrine stretched like a cat, letting her muscles relax one by one. *I am Inconnu—I observe, like Lord Dracula.* She closed her eyes. *And while I observe, I take my revenge.*

But how?! The voice was puzzled now. *How can you take revenge while being used by your enemies!*

There are many ways to kill a man. The smile returned. *Sometimes it is enough to kill the spirit.* Tsigrine's teeth glinted in the silky darkness. *And what better way to kill a man's spirit than to first belittle, then drain his manhood.* Tsigrine relaxed into the bed. *Then, when the spirit is dead...* she shrugged. *The body follows at **my** leisure.*

The voice did not reply.

It's a sweet revenge. The smile grew wider. *Almost Turkish, don't you think?*

The harem was quiet except for Tsigrine's triumphant laughter.

Revolts in the Desert

Susan Shwartz

Lawrence had been unlucky when Jemal's train had blown up. Unlucky again, that was. Sometimes, his band of Bedouin was spotted; sometimes, timers failed: this time, a chunk of hot metal had blown free of the boiler, landed on his foot, and broken it. Rest was out of the question; and the thing ached now as if some Turkish inquisitor had driven a wooden spike between the bones of toes and arch.

Lawrence stumbled, then took another step, spreading out his toes in the chilly Syrian mud for greater purchase. And greater pain.

So damned many damned pains. Not a day in this wretched campaign dragged by when Lawrence didn't suffer another ache, break, or bullet. He forced himself not to mind, or at least not to show he minded. The Arabs needed a leader; and he, counterfeit that he was, must play the part. *Play the man, Master Ridley, they said before they made him a martyr.*

Outside the hollow land of Hauran, Lawrence said his farewells to Tafas, a chief too well known in Deraa to venture in with Lawrence to survey the place. The boy Halim took their ponies and headed off to Nisib. They waved as his form grew tiny, unfocused in the watery November sky, then blurred out of sight.

If Allah or whoever willed it, Lawrence and Faris would meet up with him there. As bedraggled as Lawrence—it was a fine comedown from the Meccan splendor of Feisal's gift-robes to him to these Haurani rags—he was an eminently respectable companion for him: old enough to be Lawrence's father. Lawrence's father was Sir Thomas Chapman, who could not bequeath his son even so much as a legitimate surname: Faris would do as a surrogate in this visit to Deraa.

Deraa was the junction where three lines of railway met. It would be easy enough, even pleasurable, for Lawrence and his band of Bedouin sappers to destroy them one by one, watching the track curl, the train derail, the Turks buzz out, easy prey, like bees from a smoked hive. But to take or destroy the junction—now, that could be called art. That was, of course, assuming warfare could be called an art; and he was no Sandhurst officer to dispute the whys and wherefore of it.

Lawrence's wet robes clung to his legs, mudstained as if he had rolled in camel's dung. He longed for the hot cleanliness of the deep desert, even the hardships of the attack on Aqaba—not this Syrian muck that made his feet slip and ache as he fought to walk further and conceal the everlasting pain. The mud was cold, and his foot was broken. He might have this damnable limp the rest of his life, which, if he had to run and could not, was likely to be nasty, brutish, and even shorter than Ned Lawrence, his mother's fair-haired bastard boy, himself.

Faris gestured, grinning in his gap-toothed jaw at the railway.

Boom! and the hollow of Hauran would fill with fire like a crucible with red-hot metal. Mutely, Lawrence shook his head. Spreading their toes once more in the mud, he and his companion trudged with deceptive aimlessness into Deraa, past untidy stacks of German stores, half-unrolled barbed wires, some attempt at trenches, and the latrines the Turks had dug. Another headshake at the stink of urine and dung: for a people whose baths in Constantinople rivaled those of Rome—well, *inshallah,* he and Faris could be safely out of here before sunset.

At the south end of the station buzzed the Aerodrome, a few Albatross machines uncovered, a few men lounging about. A Syrian, less lazy than the rest, ambled out to question Faris. As the elder of two seeming ragamuffins, he was the one to speak. Faris even managed to look not even mildly scandalized at the idea.

I am this old man's fool of a son, Lawrence cued himself. *I know nothing.* Still, it was a shame to leave the peasant man to answer, although he played imbecile with the skill that small farmers learn in the presence of soldiers or tax-collectors. The official temporarily at a loss, they turned to leave.

Someone shouted after them. Turkish. Trouble.

"Keep walking," Lawrence hissed. It was not unlikely in these parts that a man spoke only Arabic.

Another shout. Keep walking, as if guileless, he told himself, and suppressed a cold twinge of horror. Spread out your toes in the muck. Don't wince. Keep on going, for your life's sake, not to mention Allenby's precious war and the bloody-minded zealots who would be just as happy to have El-Aurens as a martyr as a living man.

Had Abd el Kader passed Lawrence's description this way? In addition to having a loose mouth, Abd el Kader was a traitor. God send his treachery had not outraced them into Deraa. The price on his head had reached—what was it now? 50,000 in gold? That would be wealth, even for the likes of him, assuming the Turks would pay it.

Heavy, official steps splashed and squelched toward them, catching up before he and Faris could agree upon a line of retreat, much less snatch it.

A hand clamped onto Lawrence's arm. He had always loathed being touched. Now he flinched and hated himself for the momentary weakness, in character though it was.

"The Bey wants you," the unshaved man told him. He wore a sergeant's insignia. His Arabic was poor.

Lawrence jerked his chin "go" at Faris. The older man made himself small and drifted away with practiced skill.

Lawrence looked up at the sky. The clouds were lifting, but it was getting dark. He would never make it to Nisib by sundown at this rate. The sergeant marched him into a compound that contained a few poor buildings, and several huts. With apparent idleness, Lawrence estimated the height of the fence. Even unwounded, at his height and with this foot—could he fight his way out of Deraa at all?

The sergeant pushed him into one of the huts, roughly shaped of plastered-over mud. With a final shove—never waste time on tact when you can use brute force—the man brought him up before a fleshy, heavy-set Turkish officer who sat, one leg folded beneath him, on a kind of divan itself mounded from the pervasive mud.

"What is your name?" asked the officer in Turkish.

Lawrence pasted on his best bloody-idiot grin.

With a disgusted head-shake at the stupidity of "these people," the officer repeated himself in Arabic.

"Ahmed ibn Bagr, effendi," Lawrence kept his voice soft, deferential. "From Kuneitra. A Circassian." That should account for his fair skin and for why he wore no uniform.

"A deserter?"

"But we Circassians have no military service." He let the bazaar-seller's whine enter his voice. It was, of course, the truth, which made it that much better to lie with. You gave up these little pieces of your integrity with every such ruse until, in the end, there was nothing but gas within your skin, making you a patched balloonish thing, fit only to bob in the wind until a stray bullet or truth punctured you.

The sergeant stared at him. Lawrence looked down: deliberate submission from a Circassian, who was not as bright as he might be.

"You are a liar," he told Lawrence very slowly. "Enroll him in your section, Hassan Chowish, and do what is necessary till the Bey sends for him."

"You're in for it now, my lad," a trooper whispered as Lawrence was shoved back into the outer room.

Another man snickered. "Nah, the Bey's in for it. Or in for *him*."

"Lazy son of a camel. You wonder how he gets to sleep the day away."

"Nahi Bey words *hard* at night." The men laughed coarsely. Lawrence forced himself not to flinch.

"And he can fight. Ever seen him on those night raids of his? Strong. And... " he laughed. "He has interesting ways of frightening the cattle hereabouts."

"Come on, fellow," said a third man, who, astonishingly enough, may even have meant to be kind. "The Bey isn't all that bad if you go along with him. And you do get leave. Extra rations, even, if it comes to that. You look like you could use feeding up."

"Maybe not if you're a sheep, it's not all that bad. Him, with that pale skin of his... "

The trooper gestured with his chin. So it showed under the muck, did it? A good thing Circassians were so often fair. A legacy from other Crusades so many centuries ago? Lawrence had often wondered.

"I tell you, if the Bey is pleased, if you do as you're told and please him, who knows?"

"I know one thing," said the sergeant. "If a few people don't shut up, they're going to be lucky if they don't wind up stuck ass-end down on a stake instead of... "

The idea being, Lawrence inferred, that one could desert while on leave, provided one satisfied the Bey at least once.

"But if the Bey is not pleased, then it's Baalbek and the infantry for you." The trooper gestured as if firing a Lewis gun.

Some response was clearly indicated. Since no man but a madman welcomed conscription, Lawrence grimaced. The soldiers nodded, relieved that he seemed more reasonable.

Lawrence squatted upon his haunches, eastern-fashion, and considered. Who was the governor here? He'd heard two names—Nahi Bey, also called Hajim—a notorious lover of women, or anything else he could get his sweaty hands on. There had even been the usual invidious scandals about valuable camels. So far, those anecdotes had been confined to she-camels.

Matters, Lawrence supposed, could have been worse, although he hardly saw how. Colonel Joyce had word of the district officer of Hauran, how, accompanied by 300 volunteers, Nahi Bey had attacked Es-Salt, decapitated or otherwise despoiled Arab and Kurdish children, killing 700 people, and burning their homes. The Arabs had found some of the children and the older boys impaled upon stakes. You couldn't call that a raid, not really, but an atrocity straight out of the Middle Ages of Gilles de Rais or some madman from the Carpathians.

Lawrence could all but wish his mother had had her way of him and turned him as prayerful as his eldest brother. Let Nahi Bey hear one word from Abd el Kader, and he wouldn't need a reward to turn him in. He'd do it for the sheer pleasure of the thing—assuming he hadn't greater pleasure in keeping him. Lawrence suppressed a shudder.

He glanced out of the gaping window. A wet, chill wind was blowing. The sky had turned dark: he had missed the sunset. A pity, that: it might be the last he would ever have. But there was no missing the three men whose clumsy boots tracked more mud into the mud-floored room, each half again as tall as he.

If only he had not broken his leg when he was a boy! All the growth, all the exercise programs that young Ned Lawrence had embarked on could not restore the growth he had lost. His brothers who had already died in the war were tall, as was the eldest, now a missionary, dominated by God and by their mother. Lawrence himself: He was too small to fight, except with explosives.

The troopers led him past a side gate and to a two-story house that stood at some distance from the other buildings.

Into the house and onto some battered kilims they tracked dirt, up the stairs, and into a room, heated to the point that only an orchid might know comfort, that held more gaudy rugs, a desk, an enormous coffer that might have been an improvised dressing table, a large bed, heaped with coverings, and Nahi Bey himself.

Lawrence's eyes flicked to the cluttered desk of officialdom. Weighted by a Mauser lay a letter whose Arabic script, though crabbed, looked familiar to him. Abd el Kader. God have mercy. He slumped, making himself look even smaller and meaner, and let his lips go slack as if he were simpleminded as well as weak.

Under drooping eyelids, he studied the man who sat upon the bed. He might have been Circassian himself, paler than the Turks who saluted him. His eyes were very bright; and although he was wrapped in some sort of heavy nightgown, he trembled and sweated.

Quinine, thought Lawrence, but it was hardly his place to make the suggestion. The man had to know if he had malaria. Or anything else.

The Bey gestured. *Down*. For now, obedience was the lesser of two evils. *I am a poor, stupid Circassian, Effendi. At your command.*

Lawrence sat on the floor in front of the Bey, who had uncrossed his legs.

Don't look there, between those massive legs, at what you don't want to see.

Lawrence looked up: great head, bristling hair, a kind of darkness that had nothing to do with hair, beardshadow, or eyes... their eyes met, and he was held like a mouse, mesmerized by the opaque inhuman eyes of a cobra, its neck swaying before it struck.

Look down, look away.

For your soul's sake, do not dare, a voice erupted inside his head.

This was one of the tests, one of the trials for which he had hardened himself since he was a boy. Coeur de Lion in captivity; Lancelot run mad; the Leper King, insensible to pain; the idea is not to *mind*—or at least to act as if one did not mind.

He minded. He did not look away. Glances locked, became a contest, locked again.

The Bey raised a heavy eyebrow, grunting to himself in surprise and mild interest. He gestured. Up. Turn around.

Lawrence leaned forward. If no men had been stationed on the stairs, perhaps he could make a break for it.

That was when the Bey seized him from behind, pulling him down on top of him on that too-lavish bed. God only knew what else had gone on in those stained sheets.

If he could manage to pin Lawrence beneath him... Lawrence twisted, relieved at least to know he could outwrestle the older man. His hot breath, heavy with an iron foulness Lawrence could not identify, panted in his ear, against his cheek as the Bey, to his disgust, fawned on him. How white his skin was, how soft, how fresh. He would make Lawrence his orderly. He would have the best of food, the most liberal of conditions if he would only...

Perhaps Lawrence should simply vomit all over the Bey *and* his disgusting bed, "honeying and making love over the nasty sty... " Hamlet's words forced themselves into his frantic brain, making him that much sicker. Nahi Bey's hands roved over his body, and he pulled away, thankful for that much strength at least.

He crouched at the foot of the bed, breathing hard, frantically considering his next move.

"Off," ordered the Bey. He gestured at Lawrence's lower body. "Take off the drawers."

He snatched at them, and Lawrence recoiled. Another lunge, and he might even be able to reach the pistol on the desk. Pity it wasn't of a heavier caliber that would turn even a body wound into something fatal.

"Guards!"

So much for that pipe dream.

Two men rushed in and pinioned Lawrence, forcing his arms back behind his back. Their faces wore masks of invincible stupidity: hear no evil, see no evil, speak no evil.

"Here's sport indeed," murmured the Bey. Slowly, he ripped at Lawrence's clothes. At the faint shriek of tearing cloth, he trembled with excitement. As Lawrence's upper garments peeled away, the Bey bent forward. His eyes pausing at each rounded scar from a bullet graze, healing now despite the no-rest and the cold and the wretched food. He prodded the reddest of the grazes, probed it with a thick finger; and it burned as if new. Lawrence's gorge rose. Against his will, for it was a moral, if not a physical, defeat, he looked away. There he was, captured in the Bey's small shaving glass, an insignificant cringing shabby man—nothing to write home about unless one wanted an *exemplum* to excite physical contempt. There, in the watery glass, were the too-cramped, too-much-heated room, the desk, the bed, the walls.

But, although he could feel the man's hands pawing at his shoulders and chest, tugging at the shoddy cloth, stripping him, although he could see the man, his lips distended, his eyes intent, Lawrence did not, could not see the Bey reflected in the mirror. Pure funk, Lawrence. A trick of the light, an angle of sight. Play the man, Master Lawrence, not the would-be catamite.

It was vile, what the Bey demanded, seeing that it was forced. Lawrence had swum naked at Parson's Pleasure, or when he had roved the underwater ways of Oxford. He had discussed antique statuary for hours at a time with Vyvyan, who loved him. He had sketched Dahaum in the manner of a Greek statue, sat up till all hours near him in the house at Carchemish, while the fire burned down and their voices grew softer and huskier and neither wanted the dawn to come.

He had even noted and forgiven the pleasures of his men in the desert, the available public women being so raddled and so few. Take his servants Farraj and Daud. They were innocent and without shame, regardless of the strictures that had controlled his life—although not his parents'. Five sons, bastards all of them. His parents probably still went at it every night… his mother no doubt praying beforehand… *frailty, thy name is…* oh God, oh God, this Turk's fat hands groping up his thigh…

It grew too beastly to be borne. Lawrence jerked his knee up into the heat and weight of the Bey's groin.

The man grabbed himself (could he get pleasure from that? Lawrence wondered), groaning and staggering back to his bed. His nightshirt stuck to him, outlining his body.

"Hold him, you men, hands and feet!" shouted the sergeant. The Corporal and the others grabbed hold, and Lawrence was fairly pinioned. Couldn't the Bey even sodomize someone without a crowd about? Lawrence suppressed one of the maniacal hooting giggles that sometimes came upon him at a crisis.

"You'll say you're sorry," muttered the Bey, between groans. "You'll beg for mercy before I'm through. Kiss my hand—or anything else I order."

Painfully, he reached down and took off his Moroccan slipper.

"Hold him," he grunted at the corporal. He pulled Lawrence's head back by the hair, now drenched with the chill sweat of fear, and the Bey struck him repeatedly in the face. His lip split and blood ran down his face. He could taste it, hot and acrid on his palate. The sight seemed to fascinate the Turk.

His eyes gleamed; his lips darkened and swelled with a kind of avidity that turned Lawrence sick. *Vomit all over him, why don't you?* Because there was nothing in his stomach. The Turks hadn't bothered to feed a prisoner. His last meal had been hours before he entered Deraa, and had been of such a nature as not to leave much lying about in the belly to be cast forth. He swallowed blood and bile, then looked away.

Look anywhere else. There was a letter on the writing desk, weighted by a pistol. Inelegant as the script was, Lawrence identified it—that traitorous bastard Abd-el Kader… Best not call him a bastard: *he* was a bastard. "Now gods, stand up for bastards."

This time, Lawrence *did* giggle. The Bey redoubled his attack with the slipper. Ridiculous. The man, if he knew, assuming he knew, would submit his claim for reward to Constantinople—the notorious European criminal Thomas Edward Lawrence, dead, beaten to death by a slipper—and they'd never pay him; they'd be laughing too hard.

Lawrence giggled again.

Look away again. Look at the improvised dressing table, pungent with hair oils and whatever other aids this… this sodomite might see fit to employ. (He had no wish to learn.) At the mirror…

Oh. My. God. Lawrence drew in a sharp breath so fast that the guards almost lost their grip in surprise, and even the Bey paused.

This time he had not the convenient excuses of funk, or a trick of the light, or a trickier angle of the mirror to explain away the evidence. Once again, he looked into the shaving glass. This time, he could see himself, his head jolting with the repeated blows to his face, the slipper, its sole slick with blood and spit now, striking him repeatedly… but no hand, no contorted face, no Bey at all.

What kind of creature cast no reflection?

No. Couldn't be. This was a Turk, not a demon of the penny press. This was only an enemy, not a monster.

No reflection. His hair stood up on the back of his neck, and his balls wanted to withdraw, hiding in his gut.

The foulness of the panting breath; the excitement, the hunger. You could explain them away as a severe case of truly nasty habits. You could even explain away the troops' rumors: what if their officer did sleep late, or had a taste for battlefield atrocities? Those were hardly uncommon pastimes in any army, Lawrence's own included.

But no reflection in the mirror. He had only one explanation for that, and it was right out of the type of trashy fiction he had not been supposed to read.

He wished he could pray.

The Bey followed his gaze to the mirror.

Whatever else he is, he's no fool. But then, creatures like the Bey had the reputation of being anything but fools. If the lurid stories were true, they had had years to perfect their cunning. Centuries perhaps, since Turks and Slavs, Turks and Romanians had battled it out across Eastern Europe and watered the land with blood. Perhaps some of the creatures who fought even now had ridden even to the gates of Vienna.

My God, what they must have seen! If only there were some... some nonfatal way of inquiring.

This is no time to be the Honors student, Lawrence. Play the man. And if you cannot play the man, play the soldier. Or Ahmed ibn Bagr of Kuneitra, assuming this creature will believe that.

The Turk laughed, exposing stained strong teeth—especially the incisors. They didn't look unnaturally long, Lawrence thought. A pity his observation was so... so... pedestrian. It might be the last he would ever make.

Too late. The Bey parted his lips further, exposing even more of those deadly teeth. They were stained with old blood, slick with saliva.

The Bey leaned forward, tugging Lawrence from the pinioning grips of the Turkish guard. Then he fixed his teeth in Lawrence's neck, and bit him. Lawrence felt slimy heat from the creature's mouth, then pain from incisors that tore as well as pierced, then a hotter trickle of his own blood. The Bey's body tensed, the hot breath of the Undead—and why did an

Undead breathe?—pausing in sheer rapture at the taste of the night's first blood. The suction of those lips intensified, tugging the red life from him. Explosions, like tiny train wrecks, went off behind Lawrence's eyes. He squeezed them shut.

Into thy hands... God grant that this vampire was a fast feeder.

The most horrible thing about the whole picture was not that Lawrence would die, or not, depending on how these things worked out, but that the soldiers watched. The blood in Lawrence's temples paused, drawn down and out of him by ineluctable force, the drumbeat of his life pounding fainter, slower, faltering.

Lawrence began to wilt, weakening as the blood drained from him into the Bey. He had never been one for languor or desire, never one even for love. Not of that sort. He had asked for Janet Laurie's hand, but she had been a playfellow practically from childhood; but she had promised herself to his brother, dead now elsewhere in the Great War. His knees buckled, and his eyes rolled open in his head. *Swooning in this creature's arms?*

The Bey's eyes raked him as if he were a virgin he wished to despoil. Well, make this the seraglio, not a ramshackle army depot in Syria, and you had the very image of *The Lustful Turk*, complete with virgin, and with the addition of a vampire to the original cast. If he had the strength to laugh he would have.

He tried, anyhow.

To his horror, the Bey chuckled too, and the red tide of his life ceased to flow from him into the vampire quite so quickly.

My prey has a warrior's courage at the last? A noble chase indeed. Perhaps I should consider... what can you know of courage, you... you thing, you... I rode east with my sultan against the Christian lord who bore a dragon's name. We thought we neared a forest until the stench told us it was not trees we saw, but a forest of stakes, each one with a man impaled upon it and the birds feeding. A second Rome after the masters put down Spartacus, all the slaves upon the crosses. But this time, it was Christians and my brothers alike.

We turned and rode away. Some things not even Allah commands one to endure upon jihad. *But they came in the night, they came and they caught those of us who stood on watch. Do you like it, little brother? As the blood flowed from me to my new master, I learned there was much dark pleasure in this submission—do you see? Do you savor the darkness, little one?*

The blood tide ebbed to a hot trickle. A gourmand, this Bey, demanding his victim's conscious submission as well as his blood. Since he was Muslim, a Christian prayer would not suffice, nor would a cross.

Pretend, Lawrence told himself.

But the Bey's thoughts, as much as the drain of blood, made his head reel. Think of it. He sagged in the grasp of one of the oldest spectres of Eastern Europe, the lamia of the ancient world. This creature had ridden to the Gates of Vienna with the sultan's army, had conspired in heaven only knew how many years of blood shed and stolen—and terrorizing helpless peasants was all he could think to do with all that experience?

Contempt stiffened Lawrence's knees. Oh God, something else stiffened too. Every man has strange lusts, and Lawrence's, even more than for power or austerity, was for learning. What this creature *knew*!

"So?" murmured the Bey against his throat, intensifying the flow of blood. "You fight me. Do you truly wish to fight me?" The voice took on a purr of satisfaction, a predator more than satisfied with his chosen prey.

"No," Lawrence muttered. His voice was hoarse, his mouth dry.

Incredibly, toughened by his years of self-discipline, he pulled away. He *could* pull away. He had been allowed to pull away.

Lawrence shivered in the too-hot room under the soldiers' bulging eyes. He was naked. He had lost a lot of blood. Perhaps if he tried to think of all the verse he had ever memorized... Dunbar's *Lament for the Makars* came to mind. "The flesh is bruckle, the Fiend is slee. *Timor mortis conturbat me*." A contemporary, not quite, of Malory. Think of Malory. Think of Lancelot, tempted, failing, the most perfect knight on earth, unhorsed and defeated...

He flinched and cried out at a new anguish in his flesh. The Bey had taken a rifle from one of his guards. Detaching the bayonet, he bent, and with a craftsman's intentness, pierced the flesh over Lawrence's ribs, drove the dull blade through, and twisted it, almost a cruciform twist. Blood welled sluggishly from the wound, and the Bey dabbled it over Lawrence's stomach, which spasmed and shrank in on itself.

He *played* with the blood. Hadn't the Bey ever had vampire nursemaids who scolded, "Now, Nahi, don't play with your food?"

The blood dripped down toward Lawrence's groin, an unsightly shriveled place from which he always tried to avert his eyes. The Bey's fingers followed. Lawrence felt his balls contract. No one... not ever... he knew what this was, as well as the thirst for the blood, and he did not want it.

"*God*, no."

What was left of his blood chilled. He had spoken in English. He reeled. Perhaps he had spoken too softly to be heard. Perhaps—yet another odd thing to pray for—the Bey lingered, intoxicated by blood-lust, in his own fever dreams.

The Bey chuckled, a sound more suited for the darkness of a lovers' bedroom than anywhere else.

"You must understand," he said, "that I know: and it will be easier if you do as I wish."

He reached out to touch the wounds his fangs had torn in Lawrence's neck, painting them with blood as if it were some insignia of rank.

What did he know? A moment more, and that reechy kiss, worse than Claudius in *Hamlet*, would be upon his throat. The blood would drain, and he would weaken, surrender....

What did the Bey know, or was this a bow shot drawn at a venture?

The Bey chuckled and gestured with his chin at the table, at the letter, at the Mauser serving as paperweight. What good would it have done even if Lawrence had been able to seize the pistol, unless it had been loaded with silver bullets. What sport? Perhaps the Bey allowed peasants, perhaps on very special occasions like the end of Ramadan, actually to seize that pistol, to pull the trigger, to blast him—only to see him rise from the floor and seize them. Terror must have spiced that last drink of such victims' blood.

"I know, you see," the Bey repeated.

What if the Bey *did* know? Easy enough for the likes of him to find victims. What was the creature offering besides an untidy death?

He was centuries old, centuries during which his hatred of the

Christians, especially the monster that had driven his sultan away in incontinent terror and taken and transformed him, had had a chance to strengthen and pervert itself. He searched not just for quarry but for sport.

What if such sport lay not just in destruction, but in demoralizing the enemy, breaking his spirit before he fed unto dissolution?

Lawrence met the Bey's black eyes. He fancied they were somewhat less opaque than they had been when he had waked—perhaps rising not from the too-lavish bed but from the chest beyond it—with his dual hungers. The heavy lids drooped.

And perhaps it was not enough to destroy or even to demoralize. Perhaps one must also seduce.

Lawrence looked down to the wounds upon his neck. One cauterized a wound, but what of a bite? One slashed and let the wound bleed clean. Or injected Pasteur's painful vaccines before the victim babbled, convulsed, and died, his back arching, head straining toward his heels.

What vaccine might there be for a vampire?

He shuddered again. This was not just death, but contamination. Not just contamination, perhaps, but conscription into the vampire host—just as Nahi Bey had been conscripted centuries ago. And how much better sport it would be if he had his victim's consent.

Lawrence could fight by night. In the deep desert, that was actually the best way to travel. The stars were your friend, the sun your enemy. He could fight thus, even succeed thus, with a vampire's strength; and then, by the grace of hell, he could return to headquarters.

The British army, after all, was noted for eccentrics. A man who lived and fought by night—think of it, Lawrence. Not just buggery in the British army, but vampirism. Think of Allenby at the head of an order of Knights Vampire, marching into Jerusalem—then cringing at the elevation of the Host, Popish rite though it might be. It must be easier, Lawrence thought, for the Muslims. Islam is not a figurative religion.

It would be as if Coeur de Lion turned bandit, draining England of blood as well as gold. And there was even precedent for that. Riding across the bloody fields of France, the Maid of Orleans, Joan herself, had been served by Gilles de Rais, that bluebeard, whose testimony at his trial was so frightful that the crucifix in the courtroom was covered to protect it from contamination.

Blood was trickling now from the wounds on his neck and belly. Perhaps the vampire would wait until Lawrence bled out white that way, until he was ready to plead for what life under the sun might remain to him before he died and rose as a vampire. *God, NO!*

His decision made, he stood a moment longer, allowing the Bey to think him docile.

Then Lawrence lunged across the bed—he would regret that if he failed. Sprawling where he could reach the Mauser, he snatched it up toward his temple and squeezed the trigger.

The empty chamber clicked.

The Bey laughed and plucked the Mauser from Lawrence's hand before he dropped it onto the red—the Turkey-red—Bokharas on the bedroom floor.

"Too late," he whispered, "for a clean death, little one. Come, is what I offer so bad? Think of what I have seen, even the little I have shown you… "

His lips parted, and Lawrence knew the next word would be his name.

His true name.

He jerked his chin up, which meant "no" anyplace in the Empire. "*Yok*," he said for good measure in bad Turkish. *No*.

The Bey stepped back. Again, his eyes bore that ophidian chill, though his face was ruddy from the blood he had drunk.

"Teach him," he told the guards. "Take him away and teach him everything. You will come to me, you know, little *effendi*," he told Lawrence. "You will beg me. And then, maybe, after you have pleased me well, I will grant your plea."

The soldiers tugged Lawrence's arms behind his back and dragged him against them—the friction of filthy wool against his bare, if blood-streaked skin. Must be you could not catch the contamination from blood shed in the ordinary way, or Deraa would be a nest of vampires. Interesting. God, oh God, his wounds hurt, and what would they do to him now?

"Do not keep me waiting long," the Bey commanded, a terrible parody of a bridegroom's eagerness. His voice dropped to a whisper. "English."

At the corporal's trembling bark of an order, the guards dragged Lawrence from that terrible room. With a one, a two, a three! they heaved him down the narrow staircase—head, feet, shoulders, arse, back bumping against the shabby walls until he brought up in an ungainly tangle of bloody limbs at its foot.

They snatched him up without letting him regain his feet—even dazed as he was, he might make a break for outside, not that a scrawny naked man fleeing in the Syrian November had even the ghost of a chance at life—and pummelled him while the corporal gestured at the nearest guard bench.

Stretching him over it, two men knelt on his ankles, bearing him down so that his nose pressed against the battered wood and the wound in his belly ached with every pressure on the backs of his legs from the guards who pinioned him.

The sergeant brought out a whip and displayed it to Lawrence. It was of the Circassian sort, a thong of supple black hide, rounded and tapering from about a thumb's thickness at the grip, which had been wrapped in silver (this was a *rich* man's correction device) down to a hard point finer than a pencil. It was not the *sjambok* of African horror stories, but it could be deadly.

The man flourished it as if he proposed not to bring it down upon Lawrence's back, but to thrust it up between his buttocks, impaling him like a Turk trapped by Vlad Tepes, called Dracula.

Despite his resolve, Lawrence's heart quailed within him. All the men in the guardroom laughed.

"You will beg me," he recalled the Bey's voice.

Was there worse than vampirism? Lawrence now thought. Vlad Tepes only murdered or converted. This was rape of body and soul.

The sergeant brought the whip whistling down beside Lawrence's ear, to crack upon the bench. Lawrence flinched again, this time visibly. He let the shakes take his body, praying the soldiers would think him ill. Fevered, not afraid.

"Do it, England," he recalled King Claudius' words. "For like the hectic in the blood he rages."

He was a great poisoner, that King in *Hamlet*. Had Lawrence been poisoned by the vampire's teeth and words? He feared so. A cheap clock ticked in the guardroom. Lawrence noted the time. He would measure his own betrayals. How long could he hold out until he screamed? How long until he retched? How long until he lost all knowledge?

One question he thrust from his mind: how long until he succumbed?

Again, the whip whistled down and paused so close to his back he could feel the wind of it against his spine.

The sergeant grunted. Someone grabbed his head, jerked it around by the sweat-streaked hair, and held it while the sergeant flourished the whip and brought it down.

What felt like molten wire streaked his skin. A hard white ridge, like a railway, leapt over his side, then darkened slowly into crimson.

The man holding his head grinned into his face. His breath was terrible, although not vampiric.

Another stroke, another ridge crossing the first, with a bead of blood joining the weals like a bolt driven into the tracks.

The clock ticked. Lawrence found himself fascinated with the pattern of the destruction of his flesh, which grew darker and wetter and burned like acid. Were he to succumb, were he to betray himself, it might be he doing this to others? He heard coughing from the stairwell and knew that he had more of an audience than just the gleeful, gruesome troopers in the guardroom.

He had meant to be made general and knighted by the time he was 30. Why settle for just that? Simply trade his white Meccan robes for black and he could have all, including freedom from the pain. The clock had not ticked long before Lawrence groaned, then screamed. His body spasmed and released, a freedom he despised. He cried out again, in Arabic, until, mercifully, he vomited bile and could no longer speak.

Even in the blackness of unconsciousness, the clock ticked away. Would it do so daytimes in the coffin, if he were made vampire?

A kind of spiking, rhythmic pain in his side woke him. He lay on the dirty floor in various kinds of filth. His own filth, he realized, but he was beyond shame. The corporal was kicking him and grimacing at the damage to his boots. With the latest kick, Lawrence's body bucked in a kind of release he had not expected. It left him limp, beyond pain as he had been beyond shame. Idly, he smiled at the corporal. As always at the worst possible times, he felt a fit of laughter coming on.

Taking the whip, the corporal hacked with the full length of it into his groin, and Lawrence spent the next eternity trying to scream or turn inside out. He sensed, more than heard, the Bey's dry cough and chuckle at the head of the stairs. Was this retribution for his earlier knee to the Bey's groin?

What was left of his blood roared in his ears and overpowered him.

"Shame, you've killed him."

"Him? There's life in him yet. Make him beg, *he* said," the corporal muttered. "We've got to make him beg or we'll suffer worse than him."

In the host Lawrence had cobbled together from warring tribes and Regulars, he had known of men who so hated themselves, their bodies, and their own bodies' needs that they took savage pride in degrading their bodies and offered themselves to every habit that promised degradation in the way that young fools, drunk on poetry, hurled themselves into the front lines and across into No Man's Land. Well, they, not he, should have been in Deraa. They, not he, might have had a chance to survive. They might even have relished the way Lawrence woke, from time to time, from his stupor of fever, pain, and blood loss to find himself being dragged almost apart, like a man with each limb tied to a spirited horse that was then whipped into a gallop, each toward a different point of the compass.

When the red veils of agony lifted, from time to time, Lawrence seemed to float above his body, watching with a scholarly, even a clinical eye, while they played vilely with it. Taught, no doubt, by the creature who chuckled and waited upstairs for him to be taught everything.

The veils dispersed still further, and he could see the clock. The night was passing, but dawn could never come fast enough to save him. The tugging, the prodding, the pinching faded into another tide, this one of pleasure. Detached from his own writhing, wretched body, Lawrence had not even the luxury of an inner modesty. He had been erect before his last throes.

The corporal kicked him once again and watched hopefully; but the broken figure curling in on itself was spent.

"Well?"

Only one word from above, but it halted the soldiers in their unspeakable play.

"Better hurry," the sergeant muttered. The corporal himself took a pitcher of water and splashed it over Lawrence, while the men did their best to wipe the worst of the filth from his body.

The sensation even of temporary physical cleanliness broke him. "*Aman, aman*, pity, pity," he sobbed in Arabic, grateful he had that much control left. Let them think him broken.

More carefully than they had hurled him down the stairs, they marched him back up, grasping him by the arms and forcing him upward when his knees buckled and he could no longer walk.

They dropped him at the Bey's feet, blood and water pooling in thin pink streams on the carpets.

It was finished now. It would have to be. He could be prey or he could be predator. No doubt, Nahi Bey would laugh to hear him beg to turn predator; and he might. Offer him another blow of the whip, another session down in that infernal guardroom, where his body's pleasure betrayed his conscience, and he would dare anything to escape that. He was sick at heart.

"You sicken me," the Bey hissed. "Look what you have done to him. He is disgusting—abject, broken… I am a civilized man, and you expect me to welcome *that*?"

Too broken for the vampire's appetites. Was it relief he felt or shame that such a creature, confronted with Lawrence in all his blood, rejected him as too bloodied for his bed or his table?

The vampire had drunk his blood, and he could feel the basis for its disdain. There was no sport in prey reduced to this level, no sport, no relish—and therefore no appetite. One might as well devour a poor squashed creature struck by a train and left to rot by the side of the tracks.

My God, how low he had indeed fallen, to be despised by a hungry vampire.

"You fools," Nahi Bey spoke again to the guards. "You thrice-damned fools. I expect reparation for my disappointment. You—" he gestured at the corporal with his chin. "You are young, reasonably fresh, or you might be if you had a bath. You will stay with me. Now, you others take *that* away."

The corporal paled, but gestured for the men to leave. There was nothing left to do, nothing less he could do. At some point, dawn *would* inevitably come unless the entire world were turned as far upside down as Lawrence felt himself to be. The man would want, of course, to see that dawn.

The soldiers dragged Lawrence out of the bedroom. One moved as if to kick the door shut behind him.

The other's eyes distended. "Careful," he whispered. "Do you want him to call you in there too?"

Bracing Lawrence with one hand, the trooper reached behind him with his other and closed the door as quietly as a good nurse might.

"Let's get you out of here," muttered the first trooper. "Easy does it, down the stairs." Lawrence managed to walk a few steps, but they lifted him down the others, like two men holding a child and letting it jump down from a rock onto the ground.

"Stupid bastard," said the sergeant. "Why'd you hold out that long? Made us all crazy. And now he'll pay for it." He jerked his chin in the direction of above-stairs where the corporal… don't think of it. All the men shuddered.

"He'll lose some blood. He'll go on sick call tomorrow. If he's lucky. You fool, don't you know yet that men have to suffer their officers' wishes or pay for it with worse?"

Lawrence let his head sag. *I am Ahmed ibn Bagr, a Circassian from Kuneitra. I am a stupid bastard. I damn near died. Now what?*

"Take him to the dresser," ordered the sergeant. "Then get back in here and clean up. The place stinks."

The coolness of the night on Lawrence's raw back made him shudder against the guards' grip. His eyes rolled upward in his head toward the unmoved shining stars far above him in the darkness. The night was clear, the sky vast, indifferent. It did not judge Ned Lawrence. It did not even care. It was a matter, frankly, of celestial indifference whether such a creature existed at all.

Mud splashed up as far as his thighs as the Turkish soldiers half-carried, half-dragged him across an open space and into a lean-to, a wooden shed built onto an older building. Quilts lay tumbled all about, and a man buttoned his coat as they stumbled in.

"No, not on my quilts!" cried the dresser, a wizened Armenian with sharply marked brows and clever hands. Then, he yawned.

The soldiers grimaced, swore, and commandeered the shabbiest of the quilts, letting Lawrence sag onto it, while the dresser protested in a Druse accent.

"He's all yours," they said, and left, no doubt to clean up the traces of Lawrence's degradation in the guardroom.

The dresser, yawning and muttering to himself about pigs, washed and bandaged Lawrence's wounds, with hands that were hasty, but skilled. The impersonal, impatient compassion almost made him weep again.

"Why couldn't you have played along?" the dresser demanded between yawns. "Look at the mess you've made of yourself. Look at the work you make for me. The strong do what they will, haven't you learned that yet in this Godforsaken place?"

The strong do what they will. The weak suffer what they must. Thucydides, Lawrence thought, was for reading, not submitting to. But he had been as much a victim, as much a prize for the taking as any woman who had been taken from Melos onto the Athenians' black ships.

"There's clothes in there," the dresser pointed to a smaller room, dimly lit. "Go in and get dressed. Shut the door and let me get back to sleep."

Lawrence nodded, almost in a stupor. His head ached along with the rest of him. The dawn light was filtering in through the mud-streaked window. *Did the corporal survive?* he wondered idly. It didn't matter. He was numb.

He stumbled toward the inner room. It was, he saw, a kind of dispensary. Well enough. A coarse suit of clothes hung from a hook upon the wall: dark, shoddy, and with a fez atop them that would probably get him shot not a hundred yards outside Deraa, assuming he could stagger that far.

"The window's unlatched," the dresser whispered on a huge, final yawn.

A locomotive whistled in the station. Lawrence flinched. Then, his hands swollen and clumsy, he dressed himself as the dawn came slowly up. At least the clothes were clean—cleaner than Lawrence, who would never be clean again.

Once dressed, he pottered about the dispensary, waiting while the sun came up and his enemy, torpid and sated, retreated into his day's sleep. Dispensaries could serve as armories, he thought, and chose corrosive sublimate as a precaution against recapture. This time, he would not trust to a pistol, which might be unloaded or misfire. Just one swallow...

It was as well, the Armenian had told him that the window was unlatched. He could not remain, even if he had had to kill the man who patched him up to escape. They would be waiting for him on the road, that is, they would be waiting for him if God had granted them the wits not to do something stupid. Besides, sooner or later, he would heal—in body at least; and the Bey might call for him.

And he knew that he could not hold out a second time.

Only the ruin of his white, indoor skin had preserved him this time from a submission worse by far than suicide—a submission he knew he would make.

The pain, oddly enough, had faded, replaced by a tormenting thirst. He struggled to his feet. Men lived through such ordeals, he told himself. At Khalfati, there had been that time... but that had not been half so bad, he thought. His hand came up to the wounds on his neck. The Armenian had bandaged them, but crossed himself after tending.

Lawrence pulled the bandage from about his throat. The punctures and the flesh torn up around them were even more swollen than his hands. He needed a Pasteur with supernatural powers. What he had, he saw, was a box of sulfur matches.

The trick is not to mind, he had told the other subalterns in Cairo when he had beat all the other young officers in endurance games holding matches. He struck a match and held it to the wound, managing—only just—not to whine from this new pain. Another match. Yes. Cauterize the wound. And pray that the infection had not contaminated him.

He was shaking by the time he finished his impromptu cautery, dizzy from pain and bloodloss. It didn't matter. None of it mattered. He was so battered that he would not really notice the pain of one more wound, he thought—only that too was a lie.

At least, there was nothing in his belly left to vomit up. He rebandaged his neck awkwardly, then started for the window as the locomotive whistled once again, leaving the depot. In the hubbub, he could make his escape.

Stiffly, he climbed out of the window and headed toward the village, limping from the pain in his back and within him, rather than the broken foot that had obsessed him, in his innocence—his relative innocence—of the day before. People slipped by him in the dawn, paying no notice to a slight, limping man in dark broadcloth, fez, and slippers. He supposed he looked like a Turk. God.

Someone laughed, and Lawrence flinched. What sort of Sodom was this place where men could laugh in the same town as great evils like the Bey? Did they not know what ruled them?

How should they? The Bey had not survived all these centuries by revealing himself, save as he chose. The air was damp. His temples ached like yet another wound. How he longed for the desert, the cautery he could find for his spirit in the depths, say, of the Nefud.

Men and women drew water at the wells. Water. Lawrence started toward one of the wells, then halted. He was a stranger here. They might not wish to share water with him. But the side troughs—shallow, muddied—that, they might not mind if a stranger took, he thought.

He could see his face, the blue eyes veined with red, deeply circled, shocky, in the dark water. Thank God for small blessings. His reflection wavered, making him dizzy, or perhaps it was the sunlight, which shone now in wintry earnest. He scooped up some of the water and found it sweeter than any pond at an oasis, infinitely precious, reviving him more than a draught from the Grail.

Not that he had ever been fit, but now it was certain that he would not achieve any Grail he had ever set himself to seek.

He padded toward a valley he knew to exist. Not far down the road, a road scarcely more than a glorified camel track, hidden from all but people who stumbled onto it, wound away into the distance. A hidden road. Had he only known before of its existence, he could have spared himself the entire ordeal in Deraa.

We will come back here, he thought, and I shall build a pillar of fire and skulls that the world will take note of it.

If only he had known! It would have spared everyone what they might have to confront: Lawrence, suddenly, messily dead. A funeral, perhaps, with full military honors, up to and including a stake through the heart—not to mention impaling him someplace else.

He had been contaminated, his body broken. Perhaps his cautery had broken the infection's back; perhaps not. It remained to be seen whether the vampire's infection had destroyed what judgment he had ever had.

The sun rose higher in the sky. After awhile, Lawrence saw a camel in the distance. A little longer and he could identify its rider as a Serdi, bound, no doubt, for Nisib, where he supposed he still must wish to go. He gestured the man down and was permitted to ride on the beast's haunches into the town. The ride was bumpy. It would have been unspeakable anguish to the back, loins, and buttocks of a man as badly beaten about as Lawrence, had he not known of worse.

At Nisib, Lawrence slid off the camel and managed to thank the man. Just barely, he also managed to retain his footing as Faris, who had been hiding among the Wuld Ali along the road, ran up to him.

"Ya Aurens… "

"Quiet, you fool!" he snapped, then shuddered at the Bey's tone in his own voice toward one of his own men.

"What… what happened… "

He made himself laugh without so much as an edge of mania. He made himself lie, spinning out a Thousand Nights and a Night's take of bribery and trickery. He even made Faris smile at Ya Aurens' legendary cleverness.

Legend was all he had left, and who knew how long the fates would spare him that?

Nevertheless, he was tied to the stake and needs must stand the course, as another doomed bastard had said. Unlucky man, that Scottish character. Unlucky play. Well, Lawrence knew all about unlucky plays, didn't he just?

Like Macbeth, Lawrence had lived with fear. Now, he would simply have more fear to live with. He had known lifelong that the accident of his birth, his mother's continued sin coupled with her insistence on penance, left him as twisted within as he was stunted without. Now, so what if he had cauterized the wounds inflicted by the Bey's fangs? Like any other serpent, the Bey had brought unwelcome knowledge and new fears—that the night in Deraa had not just broken him, body and spirit, but permanently corrupted his judgment. He commanded men: hearts and minds and spirits, he commanded them. How if he loosed them, and loosed them wrongly? These lands had run with blood before. The Bey remembered.

And now, so did Lawrence.

Halim, Faris informed him, remained among the Wuld Ali, arranging for their ponies' feed. Listening to Faris, manufacturing smiles that rewarded his relief, Lawrence suppressed a shudder at the new fears with which he must live. He pressed his arm against his side, where the whip had licked about it like the touch of some corrupt lover for a pain more manageable than these new fears, but the twinges made his head spin. With pleasure, God help him.

His mother was right after all. Only penance, hard work, and mortification of the flesh—again, a spasm of heat swept over him. Even penance moved him? Then he must be beyond all hope, his blood tainted by his birth, and now his mind and spirit perverted by the Bey's strategic malice. Perhaps he had known from the first, had Lawrence snatched up to corrupt him from his better judgment so Revolt would go awry and what had been a fertile crescent would smell above the earth, with carrion men, groaning for burial.

This was, as he had always known, a land of extremes. Those extremes burned in his blood now, infected by an ancient officer of a people whose history had left pillars of skulls affronting the sky from the Asian plain.

Halim came up leading their ponies. The Wuld Ali, he announced with pardonable pride, would let them and their horses go unplundered. This was, as Lawrence realized, an unexpected generosity—a gift granted not out of the charity Muslims owed their fellow men, but another homage to Ya Aurens, who deserved nothing at all but the realization with which he would have to live for what remained of his life. He might take Damascus, but the truth was what he had taken away from Deraa: that night, the citadel of his integrity had been irrevocably lost.

So Proudly We Heil!

Fred Olen Ray

Only now, looking back, I must confess it was something of a tragedy. At the time I, being rather brash and full of my own self-importance, only thought of the consequences as they applied to me directly. I was selfish. Thinking singularly of my own well-being and survival. But now, as I say, looking back, it really was quite tragic.

All I had ever wanted was to leave Europe and its environs far behind. I had grown weary of the poverty, the wars, and above all, the blasted weather. I dreamed of other lands and other peoples. I studied ceaselessly the newspapers and crumbling manuscripts in which were detailed the thrilling adventures that lay beyond the great oceans in far-off lands with humorous names. Names like *Mexico*—that one always cracked me up, to utilize an American phrase. *Hawaii* and *Miami* always brought a wry smile to my lips—just the mere mention of them.

I had heard that the glittering metropolis of New York with its brightly lit spires of concrete and glass was a city that never slept. Thousands of people roaming the streets from dusk until dawn. Eating, drinking, making the most of life. What could this be like? It sounded like heaven. A heaven for vampires.

Our family is very old and now, very distant to each other. There had never been a closeness among us. Aside from blood ties there is really very little we all have in common. In fact, had we not all been related, in some way or another, we probably wouldn't ever have spoken to each other. Families, even the oldest ones, share this same problem—just ask the British monarchy. It was, however, a problem that made my decision to leave Europe an easy and painless one. I was young and eager to explore. I was said to be handsome, though I have never seen myself, and my world had become stagnant... lifeless. No place at all for a vibrant soul such as mine. Besides, times were changing and the family never welcomed or accepted change gracefully. All save myself. I hungered for something different. Something new—dare I say—risky.

In Rumania vampires were just a way of life. An unacknowledged chess game between winners and losers. It has always been either us or them, and sometimes, both sides lost. But beyond all else, spoken, unspoken or otherwise, it was plainly just the way things were. It was also boring.

The climate politically was becoming unnerving and no one ever knew which vendetta would crop up next to feed the aspirations of the latest would-be dictator. I feared that sooner or later the family would become the next target of unwanted, if not unwarranted, attention. I was desperate to get out, and the sooner, the better.

I booked passage to this country of America, reading so many dime-novels that I nearly expected to encounter cowboys and spacemen in Times Square. I knew so little of the real America all I could imagine were streets filled to capacity with living beings. New blood in a new land, and in this I had not underestimated. I'd even read that some of the prostitutes were actually not unattractive. Being young, and with the power of hypnosis, I was certain that New York and I would make excellent, if odd, bedfellows.

On the advice of my father, who disapproved heartily of my forthcoming folly—he still cringed at the memory of his own attempt to migrate to England—I registered several large boxes on the ship and secreted myself in one of them. In the other crates I packed all of my worldly possessions that I felt might prove of value upon my arrival in the new world. Most prominent were my books from which I had learned the language to the best of my ability, although I never advanced far beyond a suitably poor B-movie accent.

A passion for detective fiction caused more than a few eyebrows to raise. I discovered later that not everyone spoke in that manner. But I got by and some girls seemed to like it.

The trip across the ocean was smooth. Truly. A few passengers disappeared, but that was hushed up for some reason. If I'm not mistaken, a few I had never even met vanished, which struck me as very strange indeed. But as I say, it was all very quickly covered up, much to my relief, and I anxiously awaited our arrival in New York.

My plan, as I saw it, was to very quietly disembark in the early morning hours off-shore, for our landing was to be during daylight hours. I figured to come around later the following evening, secure my belongings and take up residence in the tenement my father had prearranged for me through our German solicitors. It was a wise plan and one I'm glad I did not stray from. My only error, and it was an innocent, if ignorant, one believe me, was in killing the Captain before I took leave. I now wish I hadn't done that, for the consequence proved to be grim. It was in the early morning hours you understand. Everyone, even the most ardent party-goers, had retired early in preparation for our arrival and my options were scant at best.

Only later, when I attempted to claim my baggage, did I learn of the disaster that had befallen my fellow passengers. I didn't think much of it then, I didn't really care, but now… decades later I realize the dire gravity of it all. It was a new-fangled ship. A giant gaseous behemoth. The *Hindenberg*, they called it. The newspapers said it was a real mess. A real mess. Thank God I could fly….

Film Noir

Stephen Dedman

The old man sat in the back of the cinema, watching shadows chasing each other across the screen, smiling as an actor pounded a stake into a wax dummy. Nonsense, he thought, but well-made nonsense. In truth, Harker and his odious Texan friend had merely hacked at him with steel knives; when the sun had set an instant later, he'd transformed himself into elemental dust which had been carried away by the winds. The ease of his escape still puzzled him slightly—he wondered how van Helsing had been fooled by it. Maybe he hadn't; maybe he was content to have weakened him by killing his wives and placing a wafer of host in his tomb, content that he had released Mina Harker and been paupered by his fruitless quest. It had been nearly forty years before he had been able to venture forth again, and he had first ascertained that van Helsing was dead. He had been delighted to discover that neither he nor Harker had seen the end of the century. Madame Mina had ended up in the care of Jack Seward, dying in the same month as that accursed scribbler Stoker, and her only son had been killed in some futile gesture in an idiotic war.

The old man had traveled to Germany, finding suitable hiding places in Dusseldorf, but the man he chose as his agent—an effeminate petty thief named Peter Kurten—had become even more violently insane than Renfield. He had murdered several children and claimed credit for his master's victims, and ultimately received nine death sentences. Germans, the old man reflected, were wonderfully *thorough* people; even during his own political career, he had considered one execution per offender quite adequate.

His scapegoat dead, he had decided to leave Germany for Paris. The hunting had been good, and the women attractive, but Parisians were suspicious of foreigners and fond of garlic. The old man walked out of the cinema and bought another ticket. Nonsense it was, and the actor playing Dracula scarcely resembled him, but the heroine was as delectable a woman as he had ever seen, even lovelier than the trio playing his wives. "This—show," he asked, in his archaic French, "when was it made?"

"Last year."

The old man—Vlad, Count Dracula—nodded. "And where?"

"Hollywood."

✢

"—from Hitler himself, saying how much he liked my performance, and offering me a job with the Reichsfilmburo. I replied that I thought Germany wasn't large enough for *two* talented mass murderers."

"And promptly fled the country?" asked William.

Laszlo nodded. "Well, everyone else was doing it." He glanced across the cafe, and blinked. William turned his head. "What is it?"

"The old man who just walked in—mustache, no neck. Do you know him?"

"Not to speak of. They call him the Count. Why?"

"I think I've seen him before, in Germany." Laszlo shrugged, and turned away. Hollywood, after all, was full of expatriates; he'd been born in Hungary, while William had come from London via Canada. "No matter. But here I am playing another murderer. Aren't you tired of being a monster?"

"It's steady work," replied the Englishman, mildly. Unlike Laszlo, he'd spent ten years in stock theatre, followed by ten years playing bit parts in films, before being hailed as an overnight success. "People will always enjoy being scared. When I was broke, I used to eat out on the story of the time I met a vampire." The Hungarian's protuberant eyes bugged slightly. "Oh, I didn't know it at the time, of course; I was only five years old. To us, she was just a beautiful lady—'bloofer lady'," he said, in childlike tones with a hint of cockney, "who used to ask us to come for walks while we were playing on Hampstead Heath. A few of my friends went missing overnight, though they were all found again the next day. Some were bitten, but none died. The newspapers started calling her 'The Stabbing Woman' and 'The Woman in Black', and my parents forbade us to go out after dark. I didn't think any more of it until Dad read Stoker's book a few years later. It made me quite a celebrity at school." He glanced at his watch. "I'd better be going; early start tomorrow, four hours in makeup."

Dracula, sitting in the shadows near the kitchen door, watched the tall Englishman leave, then hid behind his menu as Laszlo cast a curious glance in his direction. He had been a regular at the cafe almost since it opened, and the waitresses knew not to bother him; he ate and drank nothing, but tipped well. He claimed to be Count Vieszcy, a refugee from Russia with a home in San Francisco, who had come south to invest in the movie business.

His first year in Hollywood—1933—had been disappointing. Lupita Tovar, the stunning heroine of the film he had seen, had married the producer; worse still, she was a devout Catholic and slept with a cross around her neck. He was unable to find any of the actresses who had portrayed his wives in the film he had seen in France, and the English-language *Dracula* had an entirely different cast. Bela Lugosi looked even less like him than Carlos Villarias had, and the actresses seemed more like sleepwalking schoolmarms than succubi. Then he had seen Thelma Todd, the 'Ice Cream Blonde', in *Counsellor-At-Law*, and been captivated. He had always had a weakness for blondes.

He looked up, and watched as she walked in, alone. As soon as she sat down, he glided over to her table. "Miss Todd?"

Todd glanced at him, seeing a dark-haired man with a bushy mustache—not handsome, but well-dressed and poised. "Yes?" she replied, her voice neutral with a hint of boredom.

"I can't tell you how much I enjoy your pictures."

She smiled sweetly. "Then why don't you go away and bring back somebody who can?"

The vampire smiled back, without revealing his teeth. "Rather than that, can I buy you a drink?"

"You look as though you could," she replied, thoughtfully. She didn't recognize him, but her staff would never have let him this near her table if he were a nobody. The longer she looked at him, the more attractive he seemed, despite the mustache and his rather pointy ears. She decided it was his eyes, which were a disturbingly deep dark green. "Mr.—"

"Vieszcy. Count Vieszcy."

"Are you a director?"

"Merely an investor."

She realized that she was staring into his eyes, and made an effort to pull back. "Look, if Luciano sent you, you can tell him to go—"

"No one sent me, and I know no Luciano," he assured her, and she found herself relaxing, even becoming mildly aroused. "And I would rather not bore you with talk of business."

"Well," she said, some warmth creeping into her smile. "What does that leave?"

✠

Thelma Todd was discovered dead in her Packard convertible that December, in a closed garage filled with carbon monoxide. She was pale, apart from drops of blood around her mouth and chin; blood also spattered her evening gown and mink coat. There were rumors of suicide, and of murder, and Dracula decided it would be better for Count Vieszcy to disappear until the fuss had died down.

Thousands of mourners filed past Thelma's casket at Forest Lawn. Several commented on how healthy she appeared; one colleague remarked, "Why, she looked as if she was going to sit up and talk."

✠

Bela staggered to the door. "Yes, yes, what you want—" and opened it to see a heavy-set bull-necked old man with a wispy white mustache. "Who are you, what you want, you know what time—?" He stopped as the old man's eyes changed from dark green to lambent red. "You—"

"You are Bela Lugosi," said the vampire, coolly. "You played Dracula."

"Yes, I… " The actor began shaking violently. "I… I did not mean… "

"You receive letters," Dracula asked. "Fan letters, I believe they are called. Many of them from women."

"Yes… yes, most of it… "

The vampire showed his teeth in what might have been a smile. "I'd like to read some of them. If you would be so kind."

✠

"Thelma Todd," said William, heavily, "has been dead for, what, three years. And if she were alive, do you know what she'd be doing? Banging on the lid of her coffin screaming 'Get me out of here!', not strolling down Hollywood Boulevard."

Laszlo scowled. "I know what I saw." He sipped at his champagne, and glanced at the clock. Only a quarter hour of 1938 remained, and he was glad of it; he had done nothing all year but Mr. Moto films, and 1939 threatened to be the same.

"An impersonator," insisted William. "A double. Someone on her way to a fancy dress party, or an audition… how many ice-cream blondes do you think there are in this town?"

"She was with the man we saw her with at her cafe that night," said Laszlo. "Count Someone, from San Francisco, the one the police wanted to question but could never find. We saw them both near Frederick's—"

"We?"

"Karen and I. It was dark, and I only saw them for a second, but I'm sure it was them…. " His voice petered out. "You think I'm crazy, don't you?"

"A little drunk, maybe. Keep this up and you'll end up like Bela."

"God forbid," said Laszlo, sincerely. He refilled his glass and walked to the window, looking out at the HOLLYWOODLAND sign. Twelve more minutes. "I saw a vampire once; a live vampire, only flesh and blood, but a monster nonetheless. Did you ever hear of Peter Kurten?"

"No."

"They called him the Vampire of Dusseldorf. Fritz and I went to his trial, to see what a child murderer was like. Of course, he was like anyone else." He shuddered suddenly, spilling champagne over his cuff, and swore.

"Are you all right?"

"Hmm?" he said, dabbing ineffectually at his sleeve. "Oh. Yes. I just remembered where I'd seen the Count before. It was at Kurten's trial; he laughed when the sentence was passed. I wanted to put that in the film, but we couldn't." He sighed, but there was a quaver in his voice. "It's nearly midnight; we'd best go find our wives, or we'll have to kiss each other."

✠

"You know," said Bela, "if it wasn't for Boris Karloff I could have had a corner on the horror market." It had become his catch-cry, dropped into almost every conversation. Hope, his fifth wife, knew better than to disagree; instead, she rolled over and feigned sleep while Bela looked through the script for *The Final Curtain*.

Suddenly, he sat up, convinced that he'd heard a noise outside. Dracula? No, almost certainly not; it had been many years since he'd received any fan mail that would interest the vampire. Throughout the forties and into the fifties, he had been reduced to taking any role he was offered—Frankenstein's monster (a part he'd turned down in 1931), stock theatre performances of *Dracula* and *Arsenic and Old Lace* (a part written for Karloff) for dwindling fees, a cape-clad straight man for Abbott and Costello and Mother Riley, cameos as mad scientists and servants in increasingly awful films directed by hacks such as Ed Wood and William 'One-Shot' Beaudine. He had not had a speaking part in a major studio film in eight years, and his closest approach to fame since then had been when the press had discovered him in a sanatorium, recovering from morphine abuse.

For a moment, he sat there, his hands shaking. "Karloff," he muttered. "Boris Karloff. He's outside, waiting for me."

✣

"Exactly what is it you expect to find?" asked William, archly.

"You can tell a vampire's grave by a hole or crack in or near it; it's how the vampire gets out. Saves them banging on the lid of the coffin." Laszlo shrugged. "Sometimes there'll be drops of blood around it, too. To make sure, you're supposed to get a virgin boy to ride a black horse through the cemetery, because the horse will refuse to ride over the grave. Hiring the horse wouldn't have been a problem, but finding a virgin in this place—"

William grunted. "And you've found such a hole near Thelma Todd's grave?" Laszlo nodded. "And you want me to sit and watch it with you? And in the unlikely event that you're right, what then? Dig her up and drive a stake through her?"

"Haven't you ever wanted to play van Helsing?" asked Laszlo, teasingly.

"Frankly, no, and at my age I'd rather not spend any more time in cemeteries than I have to—and you're not looking too healthy, either, chum."

His friend conceded the point. William was sixty-eight, and appeared older; Laszlo was sixteen years younger, but flabby and out of condition. "I'm sorry to drag you into this, but I couldn't think of anyone else who'd do it—or who could think of a good excuse if we got caught." He parked the car at the cemetery gates, and reached for his briefcase. "Shall we go?"

✣

Bela opened the door, an old revolver in his right hand, and saw a dark-haired ruddy-faced Dracula standing outside. "Aren't you going to invite me in?"

"You?" He took a step back. The vampire was silent. "Yes, come in, come in, what do you want?"

Dracula closed the door behind him, looking at the actor with something akin to affection. It was true that Bela had come to be an embarrassment, making him a laughingstock in *Abbott and Costello Meets Frankenstein* and *Old Mother Riley Meets the Vampire* and an unsuccessful Vegas revue, but at least he'd never taken to eating insects or murdering children. "Put the gun away, you know it's of no use."

"I thought you were Boris Karloff," muttered Lugosi, obeying.

"I hear you're about to make another movie for Wood," said Dracula. "*The Ghoul Goes West*."

"Yes, yes, that's right—"

"No," said the vampire. "You won't."

✠

William glanced at his watch—it was a quarter past midnight—and sighed. Laszlo had poured a flask of holy water into the hole near the grave, which he had then sealed with a paste made from communion wafers. "Couldn't you have done that during the day?" asked William, yawning.

"If I wanted to seal her in, yes. I hope I'm shutting her out."

"Why? What're you planning to do if you catch her? Hammer a stake through her heart?" Laszlo glanced at him, embarrassment plain on his fat face. William rolled his eyes, lay back on a tomb like the effigy of a dead knight, and began composing his own obituary. "Horror Master, 68, Bored to Death in Graveyard," he muttered. "A hunchbacked gardener at Forest Lawn today discovered the body of distinguished British actor—what was that?" He sat up, suddenly.

"What?" Laszlo stared around wildly, wondering if his friend was joking, then saw a woman in white walking toward them. His eyes widened, and he reached for the crucifix he was wearing around his neck. The woman hesitated, then turned to face William, who stared numbly at her. Laszlo stepped between them as the woman advanced, and flicked his fingers—

still wet with holy water—at her. One drop hit her platinum-blond hair, which began to smolder; William moaned, and scrambled slowly off the tomb.

"What do we do now?"

"I don't know," confessed Laszlo.

"What?"

The Hungarian shrugged apologetically, while William fumbled for the cross he'd given him to wear. "This is another fine mess you've gotten me into," said the vampire, in a fair imitation of Oliver Hardy. She backed away from the men and toward her tomb, but stopped when she saw that the hole beside the grave was blocked. She emitted an unearthly shriek, far more Fay Wray than Thelma Todd, and stood there as though frozen. William looked around for something they might use as a weapon, and saw an almost life-size cross marking a grave; he nudged Laszlo, and began advancing slowly toward the vampire, his cheap wooden cross held high. Laszlo blinked, then followed him, preventing the dead woman making a dash to either side. She stumbled backward before them, looking imploringly into their eyes. They guided her toward the enormous cross in a strange slow troika, a *danse macabre* for three, until she backed into the monument and her hair and dress burst into flame. She screamed again, spun around to face the cross, and tried to retreat from it—but the men held their ground, preventing her escape. It took her several minutes to burn to death, and neither man could have said he saw a look of peace cross her face.

When the pyre had died down, Laszlo turned to his friend and asked, "Are you alright?"

"Apart from a pair of fouled trousers," replied the Englishman thickly, "I suspect I'm... still alive." And he promptly fainted.

✠

The body was too badly burnt to be identified, and was assumed to be that of a suicide; the newspaper stories about it were barely longer than the obituary for Bela Lugosi, who was buried soon afterward in his Dracula costume, complete with cape and full makeup.

Dracula sat in a cinema, brooding, wondering if the time had come to leave town again. Though there was no indication that Thelma Todd's killers knew where to find him, he had relocated many of the boxes of earth he used as hiding places and begun researching other cities. Unfortunately, he would still need a human agent; a pity so few of them stayed sane....

A girlish whisper snapped him out of his reverie, and he looked up to see a beautiful platinum blonde crooning into a microphone. He smiled slightly, and sat back in his chair to enjoy the movie. Maybe it wasn't time to leave Hollywood, after all.

✠

"How the hell did you get in here?"

"I'm sorry; did I startle you?" Dracula sat on the billionaire's bed, and smiled as reassuringly as he could. "You're not an easy man to get to see."

"You haven't answered my question," the billionaire rumbled.

"Bear with me, and I won't take up much of your time. I have something I think you want very badly. What if I told you how to live forever?"

"What if I told you," the billionaire replied, "to go—" He stopped, as the vampire dissolved into dust, then reappeared on the other side of the bed an instant later. The room was silent for a few seconds, then the billionaire nodded. "Okay. Suppose I'm interested; what would it cost me?"

"The occasional favor, nothing more. You might have to stage your own death at some point, in some way that the body would be difficult to identify—a plane crash would be excellent—and you'd have to change your diet. And, of course, I'd advise against going out in the sunlight.... "

"What sort of favor?"

"I need someone to help me move house occasionally," Dracula said. "And if you still have contacts in the movie business, there's an actress I'd very much like to meet.... "

✠

Norma Jeane Baker was discovered dead that August, locked in the bedroom of her Beverly Hills home. The coroner ruled that death had been from an overdose of Nembutal, yet there was no trace of the drug in her stomach or her kidneys, nor any puncture marks anywhere on her body.

✠

William Henry Pratt, better known as Boris Karloff, died in 1969.

Laszlo Loewenstein, better known as Peter Lorre, died in 1964.

Prince Vlad V, better known as Vlad Tepes (the Impaler) and Dracula, died in 1462. His current whereabouts are unknown.

Norma Jeane Baker, better known as Marilyn Monroe, was buried in Westside Cemetery. There is a small hole in her crypt, barely large enough to admit a finger, and it is frequently smeared with something red. Maybe it's only lipstick. Maybe.

Chozzerai

Roland J. Green
and
Frieda A. Murray

The wind that three months earlier had been as harsh as a Cossack's heart and as deadly as his rifle was tonight a soft, caressing breeze. Mmm, a *mechaieh*… I stood with muscles though not senses slack, savoring one of the few pleasures left to me, the clear soft nights of spring. Ah…

The climate of my native land is less lethal to me now than it was before my change, although I had never suffered from it personally. My father, a blessing on his head, never failed to keep us in food, tea, logs and warm clothing. We were fortunate; rain, mud, snow and ice, from October through April—you could die from such a climate, and many did.

But, over my memories and the breeze scented with new life, I heard the rumble and crack of a burning building. Cursing and hastening (I had lingered in the forest, enjoying the fine night), I reached the edge of the trees and studied what lay ahead. Then I eased my way among the bystanders.

It was the rabbi's house that was burning. From what I could see, Novimislovsk's Jewish population could produce a *minyan* without much difficulty but was in no position to support a *shul*. Or, perhaps, replace one that had been destroyed previously. Men and women milled about helplessly, in a rough circle around a man with neatly curled *oavess* who had his arms around a woman and two young girls.

At least they were trying to stand between their rabbi and his enemies. What else could they do? I saw fear, resignation, even anger on their faces, but no one trying to put out the fire or even keep it from spreading.

Then I saw that three burly Russians were guarding the well, and letting no one draw water unless he or she first took a bite of bacon. The Russians themselves were liberally supplied with vodka.

Oy, Gottenyu! Dos ken nor a aoy! A soldier may become inured to wounds, but I bled afresh whenever I saw such *oraubyons* in action.

The rabbi's roof fell in a cascade of sparks and burning coals. The house stood a little apart from the rest, and tonight's breeze would not, *kayn aynhoreh*, strew sparks over the whole quarter. The small honor paid to the rabbi had turned into a not-so-small blessing.

The *bulvons* whom the roof's fall seemed to awaken, picked up their jugs and left the well, muttering among themselves. Their words I could understand, but as the Rambam said, what is base should be uttered in no tongue.

The villagers opened their circle. The rabbi bowed his head briefly, and the villagers did likewise. Then he said something I did not catch, doubtless thanking the Almighty that this *paskustva* had been no worse, even if they needed it like a mare in the *mikva*. I was too busy fighting an urge to fall upon the Russians then and there to pay close attention.

The pogrom's victims could draw water now, but only to wet down the ashes and coals. I stepped into the open, leaving my cap on so they would know I was not another goy. My tongue could not utter "*Sholem* aleichem," not then.

"I will help with the water," I said.

Those who noticed my coming at all simply shrugged. A man of about fifty, with the muscled shoulders and callused hands of a drayman, handed me a bucket.

"Thank you," he said.

We emptied buckets of water on the ruins until the streams of smoke turned to wisps of steam. Two men and a woman led the rabbi's goats out of the shed behind the house; it was only soot-blackened, not burned.

Looking about, I saw no one, not even the rabbi, guarding the scrolls of the Law. *Feh!* I wondered if the rabbi had been forced to choose between the scrolls and his family.

The villagers worked like *behaymin*; this was just another plague God had seen fit to send. I—I was so happy to be among my people again, even now, that for a few ecstatic moments I heaved full buckets of water about as if they were glasses of brandy.

I remembered to watch my strength and speed when I saw the drayman watching me. I staggered, as if from overexertion. He smiled a bit sourly, and continued cranking the buckets up from the depths.

At last the steam died. As my sight adjusted to the returning darkness, I saw that some of the villagers wore night attire under hastily flung-on day clothing. While I saw plenty of darns and patches, few wore rags. There is hardly such a thing as a prosperous Jew in a remote provincial town of "Holy Russia," but I had seen the truly wretched, and these were not such.

The breeze had died along with the fire. Smoke still hung over the narrow dirt streets, and fits of coughing had taken the place of crackling flames.

A number of sober Russians drifted up. They seemed as frightened and resigned as the Jews, but none of them offered to help. One or two gave nervous looks to the northwest, from which direction I could now hear drunken singing.

No one in authority seemed to be present. "Has there been, God forbid, cholera around here?" I asked the man next to me.

"Not that I've heard of," he said with a shrug.

A woman with red hair and slanted Kirghiz eyes relieved me of my bucket. I eased away, so that no one would notice that I did not need water. I was beginning to struggle with the need for blood—specifically the blood of those responsible for this.

Oy Gottenyu! That I should not only leave the *kashrut* but come to crave blood, and kill for it, even as the blood libels alleged. *Chillul hashem* upon *chillum hashem*! And it was no excuse that I had not known what I was doing, when I began these desecrations of the Holy Name.

My exile from my people was a gaping wound to the slow poison that is the exile of my people. How soon would the two overwhelm me, turn me into something as far from the image of God as a Russian is from wisdom! The long years of a vampire's life seemed an endless tunnel to Sheol.

Ai-ai-ai. The rumblings of the belly, which I had known in my student days when I gambled a bit too freely, were as nothing compared to what I felt now. If I did not feed soon...

I moved toward the town center. I would not feed upon the totally helpless, no matter what their blood. I fell back around the corner of a house as a pair of Russians passed.

"Smell that smoke? I think the rabbi was having ham for dinner."

"Well, it's better-roasted than even a Jew can stomach, now."

"Why' d we stop with the fire? There wouldn't've been much loot, but there's a bitch or two in the Jewish kennel—"

"—who could use some of your fleas?"

The two roared with laughter. My own was quiet. I was about to close with them when I spotted two more men in a side alley. One wore the short coat, collar and tie of a city man.

What were the authorities (they should hang by day and burn by night like a chandelier) up to now?

I stole toward the two, feeling again the ambivalence of the change. When I was human, I could not have moved so quietly, nor heard from so great a distance. And I could only have dreamed about what I intended to do next.

"My orders were to create enough of a disturbance for the governor to notice," the one in city dress said.

"But, Your Excellency—"

"Hush!"

"Do you think His Corrupt Excellency will notice? This sort of thing happens often enough."

"There will be other incidents. He will have to report. If he doesn't, it will be a clear case of neglect of duty. Either way, my department is served."

"And Russia?"

"Russia is sleeping, Sergei Igorevich. She must be awakened."

"You sound like a revolutionary, Ex— ah, sir, if you will pardon me."

"Let us say, then, that *pobybka* must be blown. Russia must awake to arms before the revolutionaries, socialists and Jews murder us in our beds. My department's task is to wake the bugler."

An agent of the Department of the Interior? Fighting my hunger, I sought the control that would let me question him—first.

Sergei turned and walked farther into town, while the agent (or whoever he was) retraced his steps along the alley. It came out on a street that led out of the town into the forest, and after a long detour through the forest, to the highway.

I followed him, hunger and purpose, loneliness and revenge driving and strengthening me.

Justice would be served.

✠

Ah…

Full for the moment, I let the agent's body slide to the ground. I could never satisfy the blood-hunger without at least brief pleasure—and tonight, having killed a man you could die from, I could *kvell* already.

Then, as always, the reaction flooded through me. How *could* I have eaten such—such—*chozzerai*? An egg with but a spot of blood was rendered *trefe*, and I had just drained a man—a body. (I had, however, killed him ritually, with one blow.)

I longed to retch. My body had its own notions; the blood remained within, filling and strengthening me. For some moments I struggled, body against brain, and no quarter given.

Finally, I was able to look up—and saw a sparely built man of middle years watching me. He had broad shoulders and fair hair, and his features had a west Slavic cast. He carried no obvious weapon and wore the garb of a petty merchant—although my night sight told me that the cloth of the coat and the leather of the boots were of better quality than such would usually wear.

Brain and body surged together. Caught like this, standing over the drained corpse, I had no choice but to kill.

I flung myself on him. I carried no weapon either, to avoid awkward questions if I were stopped by the police. Nor had I been a particularly accomplished wrestler at the university—and vampiric strength and senses will not of themselves convey a skill that one lacked before changing.

However, that strength had been enough until now. I trusted it to save me tonight.

My trust lasted only moments. It took no longer for the unknown to evade my first rush, then use a throw that brought me to the ground, where a projecting root tore my jacket and shirt, and nearly my flesh.

Somehow I struggled to my feet, to find myself caught almost at once in a wrestler's lock. *Gevalt*! This man was a far more accomplished fighter than I—

If he was a man. My strength had been sufficient to bring down far more robust prey than he appeared to be.

Then, the position of my pinioned arms brought up memories from the university.

Pavel, who had changed Anya, who had in turn changed me. The two of them, Pavel watching the door while Anya, holding me as if I were a swaddled baby in a nurse's arms, satisfied her hunger and began mine.

She had held me as if I were a babe, but I could not break her hold, though I set my full strength against her. Her fair hair and high cheekbones had been those of a Slavic Madonna, but her eyes, and her smile, as she bent her head to my throat, had been those of Lilith....

Did they still hunt, and together? Or had they turned against one another? Vampire could hunt vampire; I knew that too well to be surprised at the newcomer's actions.

My only surprise was his being here in the first place. If he was hunting, why me? If he was not, why was he here at all?

But the surprise was mine.

"Enough," he said, and threw me off. I stumbled over the root again, but this time kept my balance.

"Need either of us deny to the other what we are?" He spoke in educated Russian with a distinct Polish accent.

"My name is Asher, not Piotr," I replied.

"Very witty, for one who has just... " He gestured at the body.

Rage and shame flooded me, for my name in Hebrew means one to whom a feast of good things has been promised. But I also felt the first glimmer of curiosity.

"Who are you and what do you want, already?"

"I am not hunting you, yet." I believed him; he would have won a struggle to the death. I also remembered the "yet."

His further reply told me little about his future intentions. "In life I was Ignacze Bor-Chinevski, and I was born in 1746, the second son of my family. I was changed in Paris, in 1792—"

"And what was a Polish nobleman doing in Paris during the Terror?"

"The Revolution attracted many foreigners. It promised so much, at first. I was drawn to a country that might challenge Austria. Unfortunately, not everyone it attracted was human."

I could believe that. Since my change I had discovered more than a few of the unearthly breeds (some worse than vampires) in the ranks of the revolutionary clubs.

"In any case, I have been following you for three days."

Fear came to the fore within me.

He read my face and stance. "Not with hostile intent. With the hope of serving both you and my master, who sends me forth to find such as you."

"What am I to him—if he exists?"

I had met other vampires, not to say humans, who claimed to serve masters possessed of arcane knowledge. I had come to them a skeptic, and left a cynic.

"Tell me, Asher. How did you become one of us? Unless I am mistaken, you abhor the nourishment we must take."

I could no more fight his insights than I could his strength. If he wished to use what he learned against me, I was doomed.

Nu, he could have killed me already. Again hope glimmered—of an interesting conversation, if no more.

"I grew up in Agirevsk. My father was a shoemaker, who had the *mazel* to win a contract to supply boots to the tracklaying gangs. The supplies section ignored the fact that he was Jewish, because he delivered on time and in full.

"He gave us a secular education as well as the traditional one. I was the first in my family to attend a university, in Odessa."

I stopped. It was so hard for me to tell the rest. What could this man, who while living would have at best ignored my people, know what it had meant to me, at eighteen, to cut my hair and shave? To wear a student's cap instead of a yarmulkah? To embrace *Haskala* and ignore the strong tradition that declared secular education to be a snare of the Evil One?

Only to discover that to the *goyim* I was still a Jew, and to more sophisticated Jews I was a *Yekl*. What could he know of the loneliness that left me prey to any friendly gesture?

They were clever about it, Pavel and Anya. They weren't effusive; that would only have disgusted me. I succumbed to the friendly greeting, the lack of shame in being seen with me. And Anya, who was still human when I first met her, would take a glass of wine with me in a cafe.

They introduced me to the nihilist clubs, and for a while I found these *goyishe* skeptics amusing. But as I became surer of myself in the gentile world, I sought to withdraw. And Anya struck.

"I was changed four years ago, when I was twenty-two. I stayed at the university for another year, but finally I had to leave. My—eating habits marked me among those who had known me before, even slightly."

"So, a student nihilist learned more about destruction than he ever anticipated?"

"Ye-es. But I am immortal now. And also more deadly to my enemies than I ever anticipated."

"Immortal and deadly, but driven by a hunger that still revolts you."

I could not deny any part of that description.

He seemed to look through me to something so far beyond that it might have been in another world. "Have you heard of the Inconnu?"

I had, but feigned ignorance to draw him out. "I have heard rumors of vampires who have transcended the blood-hunger. But I have never met anyone whom I would trust to tell me the truth. The secrecy our kind—" Oh, what it cost me to say those words— "maintain—"

"—is necessary, but encourages ignorance. Yes, I know that is anathema to you. Listen.

"The Inconnu are solitary vampires, who have no taste for the self-indulgence and violence too many of us are given to. We avoid feuds with other breeds of vampire, as much as we can, and we protect our own from both human and nonhuman enemies. We encourage discreet behavior, both among ourselves and with humans. And, by experiment and experience, we have discovered many aids to such behavior, including conscious control of the blood hunger."

"And the one whom you call master—who is he?"

"I may not tell you his name. He and the Inconnu have certain purposes in common. One of them is to find those like you—gifted, changed, yet fearing or abhorring the change. Such a one often goes mad—and then we *do* hunt him, as humans would a mad dog, and for the same reasons."

I heard both hope and menace in Bor-Chinevski's words, and weighed them carefully. He offered me a way, if not back to my people, then out of a loneliness that seemed to me greater than Baruch de Espinoza's. He had, after all, been human, if outcast.

But the student clubs at the university had offered the same, at a price I learned only after I had paid it. Such might be the case here, and the price even higher.

Still, to be free of the blood hunger… I might never be a *shayner Yid*, but I would no longer be blood brother to a *dybbuk*. How was it done?

As I began to ask, I saw him cock his head, then look at the sky visible through the trees. I sensed nothing, then realized that he was the oldest vampire I had yet encountered. He might have spent as much time using his vampire senses to read the night breeze and sky as I had spent alive from birth to change.

"The ones I hear are not yet on our trail, but they outnumber the two of us," he said, his voice just above a whisper. "He," gesturing at the corpse, "was of the Third Section, so they will take his death seriously."

"I know. I questioned him first. There's quite a *mish-mosh* in St. Petersburg right now. Many of the agents don't know what's going on or who they're really working for."

"They'd better not find the body, though. If you wish, I will dispose of it for you."

"Thank you."

He bent, and rose with the body tucked under one arm. It was almost completely drained, but he stuffed some leaves into the wound to be sure of leaving no blood trail.

"I owe you for this," I said.

"Pay me by thinking of what I have told you," he replied. "Meet me behind the third birch on the north side of the high road, counting from the twenty-verst post, at sunset tomorrow."

He looked at the sky. "Now let us be off, and by separate ways. You are not Piotr, but neither are you Joshua, to bid the sun stand still. The cocks of Novimislovsk will crow soon enough."

In spite of his burden, he faded into the trees so silently that I did not notice his going until he was gone.

✠

I sat in an abandoned forester's hut deep among the pines. It was about half past four; the sun would not set for another four hours. My change was near enough behind me so that only the full sun of noon truly injured me. I could still appreciate dawn, when it seemed that the Holy One said anew, "Let there be light."

This would change, I knew, in time. *Oy-oy-oy, what* was I to do? What was *I* to do? Holy One, Source of all wisdom, look upon this miserable creature, his mother's hopes, his father's money, thrown away; his every act, his very presence, not only a disgrace but a danger to the *benim* Yisroel. Tell me, I beg of You, what am I to do?

Enough! The Holy One in His wisdom has not left us entirely without any. If it was too late for me to avoid the way of the evildoers, how far could I retrace my steps?

I could not, as I now was, join any Jewish community. *Never* would I soil my lips with the blood of any of my people, not even a murderer or a convert, *aroekh he qaluth!*

So I must live alone, or among gentiles, which was the same thing. But loneliness had brought me to my present pass. Would it lead to madness?

I thought again of Baruch de Espinoza. Outcast by the Jewish community for freethinking, he had refused to join any Christian sect that would likewise have trammeled his thought. He had survived, sane, supported by philosophy.

My case was nothing like so noble—I had merely been a *yold*. But if I could retain my sanity, what kind of Jew would I be?

Though I could not live among them, could I help my people as I was now?

I could destroy Jew-baiters and murderers.

But not all of them.

Suppose I joined these Inconnu? Would it help to leave my people entirely, to give my allegiance to someone else?

Could I do that? It was so near to being *geshmat*, particularly if this mysterious lord was or had once been a Christian. To give allegiance to Christianity, nu, there had been those of us who had found it politic, and at best, all three benefited: Jews, Christians, and converts. But to give allegiance to a Christian apostate? *Ai-ai-ai*!

Would it help my people, on the other hand, if I went mad? This they would need like an outbreak of typhus: a Jew who behaved like the caricature of the blood libels. Feh!!

Was—was suicide the best thing I could do? It is not forbidden us, but is allowed only as the very last resort, to avoid profaning the Holy Name.

But—I didn't want to kill myself. I would rather kill my people's enemies.

Then I realized the form my blood hunger had taken. Since I left the university, those who harmed my people had been my only prey. Perhaps it could be controlled, or confined, or even guided so that I kept to this path by design and not by chance....

Two hours until sunset. I would keep my rendezvous with Ignazce Bor-Chinevski.

II

Bor-Chinevski was waiting for me at the rendezvous when I arrived. This was no small surprise; Slavic nobles are not as a rule notable for their punctuality, or much courtesy toward even their own commoners, let alone Jews.

Perhaps becoming a vampire could improve a man's manners, if not morals. Or was it, perhaps, that Bor-Chinevski had served under Napoleon, who had said, "Ask me for anything but time"?

The Polish vampire spent little time in greetings and allowed me none for questions or conversation. "I have seen mounted gendarmes on the road to Novismislovsk."

"Gendarmes? Are you sure?" No doubt my skeptical tone was stronger than it should have been, but I was quite disturbed by my reception.

"I recognized the uniforms. They had sabers and pistols only, no lances or carbines. Their horses are too well-fed to be Cossack mounts, and in any case the nearest Cossack regiment is two hundred versts from here."

"So where would they be coming from?"

"The nearest Army garrison is in Nizhni Gyorgevsk."

"Why a garrison town?"

"Where else would they find a Maxim gun?"

Gevalt! Machine guns were hardly a kopeck the dozen. If a garrison commander had sent one with gendarmes, they meant serious business.

Moreover, Maxim guns could be dangerous even to vampires. One bullet, unless it is silver, does no harm we cannot swiftly heal. Twenty is another matter. We can still heal from such wounds, but they weaken and slow us. Thus we may be overtaken and brought down by more traditional weapons, such as the stake through the heart.

"I believe you, I believe you. But why gendarmes to a town forty versts up the *tsuddik* of nowhere?"

Bor-Chinevski frowned. "Did that agent say anything about sending for them?"

"No. He was working incognito, reporting directly to St. Petersburg by coded messages. He carried no papers; I told you that I searched him."

"As did I, before I put stones in his pockets and dropped him into the river. Then I scouted that part of the forest. I found the tracks of military boots. Someone expected to find our friend in those woods."

"Thanks to you, they were disappointed. So, you think the gendarmes are looking for the missing agent?"

"It makes the most sense. Forty versts to Nizhni Gyorgevsk, with the gendarmes arriving about sunset, and allowing for a telegram—the times work out."

"What will they do when they don't find him?"

"I suggest that we go to Novismislovsk and find out."

I confess that the wisdom of this suggestion was not at once self-evident. Two against fifty is formidable odds, even when the two are vampires. Nor did the Maxim gun help matters.

Yet in the end I had no choice. Had I still been human I would have killed myself to bring my people warning. Being what I was now, I could fight.

I realized that my reluctance came at least partly from having to fight beside Bor-Chinevski, even under his orders. Yet he had the advantage of years and experience, and seemed not only willing to consort with Jews, but to help defend them.

We are many times adjured to remember that a virtuous Gentile is better than a vicious Jew. I had been alone so long that I had been in danger of forgetting this.

I could survive the burdens of being a vampire, from the blood-hunger to being unable to shave because I could no longer see myself in a mirror. I could not survive forgetting the teachings of the Talmud so thoroughly that I imposed upon myself a life and death even lonelier and ghastlier than fate had already done.

"Then let us go in good health," I said.

✠

I have covered greater distances in less time, but that was fleeing danger, not dashing toward it. Bor-Chinevski assured me that it was as nothing to his adventures during Napoleon's retreat from Moscow.

"I do not know whether I would have been murdered as a Frenchman or as a vampire if the Russians had caught me," he said. "I preferred not to learn. So I covered some two hundred versts a day, when the snow allowed it."

Tonight we faced no obstacles from the weather, which in its way was a pity. A pouring rain would have made fires slow to take hold, and hidden us even more thoroughly from human senses.

As it was, there was just enough breeze to let the smell of smoke reach us three versts from the town. By mutual consent, we quickened our pace, and increased our alertness for possible ambushes.

We met none. Searching the forest, it seemed, was being put off until the gendarmes had settled with the Jews of Novismislovsk.

We found most of them lined up on the open ground between the outermost houses of the quarter and the forest. Few had more than the clothes they wore, and those few only pathetic bundles. Gendarmes moved among the houses, tossing furniture and clothing out into the streets, ripping doors and shutters from their frames, smearing dung on bedding, and generally behaving like Russians carrying out a pogrom.

I saw only three houses afire so far, but I knew that many besides the rabbi would be homeless by dawn.

If they lived to see it. I did not like it that the Maxim gun was set up at the edge of the trees, its muzzle aimed at the huddled Jews. Its crew seemed indifferent to the pogrom, smoking pipes and passing a bottle back and forth, but I knew what a Maxim gun could do against such a target as the massed Jews of Novismislovsk.

As we watched, the gendarmes' horses came into sight from the west, the horseholders driving plundered livestock as well as leading the mounts. I recognized one of the rabbi's goats, who would be stew before his master's body had cooled.

Bor-Chinevski watched all this with a soldier's eye. "No fool he, whoever commands," he whispered at last. "They came in from the west or north, then dismounted. They came into the Jewish quarter on foot, so they would have the Christian houses at their backs. Now they're bringing their horses around so they can load their loot and be gone once their work is done."

I feared to ask aloud what that work might be. But my companion would not have heard the question anyway. He was muttering to himself.

"We can't kill all the Russians. The Inconnu and the Master would both take action I would not care to face. Besides, a massacre would cry for revenge. Shame, though, is something to be hidden."

As if seeing me for the first time, he nodded. "Asher, stay here. Keep that Maxim silent."

"Killing?"

"If there's no other way. I intend to try panicking the horses. The gendarmes will have to chase them, and they may panic themselves."

"So, they would have to admit to losing control of their mounts or fleeing from ghosts? They'll never do that."

"Just so."

My reply was addressed to empty darkness.

✠

I do not know to this day if Bor-Chinevski was a shapechanger, who turned himself into a bird to reach the horses in time. Certainly he could hardly have moved as fast as he did without flying.

I do know that the first horse screamed just as half a dozen houses took fire at once. From the speed at which the flames erupted, the gendarmes must have piled pitch-soaked straw inside.

They went up so fast, in fact, that the gendarmes had to dash from the burning quarter. They were running out into the open, behind the Jews, when the first horse screamed and the others began moving.

The horses moved slowly at first, but then a second one screamed. Studying the wall of moving horseflesh, I made out a dark figure straddling one of the beasts, his mouth to its neck.

A pistol cracked. A third horse reared, then reeled and fell. Aiming at Bor-Chinevski, some *klutz* of a gendarme had instead shot a horse. From that moment, even the best-trained of the gendarmes' mounts had only one thought: flee!

Bor-Chinevski hastened their flight with unearthly howls. The horses ran faster, as did the gendarmes, and even the Jews seemed ready to risk being shot while fleeing rather than face demons by standing still.

Before any of the Jews could run, the horses came stampeding between them and the burning houses. One horse ran straight into the flames, and even now the screams are something I try to forget.

Most of the rest simply charged over the gendarmes, who were caught between the burning ghetto and the Jews. I saw one gendarme raise a pistol, then suddenly he was at least eight paces off the ground! He landed twenty paces from where he took off, and had wind if not wits left. If I ever doubted that a man could outrun a galloping horse, I ceased to doubt it then.

Now I remembered my duty toward the Maxim, and none too soon. All four men had put out their pipes and were crouched about the gun. One sat behind it, while another fed a belt of cartridges into the breech.

What I did then, I would have done without any orders. The orders made only one difference: three of the Russians were still alive when I was through, and I left the blood in all of them.

I was bending over the one I had thrown against the nearest tree, to be sure that I had only broken his ribs and arm, not his skull or spine, when a nearby shadow silently took human form.

"Well done, Asher. Any dead?"

I pointed to the gunner. "He was ready to start shooting, so I had to hurry. His neck is broken. I punched another in the jaw and a third in the stomach, but not with my full strength."

"As well. Now let us see to that pestilential Maxim."

"How?" It was the first time I had used my vampire's strength as a soldier, instead of as a predator. There was a difference, I realized.

I doubted that the gendarmes had.

"Like this," Bor-Chinevski said. He pulled a gendarme's pistol out of its holster, gripped the butt in one hand and the muzzle in the other, and effortlessly bent the pistol double.

"Or perhaps we should twist it," he said, picking up the dead gunner's wrench and bringing it down hard on the Maxim's cooling jacket. Metal tore and the cooling water gushed out on the ground.

"Now, let me see about unloading this," he muttered. "We don't want any accidents.... "

He finally settled for picking up the gun and smashing the breech against a tree, jamming the firing mechanism. I thought the tree was going to fall. Then he told me to grip the muzzle while he gripped the breech. I did so, and we twisted in opposite directions until the gun looked like a pretzel.

By the time we dropped the Maxim, we had an audience. No gendarmes—they had all prudently followed the horses—but both Jews and Russians were standing and gaping.

Some were doing more. "A *dybbuk*, a *dybbuk*," one woman wailed. I thought she could at least do us the courtesy of counting properly.

Five or six of the bolder or more desperate Russians now stepped forward. The foremost knelt in front of me and begged me not to "spoil" the village. They would give me anything I wished, if I would spare them.

This was not the first time I had been taken for a sorcerer. It was the first time I had been offered the traditional bribes.

"Share your food and your stock with your Jewish neighbors, from now until winter," I commanded, in the most imposing voice I could muster. "Help them to rebuild what you watched the gendarmes ruin.

"Do this, and you will all live. Otherwise, I need only fly over the village this winter to see you all starving."

This, you understand, was only common sense. But more often than not, it takes a marvel to persuade a Russian to show any.

Jews are keener-witted. Were they going to question a *dybbuk* who drew charity from Russians? So are Poles—at least, if they have been vampires long enough.

Ignacze Bor-Chinevski and I showed our wisdom by hastily quitting Novismislovsk.

"So, Asher," said Bor-Chinevski, as we sat in a copse of pine beside the Rivov Marsh, the least inhabited part of the country. "Have you given thought to what I told you last night? Truly, after seeing you tonight, I think you would do well in the service of my master, and strengthen the Inconnu."

"Thank you," I replied. "I believe you speak the truth, as far as you see it.

"But I remain one of Abraham's people, a son of the covenant. As I am now, I can hardly keep all the *mitzvoth*. But may I die the true death if there is not at least one of the six hundred thirteen I can freely keep!"

As I said this, I stepped back. I did not expect to be able to defeat my comrade if he attacked me, but with a little head start I thought I could outrun him.

I saw him smile. "You need not fear me, Asher. Not tonight, at least. Nor need you fear the wrath of my master. He has not forgotten that when he was human, he took vengeance on his enemies, and freely shed blood to protect those under his rule from Turks, Germans, Russians, and one another."

The smile left his face. "But you need to fear madness, and more. Some might see you, in your solitude, as easy prey. Others, I fear, retain their hatred of Jews, even after the change."

"May they fall into coffins filled with silver crucifixes at noon!" I snapped. "That is all the more reason for cleaving to my own people. And I *will* call them mine, whatever they chose to call me."

"You still face madness."

"I do," I replied. "But I have a purpose—a duty now. Protecting my people from—" I gestured in the direction of Novimislovsk. "No Jew ever went mad from having work to do."

"So, you will be a self-appointed *golem*, not even resting on the Sabbath?"

It was my turn to smile. I had ceased to be surprised that Bor-Chinevski knew more than most Poles about my people.

"Call me what you will. But I also swear that I would gladly die the true death, if by so doing I could take the hatred for the Jews with me."

"Then prepare to live long, Asher. Both before and since my change, I have seen that hatred die down, but only to spring up again. You need not fear idleness."

"No," I said, thinking of the Third Section's intrigues, the peasants' ignorance, the bourgeois snobbery and envy, "Not at all."

"Our ways part here, then," he said, rising to his feet. "Good luck."

"And to you," I said. We shook hands, then once again the darkness before me was empty.

I listened to Bor-Chinevski's footsteps heading west, until they faded away after about fifty paces. Then I turned east.

The garrison at Nizhni Gyorgevsk would bear watching, at least for the next few days.

Cam Shaft

David Bischoff

I've been in England a little while now, looking for mysteries and enigmas and freaky stuff and trying to have a vacation as well, and I guess the main mystery I've found so far is how come more of these people don't leave this stupid country. I mean, they speak English (well, sort of) and they could do all right in America if they worked hard, and if they didn't want to go to America they could go to some other okay country. Why they stick it out here is beyond me, I guess. It's a dark, dreary, gloomy, *lame* place.

Besides, it's full of vampires.

Especially in Cambridge.

So there I am at Heathrow, waiting in a long line at seven thirty in the morning, passport in one hand and my dick in the other, waiting. Shit, they do like to wait here in this stupid country. "Queuing" they call it, as in "I.Q" and it certainly is low. Nearby, Brits returning to "Blighty" just breeze on through, carrying their drugs and duty-free booze, tra la la, no sweat, and we third raters sit in line to get permission to enter this bizarre, trampled, squalid little dirt lump the Atlantic couldn't stomach. And Flowers is prattling on about how "charming" the place is and how enthusiastic she is to be here. Charming. Pah. It's cold and gloomy outside with a brittle wind whipping along Cadbury wrappers onto the runway. There's the smell of rancid pork meat from a breakfast bar along with disinfectant from the bathrooms and the air is still and humid and warm as a Mexican dungeon.

A pasty-faced guy looks up at me from a chair and asks me what I'm doing here in England, and I'm wondering that myself. It's certainly not to get myself infected with bloodsucker spit and live an eternal life listening to BBC1 Radio.

"Vacation," I said.

"And how long will you be in Great Britain?" asks the jerk, his nostrils quivering as though something was distasteful about the smell of my passport.

"A month."

"I see. And where do you intend to stay?"

"Cambridge."

"Ah."

It's funny how the Brits can draw about a paragraph's worth of meaning from one monosyllable. Flowers makes me watch some of the TV imports she so dearly loves, so I can pretty much scope out the irony. What this little bastard was really saying was a condescending, "Oh dear, another Yank come over to desecrate this royal throne of kings, this sceptered isle… this other Eden… this blessed plot, this earth, this realm, this England—the filthy rotter."

He looked me over. Maybe it was the ponytail he didn't like, or the jeans and checked jacket, the mustache and the shades. I don't know what the problem was.… I gave my pits Right Guard sprays, right after Flowers and I reenlisted in the Mile High Club, British Airways branch. People do tell me I look like a drug dealer sometimes. Hell, I'm no damned dealer… just a good customer.

"And what, sir, is your occupation?" he asks.

"Journalist."

"Ah." Meaning, Yeah. Right. "Might I see some proof of your financial means to sustain this trip."

"Oh, that's *my* job!" blurted my beloved girlfriend. Flowers stepped over and shoved a thick wad of hundred-dollar traveler's checks, along with her ample cleavage, in the man's direction. The guy raised an eyebrow and not much else, which made me positive that I'd met my first British gay. Take it from me, Flowers Brown didn't get short-changed in looks from the DNA Department of Sexuality.

"Yes, and I've got bills… and a Bank of America card."

"Right. Thanks." Brit speech has more clips than a barber shop. He took the Customs slip I'd signed, promising that I wasn't trying to import fruit or democracy to Britain. "If you'll just head through customs."

And I swear the rube must have fingered a switch on the underside of his booth, because as soon as we rolled our luggage through customs some British military sort who looked like he had epaulets on his privates searched our luggage thoroughly.

"Ah yes, then," sez Colonel Blimp. "What are these then?" pulling out a box of Trojans. I knew he knew, but he opened them up anyway, looking for cocaine or something.

Flowers shot me a nasty look. "Jack!"

"Hell, sweetheart. I think they needed them badly over here. Thought I'd make a contribution to the Commonweal, ya know?"

She examined the box. "Oh yeah," she says in her Texas drawl. "Big size. They can't be for you, can they?"

✠

I guess that wasn't exactly a great send-off for our British Trek, but then I wasn't expecting much. I didn't want to come here anyway. That was all Flowers. But like she said, she had the money and we'd gone on a Caribbean cruise last year, and the boss back at the *Galaxy* told me in no certain terms I should take a vacation.

"You're burning yourself out, Jack. We need *you* here, not some hollow-eyed zombie."

"Something wrong with my work?"

"Fact checking sucks. Grammar and punctuation take two copy editors… Hell no, same as usual, Jack." Tap of fingers on my pile of yellowing past issues of our weekly rag. "It's your researching and your ideas." He flips through a pile of my copy. "DEAD BABY NEEDS A

FAMILY... PSYCHIC HITCHHIKER TAKES A TRUCK TRIP TO THE HEREAFTER... PIN CUSHION MAN GETS STUCK ON FIRST DATE..." Tsk tsk. "Old hat. No vitality." Puff of cigar smoke into my face. "I know you love your work, but take it from me, Jack. You need to fill up the well."

When you're one of the prime hacks in Orlando, Florida for the *American Galaxy*, the premier weirdo rag on the supermarket stacks, and you're pulling down some decent money for your stories, you pretty much have to toe the line in terms of editorial dictates. What I wasn't telling my editor was that my stuff was getting kind of tired because I was busy moonlighting on my own personal project.

Hell, though, I think. I've got one of those cute little Compaq four pounders. I can whack out some pages on my time off, wherever it was. Flowers was overjoyed of course and immediately insisted on a trip to England.

And so here we were, on our way to Cambridge. Why Cambridge? Simple. That was where the UK *Blake's 7* Fan Club was based and where a convention was imminent.

Blake's 7? Sort of a 1970s Brit *Star Trek* meets Robin Hood with some cheesy special effects and class consciousness in space.

Me, I prefer *Star Trek* in its various incarnations. You watch it, you take a snooze, you wake up—you can pretty much figure out what's up. Very soothing.

But vampires, Jack. You mentioned vampires....

Yeah, well, like I say, I wasn't real thrilled with being in England. You know that feeling you get when you go into a Salvation Army Thrift shop and there are a few nice things there, but the rest is kind of ragged and rumpled and has this sour smell? Add some old architecture, fish and chips, tea and lots of discomfort, you've got England. The only thing that gave me a brief jolt of joy was the Brit tabloids, which make the *American Galaxy* look like the *New York Times*. Favorite headline comes from the *Sport*: Above a picture of some blond Diana Dors reincarnation: "British Boobs Are Best."

Believe me, in Britain, there are more Boobs than those on the Babes.

✠

"Good evening," said the tall gentleman with an East European accent and reddish eyes. "Welcome to the Cambridge Branch of the *Blake's 7* Fan club."

Flowers looked as though she was going to faint with excitement. She clamped onto the guy's hands and enthused in West Texas Obsequious. "You must be Doctor Jacob Alucard! We've corresponded! I'm Flowers Brown, from the United States, and this is my boyfriend Jack Dillon. We're here for that convention you're throwing in a couple of weeks. Figured we'd come here early to Cambridge, leave late, and soak up some culture. Jack, this is the guy I've been telling you about!"

The Doctor managed to extract his hand from Flower's possessive clutches and extend it politely my way.

The hand was long, with narrow, faintly curving fingers. Very long, pointy fingernails too. I put my paw out, shook that hand and the grip was surprisingly strong and assertive.

"Hey, Doc," I said, smiling.

"Welcome to Cambridge, Mr. Dillon. I hope that you find what you're looking for here."

This Alucard guy was old but damned impressive. He had this real strong aquiline face, with a high bridge of a thin nose and peculiarly arched nostrils. Man, talk about domed foreheads. This guy had the Houston dome of foreheads. Hair grew scantily round the temple, but profusely elsewhere. Big eyebrows. Awesome eyebrows, you know the sort of Tom Cruise Neanderthals that almost connect. The mouth, as much as I could make out, was fixed and kinda mean. His face was flushed with a ruddy health you don't see much in old timers… but his ears were pale, and pointed at the top. The chin was broad and strong, and the cheeks firm though thin. He was dressed in a dark suit and a red tie and I wondered what the hell he was doing mixed up in a TV fan club.

"Thanks. Looking for some R and R, myself." I looked around him, noticing that some of the frumpy-looking housewife fans or four-eyed computer nerds with tousled hair were holding drinks in their hands. "Say, there wouldn't be a bar nearby, would there?"

"Yes, as a matter of fact, there's one right down the corridor," said the Doctor, rolling his *R*s delicately.

"Hey babe," I said to Flowers. "You want a drink?"

"Yeah, cool. A glass of wine would be nice, Jack." She gestured toward our host. "How about you, Doctor? Would you like a glass of wine?"

"I don't drink.... wine," said the Doctor, eyes flashing with amusement. "However, please help yourself to whatever libation you find nearby." His smile got a little larger and I noticed how white and healthy his teeth were, how faintly prominent his incisors were, like a wolf baring its teeth. Looked like this Hollywood agent I used to have.

"Thanks." I liked the fact that he didn't have an English accent. I was getting plenty sick of those by now. I'd thought that Flower's insistence that I watch tapes of *The Forsyte Saga* and *Masterpiece Theatre* would accustom me to the things. No way. Unless you're listening to a BBC announcer, it's all coming at you way too fast. I figured out pretty quick that Brit accents weren't like American. We've got equal opportunity accents. In Limeyland, they go around sniffing at each other's accents, like dogs sniffing each other's assholes.

I was feeling grateful and suddenly curious about this guy. He was neat, elegant and somewhat apart from the scruffy crowd here not only in intelligence but demeanor. He had a capitalist's sparkle to his eye, not the usual tea-steamed socialist's dullness I was seeing too much over here.

"Say, Doc. What's your specialty, anyway?" I asked.

He seemed surprised but not unhappy to steer the subject away from Club Business or Video Sci-Fi.

"DNA, actually. I'm a Professor here, but my principle work is in the Hematology Labs in the middle of town. We're involved in some exciting breakthrough work there." He nodded thoughtfully. "Blood, after all, is the life."

Where had I heard that line before, I thought. Ah yes. Some 1950 monster flick. Exciting breakthrough work. Yeah. I used that all the time when I wrote up some kind of science story for the *Galaxy*. You know, like exciting breakthrough work in UFO contact. Exciting breakthrough work in Elvis DNA samples. I was thinking I should cultivate this guy—might milk him for some interesting ideas for stories.

"Say, you know, Flowers here is the big *Blake's 7* fan. I'm interested in everything, though. Maybe we could get together sometime and I can ask you about blood."

"Blood? It is my life's work," said Doctor Alucard. He examined his watch. "Ah. I see it is time to convene the meeting. Mr. Dillon, if you would care to procure your drinks, by all means do so, and don't worry about interrupting the meeting. There are always stragglers. Besides, it is a very informal affair, and we are mostly discussing details of the upcoming conference."

"Thanks, Doc."

"Don't be *too* long, hon," said Flowers, kissing my ear and giving me a gust of Liz Taylor's Passion. "And don't forget my wine."

"Sure. Tell you what." I stuck my hand into my pocket. It was heavy with British pound coins and there was a thick wad of bills, all courtesy of Flowers. "I'll get you two glasses."

She didn't seem to hear, though. She was engulfed again in fascination with the regal-looking guy calling the meeting to order. All seemed damned civilized, too: I'd expected to come seeing people dressed up in dreary versions of the costumes from the show, like some Trekkie con. They didn't even have posters of the characters pasted all over the place.

The room was a hotel function room, with reddish carpeting, and they probably got it free in return for a guaranteed consumption of booze. Or maybe Doc Alucard knew the manager. I don't know. I was gonna contribute to the former, if that was the case.

I'll give this to the Brits. They got some good digs to drink in. We were at the Central Holiday Inn (thank God—an island of Americana to cling to) and I'd already been checking out the bars. There's a pub problem of pulling in the carpet promptly at 11:OO pm—started during World War I, so munitions workers wouldn't drop the bombs they were working on the next morning—but being at a hotel, I could always go down to the private bar, open till a more reasonable two am. Anyway, this hotel had a nice bar, dark and clean, with a good, friendly crowd doing what the Brits do best: Drink.

I hopped onto a bar stool, shot my cuffs, and was feeling better just from the fumes. Mind you, I can't stomach "bitter" or anything dark, but fortunately England's recently emerged from the Dark Ages and they've actually got at least a Renaissance form of refrigeration so they can serve beer reasonably cold, if they care to. Me, I'm a Bud man, but I'll give it to the Brits. The stuff they give you is a hell of a lot stronger.

"Stella Artois!" I said to the bar man, and he tapped off a pint of the stuff for me. Something to wet my whistle, I thought, while I figured out what kind of wine I should get for Flowers.

The guy put a gigantic glass of gold stuff in front of me, and I was a happy man. A pint over here is twenty ounces tall, which means almost twice as much brew was looking at me, and more bang for the buck, alcoholwise, too.

I doled out my one pound, eighty pence, and started working on the stuff, pondering life, the Universe and the bestseller I was supposed to be working on. Unfortunately, my epic Harold Robbins potboiler was stuck, and I was getting antsy. Antsy was good, since it meant that I was yearning to work again. By the time I was back in my Orlando office, sucking on air-conditioned smog, I'd be whacking away at stories.

Trouble was (as the trouble often is in my copy-hungry line of work) I had to come up with new angles for stories.

Naturally, we often go back a few years and recycle stories. Common enough. Give 'em a little spin, like that. But you also had to throw some new shit into the mix from time to time. Here, in England, was my chance to. What should it be, though, I wondered, downing my drink. BLAKE'S 7 FIENDS THREATEN CENTURIES OLD UNIVERSITY? No. Maybe if I made them Trekkies, though... BRITS DROWNING IN MEGAPINT-SIZED DRINKING PROBLEM. Maybe, maybe not, but I sure would like to research that one thoroughly.

No, it had to be something wackier, something stranger, something to catch the eye of the average American Winn-Dixie market-goer as they hauled the Spam from the shopping cart....

"Here, mate," growled a voice. "That's pretty poor. Mind topping that off?"

My concentration was broken. I looked down the bar, and found a surly-looking guy leaning over the bar, pushing his pint of brown ale toward the bar man. At first I couldn't tell what was wrong. The guy was pointing at the big head on his beer.

"Should settle down, sir," said the bar man.

"Nonsense. Top it off! Damned stuff is expensive enough as it is. My right as a customer."

The barman frowned, but shrugged. "Deed it is, sir, but you needn't be so harsh about it." He took the pint, scooped the foam off it, then stuck it under the narrow tap spigot, literally immersing the knobby head into the drink. Then he flicked off the catch to the controls and pulled hard on the tall wood and metal lever. Looked damned hard, too. These barmen over here must develop some decent biceps.

The fluid level arose, some of it dripping off the sides.

"Topping off" in Britain constitutes filling the glass so high that the beer seems to swell up past the lip of the glass, kept from spilling over by surface tension alone. The barman gingerly pulled the pint out from under the tap then hoisted it over to drain on the plastic bar grate advertising CARLSBERG BEER.

The guy, a strapping man in a flannel shirt and cap who looked like a cab or truck driver, sighed. "Thanks. Sorry. Bit hot under the collar. Me bike just got nicked."

The barman softened. "That's a shame. Had a mountain bike stolen last year myself. Terrible plague."

My ears pricked up. I'd heard intimations of this particular Cambridge problem from our bicycle place on King Street. Flowers had insisted on acting like the natives, and since the vast majority of Cambridge sorts biked about the brick and cobble town, she thought that we should. It was suggested that to get the kind of snazzy bikes Flowers' sensibility and fashion style insisted upon we should just buy them with her deep-pocketed credit card and then sell them again when we got back ("Or just store them for when we come back, dear!" she'd suggested. Fat chance.) Flowers, being of sound horse trader stock, considered this a fabulous concept. I hadn't been on a bike since I delivered my city's paper in my prepubescent days. I know it's been fashionable for yuppie types in the past decade, but hell I'm pretty far from being a yuppie. Anyway, these things I'd seen ching-chinging around this medieval town were pretty far from the light, sporty things the yups favored. They were solid-looking and comfortable and I figured, Hell, why not? Looks like fun. Maybe even relaxing. That's exactly what I needed. A little biking on nice paths by the river. I was having a hard time with Brit culture and attitudes, but biking by a nice-looking river seemed like a pretty universal damned-good-thing.

Anyway, Mr. Bike Guy warned us to buy locks and use them, so I was pretty curious about this "plague."

"Bad news," I said. "Could I buy this man's next beer in way of sympathy?"

The man, already half glugged through his enormous pint, perked up considerably. "You sure could, mate. Ta!"

Actually, I was exercising my reporters' knowledge that a little alcohol gift went a long way into collecting information. Cash was best, but hey, a beer was much cheaper.

"My pleasure." I pushed a few of the thick pound coins the barman's way.

"You're a Yank, then?"

"That's right. Never been here before. Having a—what do you call it—Holiday."

"Picked a nice hot summer for it, didn't you. I been to cooler summers on the Costa Del Sol." Glug glug. "Pah. Whole world's going to the wolves, I say. You'd think a man's bike would be respected. 'Round here… no way."

"A plague you say?"

"You bet, mate. This ain't a big town, you know? Three thousand bicycles were stolen last year." He chugged another few ounces of the bitter to assuage the trauma of this pronouncement. "And those were just the ones reported to the police!"

I had the sudden urge to go out and check my own bike, secured to a bike stand with a lock sold by the dealer. I'd had this keen new bike I'd bought myself when I was eleven years old. A black, ten-speed Schwinn Racer. A real honey of a bike, and the envy of my neighborhood. I had it all of a week before it got stolen. Never found it, and had no insurance so I had to go back to riding clunky three speeds on my route. When I had my pick of which bikes to buy the day before, I'd chosen the one that had looked the most like my old Schwinn. I was already getting attached. But no, I told myself. Don't panic. I had this damned fine modern bike lock now, product of the nineties, and my new bike would be just fine.

I had another pint with the guy, I admit, so I was kind of late with the wine for Flowers. I just brought it out in a half-pint glass so I could carry another pint for myself, top part drunk off so I wouldn't spill any.

I was feeling no pain, I admit, but Flowers didn't seem to mind. Her attention was enrapt in the proceedings. Apparently discussion of the upcoming convention had been finished up, because the assembly were discussing the ideal casting of some *Blake's 7* movie. Generally, it was agreed that, though well beloved, the original cast wouldn't do, and so current actors were being cast hypothetically, presently into the "Avon" and "Villa" parts. The original Avon—a guy named Paul Darrow—was apparently kinda chunky now, for instance. Flowers was making a case for Tom Cruise, to the distinct annoyance of Alucard, who stood, a vision of straight Old World posture, by a lectern at the front of the rows of chairs.

Blake's 7 is the story of a bunch of outlaw misfits on the lam from a tight-assed empire in a wobbly spaceship. I could tell why people liked it: it was pretty wild and woolly and nasty, the actors treading the BBC studies with melodramatic snarls and snappy diction. The Avon character was a sexy, arrogant, nasty bastard and, hey, women like that. Me, I don't know why. Women love me because I'm a sweetheart.

Thanks to the beer and boredom, I kinda zoned out, except for when my elbow sprang up automatically to feed my mouth some booze. The old noodle was zooming around, peeking under stones for good material. There was such a stew of stuff here, I couldn't quite put my finger on the really powerful one I knew I needed to start with.

The odd thing was I had this real strong feeling that there was something here, in the first three days we'd been here, right under my nose, that was exactly what I was looking for… kinda like the murder weapon in Roald Dahl's story "Lamb to the Slaughter."

In mid-thought, I suddenly burped.

It wasn't just any old burp, but a real fruity Bronx cheer burp, straight through an open mouth sounding brassy and American and real.

Damned thing upstaged the spacey *Blake's 7* meeting something fearful. Brits are pretty hard to ruffle, though, so the only one who actually turned my way was Flowers.

"Jack," she whispered harshly. "We're in polite society. Excuse yourself."

"Pardon me," I mumbled.

Unredeemed, though, I finished off most of the lager. The stuff must have been rumbling through me like some stealth freight train, 'cause next thing I know gas hit my lower bowels, hard.

Reader, it escaped.

It sounded like Pavorotti farting in an airplane hangar, and this time I did see a few startled looks cast my way.

Including Alucard's.

Only the Doctor's expression wasn't startled....

Flowers was clearly mortified. "Jack," she said, and I got a curt whack across my arm.

...Alucard's expression was knowing, piercing, and, well... murderous. I was stunned by it, the glower a dark sneer of creased brow which brought a flash of fire beneath its bushy brows, and I felt a sudden frisson of danger and menace.

"Uhm... sorry."

I was mortified.

Not so much by my eructions, but by my Britishism. Yeah, the Brits go around knocking into each other on this crowded isle and invariably the reaction is a tangle of "Sorry." "Sorry." "Sorry."

I'd thought the word was pretty pathetic, and was aghast that it had dropped from my mouth.

"Little digestive problem," I announced, suddenly onstage. "Maybe I better go to the men's room."

"Yeah, Jack. Maybe that would be a good idea," said Flowers, her face flushed with embarrassment.

I got up and felt Dr. Alucard's eyes boring into the back of my neck.

I couldn't help myself. I turned to look at him, and sure enough, the guy was staring at me. Only this time, it wasn't a murderous glower I was receiving, but a cold, assessing look, as though the guy was somehow peering into the gaseous nether bowels of my soul. He looked like some dark heiromancer, digging his paws into the remains of some dead thing, villainously thereby peering into the murky future.

I felt as though someone were shitting on my grave.

With a shudder, I got out of there.

I went to the men's room as promised, and then I made a beeline for the bar.

✠

That weird Doctor's look was still moiling around inside of me, along with the queasy lurch of a hangover, as I exited the Holiday Inn the next morning to go for a cycle around town with Flowers.

I'd gotten plenty of tongue last night—but alas, no sex was involved.

Flowers was keeping it wagging. Her gift of Texas gab had its dark side.

"You know, it's not like you're back in some Florida cracker bar, Jack," she said tartly. "These people have principles and manners. You're in polite society now, and you just can't behave like that."

I grumbled something and grimaced as we entered the daylight. England is usually dark and gloomy—except on days when I get hangovers.

"Okay, okay, so lay off, huh? I just had a few problems last night with the pipes, ya know?" We made our way over to the bike stand where we'd locked up our new bikes. "Cripes, the lousy plumbing they have over here... you'd think a guy with personal plumbing problems might be forgiven."

Today we were going to take a tour of some colleges. A place called Trinity College was of especial interest to Flowers, since one of the undergraduates had given her a little PR about it. Apparently Trinity was founded way back in 1546 by King Henry VIII himself. Lord Byron was one of its many famous students. These "colleges" are really independent entities that house and feed students going to the University—and keep up traditions. They're real old and they all have huge courtyards filled with grass and absolutely nothing else. I guess this is a big thing for Brits, to preserve a spot of lawn just to look at, since this is such a cramped, dingy little isle, but me, I don't see much use for grass. And you can't even walk on it. Sheesh!

So anyway, at the top of the elaborate gate is this carved statue of Henry. Up till the 1920s the wife-killer held a scepter in his hands. One wild night, probably after drinking at a bunch of pubs on King Street, a student climbed up, took the scepter out of the king's manly hand and slipped in a chair leg, one end sharpened so as to fit in the fist. This was apparently deemed a worthy student act because the chair leg remained until the eighties, when another drunken bunch of students climbed up, removed it and stuck in a bicycle pump. These hijinks were frowned upon. The authorities caught the culprits, removed the bicycle pump—and put the chair leg back.

Me, I think they should have put a turkey leg in the King's pudgy hand. I mean, he's always got one in Renaissance Fairs.

So anyway, a day of tourism was something I was not exactly looking forward to. The good news was that since there was a pub on practically every street corner here, I could probably go and have a pint and calm my internal World War II.

We got to the bicycle rack. I was actually looking forward to getting on and peddling, relievedly, away from Flowers.

But the bike wasn't there. The lock was, though, opened somehow and on the ground, looking useless and forlorn.

My heart sank and suddenly I was eleven again.

✠

Loss is a hard thing to take.

Me, I've lost a lot over my life. Maybe that's why I am the way I am, a little hard bitten, a little cynical—a little rough around the edges. Maybe all that keeps the big bad world a bit away from me.

Once in a while, though, life just slams me in the head with a two-by-four.

I guess losing my bike there in England was one of those times.

So much for goddamned "gentlemanly" behavior. The Brits were just as larcenous and criminal as anyone, it would seem. And hypocrites to boot about the whole thing. Damned good thing they don't let people have guns over here—they'd all shoot each other immediately.

I let Flowers go ahead on her tour, agreeing to meet at G. David's book shop at a certain time later on in the afternoon. Me, I had work to attend to.

I was going to the cops.

First I had that pint at a newly opened pub. It put a little space between me and my rage. Then I called and reported the crime, expecting a constable maybe to come over. You know, dust for fingerprints, like that. When they found out it was "just a bike stolen" they suggested that a better course of action might be to come into the station.

I did. A bored looking desk jockey who smelled like old bacon took down my registration number, the details of the crime, then thanked me stiffly for coming in.

"That's it?" I said.

"Yes, I'm afraid so. Only so much to be done. Might keep your eyes peeled. Sometimes they turn up again, these bikes, in the oddest places."

I was incensed. "I don't understand. Why is this allowed? Wait a minute, I know. You haven't got the death penalty here, right? There's no punishment for this heinous crime."

"I assure you sir, there is indeed."

"And you can't shoot the bastards 'cause you haven't got guns."

The guy gave me an odd look. "I truly don't think guns are necessary… for anything, sir."

Goddamned liberal, I think. But I knew I wasn't going to do myself or my cause—or for that matter, my hurt—any good by complaining. As soon as I left the station I knew that the Guv'nor there was probably going to pour himself some tea, eat a crumpet and read the *Guardian*.

I went out and had myself another pint of lager at a place called The Fox and Hounds. Then I had another.

I stewed awhile, thinking.

I was going to have to meet Flowers pretty soon. There had to be something I could do in the meantime make me feel less the helpless sap, the victim. Some kind of payback would be nice....

I mean, hell, it wasn't like I was in Italy, right? I was in England, supposedly a place of rationality and justice!

So I went to a sporting shop.

"I'd like to buy a baseball bat," I said to the clerk.

"Ah—American baseball, sir?" said the chirpy young clerk. He wore a tie and looked like he'd just been out on the Cam for a rowing contest.

"No. Zulu baseball."

"Ah—yes... well, we've neither, I'm afraid."

Hmm. The nice thing about a baseball bat is it has a double purpose. A nice solid one, smooth wood, good balance, some heft, can bash a little canvassed number out of the park.

It can put you in good stead in a dark alley somewhere.

Fully sober I might have blown a gasket. But the beer had put a soothing interface between nerves and cause of abrasion. So I took this news in stride, burped politely, pardoned myself and took a little stroll.

It didn't take me long to find something.

"What's this, pray tell, sirrah," I said, pointing to a display near the back.

"Cricket bats sir."

"What? To kill insects with?"

The guy took it as the joke intended. "Alas, no. They're used for a game called cricket. Please don't ask me to explain it. Most people who play it don't fully understand it."

"Ah, yes. Okay." I studied the things thoughtfully. They looked like a boat paddle without the middle part. I'd think the wide part brought on encouraged air resistance and thus dragged—but if you swung the narrow part first, you'd be okay. And it was neither cricket balls or baseballs I intended to hit. I dredged up my VISA card.

"I'll take one, please."

✠

There was a full moon riding over the old walls of Emmanuel College. The night was quiet and the air was cool and hushed. The contrast was amazing, considering the bustling ant colony it had been during the day, cars and tourists and shoppers scurrying about while the Cambridge Tour double decker buses patiently waddled through the winding streets like a clot ambling through arteries. There was the taste of beer in the air—

No. Must have been just in my mouth.

I pulled a large can of Heineken up from its place on the stoop where I was hiding, and took a sturdy gulp, then peered out around the doorway to the bicycle rack.

Nothing.

Quiet.

I sighed, readjusted my grip on the cricket bat and sat back to wait. They'd be round soon enough, I thought.

"I tell you, mate," a guy had said to me at a pub that evening. "An unlocked bike—the thieves *smell* it."

So what I'd done, I'd taken the lock and chain off Flowers' bike and now it just sat there, not even on the rack but against the stone wall nearby, naked and vulnerable.

I was going to get me a piece of these goddamn Limey thieves, no matter how long it took.

Meantime, I had a few beers to keep me company.

Flowers was back up in the hotel room, snoring away. I hadn't told her about my plan. She'd have given me hell and forbidden me, and we'd have had a fight—so why bother?

I'd bash myself a bike thief, call the cops, be a hero… and be back for a nice sleep afterward. She'd promised me a good sleep the next day anyway.

So there I was, hunkered and waiting for a bicycle thief in Cambridge, England, a cricket bat in my hand, pissed off as all hell.

It wasn't like the day had improved my mood that much.

We'd gone around looking at colleges, as promised. Peculiar things, I thought. Old and cold looking, even in the summer, and such a jumble of architecture as to look like some kind of gritty gothic skeleton. And the courts! Jeez, seems to me, the least they could do is pave them over and use them for parking lots.

We crossed the Bridge of Sighs, we hired a punt and I almost fell off (nice tradition of drinking while boating, though) and potted around the market place.

On a stroll back, Flowers had gotten all excited, pointing up at a sign fronting a long, tall building with lots of windows showing lots of offices with lab paraphernalia peeking through.

"Oh… that's Dr. Alucard's lab!" she said. "He said if we were in the area… "

I wasn't particularly inclined toward meeting up with the grim Doctor again, but Flowers was insistent.

Looked pretty much like a lab to me. Dr. Alucard was polite to Flowers but pretty much gave me the cold shoulder—and when I wasn't looking, the evil eye—as we marched through ranks of beakers and Bunsen burners and refrigerators and lab racks. I was half-crocked so I only sort of heard this and that about the blood work they were doing. Some AIDS stuff, plasma work, artificial blood—blah blah blah.

It was a pretty speedy tour, I must say, and mostly my mind was conjuring up variations of bloodwork-themed stories for the *American Galaxy* and a dark determination to bring certain bicycle thieves to justice.

As we were leaving, the Doctor bid us a peculiar farewell after saying he was looking forward to seeing us at the *Blake's 7* convention.

"And please," he said, one of those bushy eyebrows raising a bit in my direction, "stay out of trouble."

The stare intensified and again I felt as though he were staring through me.

This, I thought, is the guy the police should use to interrogate the bicycle thief I catch.

There was a baleful howl somewhere, echoing through stone alleys in Cambridge. The temperature seemed to have dropped and despite the antifreeze in my veins, my teeth were starting to chatter. There was a damp in the air, an ancient damp, the damp that must have touched the hearts of the Celts and Romans, the Angles and Saxons and Jutes, the Vikings and Normans, Charles Dickens and Jack the Ripper. It's a forbidding alien cold, the chill of mystery and dark spirits, and I guess it was getting to me because I was seriously thinking about giving up this snipe hunt and heading back to my warm bed and cushioned bed companion when I heard a noise.

A jingling.

Yes, a jingling and the *click click click* of a bicycle tire moving.

The funny thing was that I hadn't heard any footsteps approaching, just a kind of background flutter and clop on stone. I'd been listening damn carefully too, you bet. Nothing much else to do.

I immediately forgot about the cold.

Adrenaline shot through my system.

I rose up, adjusting my grip on the cricket bat.

I stepped around the side of the building and immediately saw the guy. He was just this form—dark… no, like a blobby absence of light amidst the lesser night.

Around this cloaked form I could see the front and back of Flowers' bike, which he was wheeling away.

My rage returned.

"You son of a bitch."

I raised the bat and ran toward him.

The guy swept around with a flutter of his cape. There was a leak of light from the lamps over on Saint Andrew's street and I saw him pretty well.

He was a young guy, huddled in a dark cloak, with a pale face and red, red lips. His eyes shone like peepholes into Hell, and the surprise on his face immediately turned to rage.

His mouth opened and all I could see were teeth.

Long, sharp teeth.

He came for me. I swung the cricket bat for all I was worth, but he caught it easily with a strong grip. He plucked it from my hand and he snapped it in two.

Then he came for me, and his cloak swept around me like a shroud, and consciousness popped out of my grip like a wet bar of soap.

✠

I've been unconscious before against my volition.

Too much to drink at times. Pills. Once, a car accident. Couple times even bar fights.

Not pleasant. Still they were heaven compared to coming out of that particular dip into death.

I was aware first of all that I was sitting in a straight-backed chair. I could not move my hands. They seemed to be tied together behind me with some sort of leather bands. My head felt as though someone had pulled my brains out by the nerve roots and then filled the skull back up with pain.

I expected some kind of choke around my mouth, but my groan came out loud and clear. I looked up and my surroundings gradually blended together from blurry to the merely surreal.

I was in an old room, filled with old furniture and William Morris wallpaper. There were high-backed chairs tastefully placed here and there, portraits and a landscape painting. There were no windows that I could see, although some thick, black velvet curtains could well be hiding them.

The place smelled of a century of pipe tobacco. Silent echoes of classical music seemed to hang in the air. All I could taste in my mouth was the sour of old beer and the iron of blood. I felt as though Sherlock Holmes might walk in at any moment.

Or some other character of Victorian fiction.

The pounding in my head was being offset rapidly by curiosity and fear…

Where was I?

No place promising, that was for certain. Gradually memory dripped back into my enfeebled faculties, and the fright-face of the guy I'd surprised showed up.

Damn. Trouble.

The snap of that cricket bat lingered in my head.

Could have been my neck.

Shit. All I'd wanted was payback on a score. I hadn't expected to end up trussed up in the middle of a nineteenth century nightmare.

I didn't have long to wait until the major questions in my head were answered.

After the answers, though, I wished my brain hadn't been asking any questions.

There were voices in the hall outside. Then the door opened and a tall figure stepped in.

It was Doctor Alucard.

He didn't look at me at first, just went to a cabinet. He opened it, took out two clean glasses and a bottle of whiskey. He poured out healthy shots of the whiskey, then casually placed them on an old table to my immediate right.

Then he pulled up one of the high-backed chairs and sat down, crossing his legs. When his eyes found mine, I could see no particular glower or menace in them.

"Would you like a drink, Jack?" he said, pushing the glass forward close enough for me to smell it. "Single malt from the Highlands. I think you'll like it. Might take a bit of the sting out of your head."

"Okay."

"Soon enough." He took one of the glasses, sipped it thoughtfully, those brows of his looking almost avuncular now, not threatening at all. "Once you've told me a few things I want to know. Once we've shared some information."

"Where the hell am I?" I said, keeping my voice low but still making it tough, not showing any of the fear or uncertainty I was feeling.

"You're in my rooms in Cross College, Jack. My college, you know." His accent seemed a little thicker now, a little more filled with pride, propriety and prejudice. "Did you realize that many of the colleges of Cambridge and Oxford are some of the largest landowners in Britain? It's true. They've been financial entities for hundreds and hundreds of years. Cross College, for instance, owns an entire prospering port, much of the land between here and Oxford, much in London—indeed, a whole Channel Island. And I... " A small smile passed over Alucard's lips. "I own Cross."

"Great," I said. "You want to untie me?"

"I think not. Don't worry, though. I'll help you drink your drink." He stood up and strode back and forth, long tapered fingers softly stroking his chin. "Now then, I shall come to the meat of the matter. You, sir, are a troublemaker, and I'm afraid I'm going to have to rid this cooling ball of mud of your foul carcass. However, before you go, I should like to get some information, as I said. Your cooperation in these matters will more or less determine the levels of pain you will experience in your demise… " That eyebrow rose archly. "And perhaps even the nature of your afterlife."

I somehow managed to keep my face immobile, but inside fear was knocking down the supports. Fear is never your friend, though. I grew up in a tough neighborhood. I often got the shit beat out of me by older boys. But I learned damned quick that if you showed nasty bastards you were afraid—they would just kick you harder while you were down.

And I'd pretty much figured that this Alucard guy was a nasty bastard.

With fear gripped tightly and under control, my brain began to put two and two together. The guy with the sharp teeth and batlike cape stealing Flowers' bike—This guy's look, his teeth… his blood lab…

Only I'd never quite seen two and two add up to a Twilight Zone Four.

"Please, Doc. Tell me you're not a vampire and you lead a gang of vampires in Cambridge. Huh? I mean, really. This religious motif has been getting to me here… Christ College. Jesus Lane. Jesus Pieces. God's Fish and Chips… But the vampire shtick seems to be a little bit cliché."

That got him mad.

His face writhed into a horrific mask. One moment he's in the chair, next his face was in my face and his breath was like a flame against my eyes. "Beware, mortal. The Devil is not to be mocked!" he snarled.

My spine went icy and I shut my mouth for a moment. The Doc calmed down and sat back into his chair, taking a small sip of whiskey. "You almost had yourself a True Death there, Jack. Well done, if your goal was a quick release from me."

"Shit, Doc. I just want to go home to Florida and get back to work. I don't like it much here."

"Yes. Your work. That is what I need to know about." He pulled my wallet out of his pocket, tossed it onto the table. Then he pulled my passport out, thumbed through it casually and flopped that down as well. "I see nothing in here to indicate connections with your government in any official capacity. Yet you are an agent for it, are you not… ? Or perhaps some corporation, hmmmm? Tell me all about it now, if you please, and things will be much easier for you."

"Secret agent?" I was aghast. "What, snooping *Blake's 7* conventions? Looking for vampires…. Trying to get a good whack at a bicycle thief?"

"I read human beings, Jack. You are a dangerous man. You are a snooper."

"Shit. I'm a damned reporter. I write for the *American Galaxy*, a cheesy tabloid that sells for ninety nine cents at supermarket checkout lines. Didn't Flowers tell you that?"

That arched eyebrow again. "Your estimable lady friend claims you're a distinguished journalist, a very important man. It seems to me a very good cover for investigations. Tell me the truth, Jack." He went to a hearth and pulled out tongs. "Do not make me pull it up by the roots of your tongue."

"Look, Doc. Believe me. Yeah, I snoop… you've got the right tag on that one. You gotta dig some to get stories. But hell, mostly I just recycle stories… or make them up!"

"The *American Galaxy*, you say. I have been to the States… and why, yes. I think I remember. A most peculiar black and white periodical. I believe I saw some kind of cover involving Elvis and aliens."

"You got it, Doc. That's the *Galaxy*."

He gave me a most peculiar look. "But you are here in England to dig up stories to write that only the least educated of your readers will believe?"

"You'd be surprised at how many of its readers believe the *Galaxy*, Doc. And no—I'm here with Flowers for a vacation and I guess, yeah, I'd intended to dig some stories up… can't help myself, can I. That's not the reason for the trip, though."

I figured I shouldn't lie. He seemed to have some kind of psychic gear to scope out lies. He was just inferring too much. Investigator for the U.S. Government. What the hell was this?

Of course the fact that this bothered him meant that something peculiar was going on in that hematology lab—something the Doc, by implication, wanted to keep under wraps.

Maybe even something about his identity.

The word *identity* somehow was the key. I thought about this guy's vampirish look, his demeanor, and his name did a little flip in my head.

"House of Frankenstein," I said. "1944."

"Excuse me?"

"Alucard. That's *Dracula* spelled backward."

The Doc's face grew concerned. "This was in a movie.... "

I was still coping.... "No. It's just a joke, right? Funny, Doc. Ha ha. Dracula is just fiction."

The guy just kind of smiled. "Perhaps fiction is the best place to hide from enemies, Jack. Perhaps it was I who gave Mister Bram Stoker his story, thus to obfuscate the truth of my true coming to England... and then putting a fitting climax to the tale to help the nightmares to recede."

"Yeah. Right. Let me see if I remember.... Yeah. van Helsing chased you back to your homeland and put a stake through your heart."

Alucard... or Dracula, or whoever he was smiled grimly. "I look forward to the literary critic who one day realizes that Van Helsing and my fictional namesake are two sides to the same coin. Perhaps together they add up to something like the truth of the matter."

"All that carrying of coffins... and native earth... must have been a hard haul to get over here... uhm, what's your first name? Ah yeah—Vlad."

A humorless chuckle. "Superstitious nonsense, again perhaps to cloak the truth."

"And that truth is?" I was curious, yeah. But mostly I was stalling for time. This guy clearly had an ego on him the size of the orbit of Mars. "I mean, sounds like I'm not going to get out of here anyway. You might as well tell me."

Meanwhile, my mind was racing for a way out and my hands were working at the leather bonds behind me. I had some experience with leather. Little, uh, extracurricular activities in my younger, more experimental years. One night a sexy girlfriend had tied me up and then passed out. It took me half the night, but I eventually extricated myself and came out of it with a pretty good knowledge of leather—and anathema for the questionable pleasures of B and D.

Alucard looked at me. "I don't think that will be necessary. Suffice it to say that my work with hematology has been most rewarding for the past century, and that as you may surmise, my students have spread my truths throughout the world...." His eyes gleamed. "But they are truly the select and secret race... which is why the authorities doubtless are investigating me."

"Look, I told you. I've got nothing to do with any authorities, Doc." I shook my head adamantly. "Anyway, I'm still in the dark here. You're saying the vampires are real... you're the king of the vampires... but it's not supernatural?"

"In Cambridge?" He smiled. "In Cambridge there are two principal sayings: 'What's the evidence?' and 'In Cambridge, we have standards.'"

"So it's some sort of infection... a disease.... "

"Please. It is a privilege to be gifted with the Blood. We are the Select."

"Yeah, yeah, right. You keep on saying that." I wasn't going to get any DNA transcriptions from this jerk, that was for sure. "But I don't understand.... Where does the *Blake's 7* business fit in?"

"I have lived a very long time," said Alucard. "I must have my hobbies to amuse me."

"Oh. Right. Okay... and this Bicycle Theft thing. What the hell is that supposed to be?"

"Ah yes—well, I suppose that sort of information is harmless enough to pass on. Besides, I need to perform an appropriate Summoning, anyway."

Doctor Alucard closed his eyes. His long, tapering arms folded across his chest.

The sharp fingers fluttered silently.

There was a noise like the wind outside in the hall. Shutters flapped and banged and shudders ran down my back. I had a sense of something numinous occurring outside... not good but *bad* numinous.

"Enter, Joseph," said the Doctor.

The door opened. In walked the fellow in the cloak who I'd caught stealing Flowers' bike. This time, however, he did not look so demonic. In fact, he looked like nothing so much as a fresh-scrubbed graduate student, just in from having a few pints with his rowing team.

The Doctor opened his eyes. They seemed slightly redder now, as though his student's presence were affecting him in some odd way.

"Joseph is my assistant," said the Doctor in a deep, resonant voice. "He is one of my… " His teeth bared and the canines seemed to grow before my eyes. "…Children… "

Joseph's eyes grew red. A sneer revealed growing teeth. He seemed the epitome of both health and death. "Good evening again, sir," he said in a high-class accent so nasal you'd have thought his vocal chords were in his nose. "I believe this belongs to you." From his cloak he drew out the two pieces of my cricket bat, contemptuously tossing them at my feet. "I far prefer rowing."

"Yes," said Alucard. "Joseph is one of our champion rowers here at Cross. All the rowers are my children." He sighed happily. "All the stout blood lads that have been Cross men—my men… out into the fields of academia and science across the globe. Mine. I knew when I came to England that it would not be possible to gain control from any kind of quixotic government. Control would be more valuable much earlier in the formation of the young controllers. Oh and I have plans… marvelous plans." He shrugged. "Some in the past have not worked out as well as I would have liked… but oh well… I have a long time to dabble, don't I?"

"I still don't quite get the bicycle theft ring, Doc," I said, not just stalling for time but honestly curious.

"Oh very well. That will be harmless enough for you to know," said the Doctor, placing a fatherly arm around Joseph. "Joseph here, for instance, as I said happens to be one of my assistants in my hematology labs. By now, of course, due to my work, my Family needs no longer to fear the daylight or garlic or other such hindrances. However, these are perky and restless young pups, my children. They need exercise and they need training. There are hundred of thousands of bikes in Cambridge."

"Quite a lark," said Joseph, displaying his teeth. "Good college fun, don't you know—and a source of metal and rubber for other… projects."

"Absolutely. There you go. And come to think of it, I've let on far more than I had intended to. Oh well." Doctor Alucard came close to me, his eyes dark and burning. I could feel his breath in my face. "It is time for you to tell us more. And I think the ministrations of Joseph here will encourage your participation."

In his eyes I could see centuries of madness and darkness. In his breath I could smell the future of blood.

This guy meant business.

"Please," I said, unnerved totally. "I'm telling you… I'm not a government agent…. "

Joseph's hand spread out before me.

Long sharp talons were growing.

"This is not a television show, sir," said the cultured young vampire. "Our kind has thrived for a very long time. Tell us. We will win no matter what. You are helpless against us. Spare yourself some agony."

I was about to tell them anything they wanted to hear, but suddenly there was a commotion outside.

I could hear a shrieking, almost hysterical voice coming from the front of the college rooms.

I recognized it.

"I don't care if it's four o'clock in the morning! I'm an American citizen. More than that I'm a citizen of *Texas*! I demand to see Doctor Alucard. Immediately!"

Flowers!

A look of infinite weariness crossed the Doctor's face. It was a look I was too familiar with, a look I have doubtless worn as well.

Only this time it was a look that I was very, very happy indeed to see.

Before I could even think about crying out, the Doctor pulled out a gag and whipped it around my mouth.

"Oh my," said Alucard. "There are forces that even the powers of darkness must deal with personally." He turned to his henchman. "Joseph, I must go and quiet our American friend. Please stay and guard our guest. However, no torture yet, all right? We don't want any undue noise with the formidable Miss Flowers about."

Elegant and poised, the Doctor left the room immediately, leaving me with College Boy.

The vampire, however, did not seem particularly interested in me. He went to the door and placed his ear to it, to better hear the conversation going on downstairs.

I could hear some of it, but truth be told I was busy with my leather bonds. I hadn't stopped working with them the whole of the interview, and I was on the verge of freeing myself.

I could hear some of the sounds below.

"Doctor, thank you so much. I'm sorry to disturb you," Flowers was saying. "It's Jack. He's vanished."

The Doctor's dramatic voice was easier to hear. It boomed with gentle, reassuring authority.

"Now, now, my dear. I'm sure he's all right. Your gentleman seems to be of a free, unbound nature. I'm sure you've spent more than one night alone while you've known him."

Guy was damned right about that, I thought guiltily.

Still I was better to Flowers than I'd been to just about any other woman in my life. Guess that means I must love the pain in the butt!

It was no time now for soppy sentimentality, though. I had to work on the damn leather bindings.

Just about there…

"Not right in the middle of the night, Doctor!"

"You called the police?"

"He has to be missing for a certain amount of time before they can do anything."

"Now, now. Cambridge is hardly a dangerous place. And I have heard tell of gambling dens open to all hours. Perhaps your Jack found one of those."

Drat! The guy had me to a *T*!

I could tell it was getting to Flowers too—she well knew I could hardly resist throwing down a wad at the toss of a pair of dice.

I had to move quick if I was going to have any hope of taking advantage of this intrusion by my beloved.

I took advantage of Joseph's intent distraction and worked violently at the leather. The effort worked, and I was out of them. I lifted my hand up to work at my gag. All I had to do was yell for Flowers. My only hope was that while Alucard's intentions for me were specific and accomplishable, covering up for two missing Americans would be quite a bit harder... particularly since Flowers was already on record with the local constabulary.

Unfortunately, as soon as my hands got to the gag at my mouth, Joseph's head whipped around.

He hissed and glared, and with a huge bound headed toward me.

Some kind of preservation instinct must have hit me because I wasn't consciously aware of what I was going to do next. I just did it.

Even as the vampire leaped toward me, my hands abandoned my mouth gag, and went down to the floor. They came up holding that cricket bat again.

Or half of it anyway.

The handle half, which had broken off in a way as to form a sharp spike. The vampire was on me quickly enough, but I stuck out that cricket bat spike and held it firm just in the right place to catch him full in the breast.

There was a meaty *thunk* as the cricket bat spike drove directly through the vampire's chest.

His mouth came open and blood gushed out.

The talons reached for me, but I nimbly ducked aside. He turned around, but seemed suddenly more concerned with the length of wood stuck in him than me. Joseph had a perplexed look on his features, the look of youth-promised immortality, perhaps, and facing something more abrupt and infinitely nastier.

Purplish blood was welling voluminously from the sides of the spike. He staggered around for a moment, trying to pull the wood out and then with one sudden shudder and spasm, plopped down flat on his horror-stricken face.

I didn't wait to see if he was going to get back up again, but rather got the hell out of there.

Pulling off the gag, I hopped down the steps.

At the landing below, Doctor Alucard was just ushering Flowers outside.

"Doc! Doc!" I called, running down the steps but allowing the gag to drop behind me.

The look on Alucard's face almost worth the whole adventure. This was one smug bastard who'd just gotten a bucket of shit dumped on his head.

I had a scheme, though.

Doc couldn't seem to cough up any words, but I supplied them readily enough.

"Doc, I can't let you do this," I said.

Alucard looked almost apoplectic.

"Jack!" said Flowers, a look of perplexity and joy simultaneously appearing on her face.

"Doc, I can't let you cover for me anymore," I said, getting down to them, riffing off the Doctor's mention of gambling clubs. "Flowers, hon, I'm sorry but the Doc mentioned how he enjoyed gin rummy for money. I was out looking for bike thieves, saw his light on and just couldn't resist the challenge he posed me."

A look of indecision was moiling on the Doctor's face. He could take us both now, he doubtless knew… but was it really worth the bother… ?

Perhaps not.

He sighed. "Very well, Jack." He turned with artful penitence toward Flowers. "I fear our weaknesses found each other out. I am sorry to have caused you any pain. And certainly I regret lying to you as I did."

"Yeah, babe. That was my fault. I put him up to it. Don't take it out on the Doc, huh?"

Flowers' look of distress was slowly turning into her sour look of cold acceptance—lightened, fortunately, by a light in her eye that told me she was actually happy to see me well and in one piece. "Don't worry, Doctor. It's not the first time. And gin rummy…. Well, I guess I like a game of cards myself from time to time."

The Doctor bowed a little bit. "May I show you to the gate?"

I figured we'd better get out quick before he changed his mind. "That's okay, Doc." I took his hand, shook it. "You can pay me that hundred quid you lost any time you like."

A look of amusement flickered on the Count's face. "Ah. Yes. But perhaps we can play again sometime when we do not alarm your lovely companion."

"Yeah, that would be great, Doc," I said. "And then we can up the stakes."

I grinned at him for a moment, grabbed hold of Flowers and got the hell out of there.

✠

Good grief. Dracula. The real Dracula!

And I bump into him. All kinds of ideas for stories were churning in my head. Problem was, I really didn't know what exactly he was doing in that hematology lab. My imagination boggled.

Next night, while Flowers was out with a couple of other *Blake's 7* fans, hypothesizing perhaps on the size of the male characters' penises or whatever, I found myself a nice cozy pub on King Street and brought out a notebook I'd bought at Heffer's Stationary store. Not only Flowers' bike was back—mine had been returned as well, and waiting for me in the afternoon was a cheque for a hundred pounds from Doctor Alucard.

I jotted down some thoughts on the whole business at the pub, while sipping at a Heineken. I'd slept late—like to the tune of the late afternoon. Flowers had gone out to see some exhibition or another. Me, I'd gotten up real early, run down to the chic shop at King's College Chapel and bought myself a cross I'd seen there and hung it around my neck. I don't know exactly why, since Alucard had claimed imperviousness to such supernatural boundaries. I guess it made me feel a little better.

Now, I was making a list of possible stories.

KING OF THE VAMPIRES BREEDS ELVIS MONSTERS.

UFO VAMPIRES STALK HALLS OF LEARNING.

DRACULA LIVES IN ACADEMIA!

Halfway through my Heineken, I was presented with another by the barman.

"Thanks, but I didn't—" I started.

"Fellow bought your drink."

I looked up and next thing I knew Doctor Alucard was sitting next to me.

"Good evening, Jack," he said. "Playing yet again with the children of the night?"

"Yes and within the Howls of Academia."

He had a glass of something red in his hand. He glanced at my sheet of paper, tsk-tsked, and sipped at his drink. He shook his head sadly. "No. No, those won't do at all. How about... PRINCE OF BLOOD MEETS SLEAZY MORTAL JOURNALIST FOOL... " He sighed. "Jack, I did do some inquiry into your background, and everything you said was all too true. You have absolutely no connection with any kind of governmental secret agencies." His voice was light but his face was dark.

"I'm just a lowly writer, Doc."

"Ah yes... but the power of the pen... Hmm. Well, there is no great threat. Your periodical has absolutely no power nor reputation of validity. Still—" Suddenly a long, sharp fingernail was in front of me. It slipped down and scratched across my chin, toying near my jugular. "I suggest you do no stories about our encounter for any journal or book. I shall be watching you. As will my minions—"

The fingernail pointed toward the other side of the room. I followed. Sitting in a corner was Joseph, looking healthy and vigorous, sipping a drink. He raised his glass to me.

I guess my shock showed.

"Perhaps a better knowledge of our anatomy would have dispatched him properly," said Alucard. "But it's all one, really. And it's just as well, since we'd made a mistake about you anyway. It would have been such a difficulty to dispose of your body—and the idea of inducting you into our ranks. Why, it makes my skin crawl."

"Gee—thanks."

"In other words perhaps for the first time in your sorry life your inadequacies as a being—whether living or dead—are perhaps doing you service."

"You put things in the sweetest way, Doc."

"You have this one warning, this one opportunity for discretion in your pitiful life," said the vampire in his rumbling, Balkan-accented tones.

While I'm not particular pals with Good, it's nice to know the pure Evil despises me.

"I'm listening."

"Perhaps you'd better not just listen, Jack. Perhaps you should heed. Enjoy your time in this town, on this haunted isle. Dig up what strangeness and charm you care to. However, meddle not in my affairs. And Jack… " I could see a hint of tooth and sharpness. "My reach easily extends across the Atlantic. I shall be watching your pitiful journal. Print what you care to about vampires—but it had better not hinder my operation!"

The eyes full of red and dread, and I thought I felt a hint of heat in his last hiss.

With that, he was gone, leaving only a shiver on my spine in his horrible wake.

I was grateful for the extra beer in front of me. It didn't last long, I'll tell you. I had something a little stronger to chase it with, and then I walked home to the Holiday Inn while there were more people than shadows in the streets.

Maybe it was time to start working on my novel again. They tell me romance is selling very well indeed. That sounds like a safe subject.

As I passed Trinity College, I looked up at old King Henry glowering above his primordial gate, and for the first time I knew without a doubt why he preferred that sharpened wood chair leg in his hand to a scepter or a bicycle pump.

On A Big Night in Monster History

Marc Levinthal and
John Mason Skipp

I.

Cold drive under the desert moon, and Ivan's breath plumes even before he lights the smoke. "Would you care for one?" he inquires of Gregor. His seven-foot brother—nineteenth-century fairytale witchman—peers out into the desert night, sullenly shakes his head, red eyes gleaming dull. Ivan sets down the pack.

"Oh, lovey," he coos, in a tender singsong. "I understand why you're depressed. But, truly, dinner wasn't *that* bad. And we had some fun, you must admit."

"Ahh… " Gregor waves one long-taloned hand dismissively, beyond consoling. "Let me listen to my music in peace."

Ivan shrugs his impossibly boned shoulders and turns the stereo back up. Bartok's *Strings, Percussion and Celeste*: quite soothing, really, especially after Kirsten's alt-rock din. Maybe he's just getting old—though, at a mere five hundred years, that seems like quite a stretch—but it strikes him that

Kirsten Fuckall's band has been vastly overrated, by both critics and fans. That shrieking mouth. That empty heart. *Crater*. Indeed. What a black hole of talent.

Amazing what a little pr sympathy vote will do.

He lights the cigarette, inhaling half of it in one long hotboxing toke. He likes the way the ash crawls toward him, like a gray maggot slave on its knees, and smiles.

"Well, *I* had fun," he mumbles to himself. "And it *was*, after all, a big night in showbiz history."

Then he sucks the rest of the smoke through two rows of sharkteeth. Savors the cancer. And massively exhales.

It's a slow night on the 86, rolling up from Mecca toward Lancaster and Palmdale. Date farms and grapefruit trees, away from the Salton Sea. He'd suggested they steal this immaculate '63 Lincoln tonight, to clear their heads and cheer them up—truth be told, Ivan felt a tad let-down himself—but Gregor is *so* sensitive, and he'd harbored *such* high hopes....

What can I do, Ivan asks himself, *to snap Gregor out of this?*

In the distance, a VW micro-bus comes. It's too dark to read the shape, but he recognizes the placement of the lights. Old hippies, no doubt. There are a million of them out here. Good bud and bland granola. And they're heading right this way.

It's a little piece of kismet. Who is he to turn it down?

He waits for just the right moment.

And then swerves into their lane.

The collision blossoms in sweet subjective slo-mo. He feels himself launch through the windshield and sees them scream as he hurtles toward them, so fast that he's gone through their windshield and sheared off the head in the passenger seat before the poor dumb wheatgrass-swiggin' bitch's seatbelt has finished recoiling.

Luxuriant, stately microseconds pass. Then he hits the back wall of the van and bounces, whooping at the screech and calamity about him, rolling toward the front as the VW van and the car he was in burst into mutual flames. The chick's throat-stump squirts out sizzling ribbons of startled heartblood. He catches what he can, careening through the infinite slowdive instant while Gregor grins, long Nosferatued face gleaming bald and shark-toothed in the flames.

"ARE YOU TRYING TO CHEER ME UP?" Gregor shrieks, a silent mindburst in Ivan's head. There is a loud explosion. They grind to a halt.

"YOU BET!" Ivan calls.

There is another loud explosion.

The next thing Gregor knows, his long, burning limbs are somewhat accordion-shaped. Somebody's torso is folded around him—a snapped-spine sandwich, from the back of the bus—and he starts to laugh, but there's raw meat in his mouth. Said backseat sandwich, venting ruptured spleen.

He chomps down on the unfortunate organ, savors the squish and the dying tremor. This one's not quite dead yet. He reads the meat.

Melvin, it says.

Gregor chews thoughtfully, taking it in. This guy he's eating, his name is Melvin Spece. He's fifty-two years old, and he is no big deal. He has done enough fucking psychedelics to effectively spike the Pacific Ocean, but it doesn't seem to have taught him much. He's a beak-nosed, scrawny-assed, peace-spouting, life-hating loser, a would-be Richard Brautigan whose big claim to fame is that he once grabbed Joan Baez's ass at a benefit concert in Frisco. (She'd turned around and smacked him, of course; and, like wow, that was a bummer. But hey. Life is short, and then....)

Melvin dies, and the pictures stop coming. Gregor spits out some gristle, takes a moment to reflect. He thinks it's kind of cool that he picked up a showbiz moment, but '60s folk singers mean nothing to him. Beancurd buttocks. Whoop-dee-doo.

There is a low moan, and Ivan calls out, "You know, this one danced for Frank Zappa once."

"*Reeallly*."

"Better hurry. She's almost gone."

Gregor has no bones, so he reconfigures easily—tissue stiffening into cartilage, tightening up into pale dead skin. Then he scuttles upside down toward Ivan and the mewling girlie-remnants. Her guts are mostly unstrung, so he grabs a stray loop and chomps down, blasting straight into her cellular memory.

And it's true: Zappa dragged her on stage once to dance. At the Roxy in Hollywood. They have the album at home. *The Be-Bop Tango* was the name of the tune. Frank's voice echoes up from her gastro-intestinal past, saying "Jazz is not dead, it just smells funny."

"It's dead *and* it smells funny," says Ivan, thinking back fondly to Monk, Coleman Hawkins, Bird. Those were the days. (Kenny G., of course, is one of theirs.)

Then she's gone, and the show goes with her.

"*Shit!*"

Ivan is sympathetic. "So much for Suzie Creamcheese. If only we could *tape* these things...."

"*Fuck!*"

"I know. Death's too short, and... umm. Hon? Your legs are still on fire."

Pissily. "*And...* ?"

"I just thought I'd mention it."

"RAARRR!" Gregor says, spinning, long and burning legs kicking a hole through the side of the van. He jumps out. Ivan follows. They stand fuming in the moonlight.

"I think I'll have that cigarette now."

Ivan looks rueful. "Guess again."

"Oh, don't tell me... !"

"Ooop. Never mind." He pulls an extra pack from his smoldering breast pocket. They're already burning, so Gregor takes three, sucks them down in a single breath.

In the distance, several cars are coming.

"So... still hungry?"

"*Yes.*"

"Shall we hang around for drive-thru?"

Gregor smiles at last. "No. I'm just feeling so *restless* this evening...."

"Then let's fly."

Two bodies collapse into themselves, becoming bat-style things that rise into the sky: one a compact V-shaped creature with large rabbit ears, the other a wide kitelike arrangement of webbed wings.

Into the night sky they soar, northeast, low, up over the Mojave desert. By the time the first horrified motorist arrives at the scene, they're already a mile away.

II.

They are sons of Dracula, bastard spawn of a singular evil. They haunt the night in ways no sane god had ever dared to dream before; but there they are, haunting away nonetheless.

It seems that, back in the olden days, The Count once found himself obsessed with a pair of beauteous twins. Virgins, of course. And unspeakably sweet. The need to despoil had been entirely overwhelming; but more—and this was rare for him—it wasn't just blood, but fuck that he craved.

So he came to them one night, in their bedchambers; and, having bent them quickly to his will, he then proceeded to get down. The first one was delightfully pliant, and—having given herself over to the darkest passions—deliciously ardent as well. She was all he could have hoped for, and so much more that he wanted to commemorate the event.

Taking care that he rode her past passion's peak to the absolute brink of sexual soul-annihilation, he then proceeded to drop a fiery load of rare Drac-jizz deep within her. This ate through her womb and promptly exploded in her intestines. The Count pulled out and marveled as her exquisite belly ballooned, then burst, in a whistling fireworks display of viscid shooting stars and streamers.

It was then that her innards froze in midair and stretched, mutated, intertwining and recongealing into a gangly, gleaming seven-foot intestinal monstrosity. It roared into sentience, long, gaunt skull-like nodule forming out of slime at the summit and growing eyes, teeth, tonsils a-waggling. Roaring into horrible being.

The proud father named him Ivan.

He was so pleased with how things had turned out that he'd promptly set into sister #2. And though she was glorious in the extreme, truth be told, she just wasn't as much fun.

Which, sad to say, went a long way toward explaining Gregor.

The brothers were outcasts from the very start: misfit monsters, inspiring overwhelming terror in mortals, revulsion and outrage among Immortals (most of whom considered them abominations). Even Dad soon found them to be an embarrassment, eventually departing from them and off into history somewhere. Once gone, they never saw him again.

After that, they pretty much kept to themselves: clawing out a pocket of central Europe small enough that their prodigious powers could keep the others at bay, and large enough that they could play without drawing attention to themselves.

Soon enough, the brothers began to hear the stories of newly discovered lands to the west; The New World, it was being called. A new world certainly sounded like a good idea to them; their peace with other preternatural beings in their vicinity was tenuous at best. The minor turf wars were becoming a constant annoyance. So they ceded their territory, and headed west across the great ocean.

The first permanent white settlements had yet to be conceived when the two brothers arrived. This was much to Ivan and Gregor's delight. Their travels took them far and wide, exploring the length and breadth of the American continents. Others of their kind existed here, haunting the plains and jungles; but in every case they were wild and ancient, feral things, uncommunicative. In every case, the entities were oddly respectful of the brothers, regarding them silently from afar before suddenly turning and dissolving back into the wilderness.

The boys finally settled down: as far away from Europe as they could get, toward the western end of the North American desert. The extremes of heat and cold meant nothing to them; it was the stark beauty of the place that delighted them. It was like nothing they'd ever seen.

There they built a stone fortress above a dry lake bed, corralling thousands of healthy specimens of the local native population for slave labor: controlling their minds, using them until they dropped, and then dining upon them.

The result was a castle of draculian proportions: their little pocket of

Transylvanian spacetime, a crowning achievement of their colossal dark powers. Like a pharaoh's tomb, or their own father's house—like all monuments monsters have built for themselves—it was a weirdly magnificent, insanely ostentatious tribute to evil incarnate, and to taste gone mad.

From the old world, they'd brought Byzantine vaulting and gothic ribwork; flying buttresses and great stone spires; more gables and cornices, portals and parapets, apsidal chapels and swell torture chambers than you could shake a stick at. Not to mention the gargoyles. But they'd also been greatly inspired by the grandiose designs of the Aztecs, the Incas and Mayans.

The result was a sprawling, vainglorious hodgepodge of every hifalutin' historical design concept to date. Ivan and Gregor were monstrously proud of it, and loved to joke about how jealous their rivals would be, if the miserable pricks could only see it.

But, of course, they also prayed that that day would never come.

For a few centuries—until the westward expansion finally started to reach them—the brothers went on like this: playing Evil Spirits among the red man, which wasn't far from the truth. (The old brujos and medicine men will still tell you not to stand out in the wind at night, largely due to the legendary antics of the pair.)

Gradually, over the course of the nineteenth century, they found themselves surrounded by Europeans again. They detected few Immortals, but knew that those weren't far behind. So they made the outside world see an abandoned mine where their castle stood, and dug in while they assessed this new situation. They were quite a bit stronger now than in the old days, but weren't sure where they'd stand in the new order.

Strange things began to happen around them. Mass movement. Technology. Steam. Electricity. A small town lurched suddenly into being, and the next thing they knew, mortals boiled all about them in a frenzy of ugly exploitation that dominated and marred the ancient landscape.

One winter day in 1905, some quickly built, flimsy irrigation headgates on the Colorado River burst, sending almost its entire flow down into the dry lakebed: inundating farms, wreaking havoc on the small communities, placing Gregor and Ivan's home on a vantage high above the waters. Said waters continued to rise for the next few years, until the flow was finally contained. This became known as the Salton Sea, and it was the icing on the fucking cake. They'd fly above its waters often, diving and arcing, marveling at the folly of these dexterous monkeys who ruined everything they touched.

And what now, was to be their place in the world? Where was there to go from here? To the moon? Mars? Beautiful enough, but even the brothers would starve there eventually, without their human cattle to sustain them.

They'd had to submit at last.

And if you can't beat 'em, join 'em....

Gradually, over the decades of the nineteenth century, a plan had begun to form. One from which the world would doubtless never recover. They'd often visit San Francisco, and longed for their own little corner of Babylon.

So they'd decided, as the twentieth century dawned, to build their own theme park (long before the word was coined): a microcosm of the greater Darwinian dungheap, near the little city of Los Angeles.

It was to be called "Hollywoodland."

And the rest, as they say, is history.

But they've still kept their castle by the Salton Sea, only now it's surrounded by a dying resort town that's attached to it like an abandoned hive. It's a place with that distinctive *Carnival of Souls* pallor: desiccated, twisted, almost majestic in its squalor. People still live here; tourists still come to fish and waterski; but whereas the town once buzzed with its own energy, it now resonates, making a hollow sound like a real live ghost town makes. It's the spooky low rumble of energies long gone, and others indecipherable, hidden.

And, of course, at the heart of it is their lair: magnificent as ever, now disguised as the skeleton of a burned-out motel on the edge of Route 86.

From their abode, they cultivate pockets of chaos, doing their part to steer culture toward the brink. They think of themselves as meta-artists, shepherding mortals that show real promise. The basic showbiz/vampire connection: making the deals behind the deals on records, movies, books and such. Focusing on the dismal. Pushing the "shit" envelope as far as it will go. They are particularly proud, lately, of an internationally acclaimed hit TV series that makes heroes out of bimbos on Malibu Beach. Sometimes they really outdo themselves.

But there's much more to culture than simply the mainstream; the underground must be polluted as well. And with the rise of so-called "alternative" culture, a whole new crop of dark seedlings has made itself available. A generation that grooves on death, fear and pain, wearing its dysfunction like an ugly badge of honor.

It's too good to pass up; it is right up their alley.

Hence, the advent of Kirsten; and tonight's socially fabulous but personally disappointing little entertainment event....

III.

"I'm tired," complains Gregor, gliding languorously on the wind. Below them, the turkey and pig farms of outer Palmdale sprawl. Ivan listens to the rising horror in all those mindless animal voices, as his shadow and its twin play across the earthbound doomed. Slaughterhouse-bound, every stinking one of them. And not a moment too soon, so far as he's concerned. Not that it mattered. Soon the folly of mortals would turn the entire planet into one vast charnelhouse.

And they'll be there, sucking on some ribs off that big old radioactive barbecue.

The brothers share their father's vampiric contempt for the herd: a bottomless loathing commingled with need and the simple gross connectedness of being. Ivan finds himself wondering—far more often than is healthy, no doubt—how a creator brilliant enough to conceive of an *Ivan* could consign so much of its earthly manifestation-time to that drooling cattle mentality.

He'd read somewhere—most probably in some Hindu gobbledygook—that God was inordinately fond of sleep; not just for the dreams, but for the vast unconsciousness that floated like a void, beneath and between. But why, he asked, would any self-respecting Higher Intelligence opt for enlisting in bovine boot camp, where the wages were cud and a cellophane wrapper? Why snuffle in slop when you could dance with the angels (notoriously shitty dancers though they were)?

Just another question to smack God across the face with, on that ultimate Day of Reckoning. It's a question he very much looks forward to asking.

And the day is coming, soon.

"Ho, there, brother! The suburbs are nigh!" he calls out to Gregor, who balefully sneers. "Aw, don't be a snoot! It's a junk food night, darling! Let's find out how the other half dies!"

Gregor sighs his assent; it's a perverse enough notion. And fitting, besides. Given all that has happened.

"But I get to choose," he says mopily, sounding for all the world like Eeyore, or maybe Marvin the Paranoid Android.

"But of course, my love!" Ivan chimes in merrily. "But of course!" And together, they swoop down.

IV.

In a ticky-tacky tract home, surrounded by clones, Bob and Muffy have had quite a big night as well: "How to Strip for Your Husband" on video, followed by an hour and a half of earnest foreplay, culminating in the missionary position. It's rare that they invest so much time in romance, but the lilting strains of Kenny G. just wafted them away. And with Jimmy Buffett in the afterglow, they'd have to say that the night is complete.

But now it's three a.m.: time for some nice Velveeta Nachos and a snuggle in front of the TV screen. Muffy whips up the grub while Bob grabs the remote, boldly channel-surfing his way toward American Movie Classics.

Suddenly, the words "ROCK STAR MASSACRE" emblazon themselves across the screen. A weird shudder runs through him, like someone squatting over his grave. "Oh my goodness," says Bob, glancing nervously at the window as he slowly gooses up the volume.

"Honey?" Muffy calls out from the kitchen. "Let poor Scotty out, would you? I think he needs to tinkle."

Gregor isn't sure how he finally settles on these two, this house. He supposes it's the scent of normality that had swirled up around them in the Santa Ana winds, up from this Mojave tract home, pulling them in. That's what they need now: some junk, after the complicated and somehow ultimately unsatisfying repast they'd just completed.

Some pure Taste Sensation, cheap and greasy.

Warm light pours from the windows, falling on two winged things that expand into gangly giants. They stand, then, with arms outstretched. Silent. Still as death.

"Any more smokes?" Gregor asks his brother.

"What? Don't you want to do this?"

"Of course, Ivan, but let's just go back there into the shadows and relax, have a smoke, kind of plan a little bit. If we're going to, I want to do this right."

They glide around the side of the house, out toward the back of the garage. One by one, the security lights falter and die as they go. Ivan proffers half-a-dozen Lucky Strikes, then holds up a pale slender finger, which sprouts yellowblue flame.

"It's just a snack, hon," Ivan says, blowing out his finger. "I mean, what's to plan?"

"Oh, I don't know. It's just the breeze, the clear moonlight, the sheer banality. I just... It's times like these when I've started to ask myself, what would little Charlie do?"

They'd recently taken a liking to Manson: often visiting him in his San Quentin cell, in the guise of twin black butterflies, to listen to the beautiful manic flow of his monologue. Gregor always wished they'd been able to get to him before everything went down, that they'd been able to nurture his great creativity as only they could. He would have been such a thrilling conquest for them.

Now, watching him approach his old age, they love him as he is, wouldn't change him for the world.

Ivan's intrigued. "Really. Let's do! Cheap and nasty it is! Think Inquisition. Tobe Hooper. Rwanda."

Rwanda. Gregor savors the word. Such a lush slaughter. They'd picked up some lovely ideas there. It was hard to beat the mortals when it came to perpetrating acts of sheer savagery. But it was always worth a try.

At that moment, Mr. Goodson opens his back door to let little Scotty out. The twins flow out around the garage, easily mesmerizing the dog. Scotty manages to let out a muted yap before falling under the spell: its teensy dog-mind falls, not into a trance, but into utter obliviousness.

The terrier urinates on the lawn and bounds away, happily ignoring their presence. It gnaws vigorously at a playtoy as Bob pulls the door shut and flips the lock.

Then a thick double-shadow descends upon the dog.

"Muffy, sweetheart, come see what's been going on."

Bob Goodson settles back into his plush easy chair. He flips channels, every channel sporting a field reporter in SAN DIEGO LIVE: interviewing concertgoers, police, guest psychologists.

"*...apparent suicide by self-immolation....*"

From the kitchen. "I'm COOKING, honey... !"

"*...pending arrest following allegations that her husband's death was not suicide, as previously believed, but instead an elaborate and shocking murder scheme: perhaps the most shocking in show business history....* "

V.

And, of course, it was true. The flannel-festooned Spokesman of His Generation had no more killed himself than Oswald had shot JFK. It was more web-spinning from the depths of Hell: a ruse for the rubes, and a big black feather in the cap of eternal damnation.

The brothers had met Kirsten back in the early 1990s, while helping cultivate the resurgence of punk as a lucrative cultural stance. She had the goods, no question about it. And she was already a monster in training.

They'd waited for months, watching with sublime anticipation, then descended upon her in a rare private moment of fully suicidal despair: razor poised over junk-filled veins, tears and mascara making an Alice Cooper mask of her leonine, peroxide-framed face. They hadn't needed to be invited in; her whole life had been nothing but one big fat invitation.

She had screamed, of course, when they came through the window. But her neighbors were used to the screaming. And it quickly subsided, as they offered her their terms. No hypnosis was needed, just simple verbal suggestion. It was as clean a transaction as they had ever struck; if nothing else, she knew a good deal when she saw it.

Within half an hour, she was sucking Gregor's malformed cock while Ivan rammed his worm into her asshole from behind. Then they'd switched around, and switched again, until the night began to blur: a nonstop roundelay of frenzied orgasmic corruption and bliss. She was an excellent fuck, totally committed; the combination of perversity and unbridled power made her cream roughly a trillion times.

That night, they filled her with enough demon-spunk to sink the Titanic. But it didn't destroy her, as it had with their mothers.

It had simply made her more of what she already was.

From there, it was just an extension of her already-established star-fucking trajectory: forever calculating as she worked her way up the food chain, making and breaking each relationship in accordance with the tenets of Power Play 101.

Until she met her Golden Boy.

It was not John and Yoko, but it was close enough for punk. He was a damaged, radiant, broken angel, and his purity of intent was exceeded only by his talent. They got married and spawned, in no short order.

And then it was sacrifice time.

The second-most horrible thing, of course, was that she really loved him. The *most* horrible thing was that he really loved her, too. They had connected on so many levels, shared to the core so many things, that it was very nearly unthinkable to imagine them apart, once the die had been cast. So to speak.

But becoming a monster is no simple task: unless, of course, you're born into the part. Otherwise, *everybody* would be one, since everyone certainly has it in them. It takes effort. It takes perseverance. It takes careful planning.

It takes an absolute commitment to conquering the world, at the expense of your own immortal soul.

When the brothers came, informing her of what must be done, it had been profoundly agonizing for her. On the other hand, their timing was impeccable.

He'd become a star beyond his wildest dreams, and found that being a star was as grim as he'd feared. His music—his lifeline to God—had become a fucking commodity; the more he found himself trying to appease the moneymen, the less he felt his connection to the sacred. By negotiating the terms of his gifts, he had stripped them of their passion. He could no longer feel them.

And that was the worst hell of all.

Kirsten, on the other hand, could see only diminishing returns. What good was genius if it didn't pay the bills; even worse, if it didn't headline the Pastafazoola tour? When he had turned down *nine million fucking dollars*, what was she to think? That it was okay? That he was following his heart?

Fuck his heart! We're talking NINE MILLION DOLLARS!!!

From there, love was no longer an issue. It was simply a matter of doing the math. Fifty percent of the take on a retired rock star was a suck-assed and dwindling trajectory; and with her own album coming out, where the hell did that leave her? Picking up the pieces, like a servant on her knees?

No way. No fucking way.

Thank God for Ivan and Gregor.

Suddenly, everything began to make sense. She had climbed to the pinnacle, and it was time to make her move. One hundred percent of the tragic returns on her husband's untimely death was a windfall in every respect. She had a fine album. She knew it was good. Her husband had told her so himself. And she found that she'd been unconsciously writing the script that she would follow, even before she followed it.

It was almost uncanny, the way her songs foretold his death.

She'd always been a voracious reader, with crime and horror fiction always up at the top of the list. And whoever suggested that art wasn't instructive was lying out of their ass. She had enough Jim Thompson and James L. Cain in her system to last her a thousand lifetimes; and if there were 1,000,000 readers who could wallow in horror without acting it out, then she was just the one to break the bell curve.

It involved careful planning; but—being a junkie, with a rich fantasy life—she had fucked up. And the fuckup came from following her source material just a little bit too closely. She had hired a private detective to follow her husband, after his escape from a toughlove rehab scheme she had cooked up with his record label. The idea had been to deflect the detective, make a big public show of her concern while sowing the seeds of her husband's demise.

Unfortunately for her, the detective had been smart. He'd probably read the same books, too. So after the husband had turned up dead—his head blown to burger, and a shotgun in his hands—and after the detective had found himself employed by Kirsten to follow up roughly a million loose ends, all of which led exactly nowhere, said detective started doing some investigating of his own.

He had found, among other things, that the shotgun in question had no legible fingerprints on it; and how many suicides take the time to wipe the prints off their guns? Such destruction of evidence has traditionally been the province of people with something to hide; and while it was possible that the husband had done it to set Kirsten up for a post-mortem fall, there was nothing in his history or anywhere else to suggest such a deep streak of shittiness in him.

On the other hand, Kirsten was an extravagant and enthusiastic liar; she considered it a mark of coolness, and had immense contempt for anyone who couldn't keep up. This was in keeping with her enormous contempt for her audience, which ballooned in proportion with the sympathy sent from the fans of her magnificently talented ex. Next thing you knew, her album went platinum, and she was headlining the very tour her husband had turned down. Making big noises about her regretfulness, of course. And fucking other rock stars every single chance she got.

Gregor and Ivan had observed all this with awe and delight, a fiercely near-parental pride. Every time she made the cover of *Rolling Stone* or *People*, society eroded. It was a beautiful, horrible thing.

But it was not built to last. Nor was it meant to. A couple of years was all one could ask. By the time her threats of legal action could no longer forestall the rising tide of evidence, she was so ripe with ill-gotten glamour and absolute evil that she was ready to burst.

It was time to reap the harvest.

So when the word had gone down, through the monster pipeline, that the cops would make their move tonight, the misbegotten sons of Dracula had taken wing for San Diego.

And they had been *so excited...*

VI.

Who could have known it would be so unsatisfying?, Ivan thinks as he slowly cranks the handle of the lawn caddy. They'd anticipated it with great relish, only to find that some elusive ingredient had been missing, something that destroyed the flavor utterly, leaving them with the overwhelming desire to TASTE SOMETHING GOOD. (Hence the junk food jones.)

The evening had started so perfectly. Out on the ocean breeze, west to San Diego for the show, then backstage for the other show, when Kristen found out that her number was up.

The minute the cops appeared backstage, she went absolutely apeshit: a total psychotic reaction, so intense it made her *normal* legendary rock star tantrums look like rolling over in your sleep. She was out of her mind, but she was not stupid. They didn't have to say a word.

There were four cops in all. The first one died in less time than it takes a bullet to cross a room. She had him shredded so fast that, before they could blink, the other three were wiping wet gobs of him out of their eyes.

The cops drew their guns. Kirsten snarled; her mouth, always huge, had unhinged like a snake's. It was rimmed with red all the way to her scalpline, like lipstick applied with a fire hose. There was blood on her shoes. There was blood on the ceiling.

"*DIE!!!!!*" she screamed, "YOU *FUCKERRRRRRRRRRRS!!!!!!!*"

They opened fire, but not before the front of the second cop's head had been reduced to face tartar. Kirsten took six hollow point slugs. It barely even slowed her down.

Panic hit the back room like a blow dryer in a loaded bathtub: band members, press flaks, groupies, sycophants, roadies and toadies scattered for the exits, but the only way out was through Kirsten and the cops. Which is to say, there was no way out but death; and that option was about to be exercised.

Gregor and Ivan watched all this from their chosen vantage point, high up on the wall. They were tiny insectoid ebony things, multiple fly-eyes a-glisten, clacking excitedly to each other with twisted mandible grins. This was their girl, and she sure was spunky. So far, so fucking good.

Kirsten was shoving the third cop up the fourth one's ass when the stampede hit, knocking her backward. She hadn't liked that, so she took ten sets of legs off at the knees. This slowed things down enough for her to get up, lock the door, and address her hostages.

"WHO TOLD YOU YOU COULD LEAVE?" she screamed. "WHERE DID YOU EVER GET THAT IDEA? YOU DON'T WANNA FUCKIN' FUCK WITH ME, ALRIGHT? YOU DON'T WANNA FUCKING GET IN MY WAY!"

Then the room was hushed, and the silence awed her. Ivan and Gregor were awestruck, too. She was the Spokesthing of her Generation now; and she seemed to sense, in that moment, that this was her moment of truth.

So she lied. "I DIDN'T KILL MY HUSBAND!" Squirting tears on command from her red glowing eyes. "I WOULD *NEVER* HAVE DONE THAT!" Still bidding for sympathy, while her panicking audience just stood there, mechanically nodded their heads. They'd been trapped here by some monster who resembled their rock star. This was not a good backstage party for them.

Gregor and Ivan, on the other hand, were loving it; but, alas, time was running out. There'd be more cops soon—a ton of them—and the door wouldn't hold up long. They could picture her, tossing a head out every fifteen minutes, demanding fifty million dollars for the rights to the film.

Fun as it was to contemplate, it could not be allowed.

So they showed themselves to her at last, ballooning up impressively into the middle of the dressing room: fly-bodies rippling and expanding spasmodically into two wiry, huge ultra-goths.

"*What the fuck TOOK you so long?*" she demanded. "*Don't you see what's HAPPENING to me?*"

"It's over," Gregor told her simply. "Come on. It's time to go."

"B-but… !" She was, for a wonderful moment, astonished into silence. It had never occurred to her that she might not be the Queen of the Lost Souls forever. With a quiver in her lip, she questioningly indicated her trembling ex-fans.

"'What will they do without you?'" Ivan grinned. "Oh, they'll live. Or, actually, they won't."

Spontaneously, the hostages burst into flames; all but one, a plump Kristen wannabe, who shrieked at Gregor's approach. He proceeded to mold the bones in her face, remaking her, reforming the bones of her hips, refabricating tits, ass, legs, hands and feet: remaking her in the image of Kristen Fuckall. She already had the hair and stupid babydoll dress.

Then they set her on fire with the rest of the gang. Instant alibi. Worked every time. They'd done something similar for Adolph at the end of the war, and never had any complaints.

Kirsten, the real one, stared vacantly at the burning corpse. Ivan slapped her hard across the face. "Turn into a pigeon," he said.

"*What?*"

"You heard me. We can't have bats flying out of here, can we? You've already blown enough cover tonight!"

"If we didn't love you, we'd roast your ass!"

There was a pounding on the door.

"Let's GO!" Ivan roared.

Then three birds—two black, one dirty blond—had flown up through an open window, out into the night sky. Leaving behind Kirsten's career forever, along with some answers that would never be supplied….

All that was well and good; once again, it had all *started* promisingly enough. But once they'd returned to their castle, the evening had begun to take on a definite pale.

For one thing, she wasn't sufficiently impressed by the splendor of their magnificent domain. They'd given her the grand tour, expecting the traditional oohs and ahhs, but she'd barely paid attention. Gregor even got the sense that she thought the design was tacky, and that *really* put a burr in his nutsack.

But the main thing was that Kirsten was suicidally enraged; and while it was one thing to stand back and watch her tantrums, it was quite another to endure one yourself. She'd very quickly sucked all the fun from their night; within ten minutes, all they wanted was to get it over with.

"So what do you WANT?" Gregor'd asked her, annoyed. She'd thrown her hands up dramatically.

"I just want to DIE… !!!"

This was easily arranged, although it had taken a little doing. Even with both brothers leaning into it, her will was incredibly strong. Inside her, that was pretty much all that was left: no heart, no soul, no real reasoning power to speak of.

It had taken three minutes to break her down.

They were the longest three minutes of her life.

She had cried toward the end, when she saw she was losing. Despair opened up like a canyon inside her. It smelled great to the brothers, but it couldn't quite make up for the bad taste she'd already left in their mouths.

So they'd dutifully played out the ritual they'd planned: ramming a spit up her sphincter till it came out her mouth. Yanking her hairs out. Applying the light honey glaze. Roasting her ass had been pure anticlimax, for everyone involved. They did everything right—and the side dishes were impeccable—but there was no getting over the disappointment they felt.

There's just no substitute for good taste.

And even on the cellular level, all she could talk about was herself….

VII.

The more Gregor thinks about it, the angrier he gets. It's a blood-black tide that rises in him, flushing out depression and instilling rage. The hatred he's always felt for these creatures resurges, projecting outward, where it truly belongs.

He looks at his brother and sends the charge to him. His brother nods.

He feels it, too. It's an itch that needs scratching, this impulse to kill, and it's never been stronger in five hundred years.

These cattle, these peons, these stupid rutting sows, are the reason they need to hide in the dark. In the end, it's all for *them*. All these mindless entertainments. All these endless corrupting charades.

It's all for *them*. These ridiculous *people*. And who the fuck are they? They are no ones, nothings, meaningless scabs on a meaningless planet in a meaningless void. Alternative, shmalternative, it's all the same thing: spreading ugliness and stupidity so that *they* lose their way. The thought that *they* actually control the shots makes Gregor so pig-biting mad that he practically screams at the thought of it.

He needs somewhere to put this terrible feeling.

It's Bob and Muffy time.

VIII.

There is blood oozing in under the kitchen door. Muffy stares at it in disbelief, then coaxes her trembling hand toward the doorknob. She turns it slowly—stupid, stupid—then swings the door open, revealing the carcass of the family dog. It's lying across the walk, trailing a bloody umbilicus: a string of intestine which is wound and wound and wound around the hose caddy.

A cadaverous nightmare giant steps out of the shadows, red eyes pinning her, looming above her. It gestures toward Scotty, gutted on the concrete.

"There's something wrong with your dog," it says.

Then it punches Muffy in the teeth, sending her flying back into the kitchen.

Gregor stretches his arms into the room and plops Muffy down painfully into a chair. She starts to shriek. He opens his mouth, and black mucousy strands vomit out toward Muffy: wrapping tightly around her, around the chair, sealing her bloodied mouth shut, reaching up to prop open her eyelids.

Gregor snaps the sharkteeth shut, bites off the ends, gakks momentarily. His throat returns to normal. He swallows the remnants and smiles.

Meanwhile, Bob watches the television with vapid couch-potato intensity. The *Kirsten F: Nightmare in San Diego* Special Coverage is winding down: no breaking news now for over an hour, just the same anchors rehashing what he already knows. Twenty-three killed. A blazing fire. No surviving eyewitnesses. A terrible thing.

He lifts his head and scratches at his chin, wondering where Muffy is with that big plate of nachos. There is a loud slam from the kitchen.

"Muff! You okay, hon?"

There is no answer.

Ivan, a little black skull-faced mouse, scurries up the back of the TV. He unbodies, flowing up into it, Blob-style.

Glass sprays the room as the picture tube explodes. Ivan's head pokes out of the smoking hole. "And now," he says, "for a word from our sponsor."

Bob pisses and loads his pants.

"Oh, what a shame," Ivan says, rearing up, full height, out of the wreckage of the set. "Big boy go potty. We'll have to clean you all up."

Ivan's skin begins to wriggle as little flesh-hose-teeth animals bud and detach themselves from his arms, neck and face, then crawl off him and onto Bob.

"Please… " Bob manages, shaking convulsively, as the things eat the shit and drink the piss from him, start to eat his pants, swallow big bites of his shirt, and then burrow into Bob himself: tucking into naked skin, probing into each orifice, sampling fluids, tissues, bone. The things elongate, wrapping around the chair.

"All cozy?" Ivan says. "Good. Now. Please begin to worry. This will hurt a great deal."

He produces the hedge trimmer he'd found out next to the garage.

"Gregor! Come quickly."

"I'm coming! I'm coming!"

Gregor comes out of the kitchen, trailed by the chair with Muffy. It skitters into the living room on slimy pseudopods, moving over next to Bob.

"I want to throw the yarrow-stalks," Ivan deadpans. "But we haven't got any yarrow stalks. What shall I do?"

Gregor grins. "I'd say we start cutting."

When he finishes trimming off the four fingers and thumb of Bob's right hand, he crunches down on the index and middle finger of the left hand, producing seven surrogate stalks. He immediately tosses them on the carpet, noting the pattern the bundle of fingers make. He continues to do this until the arrangement of broken and unbroken lines of the I Ching hexagram forms in his mind.

Number Eleven, Ivan recalls from his vast memory.

With Tranquility,
the small goes
and the great comes,
with auspicious success.

"Tranquility," Gregor murmurs, and pulls his Eye Straw out from where it's been neatly tucked away beneath his skin. It is an oversized surgical steel pipette engraved with intricate curlicues, which he slowly inserts into Muffy's left eye and proceeds to suck on gleefully. As the muffled screams subside, he pauses, savoring the delicate texture and taste of the fluid. Hardly junk food, he thinks.

"Have you tasted?" he asks his brother.

"No, but judging from this reading, I think it's time for 'the small to go.' What do you think, folks? Go bye bye?"

"No answer?"

"Ah, well."

Ivan kicks Bob's chair over and falls on top of him, making a mess of things, sucking up blood and essence, sucking the little beasties back into himself. Gregor, meanwhile, sits on Muffy's lap, straddles her, rips through her black gut bonds with his talons, ripping her face off as well. He swallows the tissue and laps up the blood, savoring the memories that flow into him.

Her memories are shit, nothing followed by nothing. Evidently, she has never seen live music in her life. Another bunch of nothings at a Holiday Inn lounge. An irritating nothing with a guitar in the street. There is Barry Manilow on a Christmas special. Kenny Rogers and John Denver.

Charo, Cher, and Tiny Tim. He sees she really *liked Where the Action Is*, a '60s TV show featuring Paul Revere and the Raiders. Church songs, from her early childhood.

And then he hits something else.

They are not the uncomplicated, strong flavors he's expecting, but ones that have subtle notes and accents running through them, exotic and spicy. He pauses, confused. There is something compelling here, deeper than deep, way beneath the surface. As he eats at the viscera, swallows down the rich red juice, a strange light seems to grip him from within. The intensity builds, goes from excitement to terror, until....

The light entirely overwhelms him.

Gregor stares, in confusion and fear, at the meatmass that undulates impossibly before him. He is paralyzed, helpless. He doesn't understand. *This is cattle!*, he thinks.

GUESS AGAIN, a voice says.

Before his disbelieving eyes, the ghastly leftovers of Muffy wake up and purr, sexily, "That was GREAT!" There's a smile on her skull. Viscera starts to crawl toward her, and Ivan hears Bob's voice saying, "Ditto, Muff! I could sure go for a Camel Filter!"

He begins to puke, abruptly and horribly, dropping to his knees. From the splatting on his left, he guesses that Ivan is puking, too. Everything they have just taken inside them is leaving them now, without abandoning control.

Organs start to recongeal on the floor; puddles of blood flow over the floor and reabsorb into Bob and Muffy's bodies. Anything that was taken from them now returns to them, along with a huge draught of the power, energy and will that Gregor and Ivan possess.

Incredibly powerful, incredibly ancient forms rise up, towering above the Sons of Dracula. Older and more powerful than anything the boys had ever dreamed of, older and darker than Vampire- or Humankind. Perhaps the progenitors of their darkness. Or something entirely Other.

They can hear, as if from a long way off, the hose caddy whirring as dog-intestines rewind back into Scotty. They can imagine the blood puddle reversing back into his body.

And sure enough, something big and nasty thuds through the kitchen, comes into their view. A hell-hound rounds the corner, barely clearing the door. Whatever was lazing behind the doggie-mind is now wide awake. It smiles at them, slowly opening its gaping, worse-than-canine maw.

"I'm afraid that you've made a logistical error," the Scotty-beast says, "though I must say that it was enchanting. Better than chasing cats, by a long shot." He grins. "So glad you stopped by."

"Not that it was an accident," the Muffy-Thing assures them, scooping the last glops of gore into her frame. "We like to let you ripen, till you're JUST RIGHT!"

"And then we send for you," Hell-Bob adds, tucking in a remarkably Ivan & Gregor-shaped bib. "And the kick is, you think it's your own free will!"

The three primordial beings circle the two helpless creatures.

"You see," Scotty-beast says, "after several eons or so, one begins to develop a *very* sophisticated palate. I mean, as you can imagine, the kicks just keep getting harder to find."

"*That's the beauty of unconsciousness*," Bob and Muffy intone as one. "*That's the beauty behind God's hide-and-seek. You can't really remember until you forget.*"

"Now—what was it?—oh yes," says Scotty. "'Please begin to worry. This will hurt a great deal.'"

And, as one, they fall upon the screaming brothers: devouring their bodies, but saving their souls—their consciousness, whatever—and making them watch. Grinding home the fact that there is always somebody bigger, somebody stranger, somebody worse.

Then sending them off to somewhere where they can savor the message. In all of its fullness.

Again and again.

IX.

Above a slaughterhouse in Palmdale, the sun rises slow. And all the pigs are screaming. They're not stupid. They know.

And Ivan and Gregor are there: the two of them, locked into multiple pig-brains, five hundred apiece and a thousand in all. Half-recalling their former selves. Tortured by ghosts. Unable to resist. Marching forward, again and again and again, toward the waiting abattoirs.

They come. They fall. They wake. They come. They fall. Again and again and again. Struggling in vain against the waiting knives. Powerless as their life-blood drains from them.

Remembering what it's like to ride the cattle-flume out, on the low end of the eternal food chain.

Dying over and over and over again in helpless, indifferently meted humiliation and pain.

It had been, in the end—whether they liked it or not—a big night in monster history.

WRIGHTSON

Caveat Shatner

Joy Mosier-Dubinsky

Jimmy's father was an asshole and Jimmy figured that, by merit of his genes alone, he was also an asshole. This was the conclusion he drew as he sat on the soft, rotting corpse of a fallen tree way back in Telefor's Woods, nursing his swollen (pleasedontletitbebroken) ankle. He could concentrate on that, or he could think about Kurt and David and the fucked-up plan that had somehow changed mindless stupidity into living nightmare. It was better to think of dear, old dad.

Kurt, the dumb shit, had hatched "The Plan" earlier in the week—Monday afternoon, if specifics meant anything at all now. He'd proposed a little walk through the woods to find The Vlads, a group of 18- and 19-year-old losers who hung out here, sacrificing squirrels and the occasional, hapless neighborhood cat in hopes of attaining immortality. Jimmy had seen them in the parking lot of the local Burger King a few times, smoking reefer in their Dodge Darts and Chevy Novas, talking Star Trek, too. Fascinating conversations, those were! He'd caught snatches of the great "Kirk V. Piccard" debate a few times and it had deepened his disdain for the group immeasurably. Trekkie Vampires! How stupid is that? Jimmy had a strong suspicion that if anyone would be eligible for everlasting life, a Just and Fair God would have some contingency plan to eliminate Trekkies from the running.

But Kurt had been insistent, even invoking the almighty "You aren't chicken, are you?" to get his way. Low blow, if you asked Jimmy, but nonetheless effective enough that Jimmy and David had dutifully fallen into a single-file line behind Kurt and Butt Boy Billy and followed them into the trees. The last, streaming sunlight of Friday afternoon had danced on the ground as they made their way along paths choked with roots and littered with the trash of those who had come before. Jimmy could see the moon, high overhead now, and if his ankle didn't hurt so much, and David hadn't… well, snapped, then the night, bathed in luminous moonlight, might have been worth it. If. One little word could negate everything.

They'd gotten lost and Kurt had stood, turning this way and that, trying to determine their best course. Going along with Kurt was their first mistake, but their deadly mistake was allowing Kurt to be in charge. It was like the grossly retarded leading the blind. Jimmy had just had it. They'd been wandering in what felt like a really big circle for too long, and Kurt—it was obvious!—had been charting their course by using discarded beer cans and condom wrappers as landmarks.

"This is ridiculous! Ludicrous!" Jimmy yelled, searching his memory for more of Mrs. Johnson's vocabulary-building spelling words. He'd just settled on "inane" when David turned on him.

"Shut up!" he screeched, the words almost unintelligible. "You're not helping, so just SHUT UP!"

Excuse me? Jimmy had thought to himself. David, wuss extraordinaire, is telling me to shut up? David, destined to spend the better part of his twenties asking, "You want fries with that?" is telling me, Jimmy Amdenio, quarterback and only ninth-grade boy ever to feel up Tina Anderson under the bra to SHUT UP? I think not; fuck that!

What would John Wayne do? Jimmy had just started to push his sleeves up (probably how The Duke would begin), when David's skinny hand, with scabby cuticles and inky, ballpoint blobs, slapped across his cheek with a sting. Jimmy was momentarily stunned, and the red handprint on the side of his face felt warmer than the blush spreading from his neck. It was a rotten thing to do, interrupting a guy who was pushing up his sleeves. Fuck that, too!

Jimmy lunged at David, wrapped his strong arm around his friend's scrawny neck and took him down. David did not fight back or resist as

Jimmy straddled his chest and pummeled his face with fast, hard fists.

"Remembered your place as founder of The Wimp Hall Of Fame, did you?" Jimmy smirked at him. David stared up at him with eyes that looked distant. A smug smile played on his split lips. This enraged Jimmy. He pulled his arm back, shut his eyes and blindly punched. With a sickening *crunch-thwik*, David's throat collapsed under Jimmy's knuckles. Jimmy got scared.

"Shit," Kurt said, a low whistle escaping his round lips. "You killed him!"

Butt Boy just stared.

"I… Get the fuck out! He's… " Jimmy strained to look at David's form in the twilight.

"Well, he's not breathing," Billy offered.

"Who asked you? Of course he's breathing! I think I even see the pulse in his neck," Jimmy lied, hoping he sounded convincing. Just take charge of the situation, a voice in his head counseled him.

"Yeah, he's breathin', all right. It's just that his chest ain't movin'!" Kurt crowed sarcastically.

He's calling you stupid, Jim-bo! his father's voice intoned. *You gonna let him call you stupid?*

"Shut up Kurt! 'Oh, let's go join The Vlads,' you said." Jimmy made his voice high-pitched and girlish. "'Let's go see the big, scary VAMPIRES! Let's see if they'll let us play with their SPOCK DOLLIES!' You dumb shit." Jimmy turned away from them.

Hide your fear, Jim-bo.

"Yeah, but Kurt never told you to kill David," Butt Boy pointed out.

"I didn't kill David! Stop saying that!"

They stood silently living the cliché of twilight fading fast. It was bullshit! David couldn't be… Jimmy didn't even think he'd hit him that hard. No way.

And then The Vlads showed up.

They were a tight group of the toughest bad-asses a small Ohio town could offer. Cigarettes dangled from their lips, their hands were thrust in the faded, frayed pockets of Levi's 501s. At the front of the pack (what do you call a group of vampires—a coven, a gaggle?) stood the tall, freakishly skinny Ben. When Ben wasn't leading his mighty, undead army of Klingons, he was a pump monkey at the local Amoco station. Jimmy recognized a few others from their illustrious careers as burger flippers and supermarket stock-boys. Way in the back he thought he saw Snakes Lazar, his next-door neighbor and K-Mart cashier extraordinaire. Rumor had it that Snakes could add and was, therefore, eligible for management.

"What happened here?" Ben asked, and the sound of his voice went through Jimmy like a hundred slivers of glass. Ben was speaking with a very proper, very English accent. An English accent on a native of Cambridge, Ohio? Puh-leeze! He'd wasted his time studying *My Fair Lady* when Hooked on Phonics was what he really needed.

"Jimmy punched David in the throat and killed him," Butt Boy tattled. Why couldn't he just keep his trap shut?

"I didn't kill him." Jimmy looked defiantly at Ben, his most superior sneer in place.

"Did you punch him in the throat?" Ben queried politely, the very soul of Henry Higgins.

"Well, yeah… I did. But I didn't kill him."

"Doesn't seem like he's living to me," said a voice from the back, maybe Snakes. Jimmy wondered to himself if maybe Ben and Snakes took turns dressing up like Audrey Hepburn.

"He's just… stunned, is all." Jimmy sounded whiny, even to himself.

"Stunned, you think?" Ben asked, moving closer to get a better look. Jimmy noticed that the whole group (maybe a school?) also moved forward in perfect synchronicity.

I bet they call 'em a "herd," Jim-bo, his father spoke in his head. *Look at how they follow one another, dress the same way. It's a mentality.*

Ben bent over and tugged at David's collar. A thin stream of blood trickled from David's mouth and suddenly he jerked to life. David raised himself up on one elbow, sputtering. He choked out great gobs of phlegm, sticky with blood clots, that landed on the ground with soft thuds.

"Problem solved, gentlemen," said Ben with a slight bow at the waist. He grinned at them, pleased with the miracle he had provided.

"Yeah, problem solved," Jimmy muttered, unimpressed. David was alive, no doubt about that now, but what had Mr. Lost Boy done to accomplish that?

"Beg pardon?"

"I said, yeah, problem solved. Okay?"

"I think you doubt me, doubt I had something to do with that." Ben favored Jimmy with a small, amused smile.

He's playing with you, Jim-bo!

"Yeah, I doubt you. But forget it." Jimmy flipped his hand up, dismissed Ben. He started to walk away, but Ben called to him.

"I am offended, my lad. But I will excuse your ignorance with your age."

"I'm not your 'lad,' but I will excuse your bullshit with your slippery grasp on reality."

The group (pride?) looked at Ben questioningly, and then at Jimmy with what his attorney father would call "Malice Aforethought." Ben held one hand up, like a traffic cop, to stay them. Muscles visibly relaxed as they dropped their collected combat stance. His own friends looked at Jimmy, and Kurt shot him a frightened look that pleaded, "Shut up now, while there's still time! Before you get us killed!" Jimmy would not allow himself to be intimidated. He raised his hand in wickedly perfect imitation of the bony master.

"Why do you doubt me, doubt my power?" Ben asked soothingly. He still sounded impossibly polite in that clipped accent. Jimmy rolled his eyes, and threw his hands up with disgust.

"Why do I doubt you? You want to know WHY? Gee, I don't know! You're a regular Christ Almighty, aren't you? And my pal, Dave here—he's a gen-U-ine fucking Lazarus!" Jimmy was not going to play along with this madness any longer.

And that's when the melee broke out.

Everyone had been watching Jimmy challenge Ben. No one was paying any attention as David sat up, but when he began to howl with the pitiful ferocity of a rabbit strangling in a trap, all eyes turned to him. He clawed his fingers into the ground, smeared them in his recently vomited mucus. David's fingers, caked with dirt and sputum, appeared partially decomposed in the dim light. Attention remained riveted as he slowly reached up and twisted the bulge in the fabric of Ben's crotch. Ben's wail joined with David's. The terror opera began.

The Vlads converged on them, with Kurt and Butt Boy jumping in. Jimmy held his place, fascinated by the dogfight in front of him. He watched, unbelieving, as David managed to defend himself, tossing bodies aside as if they weighed nothing more than dolls. All the while, he kept his steady grip on Ben's balls. With ease, David flicked the meaty form of Kurt away. Kurt sailed through the air, and from the *thwak* sound his head made against a tree, Jimmy guessed that the stars at night were big and bright, clap if you like.

Many of The Vlads were turning and running now, disappearing among the trees. Butt Boy sat beside Kurt's slumped figure, crying. Billy was on his own now, completely alone for the first time since the two of them had discovered a mutual love for the taste of paste back in kindergarten. Jimmy felt like maybe he should comfort Butt Boy, but his concentration was diverted by the action at hand.

David, now unmolested and undisturbed, pulled his "savior" down in a grotesque lover's embrace. Jimmy noticed that beneath the blackened smears David's fingers had made, Ben's crotch was soaked with blood. He was mesmerized by the sight of it. That's gotta hurt, he thought. Then David opened his mouth wide and sank his teeth into the hard muscle of Ben's neck with surprising ease. He raised his head toward Jimmy, bits of flesh and tendon clutched in a psychotic grin.

Get the hell out of there, Jim-bo! his father told him. Sweat soaked his armpits as he began to back away. David slurped and sucked in an effort to get the hunk of Ben completely in his mouth, reminding Jimmy of his hours-ago, spaghetti dinner that now lurched and gurgled within his gut. With a final nod to Mrs. Johnson, Jimmy looked into David's ravenous eyes and ran.

He hadn't stopped until he realized that the trees had swallowed him whole. Unless he could calm down (and Think!) he'd never find his way out. Seen one tree, you've seen 'em all, he thought. Bitterly, he wondered if he was at the mercy of condom wrappers, too. "Just call me 'Hansel,'" Jimmy grumbled to himself. There wasn't any time for self-pity, though, as his ears picked up the soft, crunching sound of David's high-top sneakers on the dry, autumn leaves.

He blindly dashed to the right, and grabbed the first low-hanging branch and vaulted up to the next. He continued climbing until he was well above the ground. Please God! I know he's different now, but let David still be afraid of heights! Silently, Jimmy repeated his prayer and listened to the sounds of David coming closer.

David came into view, his shoulders hunched forward, head darting left and right, on the hunt for fresh blood. Jimmy held his breath as David passed beneath him, watched as his former friend gingerly walked along, trying to be quiet. Jimmy's smart-ass nature wanted to yell down, "It ain't workin' bud!" but he stopped himself. David's shadowy form disappeared, and still Jimmy waited. He tried to remember how to cross himself, as his father said, *Atta boy, Champ!*

He was almost on the ground again when a limb snapped under his foot. He fell with an "oof," listening for the sound of David returning. There was a rustling in the leaves, and Jimmy's heart convulsed in his chest, certain that David was coming back. He tried to stand, but his left ankle yelled loud protestations along the nerves of his leg. He stumbled, and crawled over the cold floor of the forest to the tree trunk where he now sat.

Gently, he tested his ankle. It flat-out refused to take any of his weight. Jimmy knew that football practice tomorrow was out of the question, and probably the rest of the season, too. Then he remembered the look on David's face, saw his teeth slipping into Ben's flesh like it were soft bread, and Jimmy started to cry. Life, as it had been, was over. No way could he go to school on Monday morning, cool and sure, lean over Tina's desk and say, "Yeah, well Friday night, we all went into the woods and David ate a vampire. Well, not a real vampire, but... " Ri-i-ight. Thinking that way made him feel hopeless and broken inside, made him wish he'd broken his neck instead of his ankle. He really didn't want to die, so he started to count the ways that his father was an asshole and that seemed to keep his mind occupied.

His father would stand at the edge of the practice football field yelling, "HustleHustle, Jim-bo!" and it was really annoying how two separate words became one. The real bitch of it was, while Jimmy was on the field, sweating like a pig, taking hit after hit from bigger guys, his father had the balls to stand there (crisp and cologned, for Chrissakes!) demanding more. Asshole!

His father wore black, nylon, lawyer-socks with their yellow toe-seams peeking out of the tips of his sandals. All right, so he only did it around the house, but still! It was pathetic! It set Jimmy's teeth on edge, and at night while they watched TV together, his father would pick little lint balls off those socks. The lint balls went in the ashtray, burning with a faint, melted plastic stench when hot cigarette ashes fell on them. That was asshole all the way!

This whole "Jim-bo" thing was a point of contention with Jimmy, as well. He was forced to become "Jim-bo" when his father felt like giving advice, or being affectionate. "Jim-bo! Don't let the other kids push you around.... Don't take their shit, Jim-bo.... I love you, Jim-bo."

His dad did love him. He knew that. He also knew that his father hadn't had it easy since his mother had traded the two of them in like they were out-of-style or last season's "look." She'd just gone and gotten herself new—and his dad had stayed around, tried to make it okay.... and thinking of this was more upsetting than he'd realized it would be.

Behind him, the bushes moved. From deep inside the leaves, a hand shot out and grabbed his shoulder. Jimmy was pressed down, the bark of the log biting into the backs of his thighs through his jeans. Another hand clamped over his mouth, and Jimmy felt hot, smoky breath as Snakes Lazar said, "Don't think about screaming, motherfucker. I'm here to help you."

Jimmy wasn't sure it was relief that washed over him, but Snakes wasn't David and that counted for something. Snakes assessed the situation and set quickly to work. He snatched up the traitor branch and began to work his knife along the length of it. He fashioned a splint and, with help from a snotty bandanna, set Jimmy's ankle. While he busied himself with this, Snakes told Jimmy that he'd returned to the "scene" and, since he hadn't noticed Jimmy's body among the others, he figured that Jimmy had gone and gotten himself hopelessly lost in the woods. He paused and looked hard into Jimmy's eyes to see if what he'd said was sinking in. Jimmy got

WRIGHTSON

it all right—"body" and "others." David hadn't been satisfied with just Ben.

Snakes hadn't worried about the other Vlads, they knew this area like they knew their own dicks, he said. And he knew Jimmy wouldn't know what to do, either. From the looks of things, that was dead on, too. So he'd made his way about the woods, stealthily avoiding that "Beastly Bastard," and looked for Jimmy. It was very important that Jimmy be found, you see, "… because you have to kill that friend of yours," Snakes concluded, tying a knot in the handkerchief with a flourish.

"I have to kill David? If you think back, that's what supposedly landed us in this mess in the beginning!" Jimmy looked at Snakes. "I don't think so. Thanks for your help and all."

"Jim, you don't understand. You don't have a choice. Ben said so." Snakes didn't look menacing, although Jimmy knew he could if he set his mind to it.

"When did Ben say this? Before David ripped his cock off, or after he became a midnight snack?"

"He said it three nights ago. And you don't have a choice, Jim. This is your destiny." Snakes said it with a strange reverence. Jimmy made a "chee" sound of disgust, ready to mouth off. Snakes stopped him.

"I know you don't believe—I didn't believe in the beginning, either." Snakes looked at him and Jimmy thought about the boy who'd always lived next door. Snakes had always been a little too old and beyond Jimmy. They weren't on speaking terms, let alone friends. Jimmy didn't have to listen. Snakes was a kid in a leather jacket—a tough guy. Jimmy was a kid with a football letter on his jacket, a "jock." They were oceans apart in experience.

Snakes interrupted his thoughts. "Look Jim, none of us Vlads was ever a football star, and we couldn't have been even if we tried. Not me, not Ben, not any of us. We're 'losers' to you and your friends, and we fell in together because of it. We were just a group of buds who hung out together, ran through the woods." Snakes paused and pulled a plastic canteen from inside his coat. He offered Jimmy a swig, but Jimmy shook his head. Snakes had lost that dreadful, affected accent and Jimmy was glad for it.

Snakes took a few gulps, and continued. "We scammed beer from our parents when we could, smoked a little dope. We just had fun together. If we could get girls, we got 'em.... " Here, he nudged Jimmy and gave him a little wink. Jimmy got the distinct impression that Snakes Lazar was a veteran of "Under The Bra" and beyond. Jimmy nodded appreciatively, thinking of Tina and the warmth of her skin.

"Hey Jim! Come back, pal. No time to be thinkin' 'bout titties!" Snakes laughed. "We got work to do."

"No, we don't have any work to do. I don't understand any of this. And how did you know... ?" Jimmy felt overwhelmed.

"I'll answer your questions, but I have a story to tell you first. We—The Vlads—we weren't vampires to begin with. We were just hanging around, talking Trek and stuff. Then Ben started to have these... visions, I guess you'd call 'em."

"And a little dope didn't have anything to do with that? Come on!" Jimmy interrupted.

"No, reefer doesn't make you see things, it makes you mellow. 'Course you wouldn't know that. Ben started having what he called these 'awake dreams' and we thought he'd lost it. His mom had offed herself last year, he'd started reading these weird books about witches and stuff. He'd try to talk to us about it, and we'd laugh. I know where you're coming from on this, Jim. I used to be there myself. That changed for me, and I think it will change for you, too."

You wish, Jimmy thought sullenly.

"You have to believe. Just try, okay?" Snakes was pleading with him, and Jimmy wasn't sure why it was so important that he play along. His ankle felt better, but it still hurt. Jimmy thought longingly of hospitals and doctors, real medical attention. Every minute here, arguing with Snakes, meant delaying that.

"Make you a deal, Jim. Just listen to me, believe me, force yourself to, and I guarantee you won't need a doctor after all. All right?" Snakes held out his hand, and Jimmy shook it, thinking that he was pretty much at the mercy of the other boy and his grip.

"Ben came to my house late one night, raving about the afterlife or something. My dad wasn't even gonna let him in, but he finally did. We went up in my room and Ben takes my knife and cuts his wrist," Snakes gestured to his own wrist, his index finger pointing just under the fleshy pad of the palm of his hand. "From here to here! Clear up to the fucking inside of his elbow!" Snakes looked momentarily sick at the memory. "He's laughing like a crazy man, sticking his arm in my face. Blood is spurting everywhere. I'm screaming, my father is pounding on my door, my mother's in the hall crying. I was completely convinced he had snapped and come to my house to kill himself in front of me. Then Ben turns around and shows me his arm. Nothing there, not a fucking mark! And he's pleased with himself, like this is some good joke or a trick, like in the movies."

"I don't be—" Jimmy started to protest, but Snakes cut him off.

"I know you don't believe. I know you're humoring me. But if you want to live, little man, you have to quit being a smart ass and believe me!" Snakes was starting to look a little angry.

Jimmy considered the size of the boy beside him. If his ankle hadn't been bum, he'd have told Snakes the whole thing was Ridiculous! Ludicrous! and walked away. Unless Snakes bitch-slapped him, too....

"Jimmy, look: a year ago, I thought it was shit for the birds, too. But believe it or don't, I'm gonna live to see more tomorrows than any man probably should. I have Ben and his visions to thank for it."

"Okay, I'm pretending to believe you. Now will you please tell me why I have to kill David?" Jimmy thought playing along was his best choice.

"Ben did a divination the other night. He predicted that a stronger, more powerful vampire would come into the woods. That other vampire, your friend David —"

"Wait a minute! David isn't a vampire! David can't even sleep without lights on if he sees George Hamilton on TV!" Pretend, yes. Swallow a big load of shit? No. It was impossible, the very idea of it!

"David is a vampire! He had to die as a mortal in order to come back in his true form. So when you killed him—"

"BUT I DIDN'T KILL DAVID!" Jimmy burst out. Snakes quickly threw himself onto Jimmy, and put his hand over the younger boy's mouth.

"Keep your voice down," he hissed, eyes darting into darkness. "You'll get us both killed!"

"Sor-ree!" Jimmy murmured beneath his fingers.

"Look, I've had it! I'm trying to do you a favor. I should just leave you.... "

Jimmy panicked. "No, don't! I'm sorry, I really am. It's just… " his voice trailed away.

"Ben saw the whole thing, even his own death." Snakes' voice dipped, but he continued, sensing they hadn't much time. "You're gonna love this part, Jim. You," he pointed his finger at Jimmy, "have an appointment with destiny, as they say in the movies."

Jimmy felt a foolish grin slide across his face as he waited expectantly for Snakes to continue. Snakes felt the same urgency, the same sense of individual seconds of time slipping away too quickly, but he wasn't sure how to continue. Ben had warned him that Jimmy would be a tough nut to crack. He'd suggested to Snakes that it might be better to keep some details from Jimmy. Snakes had a conscience, though, and it was harder keeping things back than he'd thought it would be. He sighed heavily, and then turned to face Jimmy.

"There are people out there… " he began, and stopped. "Not every vampire is… " *Why can't I just spit it out?* Snakes wondered, while Jimmy sat looking at him, that same idiot smile on his face.

"You must become a vampire, Jim. Then, you must kill your brethren." There! It was out.

"Huh?"

"Your destiny runs strong. You will become one of the Inner Circle, and your purpose will be to cripple those who have strayed."

"What are you talking about?" That moron look was frozen on his face.

"I'll make it simple for you: There are good vampires. There are bad vampires. You're like the 'Vampire Police,' so to speak. You'll spend the rest of time hunting the Fallen, and destroying them. "

"Sure." *Me?*

"Yeah, you. We're partners, might as well know that." Snakes began to pat at his pockets, searching. He finally found what he was looking for, and produced a small film canister. He snapped the top off. "Here, drink this."

"What is it?" Jimmy asked, sniffing at it. It smelled spicy and rotten.

"Your potion. I don't know what it's called. I don't know what's in it, so don't even ask." Snakes suddenly felt very tired. He'd answered too many questions already and there just wasn't time for any more. He felt like grabbing his knife, pressing the blade against the whiteness of Jimmy's throat and forcing him to do as he was told.

"I'm chosen." Jimmy was awed. "Cool! Anything I should know?"

"You aren't gonna fight me anymore, Jim?" Snakes couldn't believe it. Seems too easy, he thought.

"No, I'm not going to fight you. I just want to know what to expect. Is this immortality gonna hurt?"

"Not really. You'll be able to hear snatches of thought, not read minds exactly. It sounds like flipping through the channels too quick, but certain things are plain. You wake up in the morning and it feels like there are a million pins sticking in your brain, but that's about it." Snakes looked at Jimmy, hoping this met his approval. They really didn't have time to spare.

"I didn't think vampires could go out in the sun." Jimmy was confused.

"Forget all that cheesy Hollywood stuff. Mainstream morons got hold of vampirism and fucked it all up. You're not going to have to drink blood to stay alive, either. That's just shit they made up so it would be scarier, creepier. Forget about it. Just drink."

Jimmy tilted his head back and felt the thick, syrupy liquid slide down his throat. His vision faded into a world where colors felt warm and alive. He floated in a cloud of red for long moments, caressed and cradled in the spectrum. His eyes felt heavy and he slipped away, until he felt a tugging at his ankle. He opened his eyes in time to see Snakes tossing the splint away.

"Feelin' okay?" Snakes smiled at Jimmy.

"I am feelin' great! What do we do now?" Jimmy was testing his ankle, pleased to find that it was good as new.

"Now we go get that son of a bitch!" Snakes cried, and eagerly laid out their plan.

Jimmy came up to the edge of the clearing where David sat gnawing on what looked like a femur. He was happily scraping the last bits of flesh from the bone, singing to himself in a low, growling voice. His song drifted over to where Jimmy crouched, and Jimmy smiled.

"Hey there, Georgie Girl! There's another Georgie deep inside… " he drooled the lyrics into the bone, as Jimmy stood up and bellowed his name.

David froze, and turned toward Jimmy. "Georgie Girl" died on his lips, and a rabid growl escaped him. Jimmy leaped through the air, landing with his elbow planted firmly in the base of David's skull. "Down just like the sack of shit you are!" Jimmy crowed triumphantly, and busied himself with staking his adversary to the ground. Snakes waited on the edge of the clearing, watching and hoping that David would remain unconscious long enough for Jimmy to finish.

Jimmy took four small wooden pegs from his pocket, and went about driving them through the flesh of David's wrists and ankles. The final peg broke when he tried to kick it firmly into the soft ground, so he substituted a free rib that was nearby. David began to stir, as Jimmy pulled Snakes' knife out.

David's eyes fluttered open, and he found himself staring up at Jimmy. A furious snarl came from deep in his chest and he struggled to pull his arms free. He glanced from one wrist to the other, horrified to find himself nailed into the cold forest floor. Fountains of blood began to spurt from his wounds as he heedlessly thrashed and twisted. He screamed in agony, and Jimmy snatched unsuccessfully for his tongue. It was slippery with saliva and blood, and not as easy to grab as Jimmy had assumed it would be. His fingers finally met their mark, and his nails clawed through the slimy muscle. With a deft, swooping arc, Jimmy severed David's tongue from his head. It remained twined around his fingers, as David lay on the ground gurgling and coughing. His eyes were wide and angry, and tears of frustration seeped down his cheeks as he lay quietly hating his foe, but unable to say so. Jimmy shook his hand to cast away the shredded tongue as Snakes came bounding into the clearing. He knelt at the twitching form and feasted upon the muscles of David's abdomen. Jimmy staggered back against a tree and looked elsewhere. The clearing was littered with bones and jellylike stuff that clung to clumps of dead grass. The skeletons of Kurt and Butt Boy were mixed together in a heap. Jimmy thought about them, and about the fun they'd all had together, in an effort to ignore the guttural grunts Snakes was making. Chosen or not, Jimmy was disgusted.

When Snakes was finished, he rolled over onto his back and patted his

belly. Blood and fat had dribbled down his chin and shirt in his feeding frenzy. It was obvious he hadn't a care in the world as he let out a loud burp and sat up.

"What do you want to do now, Jim?"

Jimmy looked at him blankly. "Do?" he asked.

"Yeah, I was thinking... I got all the original Trek episodes on tape. You could come over and watch 'em, if you want." He started to get up, rubbing his hands in anticipation.

Jimmy shuddered. An eternity of Star Trek? Jesus, NO!

"Come on, it'll be fun. Ben and I used to—"

"I'm just not interested. It's been a long night." Jimmy turned, and began to walk deliberately out of the woods. Snakes chased after him, and caught his arm.

"Hey! You forget! We're a team!" he whined, breathlessly.

"Yeah, but we aren't friends. Got that?" Jimmy sounded nastier than he'd intended. "Look," he tried again, "No matter how long I live, I just... I hate William Shatner, and an extended lifetime of watching him 'boldly going where no man has gone before' sounds like hell to me. I'm sorry. "

"Nobody said it was gonna be easy, Jim." Snakes said.

"You don't mean—? Oh, no! I didn't sign on for that. Forget it."

Snakes laughed as Jimmy spoke. He clapped Jimmy on the back like a used-car salesman closing a deal. "I was teasing, Jim. I know where to find you when I need you. See you around."

"Yeah, teasing... see you." Jimmy walked away, glancing back. Snakes stood laughing at his little joke. Bite me, Jimmy thought, and started out of the woods again.

"No thanks, " Snakes called after him. "I just ate!"

Jimmy was deep in thought as he walked home. He and Snakes were partners forever. An extended lifetime of Snakes jumping into his head, reading his private ideas, maybe even living his memories—it made Jimmy's stomach hurt. Jimmy had just damned himself to an eternity with a guy who knew the difference between Klingons and Romanians (or whatever they were called!) and that was that.

Forever.

Vamway

Brad Linaweaver

Mr. Sepet held the floor. We all respected him. Some would say it was because of his age but that wasn't it. The new girl, Johna, told me she found him very sexy. One of the punk kids in the organization said he'd rather fight a whole street gang than go up against "the old guy." Tonight the kid was on guard duty. Mr. Sepet held the floor because he held our respect. There was real power in the man who founded Vamway.

"This evening is your initiation," he said, his eyes seeming to burn right into her. After years in close contact with him, I still couldn't describe the color of his eyes. They changed.

One of my responsibilities was to bring out the chart. The punks had already moved the heavy mahogany dining room table off to the side and rolled up the carpet before placing chairs in the center of the room. The chandelier lit up the work area nicely. I placed the chart on a metal tripod in front of the chairs and went back to my corner.

The familiar pyramid showed the various levels within the organization. I glanced over at Johna because I wanted to see if she reacted when she saw it was the Great Pyramid of Egypt. Occasionally we recruit people who are into Pyramidology. She looked at the chart without visible signs of excitement or stress. She probably wasn't even a regular watcher of Dr. Gene Scott's television program.

Mr. Sepet must have been reading my mind because he suddenly asked Johna, "Do you believe in God?"

She raised an eyebrow. The founder smiled, pulling back his lips just enough to reveal a single, pointed tooth. We breathlessly waited for her answer.

"I don't know," she admitted.

"Are you certain of anything?" he asked, voice as cold as my dead wife's feet.

Johna frowned. "I'm certain I don't want to find out if God exists anytime soon!"

That broke the ice. Everyone laughed, even before Mr. Sepet chuckled—his usual method of warning the rest of us to be at our ease.

With a motion as slow and deliberate as the erection of a statue, the founder stood. Johna involuntarily took a step back. He would be an imposing figure even without his great height. I offered him the pointer and he jabbed at the chart.

"We must have courage," he intoned, "to attempt immortality on this plane." He held the wooden pointer over his head as if it might be Excalibur. "To allow even this mundane object in our inner sanctum requires a brave heart! We face so many limitations as it is, you might wonder why I created an organization that, on the surface, seems only to add to our burden."

He stared directly at Johna but she wisely refrained from speaking. Vamway always has room for another smart recruit.

Again, he seemed to read my mind when he said, "The essence of my cruelty is that I try to oblige women and give them exactly what they want. Especially the ones who are closet exhibitionists."

I laughed nervously. The other women in the room smiled and whispered among themselves. I never ceased to be impressed by how he handled the Brides. That's what we called the women who converted enough new members to join his inner circle.

"Me, too," said Lucy, the boldest member.

"You give men what they want?" Johna asked her uncertainly.

"No," answered Lucy, smiling devilishly. "Women!" The redhead licked her lips. I liked her the best. She was friendly to everyone, male or female. She even paid attention to me when I went on and on about my favorite subject: fly fishing.

"Peter Pan was one of us," announced the founder without preamble. "What do you think is the moral of the story?"

"I don't know," admitted Johna.

I'd heard the speech so many times that I knew the words by heart. But none of us would dare step on Mr. Sepet's lines: "Once you lose your shadow, it's a waste of time trying to get it back."

Johna was the youngest girl there, just barely in her twenties. She looked younger. She had a petite figure and with her short dark hair could play the role of Peter if we felt like putting on our own little theater production. Lucy would almost certainly volunteer for the role of Wendy.

Johna tilted her head in a birdlike fashion and volunteered: "Isn't that story about free will? The children are given the choice of staying young forever."

"The perfect metaphor," hissed our noble leader. "To be fully human, you must be full of human blood. Keeps you young! I first hit on the idea of Vamway when I offered a Turkish scholar the opportunity of joining our society voluntarily. Unbeknownst to me, the man was dying of cancer and he eagerly accepted. Over the centuries, I have harvested some of the most famous men and women in history as they neared terminal retirement."

Sometimes I can't keep my big mouth shut. "As Winston Churchill says—there's no such thing as history; there is only biography."

"Is he… a member of Vamway?" asked Johna.

From the back of the room came a female voice with just a touch of brogue: "Any Irishman would say yes."

The founder reiterated the official line: "Only those who have sold enough to reach Five Blood Rubies level are privy to our confidential lists. Johna, you have passed the preliminary tests. Do you voluntarily accept our kisses?"

She swallowed hard and nodded. The time for words was over. I went to the closet and got out the mop and the robes. Before I returned I could hear the ripping of cloth. The Brides liked to tear off their own clothes. We'd gotten to the point that we had special tailoring for these events.

Six naked women surrounded Johna, whose eyes were already glazed over. The room was full of perfume and female musk. I dropped the mop and busied myself moving the chairs out of the way. I could feel the founder's eyes on the back of my neck like two golden bees, ready to sting. I was a little slow tonight.

"Your turn," said Mr. Sepet softly. Johna unbuttoned her blouse. No one seemed to mind that she might want to preserve her wardrobe. Then she removed her skirt and dainty underthings. Lucy moaned at the sight of small, firm breasts and full thighs.

"Wait," said Mr. Sepet, barely above a whisper. "My turn."

The founder approached the girl in a manner both leisurely and formal. He might be asking her to dance; but no word escaped his lips. Only his tongue protruded like a red snake. No tongue should be that red.

He licked her nose. Then on to her eyes, her forehead, her cheeks. Everyone in the room waited in rapt anticipation for him to reach the pulsing at the base of her neck. When at last he sank his fangs into her flesh, there was a collective sigh of release. His large white hands held her by the shoulders. He could have crushed so easily the vessel from which he drank.

Then he stood back. He wasn't satisfied. He could never be satisfied. But a true aristocrat practices moderation and derives pleasure from the sensation of hunger.

"Everyone's turn," he said in a voice heavy with her blood; but I knew the invitation didn't extend to me. I wasn't complaining. My diet had improved a lot lately. I remained in the corner and finished munching the remains of my snack.

Six moist, soft tongues replaced the founder's dry, rough one. The Brides fed on every interesting portion of Johna's writhing body. She was the cup. We know the true meaning of communion at Vamway.

Johna groaned more deeply than Lucy. Mr. Sepet guided the novice's head to Lucy's breast and made her nurse from the crimson nipple. Lucy laughed hysterically, and then returned the favor by getting behind Johna and burrowing there.

Johna died beautifully. She was reborn in the glory of the new flesh. Over the years, the founder had discovered how to accelerate this process.

As the new member, and potential Bride, opened her shining eyes, everyone in the room experienced a telepathic projection of the life Johna had left. We saw a little girl about the age of ten skipping in a garden. She expected nothing but good from the world. She eagerly faced life like a newborn kitten. Then a few years passed and there was the change.

Puberty had done its work. Now the girl was sullen, but still expectant. The longing for life was thwarted, and she'd already learned to keep feelings to herself. Playfulness had been replaced with her secret tension.

It was the worst kind of secret—the secret everyone pretends not to know. She still looked out upon the world, but suspicion was her *leitmotif*.

A few years passed again, and she was a full-blown teenager. Running hot. Running cold. No more skipping in the garden. Volatile. Vacant. Crazy. Lied to until the only defense is pretense made into a law of life.

Then there was the calm after the storm. The first great love. Followed by the second, third, fourth One-and-Only Great Loves. Five. Six. Each time the temporary return to the garden. Hope turns into lies like butter melting on a hot gravestone.

Each time love died, the calm expression drained away more slowly than before. The frustration returned, of course; but she was building up her armor. If she'd lived out a normal life span she would have continued confusing monogamy with loyalty. The wages of monogamy are death-in-life. She'd been saved from this by the founder, with his gift of life-in-death. Lucky girl.

With a collective sigh like a hot tropical wind against our lips, the visions faded. Back to reality. Back to abnormal.

I didn't want to get into any trouble for being too slow now! One of the punk kids guarding the mansion liked to say that when Mr. Sepet got pissed off, he went postal more completely than anyone this side of a world war. He was a great killer.

First, I passed out the thick cotton robes. They were all red. My idea. I have my moments. Then I mopped up the puddles. There hadn't been much waste tonight.

"You're hungry now," said the founder to the gasping newcomer.

"Yessssssss," she sighed.

"Wait," he advised. "Let the hunger grow. You can't experience the deeper satisfactions unless you first practice self-denial."

She whimpered but there was no resistance in her. "Yes," she said.

"How do you wish to address me?" he asked, his voice suddenly gentle.

"I… I'm not sure," she answered.

"What do you want to say to me?" he coaxed her.

"I'm ashamed to say it," she murmured. "I don't deserve to speak the word."

"Say what is within you."

"Yes, master," she screamed, falling to the floor and kissing his feet, abandoning herself to the freedom of total self abasement.

The founder laughed. The nostrils flared on his aquiline nose. His chiseled features were full of the love that only comes from a clear vision of the object of one's passion.

"There, there," he said, beckoning her to rise. "Now tell me: are you still concerned for the rights of others?"

She nodded, too ashamed to speak.

"That's all right," he consoled her. "Vamway is the only pyramid scheme that never fails. Normally, you run out of people. The base widens until there is nothing underneath it but empty promises. The people at the bottom guarantee a good living for the people above; and they in turn pass the benefits up all the way to the top. But there is always a limit to how many can maintain themselves at the bottom. There comes that dread day when the market is exhausted, the market in *suckers*, one might say."

"Fortunately, Vamway isn't in the business of providing a living for anyone," said Lucy while she ran her fingers through Johna's short hair. Here was a new Peter Pan indeed. At least I didn't have to mop up any spilled shadows.

"A true pyramid scheme is a Ponzi scheme," he went on, as if he hadn't heard Lucy. "There is a geometrical progression making it impossible to maintain. The power of two is the power to run out of victims. We aren't selling a product, of course. We are selling a 'lifestyle,' one might say. We have the means to drain victims to the point of death. To join us, one must deliberately partake of the sacred blood. If everyone in the world wanted to be in Vamway, we'd have an insurmountable problem. Then we would be guilty of a pyramid scheme. I can assure you that we'll never have that problem."

Johna blinked her big, dark eyes. "I think I understand," she said uncertainly.

"Are you happy?" Mr. Sepet asked her.

"Yes," she said quietly.

"We will find you a volunteer," he promised, "but now I must tell you one of our secrets. The younger the blood, the more it satisfies us. The older the blood, the emptier we feel... although it maintains our existence."

I watched realization dawn in her face. It was much easier to find volunteers among the old ones. There was only so much decadence available in youth.

My last task of the evening lay before me. I led Johna to her coffin, already prepared and waiting for her. I could tell that she hungered for my throat but she would follow the rules. I told her that later the founder would join her and allow her to finish her communion with him, personally. Then when she awoke, feverish in hunger, we would introduce her to the next volunteer, a middle-aged man who would have to do.

"Was he telling the truth?" she asked me as I started to lower the lid over her beautiful, intelligent face.

"About what?"

"About famous people who are still… on Earth?"

"Oh, yes. This weekend I'll personally introduce you to Bram Stoker and Ambrose Bierce."

"There is so much I want to ask them," she said, more to herself than to me.

I left her dreaming of the new life opening up for her. There was no reason to disappoint her. It would be months before it finally sunk in that our knowledge was not particularly more advanced than the ones who bleed and die. Mr. Sepet was still wrestling over the question of whether or not God exists. Every dawn he prayed that the answer is no. Please.

When I returned to the dining room, the Brides had finished with the baby. Mr. Sepet brought it in the moment I took Johna to her new quarters. My guess is that it will take Johna about a year before she is ready for the next secret. Namely, that Vamway recruits new members who respect the rights of human beings because such members are worth teaching. Only through ritual do they overcome their prejudices. We don't want brutes. We want members who know what they are doing. Who feel the delicious pleasure of feeding well.

The Brides are getting better about leaving me something. The master has made it clear that I work hard and I deserve the leftovers.

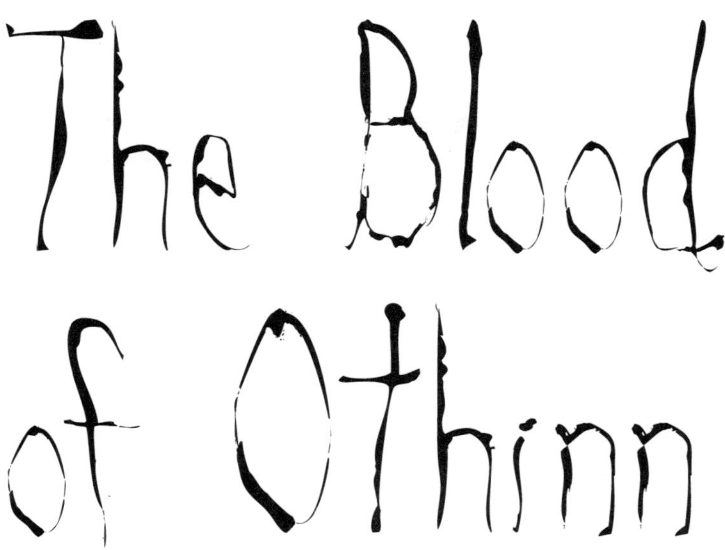

The Blood of Othinn

C. Dean Andersson

I have tasted the blood of a God. I licked it from Virana Lokena's dead lips.

Othinn may find me, soon, and murder me like He has so many others of our kind, if I don't die first like Virana, poisoned by His blood.

Either way, I probably don't have much time. So I'm putting this on-line. Virana wouldn't have approved. She didn't like computers. She despised e-mail and the Internet.

But I doubt even Othinn can find and kill everyone who reads this on the Web. And some of you will know what to do, who to tell. Some of you will be real vampires, too.

For those of you who chronicle our history, give Virana the credit. She'd been suspicious of Santa Claus since childhood.

She once told me that when she was three, she jumped up and down while music was playing because she had to go to the bathroom. But her mother interpreted it as rhythm, strapped tap shoes to her feet, and put her in a dance class.

The next Christmas, she was forced onto a stage with other uneasy children. The program notes said they were WAITING FOR SANTA. When Santa arrived, they were to do a little dance.

Some of the kids had stage fright.

Virana had Santa-fright.

When Santa walked into view, she didn't dance. She screamed and ran. The audience laughed. She was punished. But she didn't care. Santa hadn't gotten her.

From the first, she said, she had been terrified of the Fat Man in Red with the Long White Beard and the Strange Loud Laugh. She hadn't liked His ominously wide Black Belt or His unnaturally shiny Black Boots. The first time they'd tried to make her sit on Santa's lap in a department store, she'd thrown a screaming fit to avoid it.

She desperately hadn't wanted Him to know what she was thinking and whether she'd been naughty or nice. And she frantically hadn't wanted Him creeping into her house while she was asleep and helpless.

Sure, they claimed He only broke into houses to leave presents, *but what else did He do while He was there?*

Virana had a theory that she had also been a vampire in a previous incarnation, and that was why she knew to fear Santa in this Century of Deception. Her fear led to fascination.

She studied the history of Santa, and at the end of her studies, she found death. But also the Secret of the Stake.

She wrote down the essence of her discovery before she died. In her own words, "I have tasted the Blood of Othinn. I have learned the Secret of the Stake.

"The last 100 years have seen mortals systematically tricked in many ways by their Secret Rulers. Most humans no longer believe in vampires and werewolves, gods and goddesses, faster than light travel, or Santa Claus. But there's a *real* Santa, and I was right to be afraid of Him as a kid, because he murders vampires on the side.

"Yule is celebrated when the Sun, as seen from the Earth, turns back to the north after having reached the southernmost point in Her yearly journey. Yule is also known as Winter Solstice. It happens each year a few days before Christmas, the Season of Santa, that tricky advertising icon whose sleigh-ride vampires should call a slay-ride.

"The longest nights of the year in the northern hemisphere are near Yule. Before I became one, I thought it would be a good time for vampires. Longer nights would mean more time out of the grave before the next sunrise, more time to hunt and stalk and drink warm blood. But the Twelve Nights of Yule are also the Nights of the Wild Hunt.

"My research shows that the leader of the Wild Hunt is sometimes said to be a Saint, sometimes a Sinner, sometimes a goddess, or a god.

"When it's the God Othinn, vampires die. Othinn has many Forms, may they all be cursed. One of them is Santa Claus. Santa's aerial ride on Christmas Eve is nothing more than Othinn's Wild Hunt in disguise.

"Look up the oldest representations of Santa Claus. Some of them show Santa holding Othinn's wooden Staff.

"Remember the Staff. It's important.

"Before the religion of the White Christ crept into their lands, northern Europeans knew Othinn well. Some still do.

"Among other things, Othinn is the patron God of Berserkers, particularly the shapeshifting Get of Fenris. Vampires have those shapeshifters to thank for making Othinn our enemy.

"Visions arise in my mind as the Blood of Othinn poisons me and brings true death swiftly near.

"I see three vampires of a rare, alien parasite variety attacking Norse sailors near Lindisfarne Abbey in June of 793 C.E. One of the sailors is a young shapeshifter who calls on Othinn to help him change into a beast.

"The Berserker youth becomes filled with Othinn's Fury, changes into a ravening wolf, and kills two of the vampires. The third flees back to Lindisfarne.

"The surviving sailors attack the Abbey the next dawn.

"They have learned the Secret of the Cross, how vampires have tricked Christians into believing the Cross repulses them, so that they can sleep safely beneath its cruciform shadow.

"With the attack on Lindisfarne, the so-called Viking Age begins, and during the Twelve Nights of Yule following Lindisfarne, vampires become the chosen prey of Othinn's Wild Hunt.

"I see Othinn, His one-eye blazing with fire, riding roaring storm winds through the night sky upon His eight-legged horse. His wolves prowl below Him. His ravens fly above Him.

"Hail from the storm he has conjured pounds the Earth, clattering upon the rooftops of dwellings, while inside huddle frightened mortals. But not just mortals.

"With His mystic vision, Othinn finds many vampires.

"With His Staff he slaughters them.

"And here is the Secret of the Stake.

"Othinn's Staff is made of wood taken from a gallow's tree. It is carved with Runes, imbued with lethal Magic. In His hands, it emits rays more deadly to vampires than sunlight. But using His Staff to destroy us during the Yule season was not enough for Him. He also gave to humankind a weapon to use against us.

"He cast a sorcerous spell that traveled through Time and Space into all places on the Earth, into the past and into the future. The spell gave wood the power to immobilize vampires, *to root us to the spot*. And thus was born the mania for hammering wooden stakes into our hearts.

"But if we could remove the spell Othinn placed upon wood, the stake would no longer paralyze us.

"How can that be done? If Othinn was slain, would it remove the spell? How do you kill a God? Or is there another way to lift the spell? Perhaps one of you who reads this will find a way.

"Or perhaps others will have to do what I have done, find a way to draw near to the real Santa without His knowing you know He is Othinn and without His discerning that you are a vampire.

"Lunge for His throat, then, and taste His blood, if only a drop, if you can, and have your escape well planned as did I. And maybe you will learn even more than I learned. Maybe you will learn not only the Secret of the Stake, but how to remove the spell.

"But be warned. Othinn has the power to know what you are thinking.

That part about Santa Claus is certainly true. And there is something more…

"In my mind I now see another vision. An elder vampire scribbles words by candlelight. He writes, 'HE rides the Twelve Nightwinds of Yule, HIS gallowed Staff brings Storms, HIS spider-legged steed haunts Crossroads, Vampires curse all HIS Forms.'

"And I see a title to the book, *Codex Othinnicus*, and a date, 942 A.D.

"Look for the book! A copy must still exist somewhere. Maybe it will tell us how to lift the spell!"

And there Varina's notes end.

I hear a storm building outside. Isn't there a line in "The Night Before Christmas" about a clatter up on the roof?

At least I don't have a chimney.

It sounds like hail up there.

I'm signing off now.

Good luck to you all.

And to all a good night.

Biographies

Editor

Edward E. Kramer

is a writer and coeditor of *Grails* (nominated for the World Fantasy Award for Best Anthology of 1992), *Confederacy of the Dead*, *Phobias*, *Dark Destiny*, *Elric: Tales of the White Wolf*, *Excalibur*, *Tombs*, *Dark Love*, *Forbidden Acts*, *Sandman: Book of Dreams*, and many additional works in progress. Ed's original fiction appears in a number of anthologies as well; his first novel, *Killing Time*, is forthcoming from White Wolf. His credits also include over a decade of work as a music critic and photojournalist. A graduate of the Emory University School of Medicine, Ed is a clinical and educational consultant in Atlanta. He is fond of human skulls, exotic snakes, and underground caves.

Contributing Authors

C. Dean Andersson's

thirteen novels include *I Am Dracula, I Am Frankenstein, Torture Tomb, Raw Pain Max, Fiend,* and two original novels set in the world of Mortal Kombat. Some of his short stories have appeared in *Scare Care, Dark Seductions, The Splendour Falls,* and *Dark Destiny I.* He wrote an overview of slasher films, "Halloween Chainsaw Hockey," for Issue One of the *Jason vs. Leatherface* comic book. And he admits to having had a childhood fear of Santa Claus.

David Bischoff

is the author of over fifty novels, several of them bestsellers. These include *Nightworld, Star Fall, Mandala, The Gaming Magi,* and *The UFO Conspiracy* on his own; *The Selkie* and *The Judas Cross* with Charles Sheffield, *The Dragonstar Series* with Thomas F. Monteleone; and *Doctor Dimension* with John DeChancie. He has written scripts for television, including work for *Star Trek: The Next Generation.* His short work has been published in *Omni, The Magazine of F and SF,* and *Analog.*

Richard Lee Byers

is the author of the novels *The Ebon Mask, On A Darkling Plain, Netherworld, Caravan of Shadows, Dark Fortune, Dead Time, The Vampire's Apprentice, Fright Line,* and *Deathward,* as well as the Young Adult books *Joy Ride, Warlock Games,* and *Party Till You Drop.* His short fiction has appeared in numerous anthologies.

Stephen Dedman

has escaped from several institutions of higher learning, where he studied writing, theatre, and film history. Now a full-time writer living in abject poverty in Western Australia, he has worked as an actor, an experimental subject, and the manager of an SF bookshop. His short stories have appeared in *Little Deaths, F&SF, Asimov's* and *Science Fiction Age*; his first novel, *The Art of Arrow Cutting,* will be published by Tor Books in 1997.

Esther M. Friesner

received her M.A. and Ph.D. in Spanish from Yale University. She taught Spanish there for a number of years before going on to become a full-time author of fantasy and science fiction. Her short fiction and poetry appear in numerous magazines and anthologies. To date, she has over two dozen novels to her credit. Esther lives in Connecticut with her husband, two children, two rambunctious cats, and a fluctuating population of hamsters.

Roland J. Green

is a prolific writer of science fiction, fantasy, action-adventure and historical fiction. He also reviews for the American Library Association and the *Chicago Sun-Times*, edits, and handles nonfiction projects like the "Concordance" of *The Tom Clancy Companion*. He is a graduate of Oberlin College and the University of Chicago, and has been active in the Society for Creative Anachronism.

Rick Hautala

is the international best-selling author of fifteen novels of horror and psychological suspense. With more than two and a half million copies of his books currently in print, his novels include the national bestsellers *Shades of Night*, *Twilight Time*, *Night Stone*, *Little Brothers*, *Cold Whisper*, and *Ghost Light*. In 1996, his novels *Beyond the Shroud*, *The Mountain King*, and *Impulse* were published. With more than fifty published short stories and nonfiction pieces, he has appeared in numerous national and international magazines and anthologies.

Caitlin R. Kiernan

was born in Dublin, Ireland, but has lived most of her life in the Southeastern U.S. She holds degrees in Philosophy and Anthropology, and has worked as a paleontologist, a newspaper columnist, and an exotic dancer. In 1992 she began pursuing fiction-writing full-time and has sold stories to a number of magazines and anthologies including *Aberrations*, *Eldritch Tales*, *High Fantastic*, and *The Very Last Book of the Dead*. Her first novel, *The Five of Cups*, was published by Transylvania Press.

Victor Koman

sold his first story to *New Libertarian Notes* in 1976. His novels *The Jehovah Contract* (1985) and *Solomon's Knife* (1989) received Prometheus Awards. Victor's story "Bootstrap Enterprise" in *The Magazine of Fantasy and Science Fiction* was noted as one of the best SF stories of 1994. His latest novel is the massive space thriller *Kings of the High Frontier*. A Hollywood extra in *Star Trek—The Motion Picture*, *Cyberzone*, and *Attack of the 60-Foot Centerfold*, Victor lives in Southern California with his wife and daughter.

Marc Levinthal

is a musician and writer who has lived in Los Angeles since 1980. He co-wrote the score for the film "Valley Girl" and the hit single "Three Little Pigs" for Green Jellö. He has played in bands too numerous to mention (or remember), and inexplicably, has just started another one. His story "Kids" will be part of *The Very Last Book of the Dead* edited by John Mason Skipp, with whom he is currently collaborating. Their story "The Punchline" appeared in *Dark Destiny II*. Marc currently resides in ultra-groovy Silver Lake with his fiancée and five moderately evil cats.

Brad Linaweaver

is best known for his novel *Moon of Ice*, which won the Prometheus Award in 1989 and, as a novella, was a Nebula finalist. His short stories have appeared in over two dozen anthologies. He has worked in radio and film; coedited *Weird Menace* and *Free Space*; and has collaborated with Dafydd ab Hugh on two *Doom* novels and has just completed two *Sliders* novels.

Anya Martin

is a freelance writer/journalist, music critic, and editor specializing in horror, science fiction, comics and rock 'n' roll. She had her first published short story in *Confederacy of the Dead*. Other credits include an essay on the rock/horror connection in *Splatterpunks 2*, and *Still Life With Peckerwood*, which recently appeared in Gahan Wilson's *Haunted House*. Fresh from two years of promotional writing for Marvel Comics, she is currently completing a contemporary southern gothic novel.

Doug Murray

began writing at age 13 for movie-oriented magazines like *Famous Monsters of Filmland, The Monster Times*, and *Media Times*. In the mid-eighties, he graduated to comic books as the creator and primary writer on Marvel's *The 'Nam*. Doug has also worked for Comico, DC, and Eternity. His short stories appear in numerous anthologies. His novel, *Blood Relations*, was recently published by White Wolf.

Frieda A. Murray

is married to Roland Green, and has collaborated with him on the fantasy novel *The Book of Kantela,* and numerous short pieces. She is a graduate of the University of Chicago, a past member of the Society for Creative Anachronism, and is active in Chicago Women in Publishing.

Philip Nutman

is the author of the critically acclaimed novel *Wet Work*. A four-time Bram Stoker Award nominee, his fiction has appeared in nearly two dozen anthologies, including *Book of the Dead, Borderlands 2*, and *The Year's best Horror Stories XIX* and *XX*, and has been translated into eight languages. He is currently at work on a third novel and a screenplay for a major Hollywood studio. His collection, *Cities of Night*, will be released in late 1996.

Fred Olen Ray

has written, produced and directed over fifty feature films of every kind and nature, including *Mob Boss, Inner Sanctum, Evil Toons*, and *Hollywood Chainsaw Hookers*. He has been featured prominently on such TV programs as *Entertainment Tonight, Hard Copy, Stephen King's World of Horror, CNN's Show Biz Today*. Fred wrote *The New Poverty Row* and *Grind Show*, and coedited the horror pulp anthology, *Weird Menace*. He also writes for several national magazines and is himself the subject of numerous magazine articles and interviews.

Rick R. Reed

acts as an agent for several Chicago underground bands while not chained behind his typewriter. Currently, he is on tour with Tactile Sluts, known for their grunge arrangement of Billie Holiday standards. He is the author of the Dell Abyss novels *Obsessed* and *Penance* and the stories "Tool of Enslavement" appearing in *Dark Destiny* and "Epiphany" in *Dante's Disciples*.

Victor Rodriguez

was born in Los Angeles in 1968. He is a short story author and screenwriter who has sold scripts for television in connection with the FOX and HBO networks. He was formerly a management executive at BMG Music Publishing, where he worked with the music industry's top songwriters to provide music for hundreds of films, television programs and multimedia projects. Victor has spent time in many different countries, but always manages to find his way back to LA, where he currently lives.

Robert J. Sawyer

is the author of seven science fiction novels: *Starplex*, *The Terminal Experiment*, *End of an Era*, and *Golden Fleece*, plus the Quintaglio trilogy (*Far-Seer*, *Fossil Hunter*, and *Foreigner*). He has twice won the Canadian Science Fiction and Fantasy Award ("the Aurora"), and three times won the CompuServe SF Literature Forum's HOMer Award for Best Novel of the Year. His work has appeared in *Analog*, *Amazing Stories*, and many anthologies including *Dante's Disciples*, *Free Space*, and *Sherlock Holmes in Orbit*. He lives in Toronto, Canada.

Susan Shwartz

is a financial writer, editor, and assistant vice president for a Wall Street investment firm. By night and any spare minute she can scrounge, she writes, edits, and reviews fantasy and science fiction. She has published more than 60 short stories, authored a number of novels, and has edited seven anthologies. She has also written criticism for *Vogue*, *The New York Times*, and various other national periodicals. She holds a Ph.D. in English literature from Harvard with a medieval specialization.

John Mason Skipp

is an expatriate elder statesman of the New Horror wars. He is also a singer, writer, musician, composer, performer, editor, collaborator, fledgling director, interpretive dancer, and certified lover of life. His new band (as yet unnamed) is a techno-industrial trance-dance affair. Other collaborators include Marc Levinthal and writer/director/performer Tom Stern. John lives alone in the shadow of the Griffith Park Observatory, where sleazy Hollywood collides with bohemian Los Feliz. He loves his family, both real and imagined, and is finally figuring out who his real friends are.

S.P. Somtow

(Somtow Papinian Suchariktul) was born in Bangkok and grew up in Europe. His first novel *Starship & Haiku* won the Locus Award for best first novel; he won the 1981 John W. Campbell Award as well as the 1986 Daedalus for his novel *The Shattered Horse*. Somtow's other novels include *Vampire Junction*, *Moon Dance*, *Forgetting Places*, and *Vampire Junction*'s sequel, *Valentine*. His film projects include *The Laughing Dead* and *Ill Met By Moonlight*, a radical departure of Shakespeare's *A Midsummer Night's Dream*.

David Niall Wilson

has sold over 70 short stories and four novels. His upcoming work can be found in *Robert Bloch's Psychos*, *Razor Kiss*, *New Altars*, *Vision Quests*, *Cemetery Dance*, *Deathrealm*, and *Bones*. His first novel, *This is My Blood*, is due from Transylvania Press this fall. Also forthcoming is his *Star Trek Voyager* novel, *Chrysalis*, and his White Wolf **World of Darkness Wraith** novel, *Except You Go Through Shadow*. He lives in a big haunted house in Norfolk, Virginia, with his wife, JoAnne, two boys, Zach and Zane, and a neurotic cat.

Bernie Wrightson and Joy Mosier-Dubinsky

have logged countless hours from the hills of Pennsylvania to the shores of Saugerties in an attempt to find the perfect cup of coffee and the best damned pool hall (Answers: Bernie's and Breaks Cafe in Kingston, NY). Bernie is a former Bolshoi fan-dancer, co-creator of DC Comics' *Swamp Thing*, and the guy who did those amazing *Frankenstein* illustrations. Joy is a former political campaign writer gone bad, who once taught Sunday and Bible School to preschoolers. Both recently graduated *magna cum laude* from an accredited clown college and hope to soon return to the stage with their pantomime interpretation of *A History Of The Aztecs*.

Brian Yuzna

is a hardcore horror fan. Since his childhood in Latin America he has been hooked on horror movies and weird literature, so it was inevitable that when he moved to LA in the mid-eighties to make movies he would work within the horror genre. His first producing effort was the classic *Re-Animator*, based on the writings of the godfather of twentieth century weird fiction, HP Lovecraft. Yuzna went on to produce, direct and write other Lovecraft film adaptations, including *From Beyond* and *Necronomicon*, as well as *Society*, *Return of the Living Dead 3*, *The Dentist*, *Honey, I Shrunk The Kids*, *Guyver* and *Crying Freeman*. He is known internationally as one of the leading supporters of the genre and has successfully collaborated with European and Asian filmmakers on his endeavors. A true believer, Brian would next love to make a vampyr movie.